KISSING JUDAS

'The British crime novel is enjoying a second "golden age" – an age of realism – with literate writers using the form to say important and necessary things about contemporary life and the darker workings of the human mind. Frederic Lindsay is playing his part in making readers sit up and take notice' *Ian Rankin, Scotland on Sunday*

'Lindsay has used a genre often concerned with entertainment only to write a profoundly serious novel, as Chandler and Ross Macdonald did in California half a century ago' *Allan Massie, The Scotsman*

'A superb piece of crime fiction. We're going to hear a lot more about Jim Meldrum' *Neil Johnstone of Waterstones, Edinburgh Evening News*

'There's nothing like a good whodunnit to leap out of the shadows and deal a death-blow to those dark winter evenings . . . Lindsay keeps you guessing right till the final pages' *Big Issue*

About the author

Born in Glasgow, Frederic Lindsay now lives in Edinburgh, where he is actively involved in the Scottish Arts Council and Scottish PEN. He has written for the theatre, radio, tv and film, and has written four previous highly-acclaimed novels. His first novel, *Brond*, was televised in a three-part adaptation by Channel 4.

Kissing Judas

Frederic Lindsay

CORONET BOOKS
Hodder and Stoughton

First published in Great Britain in 1997 by
Hodder and Stoughton
a division of Hodder Headline PLC
First published in paperback in 1998 by Hodder and Stoughton
A Coronet Paperback

10 9 8 7 6 5 4 3 2 1

ISBN 0 340 69534 X

Printed and bound in Great Britain by
Clays Ltd, St Ives plc

Hodder and Stoughton
A division of Hodder Headline PLC
338 Euston Road
London NW1 3BH

For Robbie

And the Lord spake unto the fish, and it vomited out Jonah upon the dry land.

Jonah, II, 10, *c.* 400 BC

Back then I was in the heart of the whore.

Ex-CIA agent, *c.* AD 1990

BOOK ONE

Getting Together

CHAPTER ONE

Other nights the blind man Arthur Hull had heard footsteps crossing the room although he was alone. That wasn't pleasant, but knowing it was in his head he could live with it, and after a time the footsteps wouldn't be there any more. What was strange was they were always made by the same man, someone he didn't know. If he had thought of being haunted, he would have expected it to be by the way Francis lingered from step to step as if reluctant to raise himself from the earth. He did not expect ever to have another lover. To be haunted by Francis wouldn't have been a surprise.

Feeling his way through the hall, he imagined what it would be like if Francis had come back again. When he opened the door there would be a silence. And he would listen and hear the light sigh of a breath taken. And know. And then he would feel a hand touch his cheek. It was an imagining which had stayed with him from the first painful weeks of his loss, a habit he couldn't break.

When he opened the door, there was silence, but with some instinct of the congenitally blind he had the sense of a shape, taller than himself, and caught a smell of unwashed flesh. Though the voice was hoarse, the timbre of it was young; he pictured a young man. 'I wonder, sir, if you could tell me if the second post's been? I used to live round here, you see.'

Irish.

'What time is it?'

'Time?' The young voice sounded puzzled.

'Don't you have a watch?'

His outstretched hand rubbed against a slippery sleekness and he took a pinch of it between his fingers and felt down to the cuff where there was a flap and a press stud. A cheap anorak it would be, with a hood hanging at the back or folded into the collar. Trainers, of course, on the feet. Big ones if the width of bone across the wrist was any indication. Wiry rub of hairs and the warm firmness of skin.

'No watch,' the young man said. 'Thieves everywhere.'

'I was sleeping.' In the chair. Whisky had left his throat dry and tight. He made chewing movements and pushed the thin saliva back and through his teeth before swallowing it.

From the hall behind him the grandfather clock began to chime.

'Not midnight,' the young man said on the last stroke. 'Twelve though.'

'I know what time of day it is. I feel the sun on my face. I can hear the traffic.'

'There isn't any, sir.'

A dog in the street barked and the young man pulled his wrist free.

'I can hear it.' He could hear all the sounds of Edinburgh. 'On the main road, I can. Plenty of it. It's usually about eleven.'

'What?'

'The post. Is that not what you were asking about? The post. Did you say you live round here?'

'It'll be gone then.'

'Well, I should think so. It's past eleven.'

A girl laughed. She wasn't far away, near enough to hear his querulous old man's voice. A double note of laughter like a barking dog, thin and hard as metal. Young. Without law or fear or pity.

'Do you live round here?'

'I said I used to.'

'Where?'

'It was only for a short time, sir. Thank you anyway.'

There was the soft flap of feet across the stone slabs that made a bridge over the basement and down the steps to the pavement.

Listening, he couldn't be sure, two of them going off certainly, three maybe. A car passed just then, however, coming up the one-way street, and when it had passed they were gone.

He shoved the door shut with a bang. To calm himself he chewed a handful of sweet biscuits while he waited for the kettle to boil. In his own house it would be stupid to be afraid. He drank tea standing by the kitchen table and told himself he was angry.

The cup only half finished, he went back through the hall and out on to the front step. It was quiet. On the opposite side of the road there was a school, empty now and boarded up. At one time the air at this time of the day would have been crowded with the sounds of children playing. Not a sound. He turned from side to side, feeling the sun on his face. Nothing. He would go and talk to Mulholland.

Long practice had made locking the door an automatic movement; but this time he fumbled the key twice before getting it in. Having his back to the street made him uncomfortable.

His was a main-door flat, so guided by the railing he went down to the pavement and along into the next close. As he climbed the flight of stairs to the first floor a pervasive acrid smell wrinkled his nose.

'You've had a cat peeing down there,' he told Mulholland.

'I can't ask you in, Arthur,' Mulholland said.

'That's all right.' They weren't friends, just two ageing men who had lived in this building longer than anyone else.

'I've got the minister in.' More softly, closer so that he felt the spicy draught of breath on his cheek, 'Rejoicing over the lost lamb.'

'A young fellow knocked at my door – he wanted to know if the post had been. The second post.'

'What was he doing – a survey?'

'There were others with him. Didn't you say you'd found somebody sleeping in the back close?'

'Listen, I've got to go, Arthur.'

But he could hear that he had caught Mullholland's attention.

'Young. Wearing an anorak, something like that.'

'I never saw him. Hell, it gave me a fright. I was going out to the garden and I passed this – I thought it was rubbish. I'd gone past it to the back door and then something made me turn round and take a proper look. He was sleeping – I could see the shape of him.'

'He didn't wake up?'

'Shamming, you mean? I got out of there at the double. I was on my own.'

'But you went back, you said.'

'Later on. With Morton up the stair. There was cardboard spread out and a sleeping bag. And his case. Making himself at home. No telling how long. But what would he come back here for?'

'Maybe what you did made him angry,' he said and took a malicious satisfaction at Mulholland's sharply drawn breath.

'We just put his case out into the front close. To let him know it wasn't on, his luck had run out.'

'You went through the case, you told me.'

'To be on the safe side, that was the way Morton looked at it. He found a benefit card – left it tucked through the handle of the case. Just as a warning. So there wouldn't be any nonsense, he said.'

'As a warning?'

'He took a note of the name and number.'

Then it was time to eat. Living on your own remembering to eat was important. Otherwise they broke in to find you grinning on the floor with the flies crawling over your teeth. He fried an egg to a count of twenty, then slid it on to a piece of bread. Lately he had been thinking a lot about dying. He had held his mother's hand at the side of the grave when his father was buried. The sun had been shining that day too, but when you were only four it meant something different, itch of the unfamiliar heavy clothes, sweat in eyes that could sting though they couldn't see. He remembered the noises people made shifting their weight from one foot to the other and the minister speaking, every word separate like taps on a drum, but there must have been a field somewhere round about for there was a thin little complaining noise and then a string of responses, deep and harsh; it was the first time he had heard a lamb and sheep. When the minister bent over him later on he smelled of hair oil and cigarettes; which was the way his father had smelled, so he didn't hear what the man said that time either. Stupid to remember smells and farm noises and not what mattered, the words they needed to put you down into a hole in the ground. One thing he hadn't heard, he hadn't heard his mother crying in the car or by the grave. When they got home at last, he had thought he would have her to himself for ever.

It was the clock that woke him, though too late to tell what hour it was marking. As so often, he had dreamed the broken theme, notes coming in a succession so perfect he foresaw everything to come and knew that it would justify the misery of having existed. Waking, it seemed for a moment he could still hear it. As always, then it was gone. He sat up as the last chime lengthened into silence. The movement knocked the plate off the arm of the chair and when he groped after it he put his fingers into a smear of slime. He searched again and found the slice of bread and the egg fallen alongside. There didn't seem to be any of it eaten.

He thought about making something else. In his head went through the steps of what would be needed; he couldn't face another egg, but there was bread, he could make it in the toaster two slices at a time and there should be jam in the pot that would do. Maybe later.

He couldn't be bothered.

It was when he opened his eyes for the second time he saw the man.

'I could describe him,' he insisted the next day.

'Was that before or after you finished the bottle?' the policeman who called himself Ord wondered.

'What bottle?' You've been inside a bottle as much as me, the blind man thought, recognising the rough huskiness of a man who drank too much.

'The empty one on the floor. Other side.'

'I wasn't drunk.' Gasping for breath, he stretched over the arm of the chair to which he had retreated after opening the door. He felt safer surrounded by its comfortable familiarity.

His fingertips brushed the bottle and he set it upright on the carpet.

'Would you like to describe me?' the other policeman, the one called Meldrum, asked. A lighter voice, he sounded younger.

'How do you mean?'

'Quite a party trick. For a blind man.'

'What age are you? Twenty-eight?'

'You're not wrong.' Meldrum was laughing.

'I could tell more than you think, blind and all as I am. Six feet? Thirteen stone? You're a whisky drinker, just like this one here, I could smell it off your breath. Are you married? Of course you are. And your wife will be tired of the hours you work. That always causes the trouble, they tell me.'

'Aye, but what colour's my hair?' Not amused any more.

'You don't have to believe me. I woke up – sitting where I am now – and I saw him. He came from that corner by the kitchen door across the room. Straight ahead. Didn't even spare me a look.' Sharply he asked, 'What are you doing?' and turned his head towards the policeman Ord and the sound of wood rubbing on wood. 'Leave that drawer alone. You haven't any right to look through my things . . . No right . . .' And lost interest in that as only a distraction from the amazing thing which had happened. 'He was in a suit and tie. Thin – no – I don't know – that was the way it seemed to me. And his hair was bright. I couldn't tell you what colour it was.'

'Bright?' Meldrum asked.

'Bright was the word that came into my head. I've never seen a colour. I'm blind, I've always been blind.'

But behind the man he had seen the room in which he had lived for twenty years, *seen* not felt the bulk of chairs, the piano, the flat length of the table, light from the open kitchen door and the glittering square of mirror hung there since Francis's time. The thing was that now he remembered all of it and how it had looked, though at the time he had been conscious of nothing except the man crossing the room without a glance.

'Then he walked out through the wall,' Ord said.

'I don't know. One minute I was looking at him, the next it

was like a curtain dropped. The light was gone. I've always been blind.'

There was the noise of the drawer being shut, a bang maybe with the side of a fist when it stuck; Ord didn't make any attempt to conceal what he was doing. He said, 'You had a bad dream. Tell me about Pietro.'

'Francis? What's happened to him?'

'Were you expecting something to happen?'

And it struck him that there was no reason for anyone to think he should be the one to come to, the one who would care and need to be told.

'Francis walked out on me months ago.'

'And you haven't spoken to him since?'

'The fourth of January.' At breakfast; something he said made Francis laugh; and then he went off to work same as always, only he must have packed a case. Everything gone, fumbling through wardrobes closets drawers that night. Nothing left. 'We hadn't quarrelled, nothing like that. He just went off. Fourth of January. I don't know why.'

'But you knew where he'd gone?'

'Not at first.'

'But you found out?'

'I made it my business to find out.'

'And then you got in touch.'

He knew he should ask why Ord was asking these questions, but how could there be a reason that wouldn't hurt? 'I phoned. Sometimes he would listen without saying anything, sometimes he would hang up at once.'

'You're telling me you never went to Pietro's flat?'

'Once. I asked why he'd left me. He shut the door in my face. And the taxi had gone. I thought I'd never get home.' Into the silence he said, 'It was after that I started to phone.' A flush like pleasure warmed him; he had someone to listen as he talked about Francis. 'I didn't give up, that's not my style . . . Not even when the boyfriend answered.'

'Pietro's lover?'

'Oh, abuse the word!'

'Call him what you like – how did you know?'

'There wasn't any doubt. When he picked up the phone, I

started at once. I thought it was Francis, and then when he
interrupted he was so obscene. A vulgar, common man.'

'Did he give a name?'

'No.'

'Anything about him? Accent?'

'North of England. Newcastle, somewhere round there. Where
the mercenaries come from.'

'Mercenaries? Did he say he was a soldier?'

'I thought he might be. He was a brute. The kind of man who
would beat up gay people, who would claim to hate them. He
used all the dirty soiled words. Do you know what I mean? The
kind of men who won't admit their own natures.'

'Was that what Pietro was into?'

'How can I know? With us it was all gentleness. We were
in love.'

'And you haven't spoken to him since?' Ord asked again.

He almost said yes, but he resented them too much to tell
them anything.

'So you kept phoning,' Ord went on, not giving him enough
time to think.

'When I couldn't help myself.' Hopelessly. It wasn't true that
it wasn't his style to give up. 'To tell him how much I missed
him. I never wanted him to be lonely.'

'Yesterday – on his answerphone, you sounded pretty angry.
Did he call you back?'

'No.' It took him a moment to take it in. 'What's happened
. . . It's something terrible, isn't it?'

'You'd phoned him earlier. The two of you had talked.'

It was made as a statement, but the blind man heard the
shadow of a question underneath. The detective wasn't sure.

'No.' He was the one who had done the talking, Francis
hadn't said a word, and then the phone had gone down.

'Is he ill? He was never ill.'

You say angry things to the young because they seem immor-
tal.

'Somebody cut his throat. Very professional.'

'Professional?' Dazed, he seized on the word as if it was what
mattered.

Had he suffered? Francis couldn't stand even a little pain.

If the policeman had been talking to a woman, to a wife, he'd have found something to say even if it wasn't true, some kind pretence. He wouldn't share with them his last memory of Francis, no way that he would ever share with them the miracle now a week old that had brought Francis back to him saying, I have to talk to you about something awful.

'Not a day has gone by I haven't missed him.'

There was a pause as if the policeman was working that one out, then Ord said, 'Well, one thing, you don't need to worry about him being lonely any more.'

Some time after that the two policemen must have left and he was on his own. More on his own than before since now nothing in his loneliness could ever change.

He came awake sure that the outside bell was ringing. He was confused to find he was still in the chair and not in bed. He got up and went into the lobby. He couldn't hear anything, and then he thought he heard a little sighing of breath.

He went back into the living-room and made his way to the chair again.

Because he depended on his hearing, he could make from the sound of steps an image of sex and build; no two people sounded alike, so that he was in no doubt that it was the man with bright hair. He pulled himself up and reached out, but he was mistaken, for the man was taller than he had calculated and his hand touched between the thighs of the other. A shock went through him at the reality of flesh; this was no dream. The man stood still and he cupped his fingers under round firmness, knew the weight of it, felt flesh stir and rise against his palm. Then his hand was lifted up to a belt and the handle of a knife and afterwards trailed down the man's belly upon the endless slim length of a blade.

A hand gripped his hair, head bending back, eyes widening on a dark that would not end.

'Are you to be my death?' Arthur Hull whispered.

There was some interval of time, enough for the music to begin, notes coming in a succession so perfect he foresaw—

BOOK TWO

Foreplay

CHAPTER TWO

The morning of the day his daughter's boyfriend was attacked by policemen, Meldrum was on his way to the Borders to unsolve a murder case.

He was badly slept for in the small hours he had wakened and lain sweating in the dark. He had The Fear. It had come over him at intervals most of his life – unacknowledged in daylight, like something buried coming up a horror out of the graveyard earth – the sense that there was an abyss into which you could fall – into prison, or on to the streets, the slide into poverty, to sleeping rough. Who knows where it came from . . . from childhood . . . from his father, a man who failed slowly in a small business . . . from his mother's fear, for him on a bike, in the water, in the whole dangerous place that was the world.

Sweating in the dark, until he came properly awake.

I'm a policeman, he'd told himself, I'm forty-three years old, I have a pension coming; and went back to sleep.

Now he touched the brake, taking a look, the little town below spread out like a fan on either side of the river that wound along the foot of the valley.

Riding into town to see justice done. Wearing a white hat. That was how you told the good guys from the bad.

A watery sun was struggling from behind clouds as he backed into a parking place in the line of cars that ran up the middle of the square. Making his way along the street, it surprised him how many people nodded and smiled to him in passing. They approved of him. Being approved of was a nice feeling.

At the station desk, he waited for a yawning constable to put in an appearance, long enough to remind him of how sloppily the place was run. He had felt that from the first.

'You've missed a good lunch,' Baird said, holding out his hand. The chairman of the local council, he was a small man with a large ego.

'We all have,' said the Detective Inspector, whose name was MacLean.

'I ate at the hotel.'

'At the hotel? Didn't you know we had an invitation from Sir James – did no one tell you? To join him at Gautmuir for lunch. I've had to phone him to apologise.'

They were all still on their feet.

'You want us to go now?'

'He's expecting us. Whenever you arrived, he said. May as well save it till we get there, eh? Save you going over it twice, am I right?'

Following Baird as he trotted across the car park with MacLean at heel, it was the unprofessionalism of it Meldrum despised. Recently his daughter Betty had lectured him: You can kid yourself in the city, in the country the estate walls rub your nose in where the power is. He'd told her: Don't bring your soapbox when you visit me.

In the car, Baird said, 'If he runs true to form, there'll be a dram on offer.' And after a silence, 'It's natural for Sir James to take an interest. Ex-Home Secretary and all that.'

'And he knew Mrs Hannah,' MacLean said. 'He went bird-watching with her late husband. When they were younger, that is.'

As they got out of the car, a bird flew up off the loch that lay in front of the house.

'Great crested grebe,' MacLean said, swinging the big red ball of his face to follow its flight. 'I'm an enthusiast,' he apologised. 'Have been since I was a boy.' And quietly to Meldrum as they followed Baird up the flight of steps: 'You can park on the layby outside the gate and bird-watch in the

estate woods. Have to be careful, of course. It doesn't do to get
on the family's wrong side.'

They waited in a room which was probably called the library
– between the windows there were bookcases from floor to
ceiling. On the other hand, Meldrum decided, it could be
called the bowling alley. It was long enough. Have to move
the tables back one way, of course, and the leather couch and
chairs the other. Carpet bowls. Roll the jack up to just under
the paintings on the end wall.

He heard the door open behind him. Despite Baird's prompt-
ing, he had avoided meeting Sir James during the investigation.
His first impression was that years out of the public eye had left
him unchanged: the narrow height of the man, the loose jolting
walk, a face all bones with a jaw clenched like a trap and a
thin, bloodless slash of a mouth. Closer he saw the neck and
face were seamed with wrinkles, as if a net had been pulled
tight to contain the old yellow flesh.

'You'll forgive me,' he said when they were seated. 'Knowing
Martin Hannah as I did, I wanted to be in at the kill.'

'I'm afraid it isn't a kill,' Meldrum said.

'Whatever you care to call it.' The old man's hand, white on
black leather, brushed that aside.

It was the kind of gesture that brought out the worst in
Meldrum.

'By the time I was called in, Mrs Hannah had been dead a
week.' Make them wait for it, he thought. 'Statements had been
taken. All of them gave descriptions of a man who'd been seen
either in the garden or on the road outside . . . And then, of
course, there was the bus driver Kerr.'

The point about Kerr was that his description contradicted
the convenient agreement among the other witnesses. At mention of him MacLean frowned. The faded blue glance of Sir
James shifted to him and slid back. It was interesting to note
how the old man had picked up on that. In the same way, when
Kerr's role had been explained to him, he asked, 'Why should
he remember this passenger in particular?'

'Because he asked the way to the Hannah house.'

'Or the road. It might have been to the road,' MacLean said.
'There are only two houses on that road.'

'But then you heard from Maidstone,' Sir James said with the faintest trace of an old man's irritability, 'so that rather settled matters, did it not?'

'Inspector MacLean and I went down,' Meldrum said. 'William Hawthorne had been held overnight for refusing to pay a restaurant bill. By chance a bright young constable connected him to the description we had circulated. It was the Australian accent that clinched it.'

MacLean took advantage of the pause to enter a claim for his share of the glory. 'He denied ever being in Scotland, but when we got him up here the witnesses identified him.'

Except Kerr, Meldrum thought, and realised Sir James was watching him. Like a mind-reader. Or an old fox scenting an unwanted something on the wind.

'And when they opened his suitcase there were photographs of the countryside round about here. One even showed Mrs Hannah's house in the background,' Baird said, savouring it. 'An expensive souvenir, I'd call that. But, please, this is your story.'

'Circumstantial,' Meldrum said, 'but it added up. Going over Mrs Hannah's house, we hadn't found it easy to check on what might be missing.'

MacLean said, 'Mrs Hannah wasn't one for visitors.'

'Martin and she preferred birds to people,' Sir James said, sounding as if he felt it a reasonable point of view.

When Meldrum had flown back down to England two days earlier, he had only two items to be sure of – a silver whisky flask, a presentation cup – but each was unmistakable. Find either of them and the case was watertight.

'The Chief Inspector phoned this morning,' MacLean said, 'to say there had been a development.'

'I'd tried all the pawnbrokers in the place,' Meldrum said. 'I was ready to come back. I was in the last one on my list. Same story. No cup, a flask but the wrong one. I was standing on the pavement outside when I thought of the camera.'

It had bothered him that there had been photographs but no camera. Back inside he asked them to check their records.

MacLean was frowning again. 'His camera? I don't see what that would prove?'

'Date and time. It proved that at half-four on the day Mrs Hannah was killed, William Hawthorne was hundreds of miles away. Pawning his camera. His story about hitching south on the day before the murder was true.'

'You're sure it was him?' MacLean asked.

'He signed for it.'

Baird was blank-faced, the flesh on his plump cheeks sagging like a petulant child's. For the rest of the time, he said as little as possible. It was only when they were outside that he burst out, 'Why didn't you tell us? In front of Sir James too!'

Punching buttons in search of music on the drive home, Meldrum let his attention be caught by a mention of Farquhar Wood. There had been a demonstration against the Secretary of State in Edinburgh. By students at a graduation ceremony. Betty was only second year. So that was all right. Nothing to worry about.

Young student voices talking about hardship. Listening, he welcomed the distraction. They should come with him into the housing schemes, he'd show them what hardship was in the real world. He tuned in on an old Country-and-Western and stayed with it to find out the singer whom he half recognised.

'In front of Sir James too!' Making enemies was easy in the police, but just as stupid as in any other ambitious profession. Sir James, those fleshless jaws snapping shut like a reptile's, you wouldn't want him as an enemy. But why should he be an enemy? He must want the right man caught, not just anyone. Home; get a sleep. Tomorrow he was due at a case conference with Billy Ord. Pick up the pieces.

At parting, Sir James had laid fingers fragile as a bundle of dry twigs into Meldrum's grip. 'It's all still to do. Evidently. You were remarkably conscientious.' There was no way of telling from his face or the dry, whispering old man's voice what he was thinking. 'The pitfalls of circumstantial evidence.'

One moment the road clear in front of him; the next Hugh Keaney's face, going whiter than the bands at the judge's throat as he was sentenced to life for the murder of blind Arthur Hull. Circumstantial evidence. Thank God, he didn't swerve the car. He didn't want Keaney in his head. Keaney was in the past,

over and done with. Rooftop protests would do him no good.
Some things it did no good to remember.

What was left if you stopped being ambitious?

A different record was playing. The other one had ended
and he'd missed the name of the singer.

CHAPTER THREE

'I couldn't believe how late it was.'

The hair stood up on the back of her neck when she heard Sandy Torrance's voice.

'Some people love their pit,' Cliff the landlord said, making hoinking noises at him and pointing at the clock. Betty Meldrum and Cliff had known each other since they were children at school. 'That nice fee-paying school of yours,' Sandy called it.

Before last night she knew Sandy had been jealous of Cliff. Now as he edged round the table she was aware of his heat on her skin and a smell warmed in a burrow of blankets. All of her senses were on full alert. Last night he had made love to her. It was the first time for both of them. They were nineteen.

She watched him from the corner of her eye as he ran a little water into the kettle. She said, 'Sandy and I sat up late talking.' He hadn't looked at her yet.

'Laying plans for the revolution?' Cliff wasn't the type to be sensitive to atmosphere. Lesley would have picked up on what was going on, but as a nurse she was away early in the morning.

'That's how it's going to feel to Farquhar Wood,' and putting it into words Sandy threw up his arms and let the excitement go like pulling a cork.

'Careful!' Betty said.

All she meant, of course, was that he was spilling his tea.

He put the mug back on the table and took a bite out of the sandwich he was holding in his other hand.

'Up the workers!' Cliff jeered.

'We're not interested in your sex life,' Sandy said.

Cliff looked offended, which came easily to him. Born to be an accountant, Lesley said. It was part of her feud against him since he had pinned a note to the bathroom door accusing the girls of blocking up the toilet. Betty hadn't let it bother her. Tampax, Cliff? she'd asked laughing, where'd you learn such a word? Wash your mouth out!

As Sandy leaned against the sink sipping coffee, she wanted him to reach out and touch her breast. If he didn't look at her soon, even Cliff must guess what had happened.

'Betty!' The word exploded out. He stood there with his face going red. Now they were both looking at him.

As Cliff's glance went from one to the other, Betty got up and took the mug and rinsed it under the tap. When she turned back, she was smiling. 'I know, it's time we were going.' She felt relaxed and in charge. 'We have to meet the others.'

As soon as they were on the landing, he caught her by the arm and kissed her. Behind them the door opened. They jumped apart, but Cliff didn't seem to notice.

'I'd be a bit careful.'

'What?'

He stood in the doorway brushing at the hair that persisted in falling in a lank wave over one eye. 'I'd be careful about getting mixed up in anything outside the hall. Inside, safe enough.'

'Since when are you an expert on demos?' The idea did seem funny to Sandy, but his question came out aggressively. Hearing the harshness, she thought it was answering something in Cliff, some tension of discomfort that made her uneasy.

'At least you might think of Betty!' he cried and slammed the door shut.

Sandy took Betty's hand as they ran down the stairs.

'What on earth was that about?' he wondered.

'Just Cliff.'

As if that explained everything.

'His father's a top lawyer, isn't he?'

'An advocate,' Betty said.

'Maybe he's heard something then.'

'About what?'

'He'll have pals in the police.'

But they were out in the street now, into the daylight press of cars and people. The idea of Cliff's father getting wind of some police plan seemed foolish.

And after all, there was no secret about the anger directed at Farquhar Wood. There were two kinds of Secretary of State for Scotland, the ones who sought a high profile and the ones who kept their heads down. The latter had risen as far as they were ever likely to, often higher than they had any right to expect. They aimed for a quiet life and hoped for the right amount of nationalist success, just enough for the Prime Minister to leave them in place as a convenient bulwark, not enough to worry him when he had more important matters to attend to. The high-profile ones, on the other hand, had ambitions of being Minister of Defence, Home Secretary, Foreign Secretary: something juicy at the centre. For them timing was important; and a bit of luck if a career wasn't to stall. From London, Edinburgh seemed further away than its 400 miles, a view shrouded by the prejudice of a border crossed in the past by armies at war.

It was the ill fortune of Farquhar Wood, generally regarded as one of the quiet ones, that everything Prime Minister and Treasury had told him to do in the last year had made life worse for most people, not least students.

'What does he think's going to happen?' Sandy asked as they crossed the Meadows. 'That we're going to stand up and cheer him?'

Under its round dome the McEwan Hall had the look of a temple. Sandy had wondered to her if there might be some god in an eastern pantheon who took care of education. Somebody to pray to for rent allowances, books in the library, trips to where the great paintings were.

Already graduands in gowns and their families were getting animated with friends or into line at the doors. On the pillars of the steps leading down into the Square, swoops and whirls of Arabic had been leached in black paint into the new sandstone. Quotes from the Koran; protests against imperialism; Nojat

loves Mariam: how could you tell? Around the sunken paved
area, the concrete and glass of Bristo with the student bank and
canteens faced the old stone of Teviot Hall and the McEwan.
Like a circus with the audience gathering, she thought. Lions
being introduced to Christians. And in the middle of the
sunken area she turned all the way round, but saw only one
policeman near the main entrance.

'Do you see them?' Sandy asked, looking for the others.

It had all been worked out at the meeting three days ago: the
effort to keep Farquhar Wood out of the Hall, the protest inside,
making it hot for him afterwards. She hadn't anticipated the air
of celebration, the mums in hats. It felt like spoiling a party.
When Jimmy Campbell came up and said, not bothering to
lower his voice, 'The bastard's inside. They've pulled a fast
one,' it was a relief.

'How do you know?'

'One of the attendants.'

'Damn!' she said. 'Let's get in there.'

Sandy glanced towards the solitary policeman. His head
was bent to the radio in his hand, but his eyes were fixed
on them.

'There's a policeman watching us.'

But when they looked, he was turned the other way.

'Seeing you, he couldn't believe his eyes,' Jimmy Campbell
said, tapping the side of his nose derisively.

Sandy, learning to be a painter, drawn into Students for Change
only because of Betty, was suspected by Jimmy Campbell of
frivolity. Like Betty, Campbell was at university, doing History
though, not English. Jimmy was serious. Jimmy was a revolu-
tionary who dressed like a bank clerk; Sandy, ring in each ear,
rings through his nose and all, was at heart a gentle pacifist, a
believer in the quiet life. Any anger he had he wanted to save
for the canvas.

They had managed to get hold of tickets for the left gallery. Below, the graduands filled the body of the hall. When
the platform party with the Principal at its head processed
in, everyone stood. Tradition; like getting up for God Save
the Queen; usually she stayed seated for that; didn't seem
good tactics here. In the procession slow-pacing up the aisle,

she spotted the squat, comfortable figure of the Secretary of State.

'There he is!' Sandy whispered.

The woman in front turned and smiled at them. She thinks, Betty realised, we're here as family, for somebody about to graduate, a brother maybe. She smiled back and the woman nodded as if to share her pleasure in the day. A woman of fifty or so with lined cheeks as if she'd been ill once. The man beside her had white hair. Waiting to see their child graduate. A big day.

She felt a stab of panic as she searched for the others in the group. In theory, tickets were for close relatives only and confined to two to each graduand. In practice, through one channel or another, they had got hold of eighteen tickets. Checking everybody in sight, Betty could find only five of them. With Sandy, Jimmy and herself that made eight. Either she was missing them, or the rest had taken cold feet. If so, they were no worse than those professors who had talked of staying away in protest at the invitation to the Secretary of State. There were no gaps that she could see in the solid ranks on the platform.

The graduation itself was oddly soothing, the litany of names, the blocks of colour made by the hoods spreading back row on row from the platform, the shuffling from seat to seat as they came back like beads pushed along an abacus wire. The clapping came in little bursts with each name and Sandy joined in every time.

The plan was that five minutes into Farquhar Wood's speech there would be the first interruption, then five minutes after he got started again there would be another; then ten minutes later the third. It had been carefully worked out. There would be four in the first team of protestors, six in the second, eight in the third. Even after they were all ejected, it would be hard for anyone to pay attention to the speaker as they waited for the next outburst. Sandy was one of the openers, since it was felt the way he looked he might be thrown out on principle at the first sign of trouble.

When Farquhar Wood got up, a thin self-conscious booing from among the newly graduated was swallowed up in a wave

of applause. Some of the professors were holding their hands
up in front of their faces so that they could be seen to be beating
them together, moved no doubt by notions of the hospitality
due to a guest.

She could hear Farquhar Wood's voice but couldn't make
sense of the words. The minute hand dragged forward from
11.34. When it reached 11.39, Sandy jumped to his feet and
started yelling. They had worked out slogans, but he kept yelling, 'Bloody fascist!' over and over for no sensible reason.

As if too delighted to notice anything outside its own noise,
the amplified voice of Farquhar Wood rolled on without a
pause. Sandy glared around; he was alone on his feet. At that
point, just as he stumbled to a halt, Betty, who had appointed
herself to the third group of interrupters, said, 'Oh, hell!' and
got up to join him. Like a signal that got the others to their feet;
and listening to Betty, Sandy got the slogan right and they were
all shouting the same thing.

People round about began to object. Down below, a professor
jumped to his feet and shook both clenched fists up at them.
Sandy clutched the pew, forgetting slogans again, leaning over
to shout down at him, 'Sieg Heil! Sieg Heil! Sieg Heil!'

'You should be ashamed!' the woman with the lined cheeks
said. Twisted round to stare up at him. 'Why are you doing
this?'

And he laughed into her face as if wanting her to share his
excitement.

Betty had him by the arm. 'Come on! Come on!'

The plan had been to give up quietly. Even if all eighteen
of them were arrested, there were to be another half dozen
waiting outside the hall for the exit protest. But now Betty
was racing up the steps, pulling him with her. At the top they
ran along the passage behind the seats, circling the length of the
gallery away from the policemen. Jimmy Campbell and Danny
scrambled up an aisle to join them. Ahead Hilary and Neil were
running. The way seemed clear to the far exit. People were up
in their seats but no one showed signs of wanting to join in
the chase. Leave it to the police, the civilised way. She threw
back a glance, expecting to find one on her heels. There were
two of them, not running but walking. Taking their time. They

must know there were others covering the exits. There wasn't any point in running. She ran. Sandy ran. All of them ran.

They piled out on to the upper corridor. 'This way!' They followed Sandy, but she was sure he was running the wrong way to get out. Another policeman came out from a door at the end and they swerved into a down stair. Now it was going to be all right, went through her head, down and left and we're back at the front door. Maybe the police won't be there. Out into the Square and let them try to catch us. Any idea of protesting outside was forgotten. The stairs were stone and rang under their feet as they tumbled down the flights.

Hilary and Neil were still in front and at the bottom corridor they ran to the right. 'Wrong way!' Sandy screamed, and then she saw them. More policemen. Just standing blocking the way. As if they're herding us, she thought, but there wasn't any choice. Give up quietly had been the plan. The plan was forgotten. Once you started running, you couldn't stop.

There was an exit door that wouldn't open, then another. And then on the curve of the outer wall a door lay open and through it trees, a feathering of long slender branches, not a leaf stirring, motionless, as if painted.

At last, she thought.

From somewhere out in the open, one of the girls began to scream. Eyes wide, they stared at one another. Sandy gestured to her to stay where she was and hurried outside.

From the corridor behind, the hollow beating of feet echoed like applause. When the second scream came, the fright that had gone through her like sickness vanished. She stepped out through the doors.

Neil was on the ground with Sandy protecting him, shouting up at a policeman on horseback. There seemed to be policemen everywhere. As she watched, the horse nudged forward knocking him off his feet, and there were two men, one with a knee on his chest as he struggled and the other bent over him.

She ran at them, yelling her anger. They got to their feet, and one of them took a look at her unhurriedly, but the next moment they were gone, anonymous uniforms among the crowd.

When Sandy took his hands away from his face, she saw blood and then the loose strip of flesh that hung down towards his lip.

CHAPTER FOUR

'What's your name, darling?'
'Benny,' Clay said, which seemed as good a name as any other.

'What age are you?'

'. . . thirty-five.'

'I'm thirty-four. I'm divorced. My name's Laurel. I'm five foot five, thirty-six, thirty-two, thirty-eight. I have long blonde hair.'

None of that meant anything to him.

He waited and thought perhaps she'd gone away.

'Where are you from, darling? Up the beanstalk?'

'Carlisle.'

'Where's that, darling?'

'In the north of England.'

'Not Jack from Wonderland?'

'Carlisle.'

'Is that the back of beyond?'

'Where are you?'

'What?'

'Where are you?'

'Waterloo. In London.'

'Only a Londoner wouldn't know where Carlisle was.'

She laughed. 'Right.'

He hated the way she let a silence develop.

'What would you like to talk about? Is there something you'd like to tell me?'

'Yes.'

'Go on then. You can tell me anything.'

'How long you been doing this?'

'How do you mean, darling?'

'Talking like this, *this*.'

'Six weeks.'

'That all?'

'Oh, I've learned a bit. I thought I knew most of it, but the things you're told!'

'What?'

'The things men talk about. That gets them excited. Some of it doesn't seem to have anything to do with sex at all.'

'Yes. What? Tell me.'

'Well . . . Like getting their hair washed. They lie back over the basin and the water through their hair and getting it soaped and they're gasping and saying, oh and then oh and then.'

'I'm in a hotel.'

'What?'

'I'm on my own.'

'You're lonely.'

'I'm away from home. When I'm at home, I go to see a dominant woman once a week.'

'Is she your girlfriend, like?'

'I pay her.' Stupid bitch.

'What does she get you to do?'

'She beats me.'

'Is that what you were frightened to tell me?'

Now it was his turn to let silence lengthen. There were other things, a string of them to say, but he found he had no energy to offer them.

'That's all right then,' she said. 'Nothing to be ashamed of.'

'Not as if I murdered somebody.'

'What?'

'Not as if I murdered somebody.'

'Of course not. You sound too nice.'

'She likes to see blood.'

'Yes? . . . Well, if it was me you was seeing, I'd get you to suck my toes.' Her voice which had been listless now deepened a note and laid a faint stress on the 'I'. 'I'd be

wearing a basque and I'd have on my high-heeled boots. What
would you do then?'

'I'd lick your boots.'

'You would, would you?'

'And higher, if you'd let me.'

'No. I'd get you to take down my stockings, roll them down
one at a time and then take my boots off. I'd get you to suck
my toes one after the other.'

'Suck your toes,' he said. That didn't do anything for him.

'Not in a bossy way. If you wanted to.'

'Christ!' he said, and put the phone down.

He saw a foot, not very clean, its toes squeezed together like
a single roll of folded meat. The big toe set to one side had a
thick yellow nail.

He stared at its image in the dark.

CHAPTER FIVE

After the interview with Sir James and the long drive home from Gautmuir, Meldrum had been tired. He'd sat in the drive wondering whether it was worth the bother of putting the car away. It was only when he'd switched off, at the moment he relaxed into the silence, that he noticed the upstairs curtains were drawn. They had been open when he left.

He had got out, closed the door quietly and gone round to the back. There had been no sign of a break-in. In the kitchen the fridge had been humming as it recharged. He had gone upstairs softly and fast. The bathroom had been empty. The other three doors had been shut, to the bedroom he'd shared with Carole before she walked out, to the middle room and to the one piled with boxes and stuff he had no use for. When somebody had coughed, he had responded like a pulled switch, jumping through into the middle room, Betty's old room.

And there she had been.

He had never hit Betty. Not in all her life. But as he burst into the room, she had cowered behind upraised arms as if to defend herself against a blow. Not in all her life. What upset him was that as she recognised him the look of fear did not alter.

In what was left of the night he had slept badly, and now, following his daughter into the building, he felt the tiredness still in his bones. His dislike of hospitals went back a long way. His first year on the beat, Meldrum had ended up in a public

ward after being stabbed in the belly. They had
outside and deep inside and it ached both ends of
and through the nights there was never a time without
Like every hospital corridor this one needed a coat of pa
the ward was unexpectedly big with patio doors to a bal ny
striped by the morning sun. He saw the four neatly made beds,
one in each corner, and thought this looked like a place where
you could get a sleep.

Moving into the ward, they saw a boy on the balcony, arms
stretched out as he leaned his weight against the railing. At the
sound of Betty's voice, he pushed himself upright and turned
to face them.

'Poor Sandy! Isn't this awful?' the boy said. His name as it
turned out was Cliff. The flatmate. 'After the demonstration,
Betty came back to the flat. She was terribly upset. After what
had happened, she just wanted to go, well, home.' A polite
boy who hesitated over the complex modern geography of
where home might be. 'Betty and I were at school together,'
smiling at her.

As he followed Betty and Cliff along the corridor to the
dayroom, a stout shuffling man came out of it. 'I don't like
football,' he frowned at them.

It was hard to tell if Sandy Torrance did or didn't. A tall,
narrow-shouldered boy, he sat in the partisan noise of the
dayroom staring in silence at the screen. His nose was hidden
by a fat stripe of bandage and the upper lip carried a tattoo
of black stitches. Meldrum's first impression was that he was
in shock. Back out in the corridor, though, when Betty told
him, 'This is my father,' he responded, 'The policeman,' and
didn't sound fearful but dry, wary, challenging. He didn't
drop his gaze either; the eyes above the bandage held steady.
Considering what had happened, it wasn't a bad showing.

'The ring was torn out of his nose,' Betty had told him, her
arms down now from her face, hugging her shoulders. 'They
were waiting for us at the back of the McEwan Hall. Bloody
policemen. This one on horseback. And Sandy trying to help
– that's all he was doing, trying to help Neil.'

One day when she was still a child to him he had put an arm
round her shoulder and cuddled her. Done it without thinking

as he had countless times before because she was his daughter; because he loved her and at that time took her love for granted. She had chopped the air with her hand and pulled herself away from him. It had seemed to him the look on her face was disgust. It might have helped if he had been able to remember what they'd been talking about. No context, the moment stood alone, the gesture isolated and with it the look on her face. It was before Carole left him; he didn't think the break-up of his marriage had anything to do with it. Perhaps it was just something that happened between fathers and daughters. For whatever reason, it took away from him the ability to reach out to her spontaneously. That had been chilled.

It had left him wary of being so offended a second time.

'Sandy's face was pouring blood. And the one on the horse grinned down at me.'

If he had just disbelieved her, it might not have been so bad. But he had wanted to get at the truth, and how was he supposed to do that except by asking questions? That was his training. That was how he spent his life. He was a policeman, for God's sake.

And so it had gone on until, not able to help himself, his last question had been, 'If it's such a crime being a policeman, why come to me? Why didn't you go to your mother?'

'Because this is my room,' she had said.

Looking round at where she had been a child.

This morning he thought what she had needed was to be comforted. It did seem he might have taken her in his arms, but now it was too late.

CHAPTER SIX

'Nice case, all sewn up for the country cousins. And then Hawthorne pawns his camera! Bloody Aussie!' Ord snorted. 'And there you were getting to visit the gentry, Jim. Could have done you a bit of good.'

There was an etiquette of pissing which didn't include staring across into the next stall. Meldrum was staring.

'Truth is, you buggered it up.'

'One way of putting it,' Meldrum said, distracted.

The brilliant red streamed from Detective Superintendent Billy Ord's thick cock and hit the wall as if an artery had been severed. He gave a sly side glance and Meldrum looked away.

'No flowers by request,' he said, directing the flow to one side and the other as it thinned to a trickle. He shook himself and turned away. By the time Meldrum finished, Ord was at the washbasins watching him in the mirror.

'Eh, Jim?'

'What?'

'No flowers by request.'

Meldrum thought about that while he soaped his hands. Ord had been the Detective Sergeant he had worked under when he first came into CID. It struck him how long ago that was. The job drove you together. Civilians were cautious around policemen. Most people having something to hide. Or thinking they might one day have something to hide. Or not happy about having it drawn to their attention they didn't have anything to hide, not now or ever likely to. Next stop the cemetery.

'I like flowers,' he offered at last. 'They're a mark of respect. Not much use if you're going to get cremated, right enough.'

Ord stared then burst into laughter, a harsh noise, the big red slab of his farmer's face gaping.

'Only you,' he said. He picked up a wad of towels and started to scrub at his fists. 'Once upon a time just Ned Kellys. Now they let any colour bugger in.'

'Into Australia,' Meldrum guessed, used to the way Ord's mind worked.

'Chinks and Mafia.' He spat in the basin. 'Not a lot different from here.'

'It was never all that strong against Hawthorne. Supposing it had come to court.'

'Right.'

Circumstantial evidence.

Drying his hands, he focussed on the newspaper someone had dropped beside the towels. The front page consisted largely of a pair of breasts. The attached woman dwindled into the background behind them. Ludicrous, grotesque; not real, faked up, if they were real she'd be in pain; breasts are sexy, that was the idea, bigger the better, a kind of joke; more complicated though, if it's a joke there's a lot of anger in it, sour mother's milk. As all that ran through his head, Ord was saying something and he missed it.

Guessing again, he said, 'The one I want to look at again is the bus driver Kerr. The odd man out on the descriptions.'

Ord stared. 'Clean your ears out. I was asking about Betty.'

'Betty?'

'You got another kid you've been hiding somewhere? You said she wasn't badly hurt.'

'She isn't hurt at all.'

'So why the hospital? What was so bloody important I'd to be kept waiting?'

Five minutes. All right, ten.

'Sorry about that. A friend of hers got beaten up.'

'So?'

A trace of reluctance always gave Ord a dose of the persistents.

'She was at the demo against Farquhar Wood.'

'What demo?'

'At the university.'

'Oh, that demo.' Deadpan. You could never know when Ord was kidding you. It was hard to believe he hadn't heard about it. 'Not nice, girls getting beaten up.'

'The friend was a boy.'

'Nothing queer about old Piggy, eh?' Ord said and went out into the corridor laughing at his own wit.

Catching up, Meldrum said, 'A friend who's yelling police brutality.' Glancing at Ord, who grunted and lumbered on. 'He had a ring through his nose and claims it was pulled out. I didn't have time to check with the surgeon, but something happened to him. His face is a mess.'

'Through his what?'

'Nose, through his nose.'

'Like a bull. Boyfriend, did you say he was?'

'He's talking about getting a lawyer.' More accurately, Betty, almost back to normal, was threatening to organise him into one.

'You tell Betty,' Ord said, giving Meldrum the uncomfortable feeling of having his mind read, 'forget it. Tell her Uncle Billy says, life's too short.' And at something he saw in Meldrum's face burst out into laughter. 'Beetroot. Gives you a fright when you piss, but I love it. Ate a plate of it last night.'

Irritating bastard.

CHAPTER SEVEN

W hen Meldrum saw it, the body was pale and wrinkled.
It had lain in water for hours and the meat had been
bled from the deep gashes carved into the left wrist.

Driving back from Nottingham, it had occurred to him that
if the confession in his briefcase stood up, finding that pawn
ticket for the camera didn't matter. Which was a pity. It
had been a nice piece of work. If this confession stood up,
Hawthorne would anyway have been freed to go back to
Australia. In the end most of what you did made no difference.

It was late as always and as always he was tired.

'A case I was on,' he told Betty, justifying himself for not
being there when she came. He'd arrived home, wanting to
do nothing but sleep, and found her waiting. It was getting to
be a habit.

'In Nottingham?'

'Well, it didn't start there. Obviously.'

Betty pressed her lips together and glanced away. It was a
response he'd seen too often. There wouldn't be any point in
telling her he hadn't meant to sound so dry, so abrupt; he
wouldn't have known how to admit it even if it would have
made a difference.

So there was no way he could tell her how it had felt
driving one-way roads round that town until, like everywhere
nowadays, it didn't seem worth going anywhere. Or about the
local detective inspector who bought him a drink and said,

'Nottingham's the murder capital of England. Or was last year.'
And: 'Graham Greene started out here as a journalist. Hated it.
You've heard of Graham Greene?'

You'd have had to be there to know how empty those streets
felt on a Sunday afternoon. Or to hear the landlady when she
said, 'My husband's seen too much death. He doesn't find it
easy here. He's been beaten up twice – just for being a foreigner.
It makes me ashamed of being English. When I was out there, I
met with so much kindness.'

The landlord, a big quiet man, a refugee with his own
story to tell, was the one who had identified the dead man
for the police. He'd signed him in the night before: James
Fowler. Sometime in the early hours of the morning, the
noise of the water tank refilling had wakened the landlord
and he'd grumbled to his wife before getting back to sleep.
Next morning, the couple on the top floor had complained
they couldn't get into the shared bathroom on the landing. On
James Fowler's bedside table local police had found a letter.
It lacked detail as a confession; but he could spell Hannah
and put the old lady's murder in the right room. Meldrum
had a gut feeling it was going to check out. Another case
done with, file closed: they made up his life like bricks in
a wall.

Betty said, 'You didn't tell me you were going to Nottingham.'

Down an empty Sunday street set on a hill there had been a
statue of Robin Hood.

You've heard of Robin Hood, Betty?

Weeks could pass without her trying to see him. He thought
that but contented himself with saying, 'No.'

Before she could say anything else, he got up and went into
the kitchen to pour a drink. He wondered if she would stay
the night. If she wanted to go back to her flat, he would take
her. What age do you think I am? that's what he'd get. Run
her back anyway; it was too late for standing at a bus stop.
He couldn't bear anything happening to her.

As he settled down again, she looked at the glass in his hand
and frowned like her mother.

'You said you wanted to talk to me about Sandy,' she said.
'When we left the hospital.'

'After what happened to him, I can understand Torrance is angry.'

'*I'm* angry.'

'That doesn't do any good.'

'You're telling us to forget it? What that animal did to Sandy?'

'He's made his complaint. It'll go to the Deputy Chief Constable. It'll be investigated.'

'By another policeman.'

'By an Inspector. Or someone more senior. Probably in this case, an Inspector.'

'Another policeman,' she said with bitter emphasis.

He was angry suddenly, and for more reasons than he could have explained even to himself. 'You don't know what you're talking about. You live in a – in a dream world. Listen, not much older than you are now I was walking a beat in Gorgie. I heard screaming – I don't mean shouting. Screaming. It was a woman – he'd torn off her clothes, punched her, kicked her. She'd stepped off the pavement in front of his car. The thing is, this wasn't being done in the dark. It was the middle of the day and a crowd watching. Nobody stopped him. He was a big man and he was crazy with anger. But that doesn't cover it – if they'd wanted to there were enough men there to stop him. I stopped him.'

'You know I didn't mean you,' she said.

'I'm not talking about me. I did it because it was my job. Maybe on another corner somebody would've stopped him or tried – a guy who did judo, a Christian, I don't know. Somebody exceptional. That's why we have policemen, so we don't have to rely on exceptional men.'

'Or women.'

'. . . or women.' His anger had run down like an unwound clock, leaving him embarrassed like the morning-after memory of drunken confidences.

'I think I've found a lawyer,' she said.

'I wish you hadn't done that.'

'Because it doesn't matter. Is that what you think?'

'Since you ask, I can think of more important things.' He heard himself, dry, withdrawn. Would he never learn? He took a breath and tried again. 'I just don't want you to give it more of your life than it deserves.'

'Would you say that if it was me that had been hurt?'

'Probably not.'

'You were the one who taught me the difference between right and wrong.'

Hurt? If you'd been hurt, I'd rip the bastard's head off. He stared down into the glass, hiding the rage, for her, at her that she could even ask, watching the whisky spin under the little circling of his hand.

'People mustn't just stand by if they see something's wrong,' she said, and then after a long pause, softly so that it would have been easy to miss, 'You don't.'

But if she was claiming they were alike, she was mistaken, for she believed people were good and that made him afraid for her.

CHAPTER EIGHT

'It's different with you, Carole,' Betty told her mother.
With her mother it had always been different. If she was
against authority, it wasn't because of anything she had ever
felt towards her mother.

'Whatever else about your father, he loves you in his own
way,' Carole said. In his own way. Well, exactly. In a comfortable silence they left the office and went down the corridor to
Miss Grogan's room. As they went in, the class of nine-year-
olds looked up and some of them smiled. Once upon a time,
Betty thought, they'd have been bobbing up and tugging their
forelock, sing-songing good-morning-miss to the Head Teacher.
Things changed sometimes for the better.

The hour with the children passed quickly. During it Miss
Grogan felt confident enough to take herself off, though when
she came back it was to make a fuss about the crumpled paper
of first attempts scattered on the floor around desks. Things
didn't change all that much, it seemed.

It was Betty's third visit to the school at Carole's suggestion.
Good for you, she'd said – and good for the children, they don't
get their imaginations stimulated enough.

Back in the office to say goodbye, Betty said, 'If this is a plot
to get me to want to be a teacher, it won't work, you know.'

'What harm can it do having another string to your bow?'
Carole wondered. She pushed a letter across into a file tray
and picked up another. 'Getting a degree doesn't guarantee you
a job nowadays.'

A car had come into the playground. Black and long, so big it seemed there couldn't be room as it turned sharp left and rolled between the double line of cars belonging to the staff. A man got out on the driver's side. Young, thick-set, in a dark suit, he looked substantial and even prosperous until the second man got out; the effect was as if he had been shrunk. They stood together studying the building as a woman climbed out of the back of the car. All three began to move towards the entrance.

'You've got visitors,' Betty said.

'Oh?' Her mother eased up to peer out of the window. 'What a ridiculous place to park!'

'I'll make myself scarce.'

But there was a rap of knuckles at the door, and before her mother could respond it opened. Everything about the man who came in was big. The overcoat hung on the solid bulk of him like a black tent on a hillside. Betty guessed him at six foot two three or four inches. He had a broad pale face, a jut of nose, black eyebrows and a mane of swept-back white hair.

'John Brennan,' he said, ignoring Betty and holding out his hand to Carole as she got up from behind the desk. 'Mrs Meldrum? We spoke on the phone about Marie, my five-year-old.'

'Mr Brennan, of course. And this will be your wife.'

'My wife.' And seemed to think that enough of an introduction.

The thick-set young man stood when they were seated and was not introduced.

'I'd like to take you up on your offer to have a look around. To see what the facilities are in the school. What's available.'

'It was my impression – I was expecting you to phone back to make an appointment.'

Betty, watching him in profile, saw no trace of expression. He didn't smile or frown or blink; didn't speak; waited.

'But, of course, since you're here,' Carole said, getting up, 'I'd be glad to.'

In the flurry of husband and wife standing, Betty wondered what she would say when she was left with the young man. He, however, without a word tagged on at the end as they left. Betty

watched her mother lead them down the corridor and into
the gym. As the door opened she heard cheers and a whistle
shrilled. Too curious now not to wait for Carole to come back,
she wandered round the room. Above the bookcase there was
a little poster with a poem, MacDiarmid's 'The Bonnie Broukit
Bairn'. She read it over and then said it aloud softly to herself.
Glancing out of the window, she saw the janitor at the visitor's
car. He walked up one side, then the other, as if totalling up in
disbelief the number of cars blocked by it. Finished, he looked
around in search of advice or inspiration and, finding none,
wandered off with the air of a man who had done all that could
be reasonably expected.

'It's like a royal procession. Sorry! Didn't mean to startle
you!' The Depute had popped her head round the door. Without waiting to be asked, Betty confessed, 'His name's Brennan.
He's thinking of sending his daughter here.'

'Is he, indeed! They've been all round the place – out to the
huts – into the dining hall – they had a look at the kitchen! –
over to the infants block. A royal procession.'

By the time the procession returned, Betty had set the door
of the Head's room slightly ajar so that she could hear what
was being said as they left. Brennan's voice rumbled in the
approach all the way along the corridor, a monologue of
thunder.

'. . . but I mean a personal cheque.'

'That isn't the way we work.' Carole sounded tired but
unyielding.

'I'm sure there must be things you need. I'm offering to
help.'

'The way we do it is through the Parent Teacher Association.
They do the fund-raising.'

'Raffles and teas.' He dismissed that idea. 'Suppose I provided – what's the thing now in education? Computers?'

'We think they're important, yes.'   •

'There you are then.'

'We've laid a lot of emphasis on that area in the last few
years. From our allocation. And, of course, the Parent Teacher
Association has been very generous.'

'So what are you short of?'

'Oh, there's lots! The best thing would be to go through the Association. They do take personal cheques.'

As she heard them leave, Betty came out into the hall.

'Well done you.'

'Unbelievable,' Carole said.

Standing back from the window, they watched the car manoeuvre its way out. Betty caught her mother making a two-fingered gesture at it.

'I've never seen you do that before. What would your staff think?'

'If I hadn't won the battle there, that man would have made my life hell. He'd have taken the place over for his brat. Be on the phone giving me my instructions. I'd've been jumping when he whistled.'

'Did his wife say anything?'

'Not a word. All the way round. Not a word.'

'And the bodyguard! Or whatever he was.'

'Don't think about it.'

'Who is he? Head of the local mafia?'

'That, my dear, was John Brennan.'

'Sorry?'

'Don't you ever look at a paper? He's John Brennan the lawyer. He's quite famous.'

'The criminal's best friend?' Betty asked,

'That's the one.'

CHAPTER NINE

'It's a great bloody place Florida, but after all that Disney-World crap I needed time to myself, know what I mean? Anyway, the son's wife is lying on the sand, the kid's playing somewhere, when she sees this guy's watching her. After a bit she gets up and heads for the water. He comes after her. She ignores him. He's giving her the typical American bullshit. Big guy, all tan and teeth, with one of those thong costumes to let you study his equipment.'

They barracked him.

'Oh, she noticed then?'

'So she'd recognise him again?'

'His face, you mean?'

'Never mind his face.'

'Would you cut it out, let me finish?' Sweating and smiling; fifty years old with a grandson whose picture he carried around in his wallet; Billy Ord, the family man. 'She keeps walking. He keeps chatting her up. She keeps ignoring him. And he won't stop. Until she turns round and tells him, Fuck off! "Hey," he says, "do I detect an accent?"'

Meldrum joined in the laughter. With whisky before and wine with the meal it wasn't hard to laugh, which was just as well since Billy's idea of a tribute consisted of jokes, most of them unprintable, and more of them about himself than Dyall. By contrast, when Dyall replied it was funny but sincere in the right places and with some nice stories from when he'd been a beat constable back in the dark ages. Anyway, with retirement to celebrate, it was Dyall's night.

'Thirty years, eh? In this game,' Finlay said, sucking lips back from his teeth in disgust. 'What about you, Jim? How long you been at it?'

'Coming up for twenty.'

'Jesus! What'll you do? Take the pension and run?'

'That what you're planning?'

'Too right. Pension. Add on a wee job. That'll suit me.'

He had heard it all before. The security job, the hobby that would one day soon pay off, the brother-in-law who was looking for a partner. More and more of it as the years went by, it seemed, but even in the early days there had been the guy who got his degree paid and took off to be a lawyer and the guy who had a breakdown, the one they found blowing his whistle directing imaginary traffic through the empty canteen, and all the others whose wives couldn't stand the moods and the hours and what you brought home with you from a shift on the streets. At this kind of do there was always somebody bending your ear about his plans.

One of the young guys had put on a badge with the slogan: You've obviously mistaken me for someone who cares.

Betty wouldn't find that funny.

'What are you grinning at?'

'Nothing.'

The truth was, he couldn't imagine what he would be if he stopped being a policeman. It was something he didn't think about.

There was a bottle of whisky at each end of the tables. Everyone seemed to be talking at once. In a pause he heard the name Brennan.

'John Brennan? The lawyer?'

'The malt's from him. A present. For the occasion.'

'Billy! Billy! Fuck's sake! Billy!'

'What?'

'Isn't this from John Brennan?'

'What?'

'The Glenlivet. The good stuff.'

'You arrange that, Billy?'

Ord leaned forward and had a long slow look down the

table. Somebody started to speak and stopped. He called out in his big voice: 'We're old friends.' And, satisfied, grinned and sat back.

Later they took over the downstairs bar in the hotel and somewhere in the small hours of the morning, Meldrum found a heavy arm laid across his shoulders. 'This man,' Billy Ord told the night's survivors, 'this bloody man and I go back a long way.' He winked a moist eye: 'A word,' and drew him to one side. 'I want a word with you. On the quiet. On the square.'

'Billy,' Meldrum found himself patting the big man on the chest, 'I'm not on the square. Never, ever, have been.'

'I know that. But you were asked.'

'So I was.'

'I know you were. I should know, you bastard. And I know why you didn't take your chance.'

'Why was that?'

'Because you didn't get asked till your marriage broke up. Pride.'

'Is that what it was?'

'Ridiculous, good man like you. You should think again. The wife and you are not going to get back together, am I right? That makes a difference, eh?'

'Oh . . . it makes a difference.'

While he thought about the ways it made a difference, he missed the next bit and caught up when the big man was saying, '. . . thing about the RCs, there was a time when they had it hard, about getting a job, I mean. I knew a girl, I'm talking years ago now, couldn't get a job in most offices in Glasgow. Because she kicked with the left foot. Got a job with this big store, because it was a Jewboy place. They didn't care. But what I'm saying is, now they've the ball at their feet through there in the West, running the council, what do they fucking do, give the jobs to their own. Where's your tie?where's your belly button?where's your tits?' He mimed crossing himself. 'Flute players needn't apply. That's pape nature, Jim.'

'I'd call that human nature, Billy.'

'You know what you are? You're a cynic. Anyway, think about it. Take a look round.'

And Meldrum, looking round, recognised all the faces. They were the people he spent his life with. A glass of whisky in hand, he liked all of them, he really did.

Only, half a dozen hours later, pushing back the covers, squinting at the light, he found a grimace sour enough to match the taste in his mouth.

For him belonging came harder in the morning.

CHAPTER TEN

S taring about her, Harriet Cook sat up on the couch. Chairs, coffee table, desk, the television on its stand, were like separate presences to her. Crouched in the glimmering light like animals. In the long room, in her own flat, the eeriness made her go still, like an animal herself. And all of this wasn't because she had jabbed derangement into a vein, poured it over her throat, sucked it into a nostril, had it sprinkled on a prick and stuck into her the way it happened one night to a friend of hers.

It was only because she had lain there and thought about all she should have been doing, and when she sat up after so long a time, everything was strange to her. It was that feeling of strangeness that made her take the first drink. Sundays were like that.

When she woke up, she was drunk. It would have been easier not to go to the Pearsons' farewell party but she had been at school with Valerie. As little girls they had been best friends and now Valerie was going a long way away. A year ago, it had been Valerie who sat with her and listened while she talked about John Brennan – you had to find someone to talk to or fall over in the street poisoned by it when the bad time happened.

She felt her way along the passage, shedding clothes, dropping them as she went. Only a party but she was going to make it. Even in the worst days after John dumped her she had gone to work; she hadn't missed an hour. Standing with bent head

under the shower, she thought, Which proved I could survive.
I thought then it was about surviving. She pushed the lever all
the way over and held up her breasts into the coldness, into
its needling sudden cascade.

She dried herself and then as fat drops broke out across her
breasts had to start over again. She patted at her shoulders,
scrubbed the towel down her flanks. Sweating alcohol, she
thought. Even dressed, tucked into shirt and jeans, she felt
damp. She pulled on a light sweater. The woman who looked
back from the mirror was a surprise. Even her eyes were clear.
She had no right to look so untroubled. As she watched,
though, a line of sweat shone out on the upper lip.

At the door, she turned back and put perfume on her neck
and at each wrist.

When she got out of the car she'd no memory of the journey.
Shivering, she hurried along the lane behind the houses to the
path beside the garage that led into the garden. Light spilled
out from the conservatory and at its entrance there was a group
of teenagers. Noisy and laughing, they made her want to turn
back until one called her name and it was too late. Frances,
the Pearsons' younger daughter, took her inside and it was
crowded there, too, making her feel as if she was the last
guest; but Valerie took her hand, gave her a glass, found a
corner for her on a couch, squeezing people up. Sipping at the
white wine, waiting for it to mix into a deadly cocktail with
the gin, Harriet had an image of tumbling slowly face-down
off the couch on to the carpet.

Instead for a time she talked literature with Eddie, a grave,
bearded man who painted portraits and lived in the next
village, while he pressed his thigh along the length of hers.
She found the effect soothing rather than erotic and it was too
much of an effort to move until Martin Pearson drew her up
to talk to him. He described his new job and explained how
you had to go South for promotion. She caught cloying wafts
of his aftershave and amused herself by imagining it was called
Ambition. She had never really liked self-absorbed Martin or
believed him good enough for Valerie. Yet now when he said,
laying his hand on her shoulder, 'We're all going to miss you,'
she was embarrassed by a sting of tears.

'I don't know what I would have done without Valerie when
– last year,' she said. 'I'll miss you. Both of you.'

'Me too, Harry love.' He shook his head. 'That bastard
Brennan was at the reception at the City Chambers at the
weekend. Plus wife. The mouse lady.'

While he said this and she was remembering why she
disliked him, from the corner of her eye she began to register a
kind of attentive stillness and realised someone was listening;
a man. She looked up at him, which meant he had to be about
six feet. He had a narrow face and a lot of black hair with grey
through it. He offered a little half-grin of apology but held her
look, and perhaps it was that which made her miss his name
as Martin introduced them.

Martin asked him, 'Where's Carole got to?' and he said she'd
gone home.

'Your wife?' she asked.

'Ex-wife.'

Before either of them could find anything to add, Martin was
talking again and they became just part of the usual circle he
gathered around him.

'I tell you I was ready for a pint. I'd been there before, mine
host used to be a fisherman, it's a fishermen's bar. Good people
to yarn with.' Yarn, for God's sake! Did the man beside her
make some tiny noise, or a movement, the smallest movement?
Anyway, she turned her head to him and he was glancing down
at her quite blank and innocent-eyed, not admitting they might
have something to share, before looking back at the speaker.
Disconcerted, she did the same. 'I sat straight up on the bunk. I
mean, right out of my sleep. The storm had blown itself out and
all the water in the harbour was black dark or silver with the
moon being nearly full. I stood leaning over the rail, listening.
When I looked behind me, the houses by the harbour were like
cut-outs against the stars. There wasn't a light showing. Not
one. And then as I looked back, I saw him, his head came up
and his arm waved and then he was gone.' She could see it,
and when he dived she fell with him through moonlight into
that dark water. 'I got hold of him, too, and he got hold of me,
wrapped his arms round my neck. It was a struggle, it was
a battle, but I got him out. I lay beside him on the harbour

steps and when I got my breath back I went up and banged on the first door. And the second and the third. But at last somebody came and we got him into the warmth and got a blanket round him.'

She had heard Martin tell sailing stories often before, very often before, but this one was different. She was moved to admiration by his courage. Perhaps it was the moonlight that made the difference. Yet when she wanted to check this feeling or share it, the man beside her offered the smallest of smiles, a little ironical twitch of the lips. She stared ahead in anger.

'I wasn't expecting to be treated as a hero,' Martin said. 'Not as a bloody hero. But in the morning when I went into the pub no one would talk to me. Afternoon, same thing, I got the silent treatment. I'm a stubborn bugger though. I wasn't setting off till I found out why. I sat there till we had the place to ourselves and I said to the landlord, What the hell is all this about? I didn't expect to be treated as a bloody hero, I told him, but what's going on?'

When he told them, she took the opportunity of the laughter to move away. Valerie announced a buffet and people began to drift towards the kitchen. The couch was empty and she huddled in a corner of it and wiped at the sweat on her face with a handkerchief, swiftly, not wanting anyone to notice. She didn't feel like eating.

'Drink? Harriet, isn't it?' He held out the glass to her. She saw he was holding another one for himself. 'Your glass is empty. This is what you were on, I think.'

'No, you don't think, you're sure,' she said, but when he held it out to her she leaned forward and took the other one.

'Do you think it's a good idea to mix your drinks?'

'You're so sure,' she said.

'I'm not a great man for wine. You'd be doing me a favour.'

Giving up, she swapped glasses and he sat down.

'Wasn't it brave of him?' she challenged. 'Going into the water like that. In the dark. It would have been easy not to. I mean, no one would have known. You could have pretended to yourself – I didn't really see anything. And gone below to sleep again and when you heard about it next day, that someone had drowned, tell yourself it was a mistake, anyone can make a mistake. Even though I expect you'd know, inside yourself, but not ever admit it. Some people can do that – not admit it.' She tried to gather the thread of what she wanted to say: 'Whatever you think of him. You don't need to like him. It was brave,' and knew she was talking too much.

'What did you make of the last bit?'

'Sorry?'

'Of the yarn.' While she studied him, suspicious of the word, he went on, 'When he got the friendly landlord alone. You shouldn't have rescued him, zur. Ee'd slept with one of the other fishermen's wives. Ee'd been thrown in to drown.'

'Why the Mummerset? It was a harbour just down the coast, Martin told us so.'

'He was meant tae droon – that sound more convincing?' He smiled. 'It's a good story.'

'Why don't you believe him?'

'Like something you'd read in a book.'

'You read a lot of stories?'

'Hear.'

'Hear . . .' She stared at her empty glass. He took it from her. 'Please,' she said.

When he came back with the drinks, she asked, 'Do you teach children, the little tiny ones? Nursery rhymes. Fairy stories. Brer Rabbit.' She tried to think of another one. She meant the question to be insulting, though sober she would have argued for the value of infant teachers – and that it was a job men should do. Like nurses.

'I'm a policeman,' he said.

'I might have guessed.'

'As obvious as that?'

'You're so noticing. And so sure.'

'That's bad? I don't imagine teachers would last long if they weren't.'

He thinks I'm a bloody teacher, she thought.

'Or prison warders,' she said.

'Sorry?'

With a pleasant sense of being reckless, she hurried on, 'It's the inhumanity of officialdom. That man in the winter who was on the rooftop at Peterhead for fifteen days. And the worst winter in years.'

'Keaney,' he said, 'his name was Hugh Keaney.'

'Yes?' She hardly paid attention. 'Brought down unconscious with hypothermia and frostbite. It was such a winter. They only let him have a day in hospital. Then took him back and put him in solitary. He'd "committed an offence". That's what I despise.'

'They have to work to the rules. Anyway, they transferred him to Barlinnie afterwards.'

'It's always "they", isn't it? Or "them", we leave it to them. The way that man was treated they might as well have been trying to drive him mad.'

He shook his head in denial.

'Oh, but yes,' she said, 'he is going mad.'

'The papers don't always get things right.'

'You don't think somebody has to care?'

'If there weren't any prisons, you'd be living in a jungle,' he said.

'What are you telling me?'

'That you don't know what people are capable of.'

His sudden hard vehemence startled her.

'I'm a lawyer,' she said.

'Yes.' He acknowledged that too quickly. Did she look like a lawyer? 'After it's over. That's not the same.'

Her quick imagination supplied more vividly what he had no words for: the violation of children, the spilling of blood, the stink of fear. She read the protocols, heard it all in court, but what was being affirmed or refuted belonged to the past. She didn't need to be told it wasn't the same.

'Would you dive into the water?' she asked.

'Are you getting a lift home?'

She thought, Go to hell; held out her glass.

In the morning when she wakened she had the idea she had slept with him. She was afraid to open her eyes or move in case he was beside her. Lying still, her head felt all right. Her mouth was dry. She tested her body like somebody feeling for broken bones after a car smash.

—*The dolphin needs to will each breath. It can die between*

one breath and the next. Suicide is easy for a dolphin. Make
us the same and the world would run near empty of us.

Had she really said that to somebody? The words were there
in her mind; she said them over to herself; each time they came
clear and in the same order. As if she was saying them and
someone listening, as if to a confession, someone standing
listening, the heat of shame prickled her chest and flowed
from her neck into her face. Had she said that to him?

She opened her eyes and, of course, he wasn't in bed with
her. It wasn't her bed.

'I was too drunk to go home,' she said when Valerie put her
head round the door.

'It didn't seem a good idea,' Valerie said. 'Could you manage
a pot of tea?'

'A lake.' Sitting up came easier than she had any right to
expect. 'A lake of tea.'

'Stay where you are. It's made.'

'No.' She swung her legs over the side of the bed. 'God,
I'm hardly decent.' She was in bra and pants. 'Did I manage
myself?'

'Martin helped me.' Valerie laughed. 'Sorry. You passed out.
Don't worry. I just let him tug things off at the far ends.'

'Jesus, that sounds rude.' Her clothes must be somewhere.
She was seriously offended. She sat there, though, staring at
the naked white length of her legs till Valerie came back. The
tea went down hot and clean. 'I woke up thinking someone
was beside me in the bed.'

'Anyone I know? Do you remember dreams like that? I find
it's the good ones you don't remember.'

'He spent half the night sitting beside me on the couch.'

'Jim Meldrum.'

'Is that his name?'

'He didn't tell you who he was?'

There was something odd in the way Valerie was looking at
her.

'He's a policeman, he said he was a policeman, isn't he?'

'He's Betty Meldrum's father.' And seeing her blank look,
'The student. The one whose boyfriend is suing the police.'

'But how do you—'

'Her mother's a head teacher. School along the road from mine, the Catholic one. We're friends. She asked if she could bring him, so he could meet you.'

'But why would she do that?'

'Maybe he asked her. It is still his daughter after all.'

'And was she there last night? The girl's mother, I mean.' The wife. The thought of his wife watching last night. Stupid. Nothing happened. Ex-wife.

'She left before you came. Maybe they quarrelled. The marriage is over, of course.'

'I haven't even seen the boy yet. He has an appointment. They'd gone to see John Brennan, and he phoned me about it.'

She'd come to a farewell party, not to meet a client. It felt as if she had been used. However unreasonably, she was angry with Valerie. Last night she had come to say goodbye to a friend she loved.

'John Brennan,' Valerie said.

'He didn't want anything to do with it. Accusations of police brutality – not his kind of thing at all. So he passed them on to me. John likes to keep everyone happy.'

'Oh, Harriet.' Valerie sat beside her on the bed and hugged her closer. 'What are you going to do without me?'

Determinedly she swallowed down tears. She was over tears.

'Manage,' she said. 'Somehow.'

CHAPTER ELEVEN

'Thing about colonial wars,' Sir James said, 'you want to fight them as far away from home as possible.' He drew back the rod and cast his bait among the shadows under the opposite bank. 'What has to be done to win them isn't the public's business. Algeria was next door to France and too much of the mess leaked back. And when the shooting stopped, it got worse. Northern Ireland isn't any different. When the shooting stops, you don't know who your friends are any more.'

Waves combed by the wind made the surface of the river seem to flow against the real direction of the current. Studying the deception, the man with Sir James sighed. Farquhar Wood, Secretary of State for Scotland, was cold and uncomfortable.

'Skeletons fall out of cupboards, you mean?'

'There was a time,' Sir James said, 'when you could have stood here and watched salmon bank to bank making their way up to spawn. Great big fellows. I can't tell you what it was like to be a child looking down at these enormous shadows and suddenly *seeing* what they were. I was with my two brothers. Never forgotten that first time. Couldn't bring my grandsons here and show so many. Poachers – and stake netters over there on the English side ruining the stock legally. Courts over there keep finding for them. Know what my ancestors would have said to that? Bloody English! they'd have said.'

A man who did his homework, his companion knew that Sir James, like each of his ancestors in turn for five generations, had married an English rose for cash, land or connections. He contented himself by murmuring, 'Pollution, too, I should suppose?'

'What?'

'Might have something to do with it?'

But Sir James had nothing to add and his companion followed him a step along the bank and watched gloomily as with an unleashing movement that came all from the elbow and wrist the line was returned to almost the same place.

'No doubt about him being there. Purdie spotted him.' With a nod at Purdie, blank-faced and stolid, discreet yards away, ready when needed. A keeper. Ghillie, they'd call him further north. Had the trick of tugging the forelock without appearing servile. Just another bloody servant.

Wood was no admirer of country sports, least of all when he suspected he'd been fetched out into this discomfort as a reminder that being able to scramble half-way up the greasy pole in politics didn't make you a gentleman. In entertaining the thought he admitted a touch of paranoia; this old man, more than many a wealthier grandee, having that effect on him. Chances were there was no motive for tramping out to fish other than the blank self-engrossedness which came naturally to children and aristocrats.

'I understand what you mean about Algeria,' he said, 'but don't you believe we handle these things better than the French?'

'I'm a back number. Quite out of things.' Sir James kept his intent gaze on the drift of his line. 'I'm an old man. Why tell me?'

'It was during your time.'

'Not as Scottish Secretary. That was in the dark ages. Time you're talking about, I was Home Secretary – or just gone to the Foreign Office. Little Thompson was Scottish secretary then.'

'I've been told, in confidence, of course, that Thompson turned to you for advice.'

'. . . one journalist, you said. Doesn't do to get hysterical.'

'If you'll forgive me, that's not fair. I had it checked. That's routine. And then I found how much was . . . inaccessible.'

'For a good reason. Always best to assume that. And nothing to do with me. Not that I can see.'

'As a courtesy, in case there was anything that might get out of hand.'

'Questions in the House, you mean? The full nonsense about this Keaney, a bloody nobody Irishman?'

'I hope not.'

'Hope's no good. You'd better hope it's your imagination. If not, you'd better hope it's someone's business to see the lid's kept on.'

'There isn't anything I should know then?'

Sir James drew back the rod.

'Keep your head would be my advice. Don't want to start people thinking of you as the nervous type.'

The line snaked out in loops across the river to a darkening patch of water under the trees. Watching, it wouldn't have been hard to imagine some enormous shape easing up out of the shadows towards the lure.

CHAPTER TWELVE

By day and by night, Hugh Keaney went over it.

The wigs, white, flat to the head with curled pieces on either side, had made the faces alike, in the way members of a family bear a resemblance. When the trial began, that was how it had been for him. The judge, the defence, the prosecution, shift them around he couldn't have told them apart. If it had been his life instead of his freedom, he still wouldn't have been able to tell which one was trying to save him, which one wanted him buried behind prison walls. He dreamed about them. Awake, he went over the way the times didn't fit and searched for questions that might have been asked, could have been asked, should have been asked, he had thought of plenty. Sometimes he would think he had found a new question, then remember it or not be sure if he had thought of it before. A few were so important he found them over and over again; every time with excitement until he remembered.

Plenty of time for that, for all of that, over so many years.

If those questions had been asked, Innocent, the judge would have said.

Guilty.

In the second year he had shared a cell with a man from Inverness. A fierce little man with broken knuckles, he lay and stared at photographs of his wife and two sons taped to the wall. 'Difference between you and me,' more than once he said, 'is I've got them waiting for me.'

Guilty.

On remand before the trial, he had said to a warder, 'I've no stamps,' holding the letter to his mother, this being the year before she died.

'Do you want me to let you out to the post office?'

'You could do that, sir, and I would come back.' The words no sooner out of his mouth than he had seen himself reflected in the man's eyes: a raw boy from the bogs. 'Fuck off!' the warder said. With such contempt.

Some time after that, as time muddled here, in the fifth year perhaps, there had been a man at recreation who asked, 'Did you read about me in the *Sunday Post*? They called me the Parcel Man.'

'Christ's sake,' somebody else had said in disgust, 'you're talking to a guy's in for murder.'

'I didn't do it!' he had cried, denying it like always.

'I did the parcels,' the Parcel Man said.

For half a year the man from Inverness taunted him, 'I've got my boys. I've got what nobody in this shithole can take away from me. But you by the time you get out of here? What woman'll look at you? Maybe an old whore in a back court.'

One time he had found an answer. 'A man Mutius left all his possessions behind and went with his eight-year-old son to a monastery. The monks told him, You've forgotten that you were rich; now you must be taught to forget that you were a father. Soon the little boy was going about the place hungry and in rags. The father would watch when he was being beaten. You can't imagine what the child suffered. Being a child, I don't suppose there was any way he could understand. But Mutius never wavered because of his love of Christ.'

Father Sam loved to tell the class that story and finished the same way every time: 'Afterwards Mutius rose to a high position among the ascetics, and was regarded as having displayed in great perfection the temper of a saint.'

The things you remembered. Softly aloud. Thinking the world slept.

'In the end the boy died.'

'*Ya Papish bastard, Keaney, you're mad.*'

But then he hadn't been.

CHAPTER THIRTEEN

Clay spread the newspaper on the bed where sheets and blankets writhed; he had slept restlessly. On the front page, the way there so often was, there was a woman with breasts so large they fell to her waist. She cupped her hands under them and stared at the camera. The bitch was smiling. He sat on the edge of the bed still in his coat and twisted round to see the pages as he turned them.

The only sound in the room was made by the pages turning. Pictures of women. Advertisements for sex lines. When eventually he got to the back page where the football was, he folded the paper lengthwise and aimed it into the waste basket with a sharp downward jerk of the wrist as if thrusting a knife into wood. Contrasted with the sleepwalking lethargy of the page-turning, the energy of it seemed excessive.

It was late at night before he came back. The room was in darkness. Numerals glimmered red on a radio dial. A switch clicked and light came on. He lay on the bed and tugged a half bottle out of the pocket of his coat. For a while he was still, only his eyes moving as he looked from the wardrobe with the cracked glass to the single armless chair. As if of its own volition, his hand reached out for the phone.

The double burr of ringing sounded four times.

'Hello. Who's there?'

'. . . hello.'

'What's your name, darling, where you from?'

'George. From . . . Carlisle.'

'What'd you like to talk about?'

'I've split up with my girlfriend.'

'. . . oh, that's a shame. What age are you, darling?'

'. . . twenty-eight. She was only seventeen. We'd been going together for four years.'

'She was thirteen!'

'When we met.'

'Oh, I see. Why'd you split up? Was it her wanted to?'

'Me. It was going too far. Domination. Humiliation.'

'Oh, yes. Is that what you're interested in, love? And she didn't like it, I expect she didn't like it.'

'She liked it. It was all right at first, but then she got her own flat. Did I say she was a student? Before that I'd visit her when the house was empty. We wouldn't have more than an hour, couple of hours, and you never knew when somebody would come back.'

'What did you do to her?'

'I'd take all my clothes off.'

'You did?'

He lay thinking about hanging up. When he listened again, the phone echoed and then her voice, faint and tinny, asked, 'You there? Darling?'

'It's all about money, isn't it?' he said. 'The longer I talk the more it costs me. Your job is to keep me talking.'

'It don't mean I don't find it interesting, darling.'

'You have a nice voice.'

'Well, thank you. You sound—'

'Never mind. I'd clean out her lavatory for her.'

'Sorry?'

'I'd take off my clothes and clean out the lavatory for her. But there was always something done wrong she'd punish me for.'

'Oh, I thought it was the other way round, I see, you mean you liked her to?'

'She was young when I met her, did I say that? She learned from me. But she got to like it. She got to like it too much. She would tie me with my hands behind the loo lying on the floor looking up. When she got up she would be standing over me.'

'What else did she do to you, love?'

'Put it this way, she never needed toilet paper.'

'I've done some of that. But not, I mean not going too far.'

'She'd get me over a table with my legs spread.'

'Did she use anything on you love? What did she use? Carrots?'

He frowned at the ceiling. Carrots? Listening hard, he could hear her voice chirrup faintly. He waited.

'. . . I'm still here . . .' But there was nothing, sea noises, she wasn't there. He yelled, 'Bitch!'

'Hello?' she said.

'She used a dildo on me. She'd beat me up.'

'Did she whip you?'

He thought about it. 'I'll tell you she would take my clothes off and make me stand in the cupboard and – my hands were tied behind me – and one afternoon she put a rope around my neck. I heard the front door closing. She'd gone off.'

'You let her do that?'

'I could have strangled. If I'd fainted.'

'Yes, that's dangerous.'

'Thing is, when she came back, she'd been shopping. She took me out of the cupboard and I was in a bad way. And I said something to her, can't remember what, she thought I was being cheeky. Get back in, she said.'

'But you never did!'

'I let her put me back inside. I let her put the rope around my neck. Shorter this time. I was on my toes.'

'And she went out again?'

'She could have got into trouble. If I'd died. She doesn't care, I realised.'

'So what happened then?'

It was what he liked to think about most, being hung in the dark.

Thinking about that he must have slept, but only for a moment for she was still talking. '. . . I've done that kind of stuff.' She had flat vowels that belonged to one of the larger cities. Birmingham, was it? Manchester? 'But not, I mean, anything like *that*. Not anything extreme.'

'Do you smoke?' he asked. He had no interest in her.

'Do I . . . Yes. I'm on till eight in the morning.'

'I saw a thing about a woman who smoked fifty a day while she was pregnant. Baby was addicted to nicotine. I'd shoot someone like that.'

'Oh, you have to be careful. Have you any kids?'

'What?'

'Kids. You talk as if you're fond of kids. I wondered if you had—'

'You don't believe any of what I've been telling you. People phone you all night, telling you lies, making things up. All that stuff I've been telling you, you don't believe it.'

'Oh, I do, honestly. It sounds true.'

'What's your name?'

'Darlene.'

'Is it a working name?'

'That's what I'm called.'

He held the phone in the air, studying it, tempted to put it down and be finished. She was talking and he said over her, 'Is this being recorded?'

'Right.' She laughed. It was hard to tell if she meant: Hundreds of calls – who's got the time? Or: Blackmail, a nobody like you? Or again: Who the fuck cares?

'So you believe what I tell you?'

'You can tell me what you like, love. I won't be shocked.'

'I kill people.'

'Give me a minute, darling.' At a distance: 'Give's a drink. This one's crazy.' His head dropped to the side and slid a little down the pillow of its own weight. He'd been drinking while they talked and now the bottle was empty. He needed to sleep. 'You killed your girlfriend?'

'I don't have a girlfriend.'

'Well, you wouldn't have – not if you killed her!'

He had an image of her on the other end of the phone with breasts hanging down to her waist. Laughing at him.

'There was an old blind man.'

And added: 'He said to me, Are you going to be my death?'

But since he was already putting the receiver down to end the call, it was possible she didn't catch that last bit.

BOOK THREE

At A Touch

CHAPTER FOURTEEN

L ater, when Billy Ord asked him, Why? it wasn't easy to find an answer. There wasn't just one reason.

Anyway it was a question Hugh Keaney had asked him first. Although the walls had been painted recently, the room had the jail smell, drifting out from old tiles that had been left under the window; or maybe from Keaney as he leaned across the table.

Instead of answering directly why he had come, Meldrum said, 'You won't remember me.'

The window bars divided a little slice of sky into stripes of pearl shining above the high grey wall. It had been battering rain from Edinburgh to Glasgow all the way to the prison, now the sky was lightening.

'I don't forget anybody who was at my trial,' Keaney said.

'A long time ago.'

'And the rest. Every year, every day, I keep count. You think I don't keep count? Every minute, I keep count.'

'I came to the court, but I wasn't on your case.'

'You gave evidence against me.'

'No. I came on my own time.'

'To look at the animals. Like going to the zoo. Telling lies is what you get paid for.'

'Not all that much,' Meldrum said, studying him. It was a face the colour and planes of a carving in bleached wood. The hair was shades of straw and thinning. He remembered it from the time of the trial as red, the colour of fire.

'Every one of you knew I didn't do it.'

'No.'

'Now you're not sure though. You've come to find out if I'm innocent.'

'A jury decided that.' He said the first thing that came into his head, shocked by Keaney reading his mind or perhaps just by hearing it put into words. Was it that simple?

Was he being that stupid?

'A policeman's answer.'

'I'm a policeman.'

Keaney nodded and then went on nodding, head going back and forward. Like a fucking straitjacket rocking on a cot, the image came unwanted to Meldrum. What was he doing here? If Keaney asked him again, he should tell him, I don't know, I don't know.

'Do you think you can tell just by looking at a man?' Keaney asked. 'Whether he did it or not?'

'When I was younger. Not so often now.'

There had been times. But then over the years he'd seen colleagues too sure wasting a case or worse.

'I read about you getting out on the roof,' he said.

'Which time?'

'There was more than one?'

'Five years ago. They conned me down in three days. This time I didn't swallow any of their shit.'

'From what I read, you were in a bad way. Get any smarter you'll freeze yourself to death.'

'Are you a Catholic?'

Meldrum shook his head.

'Are you a Christian?' And when he got no response, 'It's not so easy to die. When they got me down off the roof they took me to a hospital. A real hospital, I mean,' he nodded at the window, 'one outside, not in here. That's how bad I was. I was only there the one night for they decided I wasn't going to die after all. I have a kind of a memory of a nurse who said, Poor thing. Not a woman, a male nurse. Wouldn't you think if it was a dream I'd've made it a woman? That and white sheets. Well, there would be, I know that. But the other thing was this smell. There must have been all the usual ones, piss and all that. But there was this one that was different. The night they brought me back I sniffed the air like a dog and could smell nothing but piss and fright sweat. I wanted to die that night. Only what kept me from it was that I didn't kill the old man.'

Meldrum didn't need anybody to tell him a prisoner pleading innocence proved nothing, not even if he had kept at it for years. Get an idea stuck in your head and how much competition would it find in here?

Keaney watched him with eyes bright and flat as if stamped out of blued tin.

He didn't need anybody either to tell him innocent men did get jailed. But he hadn't knowingly put any of them there.

'Are you a Christian?'

'You asked me that already. The answer's no!'

How many Christian, how many Catholic, policemen have you had round offering to help?

'But there's something in me, in what you know about me, that you put faith in?'

What was he claiming? To be Saint Hugh? Some kind of a martyr? As if martyrdom proved anything; only that you were a certain type, one of the kind who believed in the cause with every inch of their suffering – and maybe kept just one little dark room in the centre of inside where they'd locked away their lack of innocence until it might be useful again.

'It doesn't matter what I believe.'

'I say it does.'

Manipulators, the claimers of innocence had to work at making every contact with the outside count. But that wasn't what silenced Meldrum. It was the thought that the more guiltless a man was, the less chance there was of him knowing anything that would help him to prove it.

That was the problem with innocence.

'If you believed in me,' Keaney said, 'you could make a difference. I know these things. Listen to me when I tell you it's so.'

Not looking crazy, just old or ageless, not any age at all. It was as if he had bleached out like a cloth lost in a corner of a yard. Maybe if he got out one day in the distant future, he wouldn't be crazy just faded. That would be something to look forward to.

CHAPTER FIFTEEN

Coming out of Number One Court, John Brennan nodded and then, to Meldrum's surprise, stopped. 'Not proven! Don't tell me you expected me to pull that fish off your hook.' He ran his hand back through the mane of white hair and showed big teeth like a horse.

While he was making some kind of answer, Meldrum tried to put out of his mind how the dead woman's face had looked with all the bones that gave it shape broken. You worked on a killing till it was done with or you had to move on. Cases took time to come to court. It was more than a year since he had stood in an alley and looked down at Not Proven's victim.

'Be honest. Not in a month of Sundays.'

'Nothing juries do surprises me.'

'You thought, that's one in the bag.'

Stopped to gloat, it seemed; which was his style and wasn't. Brennan liked victory and made no secret of it. On the other hand, mostly he preferred to take it in his stride. He had, after all, been winning for a long time.

'Juries,' Meldrum repeated.

Brennan mimed playing the violin, bowing with one hand and tapping the air delicately with the fingers of the other. 'Yes?'

'Playing the xylophone?' With a bunch of sausages.

'Like an instrument. With fifteen strings. Pluck them right and the jury will play the tune you want to hear.'

'Not Proven.' Also known to local cynics as, Go away and don't do it again. 'He'll do it again.'

'Allow the human heart some of its mystery, man.' Brennan had a big voice. The man drew attention. Meldrum never felt comfortable talking with him. 'Leave the future to God. You put some poor devil in the dock and fellows like me rake about and turn things over. The past and what's to be done about it in the present. That's enough to fill our plates.'

'You're right, it's not my business,' Meldrum said, wanting nothing but to get away. A face like the dead woman's was dangerous to brood on; anybody who lasted had to learn that. In the last year he had seen others dead. And, not often, but in his time he had seen worse. It was just that he hadn't been prepared for the trial bringing back a trace of fog in the air and the way she'd lain among rubbish blown into a corner of the alley. He wiped his hand across his mouth and felt the resistance of teeth and bone. 'Once the verdict's in, it's over.'

It was disconcerting. He found himself being gazed at without expression by a face from which all the good-natured malice, all the life, had drained. It was as if something inside had been switched off. It couldn't have lasted more than a moment, though a moment that stretched, then Brennan said, 'You believe that?' and blinked his eyes like coming awake.

'You can only try them once.'

'If they're found innocent, but what if they're found guilty?'

'I have to go,' Meldrum said, looking at his watch.

'I've quarter of an hour spare. I'll walk you outside for a breath of air.' There wasn't any way to refuse. 'If it's guilty, there can be an appeal. And if that fails, there's still the chance of new evidence. Even years later. Am I right? Years later. Would you agree?'

Stone cladding had come off a window column in this new building exposing concrete the texture of crumbling cheese. The old one had lasted for 150 years. He had been there with Billy Ord on its last day to give evidence in some case or other. What he remembered was the dark shine of wood panelling and the way justice smelt, of sweat and disinfectant and cigarettes cupped behind hands in corridors.

But here grandeur had been bypassed; the shabbiness was instant.

How long had this place been up?

'Fourteen years, fifteen soon,' John Brennan said as they came through the swing-doors and paused at the top of a flight of granite steps. A light rain drifted across the street.

Startled, Meldrum said, 'Not so long, surely.'

A horn sounded. On the opposite side of the road a car had braked suddenly, causing another to swerve round it.

'Since Hugh Keaney's trial? Believe me, that long. I hear you paid him a visit.'

The car's reversing lights came on. Between a red Cortina and a van there was a gap but it didn't look big enough. On the pavement a policeman and a traffic warden watched as the car edged back into the space.

'How do you know that?' How the hell, he meant.

Brennan raised a hand as if to give a blessing. 'A colleague,' he explained. A woman stood beside the car, the driver's door lying open, looking across at them. She waved back. 'I take an interest.'

Meldrum recognised Harriet Cook. She was bareheaded. It was as if she didn't care that it was raining.

'In Hugh Keaney?' And then he remembered that the Senior Advocate for Keaney's defence had been John Brennan, but still, as had just been pointed out, that was a long time ago. 'Why?'

She hadn't moved, standing waiting. He had the strange impression it was him her eyes were fixed on, though she was so far off.

'I'd better let you get away,' Brennan said, watching her on the other side of the road. He turned to go in, and then over his shoulder wondered, 'Oh, why indeed?'

As he crossed the street, the policeman and traffic warden were lined up facing the woman across the car. The idea of a lawyer getting a ticket amused him. Before he could say anything, she asked, 'Can we talk?'

'If you want to. I mean, of course.'

'In the car? I'm due for a client at eleven.'

He went round to the passenger's side.

The traffic warden said, 'It was a nice bit of parking.'

'We were telling her, she drives like a man.' The policeman was a lanky rawbones, still in nodding distance of puberty.

Meldrum grunted and leaned in to lift stuff off the seat. The footwell was stuffed with bags, the backseats littered.

As she swung the car out of the space, the two stood watching.

'Like a man?' Meldrum said. 'I thought you'd have cut them off at the knees.'

'Not worth the bother.' She glanced in the side mirror, then pulled across the traffic, heading for the reserved parking behind the Court. 'Is that the impression you have of me?'

'After one meeting at a party, you mean?'

'I didn't expect you to remember me.'

'You talked about dolphins. That made an impression.'

She frowned and switched off. They sat facing the wall.

'Anyway,' she said, 'my tax disc is out of date.'

'Wait till I get my notebook out.'

She didn't smile.

'You know your daughter's boy friend Sandy Torrance came to see me?'

'And you told him he had a case against the police.'

'I never doubted for a moment that he was telling me the truth. Your daughter had enough anger for both of them. For him I thought it was more a question of integrity.'

'I spoke to Torrance in the hospital. He couldn't identify anyone.'

'That's often the first reaction. When the victim is still in shock.'

He couldn't see the wall. The side windows were fogged as well. He felt an odd sense of intimacy. His voice was quiet when he said, 'I was concerned for the boy. And my daughter.'

'I thought Sandy Torrance had character,' she said. 'That's why I was surprised when he came this morning and said he'd decided to drop the action.'

He was relieved. 'It's probably for the best. These things can get messy.'

'He wouldn't tell me why. Did you have anything to do with it?' He looked at her in silence. 'Did you threaten him?'

He opened the car door. The strength of his anger took him by surprise. He said, 'The only person I might have spoken to about that case was you.'

'At the party the night we met? So why didn't you?'

'You were too drunk.'

Dolphins.

Walking away, he tried to tell himself she was a bitch, one of John Brennan's cast-offs, and he didn't care how much, looking vulnerable if only for an instant, she might have been hurt by what he said.

CHAPTER SIXTEEN

'I tell you, boy, if I'd a prick a foot long I'd stick it up Jesus.'

He lurched at them out of the press and hurry of the street, and as he reached for the minister Meldrum knocked his hand away.

'Don't hurt him,' the minister said, and at that the man made an extraordinary face. It seemed like anger, long strings of grey hair flying as he shook his head, but there was something there that looked like contempt as well, though there was no way of telling how much of that might be for himself.

'You know him?' Meldrum asked as the man wove away through the crowd.

'No. It's the collar does it.' A bulky man in need of a shave, the Reverend Tommy Wright smelled of sweat which perhaps prejudiced the fastidious Meldrum's notion that the clerical collar and shirt weren't too clean. 'A magnet.'

'For drunks.'

'I don't think so. Did you hear what he said? Garbage, but it could stick in your head. As if there was some meaning it would be better not to think about. The mad are coming on to the streets. Haven't you noticed we can't hide from them?'

Meldrum had stood looking at the front door that used to be Arthur Hull's; walked twice round the block telling himself not to be a fool; then climbed two flights of stairs hoping the upstairs neighbour Mulholland had moved or died. The brass plate screwed to the side of the door had been rubbed smooth. It would have been easy even then to turn away.

'Yes?'

The man in the doorway was too young; and then of course there was the back-to-front collar.

'I was looking for Mr Mulholland, John Mulholland.'

'Can I ask what business you have with him?'

Meldrum thought about that, then showed his identification. 'Police business.'

'You'd better come inside.'

The lobby was narrow and dark; and, hesitating, Meldrum was unpleasantly startled by a noise from the room at the end of the passage.

'He's asking, Who's there?'

It came again, like a dog with a broken jaw trying to yelp.

'He's had a stroke. I can understand him, only most of the time, I'm afraid, but if I can be of help.' He held out his hand. 'I'm Tommy Wright, John's minister.'

Mulholland was in a chair with a shawl round his shoulders. Staring, one eye was bigger than the other. At the mention of Arthur Hull's name, water gathered and leaked in a dragging line of tears.

'He says, poor Arthur didn't deserve—What happened to him, I suppose he means.'

'You know about it?'

'Oh, yes.'

'Were you his minister then?'

'No, no, no. I came to this parish afterwards. But John's talked to me about it a lot, isn't that right, John?'

But to Meldrum the old man's condition was like a sign. He hadn't come with a theory or a neat set of questions that could be answered with a yes or no, a grunt or a nod. Mulholland wasn't dead or moved away, but something in his head had died, taking with it the kind of talk that sometimes by luck stumbled on the answer to a question you hadn't even known to ask. He'd come on a fishing trip but the river had dried up in a drought.

His first impulse was to get out. The room's dim corners soaked up yellow light from a single unshaded bulb. It smelled of being sick and old. If alone had a smell, it smelled of that too.

'He can't understand why you're here,' Wright said. 'He says it was such a long time ago.'

After a time, 'You're doing very well,' Meldrum told the old man. 'If I can ask you a couple of questions more then I'll be done.'

'You're not too tired, John?' Wright asked. 'I'll get you some more tea. Would you like one?'

Meldrum refused with a shake of the head.

'The afternoon of the murder you went down to see if Arthur Hull was all right. Did you often do that?' The old man rubbed at his mouth with his good hand. 'You said at the trial you were worried about him.'

Mulholland nodded and made a noise that might have been a repetition of 'worried'.

'Because he'd told you about the young man who'd come to his door.'

Behind Mulholland, the minister stood cup in hand making big silent shapes with his mouth. 'Ask him . . . Ask him about . . .' Meldrum couldn't make out the last word.

'So you went for your neighbour. Morton, yes, I understand. And he came down with you. That's what I want to ask you about. Just to think about it one more time. I know it's a long time ago.'

Mulholland had come out into the street with Morton dragooned to keep him company just as the door of Hull's flat opened. The man who came out watched them over his shoulder as he pulled the door shut. 'He gave us a good look at him,' Mulholland had insisted against the defence lawyer's effort to create a doubt at the trial. The man had come down the three steps on to the pavement and walked away from them towards the main road and the muffled sound of traffic. Not quickly, you wouldn't say exactly quickly, but not slowly either; he didn't seem in any kind of a hurry.

The old man sipped tea out of the cup. The minister sat beside him, working out what he was struggling to say, trying to fill in the gaps. It wasn't a procedure any lawyer would have credited, but to Meldrum it seemed they were mostly getting it right. Mulholland remembered not being able to get an answer to their ringing at the door, how Morton and he had decided to call the police, and that one glimpse he'd had before the police hurried him out of the flat of Arthur Hull leaning sideways in his chair with what looked like a red scarf round his throat.

There was no faltering in the old man's conviction that it was Hugh Keaney he'd seen come out of the flat that afternoon.

Meldrum had given up and was ready to leave when Wright gave him a piece of paper, shielding it with his body from Mulholland. He'd printed on it in pencil: ASK HIM ABOUT CLAY. When he looked up blankly, Wright squeezed up his eyes at him in mute encouragement.

'Oh, one other thing. Can I ask you – there's a name cropped up – do you know anything about somebody . . . called . . . Clay?'

The left side of Mulholland's face remained still while the other went into a jig of tics. His eyes rolled from one to the other, then it was as if the old man tried to escape them by retreating somewhere inside himself. One eye closed. The other, wide as ever, stared at Meldrum.

'They challenge us,' Wright said once they had left the flat. He was talking about the mad, though it was hard to hear him as they dodged among the traffic.

'Could we find somewhere quiet to talk?'

Meldrum, associating until proved otherwise priests with chastity and ministers with temperance, didn't suggest the pub which faced them as they reached the opposite pavement.

'In here,' Wright said, 'it should be quiet about now.'

Watched by a couple of morose mid-morning drinkers, they went from the bar to a corner bench.

'Clay? Who or what is he?'

'Can I ask you something first? When you were questioning John, you asked him if Hull had told him about hearing a girl laughing – the day the young man Keaney came to his door. What was that about?'

'According to Keaney, there was a girl with him when he called at Hull's door. She lived with this other man who gave evidence at the trial. They'd all been living in a squat together. They were a shiftless bunch, which didn't help Keaney with the jury. This man claimed Keaney had told him he killed the old man. And then the girl got into the box and swore she hadn't been with Keaney. She'd never been near Hull's house, hadn't an idea where it was. She knew nothing, if you believed her. All right? Your turn then. Clay?'

'It was the evening before John became ill.' Wright sipped at a half-pint. 'Normally he was a quiet man, but that night he couldn't stop talking. I had other calls to make, I didn't intend to stay for more than a quarter of an hour. But every time I tried to leave, he'd start again. It was as though he was bribing me to stay by finding things that would hold my attention. If I'd realised − I did think he might be coming down with flu, something like that. Of course, when I heard about the stroke I blamed myself for letting him get too excited. A doctor friend assures me it would have happened anyway. They found him on the floor. He'd been lying alone like that for hours.'

'That night he talked about Hull's murder?'

'He'd talked about it before. He knew it interested me. And this time, he added things he hadn't talked about before. Like Arthur Hull's lover—'

'Francis Pietro.'

'Yes. He said that Pietro left Hull for a man called Clay.'

Meldrum shook his head. 'New one on me.'

'But you knew Hull was homosexual?'

'We heard.'

'Pietro and Hull had lived together for years apparently. One of the neighbours, Morton − he still has the flat above John − was unpleasant to them. John's attitude was live and let live. He told me he felt sorry for Hull when Pietro left. And then one morning Pietro knocked at his door, and John asked him in. He'd come to see Hull but couldn't get an answer. Anyway, he sat talking. And that's when he told John about this new lover he'd got himself, this man Clay. It was because of Clay he'd left Arthur and gone off and found a flat of his own. He called Clay a violent man.'

'Why would Pietro confide in Mulholland?'

'Well, John had been a good neighbour to Arthur Hull and him. Anyway, it's been my experience people need to talk to somebody when they are distressed.'

'When was this?'

'Not long before the murder. John didn't say exactly when. Perhaps after so long he couldn't remember exactly.'

'A violent man . . . What else did Pietro say about Clay?'

'That was it, really.'

'Did Pietro say he was afraid of being attacked by Clay?'

'John didn't say so. After a bit, Pietro got up and went off to try Hull again. And that was the last John saw of him.'

'Did Mulholland tell the police this at the time?'

Wright looked at him in surprise. 'I suppose – I took that for granted.'

In his turn Pietro had been found dead. Naked in bed. Strangled, then cut. Rough stuff gone wrong. It happened. A pick-up. They'd been told there was a regular visitor, a lover. But he came and went. No one had seen him recently. Neighbours' descriptions didn't lead anywhere.

Clay.

Would it have made a difference if they had been able to put a name to the mysterious lover?

Wright's voice lapped against his silence. 'I smiled to myself when you wouldn't take a drink of tea at John's. It reminded me of when I went to my first charge. The retiring minister told me of being offered a cup of tea by an old lady. Both she and the kitchen were so dirty he decided as a precaution to drink from the wrong side of the cup. "Oh, minister," she said as he finished, "I see you're left-handed like myself!"' He nodded as Meldrum glanced up. 'He described it to me as a parable. Thing is, Tommy, he told me, you can't afford to be too finicky in this job.'

CHAPTER SEVENTEEN

'What the hell were you doing there?'
Ord asked the question without preamble and Meldrum,
who had just walked in the door after being summoned,
assumed it was about his visit to Mulholland the morning
before. It came into his head to protest that he could do what
he liked on his day off; for a policeman, an idiotic notion.
Then he froze on the amazement that Ord could know. What
was going on?

After leaving the minister Tommy Wright, he'd wandered
around the New Town trying to decide the next step. Should
he talk to Morton, the upstairs neighbour? Where would the
girl be now, what was her name, the one Keaney claimed had
been with him when he went to Arthur Hull's door? And
what about the man who'd given evidence claiming Keaney
had confessed the murder to him? He needed another look at
the transcript of the trial. He had wakened this morning his
head full of the same questions as if he hadn't slept. Clay had
made the difference. From the moment he knew the name the
man's existence was real to him. He wanted to find Clay.

'Would you believe I was just passing?'

'Don't fuck me about.'

'I wasn't trying to.'

'You just happened to be in Glasgow?' And Meldrum almost
said, What's Glasgow got to do with it? Mulholland living
half an hour's walk away from where they were sitting in
Edinbugh – only Ord went on, 'And then you just happened

to pass Barlinnie and thought you'd drop in and say fucking hello. That what you're telling me?'

The visit to Keaney! First John Brennan, now Ord. He should have put a notice in the paper. That way the whole world would have known.

'Can I sit down?' Ord nodded him to the seat to the left of the desk.

'I wanted to take a look at Keaney. Does that sound stupid?'

'*Sound?* So you looked at him. Moved your mouth as well, did you?'

Meldrum settled his weight in the chair. He'd been told how it affected people when he did that, like a boxer squaring up. And an expression on his face, God knows what it looked like. When he was in police training school an old sergeant had said: You young bastard, in the army we called that dumb insolence. And somebody else: You can't give orders, unless you can take them first. The stupid thing was, he believed in authority. He believed there had to be a hierarchy, that somebody, and in any country a whole class of somebodies, had to be in charge. Betty and her mob of armchair anarchists could ignore human nature only because they didn't know what a jungle the world was. At times like this, though, what he believed about the rightness of authority somehow made no difference. He settled his weight in the chair.

'We talked,' he said.

'What did you say? No, I don't even want to imagine what you would say. What did *he* say?'

'What you'd expect.' And as Ord grunted and stared, eyes as pink as a boar's teetering to charge, 'Claimed he was innocent.'

'You could have read that in the papers. That's what he climbs out on fucking roofs for.' There wasn't any arguing with that. 'You believe him?'

'Lot of people inside claiming that.'

'. . . so there are. But they don't all freeze their balls off on a roof. Is that what's bothering you?'

'He didn't say anything that made me believe him.'

He held Ord's stare for what seemed a long time. With a sigh, Ord got up and pulled out a drawer on the left-hand filing cabinet. He held the two glasses in one hand as he poured stiff shots from the bottle. The high colour had ebbed, leaving the flesh of his cheeks sweating like pale stretched dough. 'You're a bloody fool sometimes.' He held up the hand with the glasses as if to forestall an answer. 'To yourself, I mean. In this job you need friends. I tell you honestly, Jim, you don't have many in this place.'

Meldrum took one of the glasses. Ord's bulk blocked the view from the window, which didn't matter, brick walls he'd seen before. He watched Ord drink.

'But,' Ord said abruptly, 'you're a good thief-taker. When you're on your game. I've said that where it matters.'

The whisky was malt, warm in the mouth and lingering after it went down.

'I can't understand why Keaney,' Ord said. 'Even if you wanted to play the Lone fucking Ranger, why go back that far, why go back to Keaney at all? It wasn't your case. Is that it? Is it because you got pulled off it?'

At the time, it had rankled. When it had been decided that after all the murders of Francis Pietro and Arthur Hull weren't connected, he'd been put back on the Pietro killing and found himself working with a new boss he despised. And on Hull, they'd got a result: Keaney caught, tried, convicted. Everybody on that murder had done themselves good. Ord had gone up the ladder fast since then. While the death of Francis Pietro had been a dead end. No brownie points.

'No way,' he said.

As for friends, it struck him, for what it was worth, the nearest thing might be Ord himself. What would he say if he told him about the visit to Mulholland? Not hand out a medal. Mulholland was too damaged by his stroke to be a credible witness.

What would he say if he told him about Clay?

'I'm glad to hear it,' Ord said. 'Now get your head on straight. You're a policeman, not a loose cannon. Last warning.'

Sooner or later he would have to tell him.

Ord drank and grinned suddenly. 'You want to know what I think? Pawn ticket on the Hannah murder. Neat that was. A nice bit of work. Even if it did annoy the country cousins.' He pointed a thick finger. 'You've decided you're Sherlock fucking Holmes.'

Bastard.

Sooner or later he'd tell Ord everything.

But not right now.

Being laughed at didn't come easily to Meldrum.

CHAPTER EIGHTEEN

'By the way, don't bother passing Barlinnie again. They've moved Keaney back to Peterhead.'

He had been at the door on his way out when Ord said that. He'd turned, wondering how to respond, not finding anything to say, and after a moment Ord took the grin off. It occurred to him Ord might have suddenly wished he'd kept his mouth shut. Prisoners did get moved. From Barlinnie to Peterhead, though? A long way away. Up on the cold farthest edge of the country where raw winds off the North Sea scoured grey granite walls. And why now? And where had the order come from? The odd thing was that it didn't give him any sense of his own risk, not then.

It didn't stop him going to see Morton, Arthur Hull's upstairs neighbour.

'Your wife isn't in?' he asked him.

'She never is,' he said. He had the air of a disappointed man.

'It's just that she might remember what you said to her at the time.'

Morton at the time of Hull's killing had been a polished shoes type, tie matching the shirt, very neat. A precisely spoken man, holding down some kind of job with an insurance company. The kind of job, had been Meldrum's impression, you got by having been to a local fee-paying school; one of the schools with a reputation for looking after their own, and not least the stupid. At that time, certainly, he had seemed pleased enough with himself.

'Of course, there's no reason you should know my wife is dead,' he said.

Morton's wife had been very round and soft with something about her that suggested she would like what happened in the bedroom. Meldrum's mind didn't usually run along those lines, which was why he remembered her.

Anyway, her death could account for why Morton hadn't shaved this morning. Why he didn't look so sleek any more. The years had not dealt well with him.

'I'm sorry.'

'I don't want your – sympathy.' He stumbled on the word. Had he been going to say 'pity'? 'Even if she was alive . . . Hearsay. That's not evidence, is it?'

'Not in a court.'

'I said at the trial it *might* have been Keaney I saw coming out of Hull's door that day, that's as far as I would go. It was Mulholland who was in no doubt.'

'But the impression you left was that it was more likely than not. You sound less certain now than in court.'

'I can't see why you're stirring it up after all these years unless something new's turned up. That would upset Mulholland. He was so sure.'

'He still is.'

'You've seen him? How did you manage to speak to him?'

'The first time his minister helped. This time he printed his answers for me. As you say, no doubts at all.'

'He's always been like that, of course. Wouldn't listen, a dogmatic man. Not that he really knows much about anything. He left school at fourteen.'

Sometimes you took a dislike to a man for no good reason. If a householder found a down-and-out sleeping rough on the stone floor of the close, it made sense to put his case out as a warning he shouldn't do that any more. It didn't matter that it was winter. Meldrum had no problem with that. It was the fussy cautiousness with which Morton had noted the name and security number off Keaney's benefit card, 'just in case', that for some reason stuck in his throat.

'It was the hair,' Meldrum said, 'that made Mulholland so sure.'

'Well, there you are,' Morton said emphatically, 'I mean that's exactly why I wouldn't be. The pair of us saw this man pulling Hull's door shut. As we stepped into the street he looked over his shoulder at us.' That looking back was the detail Mulholland had dwelt on too. Both of them must have caught something strange in that look, though for all they could have known then the stranger might have been an acquaintance of Hull's or someone there on business. What had there been in that look to signal how badly the world had gone wrong that afternoon?

'Keaney had red hair,' Morton said. 'The thing is, I don't believe the man I saw had red hair.'

'Did you say that in court?' Meldrum couldn't remember that.

'No. I talked about it to Mulholland. He didn't say about red hair – I really don't think so – not until we saw Keaney. The man I saw had light hair. With a sort of glow. Because of the sun.'

'You must have been asked to describe him.'

'I told the policeman in charge. Blond. Or it could have been white hair. But there wasn't anyone like that in the line of men they asked us to look at. Apart from Keaney. I go over it. And then I think maybe it *was* red. The sun catching it like that.'

In his pocket Meldrum had a piece of paper Mulholland had scrawled with laborious print.

FRIGH—

Frightened? he'd asked.

YS.

Pietro said he was frightened? Was it Pietro who said that to you?

YS.

'Did you ever see Pietro after he stopped living with Hull?' Morton blinked at the abrupt change of subject. His mouth turned down in contempt. 'My father would have called that creature Pietro a bum boy.'

'I have reason to believe he came back to see Hull.'

'They found him in bed naked. He'd been strangled and then stabbed with a knife. It was in the papers.'

'Did John Mulholland ever talk to you about a man called Clay?'

Morton shook his head. 'Why?'

Frightened? Of this man Clay?

YS.

And at the bottom of the sheet he'd printed the word SOLDIER.

Clay was a soldier, is that what Pietro said?

But, the sheet filled with long straggling letters, Mulholland wouldn't answer any more.

A man with bright hair. What had been the colour of Clay's hair, Meldrum wondered.

CHAPTER NINETEEN

Driving to see his daughter Betty at her flat, he tried to remember when he'd last taken some leave. Then he tried to remember where he'd gone. If he'd gone. One time after he'd finalised the divorce from Carole he'd shut the door and got drunk for a week. After that he'd stopped drinking altogether for a while.

He'd thought about a divorce after they'd been separated for two years, but she'd have had to give her consent and, deciding that as a Catholic she wouldn't, he didn't ask. After five years he didn't need her consent and so he did it then, which she didn't just accept but in reality might even have been glad to have. She after all was the one who had wanted the marriage to be over.

By that time, Betty had taken her Highers, English, History, French, Biology, and was waiting to go to university. It had never occurred to him getting the divorce from her mother might make her angry. Why? she'd asked. To which the only answer was, Why not?

Either you were married or you weren't. He had a tidy mind.

It wasn't Betty who opened the door.

'Mr Meldrum? Betty isn't here.'

Cliff, the boy he'd met at the hospital. The landlord.

'Is Sandy Torrance? I'd like to speak to him, if he is.'

The boy hesitated. Did he imagine he'd come to act the heavy father?

'. . . if he's having a drink, he'll be in The Crusader. That's where he usually goes.'

'Is Betty with him?'

'I shouldn't think so.'

'Why not?'

But before the boy could answer, a man emerged into the lobby behind him. 'Everything all right, Cliff?' A bulky, authoritative man who managed to give a jersey and denims the air of a three-piece suit, his heavy features matched the boy closely enough to leave no doubt this was Daddy rumbling to the rescue.

'This is Betty's father.'

'But of course it is. Mr Meldrum. I'm Clifford Aitkenhead.' He held out his hand with such good will that the idea of being pulled on to a punch did no more than flick on as an embarrassing reflex at the back of Meldrum's mind. 'We met at one of the open days.' School. It took a moment to work that one out. 'Just the once, I think.'

'Usually I was working.' Working on open days. Working when he should have been at the school concerts. During the run of the school play. Missed even a prize-giving more than once – that had gone down well.

'I tried not to be if I could possibly help it. But then it's my old school. No girls in my day. The girls came later. Not everyone was in favour of *that* change. You'll be glad to hear, I've come to think the presence of girls like your Betty was a civilising influence. Won't you come in? All the young people are out, so I have Cliff to myself.'

Father and son had been sitting in the shared living-room. A chair on either side of the fire, a glass of beer beside each chair. Happy families, Meldrum thought sourly, and sat down without being asked.

Cliff asked if he wanted a beer and went to fetch one.

'I've been saying to my son— We've been sitting talking. It's one of my pleasures, talking to him. Do you have a son?' Meldrum shook his head. 'We talk about politics and things. Two intelligent people talking things over. I think that *opportunity* in their lives is something a lot of men just let go. When you knocked I was saying to him . . .' He stopped to reflect. 'Hyperinflation! It could happen. I buy property – like this place. But everything could go smash.' He had sat up for emphasis and now sank back. 'Of course, I'm not an economist. I'm an advocate.'

'I know,' Meldrum said.

The two men sat in silence till Cliff came back with the beer.

Daddy said, 'Someone like your Betty would be an asset to any school. Bright, from what my son tells me. And a fine-looking girl.'

How many beers had Daddy had?

'Thing is,' Cliff said, 'I mean, I don't think Sandy and Betty are particular . . . friends any more.' He studied Meldrum shrewdly: an if-you-know-what-I-mean look.

'Why would that be?'

'It's my impression Betty's angry with him for dropping the action.' Meldrum didn't say anything. 'For assault . . . Against the police.'

'Oh, that action.'

Daddy to the rescue again. Stretched out, a beer balanced on the comfortable mound of his belly. 'Wise to drop it. They never get anywhere with that kind of thing.'

'He couldn't identify the men involved,' Cliff said.

'I expect they're safely tucked away.' A conspiratorial grin directed over the belly at Meldrum. 'I expect they weren't there at all that afternoon. I expect they were miles away. On traffic duty.'

'It doesn't work that way,' Meldrum said.

Cliff said, 'I suppose one should say "alleged to be involved". But anyway he couldn't. Identify them, I mean. So he didn't see any point in going on. It was his lawyer, some woman, who wanted to – and Betty sided with her.'

'Not well advised.'

'Not if there isn't any evidence,' Cliff agreed with his father, 'although I suppose if the lawyer woman got to hear there was talk of trouble before—'

'Cliff!' his father said.

'What talk would that be?' he asked the boy.

'Rumours, you know. Nothing really.'

'Tell me about them.'

'That the police might be planning to teach them a lesson.' His father sighed. Cliff said defensively, 'I expect you heard them yourself.'

'No,' Meldrum said, looking at the father, 'I didn't.'

'Is there any point in going on with this?' Aitkenhead sat up in his chair, not even a little bit relaxed any more. Like that, he looked suddenly shrewd and aggressive, the way he must in court.

'I always wonder where a rumour like that starts,' Meldrum said.

'You won't think me rude if I remind you how much I enjoy a chat with my son. I don't get the chance as much as I would like.'

'And you won't mind if I sit here and wait for my daughter to come back. I have something to talk over with her. Being a father, you'll understand.'

'But she won't be back,' Cliff said. 'She's gone off to stay with her mother. I'm sorry, I took it for granted you knew that.'

With being her father . . . Though, to be fair, the young bastard might have expected him to know anyway, policemen being in the finding-out business.

'Your phone call surprised me,' he told her.

'I should thank you for coming.'

'I didn't have anything else to do. Sorry, I didn't mean that the way it sounded,' he said, and then, 'I keep having to apologise to you.'

'Apologise to me?'

'I owe you one.'

'You mean because you called me a drunk last time we met? Don't worry about it.'

'I didn't call you a drunk. I might have said you had too much to drink – on that occasion.'

'That particular occasion.' Harriet Cook glanced round. 'Do you think that's why I suggested we meet in a bar?'

She was pale with very white skin and her eyes were green, not light but with an effect of dark intensity. She kept her gaze on his face, fixing on his eyes and then on his mouth as he spoke. It was as if she was trying to test the truth of what he might say. Taught by experience, he didn't think there was any easy test for truth.

'Betty's left the flat. She's staying with her mother.'

'I knew that,' Harriet said.

'I wish somebody had told me.' Hearing his words, he regretted them. They sounded too much like self-pity. 'And Torrance was out somewhere, so I didn't get speaking to either of them.'

'Why did you want to see Sandy?'

'Not to threaten him.'

'I think it's my turn to apologise.'

'You've decided I didn't threaten him?'

'I know more about you than I did last time we met.' When he didn't answer, she said, 'I asked around. It doesn't mean everybody liked you, but you got the vote as being straight. Absolutely, for everybody it seemed to be the first thing that came to mind. Or at least the second.'

'I'm not bad at my job either.'

'I didn't say you weren't.' She laughed. 'Like a photograph.'

'What?'

'Show most people a photograph – a wedding say, with the bride and groom up-front smiling – and they take a look at themselves in the back row and say, My hair's standing on end.'

Before, he hadn't taken in how dark her hair was. Its darkness shone.

'My hair's standing on end,' he said.

He hadn't expected to want to touch her hair. He hadn't expected to like her this much.

'I didn't have anything to do with Torrance dropping the complaint,' he said. 'Didn't even know until you told me. So I got curious. That's why I went to see Betty. I wanted to ask her what it was about.'

What was he saying? That he needed an excuse to talk to his daughter?

'And have you seen her?'

'If you mean did I go to my ex-wife's, no, I haven't been there.'

'I've been wondering if Betty might after all have decided Sandy was right to give up. All the hassle. For his sake, she might feel it wasn't worth it.'

He shook his head at the idea. 'She quarrelled with him about giving up. That's why she left the flat.'

'He didn't tell me that.'

'That's the flatmate's version. Cliff Aitkenhead. Named after Daddy, QC. Who was there too. You probably know him.'

'Yes.' She was silent for a moment, thinking. 'He's a friend of John Brennan's.'

Wasn't everybody?

'The boy Aitkenhead's full of theories. According to him, Torrance gave up because he couldn't identify the police who assaulted him. If the police assaulted him.'

'Is that why you think he gave up?'

'It seems plausible.'

'Except that Sandy and I had already been through that. He knew the fact he couldn't identify a particular individual didn't stop him from bringing a general action – for damages, say. He wasn't vindictive. He didn't want any kind of revenge on an individual. For him it was a matter of principle.'

'Well, yes.'

'If you have something to say, say it.'

'Principles.'

'You think nobody has principles?'

'I hear people talk about having them.'

'Sandy Torrance didn't talk about them. He showed them in . . .'

'And then he changed his mind.'

He wondered what was wrong with him. He didn't want to quarrel with her.

'Would you like the same again?' She nodded and he caught the waitress's eye. It was an expensive hotel and the service in the bar was good. On the tables were little bowls of Indian mix and peanuts. She was drinking tomato juice; no alcohol, so maybe she was making a point.

'I had another reason for phoning you,' she said.

He sipped at the second whisky, looking across the glass at the dark gleam of her hair.

'Have you met a journalist called Brian Worth?'

He blinked. 'No.' Whatever he had thought might be coming, it wasn't that.

'He said you hadn't. I just wondered. You've heard of him?'

'Selling the land at Bellcroft cheap. That was a big story at the time. And a few years back, was it him who did the stuff about the old folks' homes?'

'Yes. And the Chalmers and Black takeover.'

'Was that him? Chalmers and Black – I was a constable on my first beat. What were you? Ten?'

'He's been around a long time. And now he's out of a job. After thirty years. I researched him.'

'Researched him, researched me. You've been busy.'

'There's a connection. He wants to contact you.'

'So why ask you? Is he a friend of yours?'

'I spoke to him for the first time two days ago.'

'So what does he want to talk about? And don't tell me I should ask him. I'm not that interested.'

'If it helps, I was at a party. I noticed this man on the edge of the group. He never took his eyes off me – but it wasn't, I don't know how I knew this, it wasn't about me, it wasn't personal. Looking over someone's shoulder at me, this round face, bright small eyes. He was just listening, but so intently. Not many people can really listen.'

'Brian Worth.'

'Yes.'

'And then he came up and told you he wanted to talk to me.'

'Well, it wasn't quite as abrupt as that. He knew I was a lawyer. We talked about the things I was working on.'

'Lawyers aren't supposed to do that, are they?'

She stared at him.

'I wasn't drunk,' she said.

It hadn't occurred to him, but her saying it made him think she probably had been.

One of the things he missed was sitting in front of a real fire. Even on his days off he used the electric one. Setting a fire was like cooking; it didn't seem worth the bother when you were on your own. It was stupid how often he visited his ex-wife and how at home he felt here. A good meal and a fire.

Making his point, he leaned forward and felt the heat like a hand cupped against the side of his face. 'I don't see why Brian Worth would be sniffing round. A story about police brutality – Sandy Torrance getting attacked, maybe getting attacked. It's not a big enough story for him.'

'You said his paper had made him redundant.'

'So?'

'Maybe he has to take what he finds now.'

'If the complaint's been dropped, where's the story?'

He sat back, and something in Carole's look put it into his head that at some level, under their talk, while they were discussing Harriet Cook and Worth, she was also somehow registering his pleasure in the warmth of the fire on his cheek. If so, it wouldn't surprise him. They had been married a lot of years and waited together for a child. It felt to him they had parted more in sorrow than in anger, that old cliché.

'What did you think of her?' she asked.

'Harriet Cook? She's not stupid. I don't know how good a lawyer she is. And I'm glad we don't have to find out.'

'You should have phoned. I could have told you Betty would be at a meeting tonight.'

'Political meetings won't get her a good degree.'

'She's an idealist. That's a good way to be when you're young. It's later all the compromises have to be made.'

'Compromises?' he wondered. She was a head teacher in a school with small children. Her work hadn't ever been very real to him.

'You're glad Sandy Torrance is letting it go.' She spelled it out. 'So am I, if I'm being honest. But Betty's furious. Same as always, she takes hold and won't let go.'

A rush of flame rose up white as a log settled into the coals.

When he didn't comment, Carole went on, 'She called Sandy a coward. And now she's sorry, you know what's she's like. Not that she'll admit it, of course, not even to herself. The whole thing's such an awful bloody shame. I feel so sorry for her.'

It seemed to him a fuss over not very much. Instead, he

was thinking about Harriet Cook and how he had chilled the atmosphere between them with his stupid abruptness about Worth's approach to her. If I told her I was concerned about my daughter, he thought, would she accept that as an apology?

Carole said, 'Your daughter's not very happy.'

'She'll get over it,' he said.

'You're not thinking about her at all, are you?'

'Sorry?'

'Staring into the fire. You're thinking about some case you're on. Work doesn't leave any room in your life.'

It was a complaint that had become familiar to him before their marriage broke up. Now, however, she made it softly, almost languidly, staring into the fire herself. There was so little lingering energy in it that almost at once she began to tell of a dream she had had the previous night. For some reason he never dreamed, and there had been a time when that lack had been made up by listening to her, a prolific dreamer.

She had been a child in bed in a room with a fire and out of the fire a red dog had jumped. It was strange how in a dream you looked out through eyes that weren't your own. She didn't decide to close her eyes, the child made the decision – and when they opened again the dog wasn't there. Eyes shut, eyes open, and this time the dog jumps out of the fire and runs round the room. The child waits till it is by the bed and throws a blanket over it. Child's turn to jump, jumps out of bed, piles wood on blanket. The blanket moves, wood falls off on to the floor. The child beats on the blanket with logs of wood. Beats and beats and beats. Nothing moves. The child leans down, head close to the blanket, and hears from under it a *whuffle*.

'It was the noise that upset me,' Carole said.

He tried to think of something to say, but he was out of practice. If he'd ever been in practice. It occurred to him maybe that had been another of the ways in which he'd let her down.

'I don't think I'd tell that one in class,' he said.

She sighed. 'Do you want another coffee?'

'No,' he said. 'Thanks.'

'I'll make another one.'

'It's about time I was going.'

'You don't want to wait until she gets back?'

'It looks as though she's going to be late.'

Carole said, 'Harriet Cook was supposed to come, remember that night at Val and Martin's farewell party?'

'She came after you left.'

'When John Brennan brought his brat into the school, I thought, Imagine a woman breaking her heart over you.'

'One of the many.'

Women were fools. It would be stupid to let it matter to him.

While that ran through his head, he heard himself say, 'It'll fall apart at the first touch,' and took a moment to realise he was telling her about the case against Hugh Keaney.

What was he trying to do? Share his life with her now it was too late?

He thought, Men are fools, but wasn't sure in how many ways, since at the moment it seemed he had a choice.

CHAPTER TWENTY

'What brings you here?'

The hard nasal edge on the muttered question had no trouble cutting through the noise. Not as much noise in The Crusader as there would be later, but still plenty: from getting started on the drink talkers and a few of the never-mind-about-eating contingent loudly left over from the afternoon; above their heads on the big screen the elegant Asian woman mouthing the evening's bad news from London.

Meldrum recognised the man though it took a second glance to place him. Bell, that was it. He picked up his pint and took a long slow pull at it before responding.

'Thirst. The usual reason.'

'The best one, right.'

'What about yourself?'

'Nice to see you again.' He spoke without turning his face fully round, glancing at Meldrum out of the corner of his eye. Scooping up his change, he gathered up the three glasses. 'Take care.'

Being in bars was part of the job and Meldrum had been at the job for a long time. That meant being recognised by a lot of people. It would be paranoid to worry about one of them saying hello. He felt paranoid. He took his time over the pint and had it almost finished before he looked round. Bell, couldn't remember his first name, was seated with two others near the door. Three of a kind.

The majority in the bar were young, but that was true of most places. A cluster of them at the far end burst into laughter. As one turned to get drinks, Meldrum caught him in profile. An earring and a nose lumped with a thread of white scar. Sandy Torrance. Someone else Meldrum recognised.

While he was registering that, he felt the touch of a hand on his upper arm.

Thinning hair combed forward, a round face, bright small eyes. About fifty.

'Mr Meldrum?' And once they were settled at a table, 'Plain mister the best idea, eh? No ranks no pack drill. Never know who might be listening.'

'I made a bad choice of meeting place,' Meldrum said, 'if that's what you wanted.'

Deliberately, he'd got his back against the wall where he could watch the room. Over Worth's shoulder, he could see the table by the door with Bell and the other two Special Branch officers.

'If you want to be private, meet where it's busy,' Worth said, not understanding. 'And this place is out of the way.'

'No hacks.'

'No colleagues. Ex-colleagues, I should say. When the old set of bastards sold out to the new set of bastards I knew heads would roll. Just never thought one of them would be mine.'

'I'm not a social worker.'

'Sorry?'

'If you phoned for advice on being unemployed, you've made a mistake.'

'Nice one,' Worth said with a smile that looked genuine. 'But I've been in the game from hot metal to wee screens. You don't stop if you've got it in the blood. I'm a freelance, back where I started.'

'Peddling stories to the highest bidder.'

Elbow on the table, Worth rested his cheek on his fist and peeped up under his brows like a garden gnome. 'I didn't expect you to be so hostile. If you hate newspapermen on principle, why agree to see me?'

'To tell you to forget it.'

'Forget what? You haven't given me a chance to tell you.'

On impulse, Meldrum got to his feet.

Worth stared up. 'You're not going?'

'Somebody you should meet.'

Sandy Torrance stood in a group at the end of the bar. Automatically, Meldrum checked out the others. Four probably students, one more interesting, older, unshaved, a face that had seen hard times. He watched Torrance place him and then, to his surprise, the boy smiled and held out a hand. 'Great to see you.' And to the others, 'This is Jim. He was a neighbour in my last flat.'

Meldrum tightened his grip on Torrance's hand, pulling towards himself. 'Have you a minute? There's another neighbour over there wanting to say hello.'

The older man watched suspiciously, scrubbing fingers across the bristles on his chin.

The room was filling up. Busier than Meldrum would have expected for a Tuesday night; no music blasting but noisy; and a muted excitement, a waiting for something, that set him on edge.

'Sorry about that,' Sandy Torrance said as they went over, 'I didn't want them to know you were a policeman.'

'Sit down,' Meldrum said.

They sat looking at one another. In an instinctive reaction to the noise they bent forward across the table. Meldrum waited for the journalist to say something. Worth stared at the boy who covered the scar on his nose with his hand, then, as if realising what he'd done, took it away.

Meldrum said, 'I picked this place on the chance he would be here,' nodding at Sandy.

'Who is he?' Worth asked.

'You tell me, you're the one after the story.'

'What story?'

'Story?' Sandy Torrance echoed.

'Mr Worth is interested in police brutality.'

'That's all over,' Torrance said. 'If you ask Betty, she'll tell you.'

'You hear him?' Meldrum said. He wanted Worth to understand there wasn't going to be a story for him.

'Anyway,' the boy said, 'I've already been warned off. You people should keep in touch with one another.'

'What?'

'Just keep away from me,' the boy said. He looked at Meldrum, his mouth twisting as if on something sour. 'Ask your friends. It's not myself I'm afraid for.'

He shoved the chair back and stood up, stepping away as though they might try to stop him, jiggling an elbow so drink spilled, apologising, edging his way off back to his friends.

'You could be right. There's a story there,' Worth said.

Somebody was shouting. Over by the door. Meldrum turned to look. As he did, the cry was taken up. 'They're here!'

People were jumping up. Meldrum found himself on his feet. He saw Sandy Torrance and his friends among those heading for the exit. He had no idea what was going on. He saw Bell and the other two Special Branch men, among the last to leave. Half the place had gone. In his confusion, he thought, Too many, they can't all be police.

'What's that about?' 'What's going on?' 'Who the fuck cares?'

As the guessing began, Meldrum headed for the door.

He was outside before Worth caught up with him.

CHAPTER TWENTY-ONE

'Hacks work under pressure. I'm not just talking about time, though it's time as well. Any story's in the process of being written before they get near wherever it is. It's going on in their heads already, the lead-in, the background. Once they get there, what happened, what actually happened, that fills in the gaps. And that's the way of it even when they haven't been told what to think, you know, the political stories, the union stories. It's easier to arrive with the stereotypes in place and then make the events fit.'

'"They". Not "we"?'

'No one tells me what to think,' Worth said.

For a man who'd had a heart attack he was looking surprisingly well. His jacket was hung on the back of the chair and he was forking through a mound of rice and curried chicken.

'Should you be doing that?' Meldrum asked, gesturing with his own fork at the other's plate. Worth shovelled in more food and raised his eyebrows in question. Sweat shone on his forehead and upper lip. 'I mean, you're not intending to try and die again.'

'I only die once a night. It was the excitement.'

They'd followed the group that left the pub, or rather followed Bell and the other two following them; it was a procession.

'Who are they?' Worth had asked. 'Those three guys?' He was panting with the pace that was being set.

'Special Branch.'

'I don't like that.' He stopped in his tracks. 'You know them?'

Meldrum turned. 'One of them.'

'I saw you talking to one of them. When I came in. I almost asked you – then I thought it was just talk to a guy at a bar.'

'His name's Bell. Used to be Drugs. Then he joined the politicals.' He looked over his shoulder. 'We're going to lose them.'

'Did you know they were going to be there?'

'I wouldn't have remembered who the hell he was if he hadn't spoken to me.'

Without waiting he started off. They were gone. He began to hurry. Behind him he heard footsteps and Worth gasping for each breath.

At the corner he stopped in disbelief. A quiet side street with distance measured by light pooled under the lamps and nobody in sight. He could see where at the far end it joined a main road, a bus, cars passing.

Worth caught up and said, 'Bloody hell! Must be another street. Must be.'

It was at the end of the block. Not a street but a wide lane, and he heard the shouting before he could see anything. His first impression was confused, a crowd jostling, filling the space. He saw an entrance and some kind of building set back behind a low wall. The lane was badly lit, as usual probably or because some lamps had been smashed for the occasion.

He didn't like crowds, and most of all he disliked ill-natured ones, edgy and ready for violence. Pushing his way through, he felt the crackle of resistance, bodies stiff with anger and excitement. At the entry, the focus of it all, a line of heavy-set men barred admittance. They looked in their twenties, except for one in the middle, beefy-necked with hair black enough to be dyed and sagging jowls, who was shouting, 'Because this is a fucking *private* function, that's *why*!' Facing him was Sandy Torrance. Oh, shit! Meldrum thought. He could see what was going to happen. What he couldn't see was any sign of a blue uniform or, come to that, of Bell and his two colleagues.

He remembered the ACPO Public Order manual, long shields, short shields, tear gas and baton rounds and if that doesn't work shoot the bastards.

A hand gripped him by the elbow and he clamped it against
his body as he swung round. A boy wearing a student scarf
tugged to free his hand in sudden fright and gabbled, 'Better
see to your friend, I think he's ill.'

And there Worth had been, on the cobbles, sprawled against
a garage wall, clutching his chest.

'Give me a choice and I'd take Indian every time. Over Chinese,
that is.'

His colour was back and there was nothing wrong with his
jaws, which hadn't stopped moving since the waiter served
them.

'Do you always eat this much?'

'Recalled to life,' Worth said, keeping the fork clutched as
he used a finger to brush sweat from his forehead. 'That gives
me an appetite.' He scooped and gobbled; grains of rice spilled
from his lips. 'Grateful to you for getting my pills into me.'

'Thank the guy who fetched me.'

'I was having a nice little chat with him when I hit the deck.
He was one of the ones in the pub. It's like a game apparently.
The fascists try to fool them, so their lot have people watching
the stations. The rest wait somewhere till they hear what's up.
Get the word and they take off. Of course, when they all start
jumping up, people like us sitting having a pint don't know
what the hell's going on. The kid liked that. Tonight they were
lucky – didn't even need the motors. That pub's one of their
favourites. Did you know that?'

'Stations?'

'Rail stations. Some history bloke was due in town. To
explain how the last war was a Jewish plot. Roundabout
way to get to Israel, you or I might think, but he'd've been
preaching to the converted. Came by train instead of flying,
only the anti-Nazi lot had somebody at the station. Nice bit of
chicken, this. Can't beat a tandoori oven.'

'Swing it!' the man at the next table ordered. His companion,
heading down the restaurant for the Ladies, grinned back at
him. She had on a red dress tight across the hips and when
she swung them the effect was more or less what it was
intended to be.

'It's been a funny old night,' Worth said. 'At least we missed the fighting.'

Meldrum's last glimpse had been of the heavy-jowelled man poking his fist out at Sandy Torrance. It happened suddenly, the way it always did. Men lashing out; at one angle their arms seeming short like those of children, till the blood came. Helped by the Samaritan, he had got Worth out to where they could find a taxi. They had been on their way to the hospital when Worth pulled his Lourdes stunt and announced he was hungry.

'I'm enjoying this,' Worth said. 'Since I got the order of the boot, the bullet from those bastards, I've missed the companionship – well, and even before that it hadn't been the same for a long time. You can't climb the ladder in any organisation without the barriers going up. You find that? Newspapers aren't any different. And then, the last year, longer than that, all the rumours, money problems, should we do a buy-out? and then the sharks swim in. There was blood in the water.' He gazed around, his face went slack, almost stupid, then he blinked and smiled. 'People have the idea being a journalist means you're never short of company.'

Christ! He wants me to be his chum, Meldrum thought; and then, Recalled to life, it'll have worn off by morning, thank God! The last thing he needed was a friend.

Worth belched into his fist. 'I feel more human,' he said. 'Food never tasted better. I seem to have lost half the evening. Did we talk? I mean about why I wanted to see you.' Meldrum shook his head. 'I didn't see any policemen.'

'Policemen?' Meldrum took a second to catch up. 'Back there, you mean? Somebody would call them. We left before they arrived.' He wondered if the boy Torrance had got himself arrested.

Worth frowned. 'There were policemen, though, weren't there? Didn't you say something about— In the pub? I'm sure there was something.'

'Three from Special Branch.'

'Did they know you?'

The tone of sharp anxiety took Meldrum by surprise.

'One of them did.'

'And they saw us together?'

'If it matters.'

'Why would they be there?'

'Your historian, the Nazi? He must be a big fish.'

'I just hope they don't make a report about you talking to me.'

'Why should they? Even if they knew who you were. Torrance isn't that important.' And when Worth stared, 'Sandy Torrance – that's why I suggested meeting in The Crusader. I hoped he'd be there.'

'So what if he was?'

'Because I wanted to stop you chasing the police brutality story;' but already he could see something wasn't right, 'stop it in its tracks.'

'I don't care about Torrance.'

'Why talk to Harriet Cook then?'

'I needed a contact. Somebody who'd fix it so you and I could talk. No official channels. Just you and me.'

Meldrum pushed his chair back, rested his hands on the edge of the table, getting ready to leave.

'Listen to me.' The journalist's voice had the same echo on it as Meldrum's father's before his heart killed him. 'I've been keeping tabs on a story for fifteen years. A bit of information came to me and I didn't have the guts to follow it up.'

'I'm a policeman. Official channels are what I'm about.'

'There's a man in jail I believe is innocent. It's my guess you think he is too. Isn't that why you visited him?'

For the first time Meldrum felt . . . a kind of fear . . . as if a net was being folded down about him. And then the anger.

'Somebody's been feeding you crap. You've lost your touch as well as your job.'

Worth leaned forward and didn't so much say as breathe a name, making its shape with his lips. 'Hugh Keaney?'

The woman in the red dress was coming back.

'Five years we've been married,' the man said, 'and she can't boil an egg. I cook or we're in here. She's only good at one thing and I'm exhausted.' He leaned over to give Meldrum the pleasure of smelling his breath. 'Painting and decorating? That's what I'm thinking about. You must have a dirty mind.'

Sometimes punching somebody in the mouth didn't seem such a bad idea.

'All I want you to do is listen,' Worth was saying. 'I have to tell somebody about it.'

BOOK FOUR

The Jizz

CHAPTER TWENTY-TWO

At that period fifteen years earlier Worth spent some of his drinking time in the bar of a club theatre. One of the divisions by which he sorted his colleagues was into those who read newspapers and those who read books as well. Among the latter was a sub-division for those who read only non-fiction; from the ones who were left came most of the people with whom he preferred to pass time. As well as eating, the woman who did the restaurant column liked books and kept him company when he went to the theatre club. In a tiny floor space, the audience on ranks of cushioned steps all round, it was a place where people were made to think and sometimes so hard, he said to her after a couple of bottles of wine, that chamber work resonated like grand opera in the memory.

The bar was a popular rendezvous for homosexuals and they would watch that by-play also and joke about it.

On this evening she had gone down with flu at the last minute and cancelled. At the interval he hadn't seen anyone he knew, which was unusual. The play had been coolly reviewed and the audience was thin. He had made up his mind to go home at the end, but didn't, and wandered into the bar. After a second gin he thought again about going home, but fell into conversation. The man was thirty-something, slim and dark; a woman would call him good-looking, Worth thought. He talked sense about the play, and it seemed to Worth he must go to the theatre a lot. He said it was the great love of his life, opera above all; and that he lived in hope of converting his friend who wasn't keen on the theatre.

Often even when the play wasn't popular the bar would fill up anyway as it got later. This night, though, it stayed quiet and it was easy and pleasant to sit and go on talking. As they were leaving, an acquaintance coming in nodded to Worth. The incident was trivial, but it affected him like a crossing of the Rubicon. It had happened, and since it had, whatever else was going to might as well happen too. Knowingly from that point he let go, allowing himself to drift passively as if through the actions of a dream.

When he had wakened, light glowed. He knew it must be day and as he stared with closed eyes, behind his eyelids lozenges yellowed and broke into lines and stepshapes that tumbling began to recede. He remembered the acquaintance who had nodded to him the previous night. Just an inclination of the head, but the man's gaze had flicked from him to the other. The bastard couldn't have known – he'd known, he'd known. Oh Jesus, what have I done? At the terror of the thought, his eyes snapped open. Sunlight and a high narrow patch of sky. In his bedroom, the bed didn't face a window. He wasn't in his own bed. There was the noise of a door opening and a voice that said, 'How would eggs do?' Very cheerful, wearing only underpants and swinging a dishcloth in his hand.

Francis Pietro.

In the best tradition of Worth's profession he'd made his excuses and left. But gone back; not just to the theatre, although he did that twice on his own in hope of seeing him, but to the door and knocked and waited abandoning self-respect until Pietro came who took a moment to recognise him and then said, 'You're lucky I'm on my own.' He had been made to pay a price for going back – for having defined the extent of his need.

The next three weeks were the most vivid, the most exultant, the most fretful and finally the most terrible of his life.

At the beginning of the first week of the three, he had sat looking out through the glass of his office at the floor of journalists, working the phones, occupied. A woman leaned on the nearest desk, scribbling; finished, she stuck a yellow reminder note beside a line of others on the space above her computer screen. A man with grey hair was laughing at something. A man he had worked with for years; he couldn't remember his name. He could see the man's mouth stretched wide but he couldn't hear the laughter. His door was open, it was always open, the room out there was full of noise but he couldn't hear anything. It was as if he had gone deaf.

He saved himself from a breakdown by falling back on the habits and strategies of his trade. The industry he worked in had information as its raw material. He set himself the task of finding out.

Francis Pietro held a job in the Finance Department of the City Council, not much of a job, what they'd have called once a clerical post; men at high desks with pens behind their ears; what did clerks do now? His real life, though, was the theatre and music, he had a passion for music. Somehow through that passion he had met Arthur Hull. Hull had been a composer, whose gift briefly appeared larger than it turned out to be. He had played the piano almost to concert standard. He seemed to know almost everyone in the musical world, not only locally but among the great names who passed through the city during the annual Festival of the Arts. It wasn't difficult to see how all that could make its appeal to someone like Pietro. There must have been an attraction, too, in the name Hull had made as a music critic; the column in the morning paper for enough years to seem a fixture, a tradition of sorts for those who cared.

Worth, in fact, knew of Hull as a fellow journalist; if only in a way, and as one who hardly ever had set foot in the building, his columns arriving over the phone, judgements in honed sentences all held in the blind man's head and right in length to the last exact word.

One day at the beginning of the year the columns had stopped coming. No surprise in that; the old man was past the pension age and everyone now seemed to retire early. What Worth hadn't known when they stopped, of course, but understood now, was that Hull had given up his column the week after Francis Pietro left him.

His enquiries didn't run up against a difficulty until he

arrived at the question of why Pietro should have walked
out on Hull after eight years together. Most of what he had
learned till then was easy; the stuff of office gossip he could
have picked up any time if he had been interested. The simple
answer to the break-up would have been a young man with an
old one; say that sooner or later for an odd couple breaking up
was bound to happen and leave it at that.

But what had held Pietro for so long in the first place? Hull
had a private income but he wasn't rich. The music? Tone
deaf, Worth hardly knew what weight to give that. Vanity and
curiosity: for an obscure young man, just into his twenties
at the beginning of the affair, a grey Monday morning in
the office must have been lightened by dreams of weekend
mingling with the admired, sometimes the famous. Celebrities
didn't command Worth's admiration, but he had interviewed
too many to underestimate the potent mystery of fame.

For whatever mix of motives Pietro stayed those eight years.
And for obvious reasons Hull put up with his young partner's
indiscretions on the side. Plenty of them. Cock on a conveyor
belt's what that one wanted. Someone said that to Worth, who
managed a smile.

Then after eight years, one morning packed and gone? But
again, of course, it happened. Slowly under the surface, hus-
bands, wives, lovers could get tired of one another. If there had
to be a particular reason, someone new was the obvious one.
The night he met him, Pietro had spoken of a 'friend' who
didn't care for the theatre. This was a small city, and in one
of its little worlds Pietro had become a known face at least.
There should have been gossip but Worth couldn't find any,
which maybe meant nothing except how unimportant Pietro
was once separated from Arthur Hull. Even so, it was possible
the friend was a married man, someone with a need to keep
the affair secret. Someone in public life?

Added into the fever of his shameful obsession, Worth felt
a stirring of the unshamable inquisitiveness of his vocation.

When he tried to question him, Pietro was at first amused
and evasive, then suddenly angry.

'He told me to get out. We were in the living-room of his flat
and he stood up and pointed at the door. Just like a melodrama.

We'd both had a lot to drink, of course. Only then to me it felt unbearable, the worst thing that had ever – as if he was telling me my new life was over when it had hardly begun. I never thought I'd ever beg. It wasn't something – would you believe I went on my knees? I told him I'd do anything. And he thought of some things. And so I didn't have to leave. But when he'd done he said to me, "This doesn't make any difference. I want you out of here in the morning. Don't even think of coming back." He turned over and went to sleep. An hour later, two hours later, I'd just been lying there, I got out of bed, carefully so as not to wake him. I went into the next room not for any better reason than that it was the first door I came to. The curtain at the window was open and there was a moon, enough for me to see, I didn't want more light. There was a record deck and speakers, expensive stuff, it was where he listened to music. I think that's where the best of his life was – not in the bedroom at all. He brought other people to life in the bedroom. He didn't have any gift for music – maybe it would have been different if he had, he wouldn't have needed— Stupid. It was part of him, making men need him, call it what you want . . . love him. And he must have had so many. They do, you know. Homosexuals, I mean. Have one-night stands. Only with him – I can't have been the only one – one night was enough to – I've never taken drugs but I think that's what it must be like. He was an addiction and one that happened very fast. You don't work at getting a gift, you're born with it. His gift was a dangerous one to have. All that went through my head by his desk in the moonlight, and it came into my mind that he hadn't been angry with me but frightened. Out in the hall again, I had to feel my way by touch. When the light came on I was blinded by it. First impressions, a great black shape, a giant of darkness, at the end of the hall where the outer door was. It ran at me and it was only when I smelled the drink off its breath I realised it was a man. The next minute my head was battered off the wall and I was on the floor. Then Francis was behind the man screaming at him, "I just met him – I don't even know his name!" and crying and pulling at him, for the man had a gun, you see, and he had it in my mouth asking if I wanted to die. "This was supposed to be a celebration, you bastard," he said to Francis. They were like a pair of madmen. Months later, when I heard Francis was dead, I wasn't in any doubt about who'd killed him.'

'But you didn't go to the police.'

'Go to the police? Is that your answer to everything – why didn't you go to the police? Because I'd have had to tell the police about Francis. Because I'd found out what I was. For Christ's sake, I wasn't a policeman. I was just somebody who'd met Francis Pietro. Why didn't I go to the police? Because before I got away that night that madman shoved his gun up my arse. For a joke. And it was a joke when he pulled the trigger and when he said, Fuck, thought I'd one still up the spout, that must have been a joke too.'

CHAPTER TWENTY-THREE

When the phone rang Meldrum didn't feel like getting out of the chair and when he heard Sandy Torrance's voice he wished he hadn't.

'Tonight?' He was home at the end of a long day. 'Not tonight.'

'I have to talk to you.'

'You know where to find me.'

There was a pause and then the voice thinned on a question so that for the first time he sounded his age, just a boy.

'. . . you want me to walk into a police station?'

'That's where I work.'

'I can't do that.'

'That's your choice,' Meldrum said.

There followed that change in the sound, like stepping into an unoccupied room, which meant the other phone had gone down.

It was an hour later and he was still in the same chair, too tired to go to bed, when the phone rang again.

'It's not for me,' Sandy Torrance said. 'It's for Betty.'

For Betty's sake, Meldrum got into the car. Torrance had said he would be at The Crusader. Ten minutes: nowhere was far from anywhere else in this small city.

Going in, it felt for a moment as if Brian Worth should be in á corner waiting for him. Compared to that night, The Crusader was deserted. Not seeing Torrance, he almost turned and walked out. They watched too much television, these

kids, learning tricks of caution; he wasn't in the mood for
silly-bugger games. On the other hand, the boy might be taking
a leak out of nerves. He bought a drink, and sipping it walked
to the end of the bar nearest the back of the room.

There was just one group at a table. The girl got up and went
to the lavatory. One of the two boys left behind nodded after
her and said to the other, 'I'm on a red hand tonight.' The age of
chivalry. Most of the young he came across, feckless, violent,
unhappy, produced in Meldrum a feeling of distaste. Usually,
it didn't show on his face. The second boy turned his head,
looked at him and, getting up, came over.

'I'm not really with those two,' he said. 'I was waiting
for you.'

It was Cliff from the flat. 'Let me guess,' Meldrum said. 'You
have a message for me.'

It had to be presumed he too was doing it for Betty, and
maybe that was why instead of giving up and going home
Meldrum followed instructions and went to The Filmhouse.

Sandy Torrance was sitting in one of the booths against the
wall with a coffee in front of him.

'I'm sorry about this,' he said. 'I tried to phone you back but
you'd left.'

Meldrum slid in opposite and faced him in silence.

'Can I get you something to drink?'

'Coffee,' Meldrum said and added as the boy got up, 'something to eat.'

At the counter, Torrance spread coins on his palm as if checking he had enough. Students were often short of money. On the
other hand, Meldrum hadn't eaten since mid-morning.

'Is that all right?'

He unwrapped the roll. It was filled with prawns and shreds
of lettuce. This wasn't the kind of place where rolls came filled
with bacon or a fried egg or bacon and a fried egg. He bit into
it and felt the pink dressing ooze out round the edge.

'It was after I spoke to you, I realised how stupid it would
be to meet in The Crusader. You can't tell who'll be watching
in there.'

'It was half-empty.'

'Your lot keep an eye on it. I asked Jimmy Campbell to tell

you I'd come here. I thought of using the flat, but Lesley's got people in – friends from the hospital. Then I thought of here.' He looked round. 'It's all right.'

'Jimmy Campbell?'

'Just somebody I know,' he said vaguely. 'He didn't want to. So then I asked Cliff.'

Meldrum looked at his watch. It was after eight.

'I know you wouldn't have come here for me,' Torrance said. 'I've been turning it round and round in my mind.'

'What?'

'The problem is, I don't know how much you care about Betty.'

Meldrum pushed his plate from in front of him.

'You and her mother are separated,' Torrance hurried on. 'I never heard you phone her at the flat. She doesn't talk about you.'

'Maybe you just don't know her very well.'

'We've slept together.'

Meldrum thought, You have a lot of nerve; or they don't think it matters any more. He asked, 'Does that mean much any more?'

'It does to me. And if you knew her at all you'd know it did to Betty.'

'Touching. Except it didn't last.'

'That's what I want to talk to you about.'

He remembered a lapel badge he'd seen somewhere, Do I look like somebody who cares? You have a problem: write to a women's magazine.

Why was the boy looking at him that way? What did he expect him to say?

'Betty thought I dropped the assault complaint because I was frightened.' The damaged nostril looked out of line and white as if not enough blood was getting to it. 'I'm not a coward.' Meldrum had seen him at the front of the anti-fascist protest. He nodded; but Torrance misunderstood. Frowning he said. 'It wasn't me those bastards threatened, it was Betty.'

He explained he'd been to a meeting of the activists. Before the demo against Farquhar Wood, he had avoided as many of those as he could. He came from a family that didn't care about politics. His father, who'd started on the shop floor and improved himself by his own efforts, always said politicians were all the same, out for themselves, one lot as bad as the other. He'd got mixed up with all that stuff only because Betty was. It wasn't true, though, that he had taken what happened to him at the demo in his stride. When he came out of hospital, that's what people said; they admired his calm, his balance; he'd 'taken it in his stride'. He had bad dreams and kept them to himself. The injury he'd received gave him a new credibility, even with Jimmy Campbell the hardliner. No one knew how full he was of anger. He poured it into visits to Harriet Cook to prepare the complaint. Before, in his innocence, he would have expected anger to go into his painting; artists turned everything to account; for the first time he wondered if he was good enough to be the kind of artist he wanted to be.

Going to the meetings helped. If the fascists wanted a fight, he was ready for them. On the way home from a meeting on this night a car went by and pulled in at the kerb. A man got out on the passenger side and came towards him. The car's engine was running; then it stopped. He knew something was wrong even before the door opened and the driver got out. If he'd gone by instinct he would have turned and fled, but pride muddled things so that, unsure, he kept walking towards them. It was only at the last minute when they raised their heads he saw their faces were covered by ski masks.

They took him when he was off-balance between steps and threw him into a doorway. They accused him of trying to fit up their mate. They put it that way as if neither of them was directly involved, though that might have been a pretence. If he didn't drop it, they would be back not for him but for his girlfriend; they described what they would do to her. When he said she was the daughter of a policeman, they beat him up, together and then one stepping back to give the other room.

The dressing had smeared pink on Meldrum's plate. Staring at it made him feel slightly sick.

'I don't want you to tell Betty any of this,' Sandy Torrance said. 'You know what's she's like. I don't want anything to happen to her.'

'I'll find out who they are,' Meldrum said.

'Please, don't! Let it go.' He touched his hand to his face. 'I don't care about them.'

'Why tell me then?' He had his own anger for Betty now; in check, his voice quiet.

'I didn't know what else to do. The thing is, I worry about her all the time.'

CHAPTER TWENTY-FOUR

Like every other detective in the building, Meldrum's desk was piled high with work. With Keaney haunting his thoughts, it had struck him at once as a bad omen to come in that morning and find the collator's message offering him more unfinished business out of the past. Even as he'd walked along the corridor to tell Ord about it, he'd had a bad feeling.

'Tonight, is it? Doesn't leave you much time, Jim. You could do with a bit of help.'

'Well, there's Stoddart—'

'Bugger Stoddart! Rank has its privileges,' Ord had said, grinning like a shark. 'If I want to go hands on, I go hands on.'

And that was what he had done; getting out from behind the desk and taking charge of the stakeout in the long shadowed aisles of the warehouse in Leith. For both of them the tip-off had revived an old file, the killing of a security guard, which had followed the not unfamiliar curve from frantic activity through to what, for years now, had seemed likely to be the depressing last stage of gathering dust. The informant had thrown in a mention of the earlier job casually, and the collator had been alert to spot the connection and get it to Meldrum's attention.

That whole day had seen everything speed up, including the bad feeling, from the moment Ord decided to come out from behind his desk and go for the laying on of hands.

'For old times' sake,' as he'd put it, 'I always had a feeling about this one. Sooner or later, that's what I felt.'

It was the first Meldrum had heard of it, but since he wasn't in a position to argue Ord had to be there with him in the warehouse and, when the unexpected happened, to be defended with fists. The fracas had ended for Meldrum in an ambulance trip.

'How's the head?' Ord asked.

'Fine.' Cracked, which was the effect contact with an iron bar tended to have. Spongy. Fragile.

'And the shoulder?'

'Fine.' These were not questions supposed to elicit a detailed list of symptoms.

'That's the way,' Ord said.

He hadn't put in an appearance at the hospital. Meldrum had got back from it the night before and spent a restless night in his own bed. When the doorbell rang about eleven, he was in his dressing-gown in front of the electric fire. He didn't get out of the chair at first, hoping the ringing would stop. When he did go to the window, the police car was sitting outside, and from the way the driver turned his head it was obvious he had seen him. On the step, Ord grunted, 'About time,' standing there holding a wicker basket with a red and white checkered cloth the size of a napkin thrown over the top. Later, on his own, Meldrum unpacked the contents: marmalade, coffee, oatcakes, cheeses, a bottle of malt whisky from Safeway's. Captain Billy, an officer and a gentleman, visiting the wounded; not naturally to say thanks, though it was his thick skull that would have been cracked if Meldrum hadn't got in the way.

Years ago he had seen Ord take out three men on his own. He could still feel the moment of shock as the big man sprawled helplessly against the pallets, not defending himself. In the chair opposite, he was bulky and looked rock-solid. In the warehouse, he'd been flung about like an empty sack.

Age had caught up with him; or maybe he'd waited too long to come out from behind his desk.

'My younger son Malcolm's about ready to splice the knot. You'll get an invite,' Ord said. 'Put it in your diary.'

'I'll look forward to it,' Meldrum said untruthfully. He took it as Ord's way of, after all, saying thanks.

'And the grandson's christening, week after next, church and back to the house for a meal,' he added expansively. 'Unless you're working, of course.'

'No. I won't be back by then.'

'You're not that bad,' Ord said sceptically, the officer taking over from the gentleman. 'Tough bastard like you.'

'I'm due leave – thought I might as well take it.'

'Uhh, right.'

That should have been it, duty done and leave. For some reason, Ord sat on, not saying anything, elbow on the arm of the chair, rasping with the two middle fingers of his right hand at a patch of stubble on his jaw. It made a faint irritating sound in the silence. Keeping Worth's story, or Sandy Torrance's, to himself had never been an option for Meldrum. That wasn't how he had been trained. The only problem had been picking the right time. It was a relief to begin and be listened to by a professional, in silence, uninterrupted.

When he finished, Ord asked, 'What's the connection?'

'How do you mean?'

'You tell me about Brian Worth. And then you tell me about the boy Torrance being threatened about Betty.'

'There's no connection.'

'I think there is. You've got them mixed up. You need to get your head on straight. If some bastard's threatened Betty, that makes me angry.'

'Torrance wasn't lying.'

'We'll check him out. But let's say it's true. When I find out, police or not, I'll put them the whole fucking road. That's a promise. I'm making you a promise. Just don't get it mixed up in your skull with all this crap about Keaney.'

'Worth struck me as—'

'No, hold it right there! Who are we talking about here? A guy that's been fired – no more expense account, no more cheque at the end of the month. Worth's back where he started, but thirty years older. He needs a story, any story, but he's scrambling if he has to go back to the Pietro murder for it.'

The pain throbbing behind Meldrum's eyes picked up in rhythm, making it hard to think.

'Well?' Ord said.

'. . . am I supposed to ignore him?'

'You could do worse.' Shrugging as if to get a stiffness out of his shoulders, he stood up. 'I should be on my way. Don't bother getting up.'

But Meldrum did, and followed him to the door.

They stood side by side on the top step. The driver in the police car after a glance sat carefully eyes front.

'This could be a nice garden,' Ord said. 'You shouldn't let it get like a jungle. Not fair to the neighbours.'

'I'll get round to it.'

'You should make time.'

'If we'd known about Pietro's lover . . .'

Worth had said, When I heard Francis Pietro'd been killed, my first thought was, I know who did it. Clay.

'Pietro had more men than you've had hot dinners. What difference would one more have made?'

'This one sounded like a crazy man.'

'Maybe Worth made him up. Maybe he met him in a wet dream.' Ord shook his head in disgust. 'Poofs!'

How much, if anything, had Worth left out of his story? Face grey and leaking sweat like water out of a squeezed sponge, he'd suddenly looked as if he was about to have another heart attack right there in the restaurant, and Meldrum had seen him into a taxi. Next day all he'd been able to get on his calls was Worth's answering-machine.

Watching the police car accelerate away from blank windows and neat suburban hedges, Meldrum let the admission surface that, in his turn, he hadn't told Ord everything. He still had to confess his visits to Mulholland and Morton, Arthur Hull's neighbours.

Unfinished business. Despite common sense and his own best interests, unfinished business.

CHAPTER TWENTY-FIVE

'The strapping's due off any day now.' He fingered his shoulder. 'It was a straightforward break. The kind of thing jockeys get falling off a horse.'

'So it's not as bad as it looks,' Carole said.

'It's a bloody sight worse!' Meldrum said mock indignantly, and after a beat they both laughed.

Laughing with her, he felt better. He'd come on impulse, unannounced, and it had been good to find her on her own.

'How do you like having Betty back with you?'

'We get on well. She's good company.' She glanced at him. 'I don't suppose it'll be for long.'

It was as if she was, not apologising for being closer than he could be to their daughter, not apologising, that would be ridiculous, but trying to gloss it over so as not to hurt him. That would be very like Carole.

He had felt low that morning standing at the bedroom window. His shoulder ached; the pain in his head made him squint. Grey sky and a howling cold wind; the only way to tell it wasn't winter, sodden leaves huddling and thrashing on the trees.

'You're not used to having time on your hands,' she said.

'I'm a quick healer.'

'So when are you going back?'

'I'm thinking about taking some leave.'

'Good!' But then she frowned and asked, 'Is there something you're not telling me?'

Her question took him by surprise. In telling Ord he intended to take leave, he'd set up an opportunity to pursue the question of Hugh Keaney's innocence. Or guilt. Carole had felt that somehow; he could still be surprised by how well she knew him.

'The doctors haven't said something, have they?'

'Doctors?' he asked in bewilderment.

'What the hell were you doing anyway, getting involved in a fight? At your stage – you should have more sense – beat constables get battered round the head – that's what they keep them for. I hated it when you were on the beat.'

'Don't blame me, blame Ord.' But she had no patience with that, and his grin faded. 'I'm fine, honestly. I have a hard head. When I'm working, there's always so much piled up, I can't imagine how they'd manage without me. How often have you told me the world wouldn't stop if I took a break? A knock on the head and I see the point. So I'm taking some of the time off they owe me.'

'What are you going to do?'

It was still raining outside, but the room was warm; his chair was comfortable; she sat opposite him on the couch. He stretched out his legs and yawned. 'This is nice.'

'Tomorrow's Monday. I go back to work,' she said. 'You should go away somewhere. Take a proper holiday.'

Things to do.

'I used to like it when you told me what was happening in the school.'

'No, you didn't.'

'Yes, I did,' he said, pantomime-fashion, thinking she would laugh.

'No,' she said, unsmiling. 'I told you what had happened at work because I like to talk, and you'd nod and smile and then I'd realise you weren't listening at all. You were thinking about the next day, brooding over some eighty-year-old beaten to death or a child raped. And I'd feel foolish. You were the one with the stories. But, of course, you never told them.'

'You make me sound like a shit.'

'Hmm.' But then she repented and said, 'No. I never thought

that. I always knew you cared. I sometimes felt if you could share some of it, it wouldn't be so hard for you.'

And because he had no answer to that, she began to tell him about a boy she'd had for a time when she took Primary 3 while its teacher was off ill. 'I would say to him, Be a golden boy for an hour. And at the end of it he'd ask me, Was I a golden boy? And then for half an hour he'd be hell on wheels, it had been such a strain. But if I'd had him all the time, he would have been more golden than not.' Then his parents broke up. His father's new partner rejected him. 'By the time he got to Primary 7, he *was* something of a shit and well on his way to disaster. But on Friday I caught him misbehaving in the corridor and I said to him, Matthew, you can do better than that. That's because you knew me in Primary 3, he said, I was good in Primary 3. Oh, dear, I thought, I had him two or three hours a week – for what? Six months? I said to him, I always thought that was the real Matthew, that all this other stuff was just laid on. *Depends*, he said, but he gave me a look – he knew he could do it – but there wasn't anybody to say golden boy.'

It was a pity Meldrum didn't like that story.

'That depresses me,' he said.

'I have the optimism of a teacher because I see what people might be.'

'That's nice.'

'You have the pessimism of a policeman because you've to deal with what they are.'

'Not much might-be about your Matthew.'

'You and I are not compatible,' she said.

'Maybe if we had the time . . .'

'No,' she said. 'We've been through that.'

All the same, he felt like talking. He told her about going to Barlinnie Prison to see Hugh Keaney and about Mulholland and the Reverend Tommy Wright and about Worth and the lover whose name might be Clay and what he'd admitted to Billy Ord and what he'd left out and what he thought would be the next step.

More or less he told her everything, which later he regretted, feeling it as the kind of loose-mouthed breach of confidentiality a good policeman shouldn't make even with someone he loved.

Monday morning the sun was shining, and those who had jobs were going to them. A distraction of birds quarrelled on the tree outside the bedroom window. On not much evidence, Meldrum decided he was feeling better. Among the untidy mess of gas bills, old letters and receipts in the desk, he found the sheet with the information from the police computer and took it with him into the kitchen. He leaned his elbows either side of the printout and stared at the names: Tracey Connolly, Andrew Fisk. Two witnesses who as much as anybody had made sure Hugh Keaney went down for murder. A long time ago, but both of them had form, so there they were on the database – along with more honest people, come to that, than it would have been good for the general public to know. The current address for Fisk was a flat in Livingston, an invention of the Sixties scattered as a town on fields to the south of the city.

On the way there, he was forced to pull in at the side of the road. When the wave of sickness passed, he sat for a while and thought about going on, then turned the car for home. Fisk would have to wait.

When he got to the city outskirts, though, instead of running through the first roundabout for the city centre he swung left for the scheme where Tracey Connolly lived. At the time of Arthur Hull's death, she had been fifteen. It was Keaney's claim that she had been with him on the day he had given in to the unlucky impulse to ring the bell at Hull's flat and ask if the postman had been round yet. According to him, she'd stood in the street laughing at the old man on the steps above her. For her part, she'd called Keaney a liar and the police had believed her.

Either way it might not seem to matter. Keaney had never denied that he had gone to the flat to make a nuisance of himself, working off his irritation at being moved out of the close where he'd been sleeping rough. On the other hand, if evidence was hard to check so many years later, at least the girl was a link in the chain that could be tested. In the end what mattered was whether Keaney told the truth or not. Catch him out in one lie and everything he had said might be another.

Verdict: Guilty.

He thought he knew where the street was, but got it wrong and didn't have a map. Flats and houses in lines; high boxes and low boxes; it was a place without landmarks. Giving up, he parked at a shopping precinct and went in search of directions. At midday the shops had their shutter grills down; not a Marks and Spencer's in sight. The nearest had a door of temporary boards where its glass had been smashed.

Inside, instead of the gloom he had expected, a hard brilliance of fluorescent light fell on a couple of aisles piled spilling high with packets, cans, bread. There was milk in a chill cabinet and he squeezed in past a chest freezer of tandooris and pizzas. If you had to lay in stock for a siege, it looked like the place to come. The shopkeeper shrugged his indifference to local geography, but two women customers competed in the game of find the street.

The houses were four in a block style, two up two down, four flats under one roof. He idled past them, checking the numbers. On a gable end, white paint shaped out in ragged letters: TOMMY THE GRASS. The flat behind it had been burned out, round the windows streaked black where fire had raged. Tommy Nolan, of course, and one he certainly had been – a grass, that is, who'd made a regular income over the years putting his neighbours behind bars. Eddy Short had run him; and for so long Eddy had stopped caring about being discreet. Burn out time, as they said on the floor of the Stock Exchange.

The next number he registered told him he had gone too far. He left the car and walked back. There didn't seem anything to do but curse his luck when it turned out the flat with blank smeared windows under the burn out was the one he wanted. He was turning away when it occurred to him that in this area if a flat was empty they'd have boarded the windows to make it vandal proof. He went up the path.

She had to be thirty by now, but his first eerie impression was that Tracey Connolly was still only a child herself, despite the

baby on her hip. Behind her, a girl of about four wearing a pair
of soiled knickers squatted among the rubbish on the floor.

When he told her why he was there, she said, 'I didn't want
any trouble. I was pregnant – they could have done the father
for that – me being fifteen.'

'The kind of trouble Keaney was in, that wouldn't have
seemed very important.'

'Eh?'

She didn't have a very expressive face, but the questioning
grunt suggested to him the possibility that Keaney might not
have been the one who'd made her pregnant. At the trial the
prosecution had found a way to bring the relationship into
evidence; it had made a newspaper headline; in his summing
up the judge had referred to it with distaste. It had done
Keaney harm.

'Are you telling me Keaney wasn't the baby's father?'

'Him and me only did it the once.'

'That's all it takes.'

She stared blankly, and then gave a slack mechanical grimace
as if accustomed to placating men's sense of humour.

'I was already up the spout. I'd missed for a couple of months
and I told Andy.'

'Andy?'

'Andy Fisk. Hugh – Hugh Keaney – came into the flat when
Andy was giving me a hammering for being such a stupid cow.
Hugh tried to stop him. Hugh didn't know why I was getting
it, see.'

'He didn't know you were pregnant?'

'He knew Andy was riding me.'

'So Keaney came in while you were getting beaten up.'

'He was stupid having a go at Andy. I never asked him to.
Everybody in the place was frightened from Andy. He gave
Hugh a kicking. Threw him out the door and threw his case
out after him.'

There had been half a dozen of them in the flat, paying their
social security giros to Fisk, collector for the landlord from that
and whatever other properties.

'And that was the last you saw of Keaney?'

'No.' Blank monosyllable, as if to say don't be stupid.

'You saw him after that?'

'About a week maybe. I came out the close and he was waiting for me. He always liked me. I went away with him.'

'Where?'

'We just wandered about.' Her smile this time was different, like something that belonged to her. 'We met this old couple and walked right across the Meadows talking to them. About how it felt sleeping outside and things. I thought Hugh would tap them for money but he didn't. He was like that, right soft. And the old shites didn't offer. She was friendly and that, but.'

'Did you go to Hull's? The old man. He was blind. Were you with Keaney when he knocked at Hull's door?'

'That was the next day. Slept all night at the foot of a garden. Had to run for it in the morning when they let the dog out.'

'You were with Keaney when he went to the old man's door?'

'I said I was.'

He nodded, thinking about the next question, feeling the excitement build in him.

'And what did you do after that?'

'Just the same. Did a bit of cadging at Waverley. We had a laugh.'

'Where did you sleep that night?'

'Can't remember. Somewhere.'

'But you were with Keaney?'

'Oh, aye. We got a bottle of wine. That's when he shagged me.'

'When did you split up?'

'The police lifted him. I'd gone for a pee and just as I came up the steps I saw them putting him in the car so I went back down again.'

'You were with him all the time?'

'I told you.'

'Two nights and two days. All the time?'

'We were having a laugh.'

'*He had an alibi.*'

She stared at him blankly.

Before he could go on, a voice behind him demanded,

'What's the good of talking to him in here? Here, you, come and see the state this ceiling's in.'

'Don't be stupid, Mammy,' Tracey said.

'It's a damned disgrace. You wouldn't keep pigs like this,' Mammy said. She was in her forties, with the same lank yellow hair as her daughter. It was a face that had seen hard times, but would still have passed under a streetlight with the war paint on. As she gestured, glass in hand, liquor splashed on to the floor. 'Smell it, you can smell the burny smell. Why should we have to suffer for that swine upstairs? The water brought the ceiling down.'

'He's nothing to do with the Housing, Mammy.'

'You shut your face, you're too soft.'

But something must have penetrated, for she headed for the couch under the window, giving the momentary disturbing impression that she was about to trample over the child on the floor instead of steering round her.

'Hugh Keaney must have been with you when Arthur Hull was killed. Isn't that right?' Tracey nodded. 'Did you tell the police that?'

'How do you mean?'

He said it slowly as if to a backward child: 'Did you tell the police that Hugh Keaney and you had been together all that time?' She nodded. 'Can you remember the names of the policemen you talked to?'

'I can't tell you more than I told the other one.'

'What?'

'One of your lot's been here already.'

'Somebody's been here – recently? Asking about Hugh Keaney?'

'Like I said. One of your lot.'

'Did he tell you who he was?'

No more than Meldrum had.

'I told him Hugh and me'd had a laugh. I told him Hugh never went back to the flat. Go back and start drinking with Andy Fisk? After Andy gave him a kicking? Aye, that'd be likely.'

'Fisk claimed that's when Keaney told him he'd killed somebody.'

'He was with me.'

'Two or three of the others in the flat said Keaney came back.'

'Them? They'd have eaten shite if Andy told them to.'

Meldrum had moved so that he was blocking Tracey's view of the couch. Now from behind him there came a little explosive sound of disgust. 'What have I not had for a long time?' Mammy asked.

'Your own teeth?' Tracey speculated.

'No!'

'A man?'

'Stupid wee whore.'

They fell silent. It sounded like an exchange they might have had before.

'The baby died,' Tracey said. 'After I went back to Andy Fisk. I lost it during the night. I got up one morning and it was dead. I'm not frightened of any of them. Not now.'

'But you were frightened then? When you gave evidence at the trial?'

'Then I just said whatever Andy told me.'

To get out, Meldrum had to shift the child who had bumped over and was sitting with her back against the door. As he touched her, she gave a kind of shudder under his hands. Her mouth hung open and drool ran over her lower lip, hanging in strings like a dog in summer.

He lifted her gently and smiled at her, but the eyes stayed on him wide and empty.

'Now I don't give a fuck about anybody,' the girl behind him said.

Depressed, at home he hung on until the walls seemed to be closing in, then he rang Carole.

'Could I drop in tonight?'

'Not tonight, Jim.'

'. . . fine.'

'I'm expecting someone.'

There was a pause. He waited it out.

'You don't know him,' she said.

CHAPTER TWENTY-SIX

Meldrum would tap back and forward across the channels, looking for talk or Country-and-Western depending on the mood he was in. It took some of the curse off being in the car, all those hours on the way to something or coming back, that nothing time in between.

When he pulled in to the court at the front of the flats, the voice on the radio was still explaining why there was no need for alarm about the latest health scare. He liked things explained, and switched off the engine to listen and see if this voice made more sense at the end than it had in the middle. As he listened, he wound the roof shut. The heat felt solid as if you could lean into it. In this northern city three hours of sunshine could come on like a heatwave. The voice stopped in what sounded like mid-sentence as if the speaker had lost heart. Light glinted in the rear mirror. A man coming out had swung open the glass door at the front entrance to the flats.

Meldrum recognised the Special Branch detective, but too late to stop himself putting the radio off, so that as Bell crossed towards the line of cars the aerial whined down in the silence. He bent his head, resisting the temptation to slide down in his seat. A door slammed; an engine started up. Briefly, a car reversed into view and was gone.

In the Thirties, the flats might have had a caretaker to keep an eye on visitors. Now there was an entryphone system, and someone had left the lock off. So much for security. Light from a high window on the half-landing flooded down a wide stairway into a hall that could have done with a fresh coat of paint. It smelled nicely, though, of polish and faintly of roses. At the back there was a vase of them on a table littered with shed petals. There was a lift there too, he was glad to see. His bones still ached from the beating.

'I hate that thing. Claustrophobia,' Worth said as the lift gates slid back. He was waiting in the doorway of his flat. 'I've left instructions if I die here they've to take me down by the stairs.' He didn't stop talking as they went in. 'Ever hear about the chap whose wife died at the top of an old tenement? They had to stand the coffin on end to get it round the first turn of the stairs and there was this banging from inside. Took her out, she lived another ten years before she died. The same undertakers came back the second time. Started down the stairs with her. For God's sake, take it easy on that bend, boys, the guy shouted. Can I offer you a drink?'

A big room, surprisingly big, with cream walls and mirrors that bounced the light back from a line of windows. If there was a television, it was out of sight; no paintings, but plenty of books, lots of them piled round a scuffed leather chair with a plate of food balanced on one arm. A room where a man lived on his own. Meldrum recognised the signs.

'You don't seem surprised to see me.'

'I saw you getting out of your car.'

Meldrum went to the nearest window. He could see his car and beyond it the space from which Bell had pulled out.

He heard Worth behind him murmur, 'Isn't it a wonderful view?' and lifting his gaze saw the city spread out with church spires and the castle on its hill.

'Did you say? About a drink?' Worth was sweating, a line of drops gleaming on his upper lip. 'I was just going to have one.'

When Meldrum nodded, he went out. It felt good to sit down, but he got up again so that he was on his feet when Worth came back carrying glasses.

'You're privileged,' he said. 'I don't entertain here. I've always kept my work and my private life separate. If you're going to argue, do it in a restaurant, and no washing up afterwards. John Prebble said to me once in a restaurant, the

Canadians are like the Scots, they think too many of their men were killed in the war. He felt everybody was unfair to the English. Such a nice man to talk to. I hear you've been in the wars. When that warehouse thing in Leith went wrong.' He paused in his rush of words and had to look up at Meldrum, who when he took the glass had stayed a little too close, crowding him. 'I'm glad it wasn't worse. I hear you saved Billy Ord's bacon.'

'You don't want to believe what you read in the papers.'

'I still have my contacts,' Worth said. He swayed a little. 'I'm sorry, I have to sit down.' He took the leather chair, pushing books aside with his foot. Meldrum ignored the chair he was being waved into and took one nearer the window. 'There was someone here just before you came. He upset me.'

'Why was that?'

'You don't ask who it was.' Worth screwed up his eyes, staring against the light. When Meldrum didn't answer, he said, 'You must have seen him leaving. Don't treat me as if I was stupid.'

'Lot of people apart from you in this building.'

'Oh, it was me he'd come to see. He was the one in the Crusader bar – I remember faces and names. Mr Bell, I said, as soon as I saw him. He didn't like that. Stupid, I can be stupid sometimes.'

Meldrum kept silent. He agreed it had been stupid.

'After that he didn't introduce himself. I knew he was Special Branch, because you'd told me, but he didn't bother to say so. He just came in as if I had no right to refuse him.' He stared at the glass in his hand as if not understanding how it had got to be empty. 'I need another drink.'

'What did he want?'

But Meldrum thought he knew: questions about the night at the Crusader bar, about Sandy Torrance and the fight afterwards with the neo-Nazis. Thank God, Betty hadn't been involved in any of that.

'He asked me about Arthur Hull's murder.'

Meldrum was glad he had his back to the light.

'And I tried to talk as if I was just remembering it as a story, the way any newspaperman would. He asked about you. How we'd met. How well I knew you.'

'What did you say?'

'I told him we were friends.'

'Friends?' Incredulous.

'We were having a quiet drink in The Crusader, I said, and then when everybody rushed out we just went with the crowd to see what it was about.'

'How long are we supposed to have been friends? That kind of thing isn't hard to check on.'

'I told him I was taken ill and you looked after me. Anyway, I told you it wasn't that night he was interested in.'

'Did he say anything about Francis Pietro?'

'Nothing! And, God knows, I didn't mention him.'

He thought about that while Worth fetched the bottle. He sipped and watched the other man drinking. Worth didn't bother to offer after the first refusal, just kept emptying and refilling his own glass. It didn't seem possible that Arthur Hull on his own could be of any concern to Special Branch.

After a time, the two of them sitting without a word and the only noise the clatter of the bottle rim on Worth's glass, he wondered quietly, 'He didn't say anything about Clay?'

Worth shook his head. 'Just about Hull. I told you, he never mentioned Francis.'

'When you told me about Pietro's lover coming back, bursting into the flat waving a gun about, you didn't say his name was Clay. I had to find that out for myself.'

Worth looked up with sudden drunken shrewdness. 'You don't know fuck-all, do you? Or you don't want to. None of you wanted to. Forget it.'

'No, I don't think so. Don't you forget, you were the one who came to me.'

'I shouldn't have done that.' The hand holding the glass shook.

'That night Clay burst into the flat he talked about having something to celebrate. What was that—'

'I never said anything about Ireland!'

'Ireland?'

'You didn't hear that from me.' In his agitation, he gestured

a denial, splashing drink across his knees. 'Look, when I was
sick you helped me. A friend couldn't have done any more.
You've a good job. Don't spoil things for yourself.'

'Had Clay just come back from Ireland?'

But Worth had taken fright. To every question, he answered
with a shake of the head. Meldrum's questions came more
slowly. After a while, he held out his glass and Worth shuffled
forward in his chair and poured a full measure.

As they drank together, the heat of whisky running back the
length of his tongue, Meldrum felt the ache of each bone where
it had been struck. Pain bored between his eyes. He sipped
from the glass, waiting for the energy to go home.

At some point, Worth said, 'First paper I worked for, good
paper, went to the wall years ago, this was years ago. The
Black Forest Holiday Company. Innocuously named, I said.
The innocuously named Black Forest Holiday Company. For
those who wished to play the role of concentration camp
victim or guard for a week, fortnight, month. And they claim
Scottish papers don't do investigative journalism, I said. That
was the point, I think that was the point. Or maybe I was tired
of doing that column, maybe I wanted them to throw me out. I
was young then. Listen, forget irony. You wouldn't believe the
letters of enquiry I got. The paper folded, this was years ago.
The point is, Jim – can I call you Jim? There was a market. I
could have been an entrepreneur. Got a grant from the Scottish
Tourist Board. Knighthood from Mrs Thatcher.'

Meldrum decided it was time. From somewhere he found
the energy, got up and went home.

CHAPTER TWENTY-SEVEN

It rained all the way to Peterhead and as he went north it got colder. He drove through Aberdeen though he'd meant to stop there to eat, and by then was so early for the prison visit that on impulse he swung on to the hard shoulder when he saw the name on the sign. He was almost past before it registered and had to back up to check before turning into the side road. None of it was familiar to him, no landmarks, the sign hadn't given miles, just pointed the way to the bare name of a place he remembered. He'd been on this road only once before, aged just fourteen, with somebody from the undertaker's to drive them in the car behind the hearse. It had been raining then too, but it had been winter and he'd sat beside his father and watched the leafless trees go by.

Now, in the abundant season, heavy foliage on either side shrouded the view so that the place came on him like a surprise. He knew it by the squat towered spire that to a boy had seemed more like a castle than a church. The little crowd of mourners had stood in the rain and as the minister went through the routine of consigning his grandfather to the earth he'd taken a cord and looked across the open grave at the grim-faced strangers to whom he was related. Later at the meal he had been watching a girl, dark hair, cream skin, perhaps a cousin, wishing she would see him, when he heard a man's voice in a near shout and his father answering more quietly. The two brothers made a silence and fought for a time in it with such a ferocity of bitterness it tore the afternoon apart like a wound. It was shameful, and he could see which of the two men was being blamed for the outburst by everybody, everybody was blaming his father and it wasn't fair. Not long afterwards they had left. And he had no idea what it had been about, but wished afterwards he had been able to defend his father.

He pushed open the gate of the church and walked about in the rain among the stones. Dates of birth and death. Two in their nineties; in the eighties, in the seventies; a good stock. His grandfather had lain in an open coffin with a white covering over him through which his hands poked, broad hands with big knuckles and blue half-moons at the end of each nail. A fly had gone back and forward in the still air of the bedroom. It had made him think of things that rotted and the smell death must have, so that he was glad there was a kind of net laid tight across the coffin and stretching down to the floor. Behind him a woman whispered, 'It's been flying round in here every day. I was thinking it might be our Lizzie. You know how fond he was of her.' And a man's breath blown out in a great dismissive blast so that he could smell the tobacco, and his voice saying, 'And here I was away tae gie it a swat.' His grandfather looked as if he was asleep, as if he was peaceful, things like that they said, with the skin tight on his brow and cheek-bones and the fierce curve of his nose and the thick moustache curling down to touch his lip in separate visible white hairs.

But the closed eyes bulged and the horror to the boy had been not that they might open, but that if the lids were pulled back there would be no eyes there at all, only cottonwool or cups of white plastic.

When he found his grandfather's headstone he crouched down beside it in the rain. Under the scouring weather of the place the black letters incised into the granite were like memory already fading. Thinking about it over the years, he had guessed the quarrel at the funeral meal might have been about money or how work on the farm was split by the grandfather among his sons or even inheritance, something like that. His father died without speaking of it; but after his death in a drawer under a drift of receipted bills he had come on a bible. It would have been the last thing he expected to find. His father mocked religion and held the religious in contempt. He had turned it in his hand, a compact black book; published by Collins in Glasgow, and in ink on the blank page opposite the title: *To my Daughter Lizzie for her Birthday with love from her loving Father Oct 5–10–33*. As if to mark a place, in the middle of the book there was a photograph of a man in his middle years with a girl on one side and a boy on the other. There seemed nothing of significance to have marked out that page: a listing of the descendants of Esau, duke Timnah, duke Alvah, duke Jetheth, duke Aholibamah, duke Elah, duke Pinon, duke Kenaz, duke Teman, duke Mibzar, duke Magdiel, duke Iram, and so on in print tiny enough to challenge piety. The man in the photograph he had recognised as his grandfather though the great curve of moustache was black not white. The girl, he supposed, might be the daughter Lizzie, who had died at nineteen in London. The boy, Meldrum's father, stood as if to attention, looking up at his own father who, as it happened, had turned his head away to smile down upon the girl who held his hand.

At the end of the cemetery there was a wall and beyond it a paddock where two black horses cropped the grass. When his father had been young, to work on a farm was to labour. It occurred to him that perhaps the bitterness at the funeral had been about nothing more than his father's choosing to walk away from all that, the eldest son leaving his brothers to the driving of an ambitious father.

That might be seen as a kind of desertion.

Yet what ideal had his father ever held higher to him than duty? The duties of a child, of a man; duties to vote, to be an honest worker. His duty to the law when he became a policeman.

It was hard to decide what his father would make of what he was doing now.

He had seen prisons all over Scotland and a few in England. None looked bleaker than this one set down where the land stopped by the edge of the North Sea. He stepped out of the car into a wind that tasted of salt and headed shivering across the reception park for the first gate.

He was so busy working out what he wanted to ask Keaney

that he didn't register at first that something was wrong. He'd applied and done the paperwork, followed a silent warder from one gate to another, waited on the heavy tumbling of locks; the usual routine; which didn't routinely end as this one had done. There was a grey metal cabinet and a couple of chairs against the wall: every prison kept rooms like this tucked away at the ends of anonymous corridors. The warder was in his twenties with a heavy jaw and little full lips that made him look petulant; the type who would break the peak of his cap and glower out from under it, pretending to be a Guardsman. He kept glancing at Meldrum as if expecting him to ask what was going on. In the end, he was the one who spoke.

'Say one thing about this place, the grub's not bad.'

Meldrum grunted.

'It matters, you know.' The accent was broad and local, somebody else escaped off a farm. 'We do long hours.'

Meldrum didn't care one way or the other about that either.

'Same as you, putting in the hours, eh? . . . Only you get doing some of it over a drink, eh? . . . You catch them, we hold them. Right? . . . Fuck it, we're on the same side, right?'

'Right.'

'That's what I'm saying! Doesn't make fucking sense any other way.' He stared at Meldrum like a man starting an argument, then changed tack abruptly. 'Aye, the chuck matters. Gob a few times in a guy's semolina and it spoils his appetite. It's not easy being a hard man once you've a stomach full of ulcers.' He gave Meldrum a smile as if thinking of a joke too good to share.

They passed the rest of the time, almost the length of an hour, in silence until there was a tap on the door. Following a new warder back through gates he'd passed on his way in, Meldrum gave up on his chances of seeing Keaney. As he followed up the flight of stone steps, he prepared himself for being shown into the Governor's office.

The waiting time had been used to check up on him. Certain ways of putting things suggested Billy Ord must have been one of those summoned to the phone. The man behind the oak desk knew Meldrum was on sick leave; and the reason for it. 'Got a bit of a beating about the head, I understand.'

And as for Keaney: 'not something you were involved with
– the investigation, all of that. No, quite. Yet I'm told you
visited him when he was held in Barlinnie.' The Governor
gave the appearance not so much of being angry as of honestly
puzzling over a curiosity. 'A man with your fine record.' And
that took him back to the ambush in the warehouse in Leith:
'Quite a battle by all accounts. You took a knock on the head
I hear.' Second time he's mentioned that; is he waiting for me
to plead insanity, Meldrum wondered. It didn't seem the most
certain way to save his career. A wry trace of that reasoning
might have shown in his face for the Governor's tone became
drier and the old combativeness in Meldrum rose up to meet
it in defiance as always of common sense.

'All the same, I'd like to see the prisoner, sir.'

'Would you, indeed?'

'He asked to see me, and I think that's within his rights.'

'When did he do that? He's been in solitary the last forty-
eight hours, and he'll stay there as long as I can keep him. He
attacked one of my men.'

The Governor looked the kind to whom that would matter,
hard but fair, not the sort to spit in anybody's stew. Thinking
about the guard who'd talked so much about food, Meldrum
had an idea. 'Has Keaney gone on hunger strike?'

'That is none of your business.'

But the Governor had blinked.

The walls of that prison were high and every window barred,
and in one part cages had been constructed, a cell with a
second one built around it, so that the man inside could
be held without danger to his keepers. Meldrum knew too
much about what some men did in the outside world to be
sentimental about conditions inside.

Yet standing by the car looking across the choppy water of
the bay to the prison, where despite walls and bars the grey
wind from the sea would search every huddling corner, he
couldn't bear to think of Keaney. Day and night alone, always
alone, as if lying in a grave.

He swore a vow in silence that he would get Keaney out of
there, for the first time made a promise to himself to go on to
the end whatever the cost.

CHAPTER TWENTY-EIGHT

The day started badly for Harriet. She didn't like having to say no. The easiest thing would have been to make some excuse when Eileen phoned asking if they could lunch together. Agreeing to meet cast a shadow over the morning. They had known one another since university, student lawyers, members of the same circle, but always with more of an edge of rivalry than friendship between them. Probably they were too much alike. Good-looking, strong-featured girls, they might have been mistaken for sisters. They attracted boys, but neither of them it seemed was a good picker. While their contemporaries were meeting the men they would later marry, they were having affairs that went sour, in third year with the same man. They didn't let it spoil their work, however, knowing they had plenty of time ahead of them. They were clever, too, enough that each was tipped at one time or another to take a First. In the event, both ended up with a Two: One.

She went to lunch sure that sooner or later she would be asked about the job which had just been advertised. Against advice, Eileen had gone to work in a one-man firm and for a lawyer who specialised in criminal cases. A year ago he had been attacked with a broken bottle. The assumption in the profession was that things like that happened to those who crossed the line in dealings with their clients. Even if due to nothing more than a need to keep such horrors out where they could only happen to other people, that was the assumption and Eileen had been tainted by it. She hadn't worked since the firm closed down.

It was a brittle lunch that moved towards 'Put in a good word for me'; and a fraught one after Harriet explained why that wouldn't do any good. The advertised job, after long leets and short leets and interviews, would go where it had always been intended it should go, to the senior partner's oldest friend's nephew.

'The thing is,' Eileen said, 'since the attack Simon won't see me or talk to me. He wants a mummy – and his wife's had plenty of practice. They've got five kids.'

She too, it seemed, had slept with the boss. Sitting at her desk, Harriet kept thinking about that. They were alike in so many ways. Both of them bright and competent, good lawyers, pass your exams, start your career, network, everything straightforward, except being a woman, spread your legs, get fucked by the boss, everything complicated, everything dirty, stupid stupid stupid, and falling in love, stupidest of all, except that she hadn't been as stupid as Eileen, a better picker that time, John Brennan being a success big man well regarded, get a job anywhere on his recommendation once he felt it was better for you to leave, get on with your career or was it your life? Brennan's Discards, they should form a club . . . Maybe in other people's eyes they already did.

An unpleasant thought. She was thinking it when the phone rang. 'A Mr Meldrum. I asked him what he wanted, but he said he'd rather speak to you personally. Shall I put him through? . . . Miss Cook?'

'All right. I mean, yes, put him through.'

Not such an uncommon name; it might be another Meldrum. But it wasn't.

'If it's about—' Her mind went blank and she had to start again, searching for the boy's name. 'If it's about your daughter's friend, Sandy Torrance . . .'

'Ex-friend, I think.'

'He hasn't been back to see me. As far as I'm concerned, that's the end of it.'

'Yes, I can see that.' There was a pause that went on so long she thought he had hung up. 'Would you like to have dinner with me?'

I don't think so.

Not tonight.

Saying no. That shouldn't be hard to do.

It was a Chinese restaurant opposite the Lyceum Theatre, a place with a good reputation and handy for parking, which was always a problem in Edinburgh. The plan at first had been that she would meet Meldrum there, but then there hadn't seemed any sensible reason to refuse his offer to collect her from the flat.

She didn't get a proper look at him until they sat down to eat. On their previous meetings, his height, his abruptness of manner, had matched pretty exactly her experience of one kind of policeman. Tonight he seemed physically depleted and when he talked it was with a contained bitterness. At one point he said, 'I've done my stint. I've met the criminals on the street – and in the Force. I wouldn't mind seeing my time out in some wee country town. In the city things get desperate. It's so much them and us – and to curb the them the us get just as bad. The worst are the ones who come in as idealists. They finish . . . they're so anxious to make the world perfect . . . they finish up way beyond anything.' She wondered what he had done before he joined the police. I was a carpenter, he said, and she understood with a shade of amusement his hesitation must be because that placed him as working-class in a way being a senior police officer didn't. But when he spread his hands on the table and said, I served my time, there seemed some pride in the claim and so maybe she had got that wrong. He drove her home and they sat in the car. He yawned, and she seized on that: You're tired. Just with the travelling, he said, I had to go to Peterhead today. He switched off the engine and she listened to the silence and thought, why not?

In bed when he came over on top of her she saw a wart low down on the side of his neck. Some of the hairs growing from it were grey. It was typical of her to see it and having seen it not to be able to put it out of mind. All the time her body responded, some fragmentary part of consciousness held its image, the colour of it, the shape, the growth of hair, something unpleasant, an imperfection. She cried out and he sighed and came down upon her and as they lay together she imagined it touching her shoulder, brushing against the skin. He slept, and quite soon she did too. They had come together in fierce need. You couldn't call it making love. It seemed to her just before she went to sleep like nothing more than part of an old pattern.

In the middle of the night he struck her, and as his arm flailed again she came awake and struggled up in fright, then got angry and scrambled across him to put on the bedside lamp. He was asleep, lying on his back. His forehead was covered in sweat. He gave a groan and threw up his arm again, but when she caught and held it he gave in at once. She pressed it down and lay across him, holding both arms by his side. 'It's all right,' she told him, 'you're having a bad dream, it's all right, it's all right.'

Even when he quietened, she held him against her and lay like that while the light from the lamp faded gradually into the morning of another day.

CHAPTER TWENTY-NINE

H e phoned Harriet Cook and sat at his desk wondering as the ringing went on if she was there with somebody or just didn't want to answer. Maybe she had gone out for the evening. Maybe she already regretted what had happened. He put the phone down.

Since the split with Carole, he had got into the habit of eating out. If he was late, and he was usually late on a Friday, he would go to an Indian restaurant in Stockbridge and linger over his food until it was time to go home and try for sleep.

Oddly enough, it was the other man he recognised first. People leaving cleared his view to the table in the corner. He attached a name and crimesheet to a face, idly, out of habit. Then he realised the man's companion, sitting with his back to him, was Worth.

He pushed aside his plate; he had stopped being hungry half-way through the mound of rice and cooling meat. He emptied the last of the bottle and took the glass with him to their table.

'GBH, wasn't it?' He took the seat beside Worth and nodded across at the man. No doubt about it: round head like a cannonball, the hair cut short, lips ready with a grin or a sneer. 'I thought you'd still be inside.'

'You know me?'

'Don't be a clown, McArdle. Why don't you have an early night?'

'An early night?'

'This man and I have business.'

'So did him and me.' He rubbed a palm over the bristles on his head and grinned. 'We were going to have a wank in front of the fire.'

Worth sat with his head down, stirring a fork round his plate.

'Rough trade,' Meldrum said, watching McArdle leave. 'You should be careful.'

'If I needed a policeman, I'd have phoned.'

'I mean, even apart from him getting violent once you're on your own. Plenty of people have McArdle's card marked. What happens if one of them sees you with him? I thought your reputation mattered to you. Wasn't that why you kept your mouth shut about Clay, and to hell with Hugh Keaney?'

'There's something you should know about,' Worth said. 'I didn't have the guts to tell you that day you came to my flat.'

Meldrum hadn't doubted there was more to learn from Worth. What he hadn't expected was Worth to volunteer information. If he was a fruit, he'd assumed it was one that would have to be squeezed.

After a moment, he prodded, 'Tell me what?'

'About somebody you should talk to. I can fix a meeting.'

The world moved, not on maybe, but along, so that even to stay the same it had to be changing. Near the start of the previous decade, the Israeli ambassador had been shot one June day in London; and the next year three Arabs had been sentenced for his killing to thirty-five years in an English jail. The day after the ambassador's death Lebanon had been bombed by Israeli jets. Two days afterwards the Israeli invasion crossed the border; a month later their armour broke into West Beirut. In Paris six died when a grenade was thrown into a Jewish restaurant. Days later Israeli jets bombed West Beirut for eleven hours. That same month IRA bombers ambushed a detachment of the Blues and Royals trotting on horseback along South Carriage Way in Hyde Park on their way to the changing of the guards. In September Bashir Gemayel, president-elect of Lebanon, was assassinated; four days later Lebanese Christian militia were unleashed and took their revenge on the Palestinian refugee camps. Bodies of men, women and children lay piled on the mean streets of Sabra and Chatila. In August in Ireland a supergrass gave evidence and an IRA cell's members got sentences totalling more than 4000 years; its leader alone sentenced to 963 years for conspiracy to murder and murder attempted. In October young Palestinians drove suicide lorries packed with explosives at the head-quarters of the peace-keepers and killed young Frenchmen; and young Americans, 248 of them. And at the very end of the year, after a three-week war in the camps, Yasser Arafat was forced to leave Lebanon.

Meldrum stared down at the newspaper clippings. As he'd finished glancing at each, he had let it drift from his hand. Now they lay scattered across the carpet as Worth would have been if his evening had gone according to plan.

'So what?'

'I have one more.'

He'd passed them across one at a time from a box-file balanced on his lap. He took out the last one, and sat with it in his hand.

'It's too late now to change your mind.'

'Since Francis was killed I've been frightened. That's a long time to be afraid.'

Meldrum reached out and took the clipping from him.

It described how John Fields Laverty, personal assistant to the American Ambassador in Dublin and forty-eight the morning he died, had met his end. He had only been in the country four months and in interviews had made a good deal of being a second-generation Irish-American; in one quote talking about 'roots' and even in another of 'coming home'. The photograph showed a thick-necked, high-coloured, smiling man, handsome after the curled bullock fashion. He had his wife, a pretty woman almost twenty years younger, on one side and his eight-year-old daughter on the other. They had been in the car and died with him when the bomb went off.

'Nobody claimed it. Nobody was ever arrested. But it came out who'd done it and why,' Worth said. 'Laverty had come to Ireland from the embassy in Israel. There was a suggestion he'd been CIA, some kind of intelligence man. Every embassy

has them. Whatever he'd done, he was a marked man. The
Palestinians wanted him dead. They offered money and arms
to get it done. The IRA wouldn't touch it. But they'd a splinter
group just broken away, led by one of the real crazies. In
America they didn't bother about the distinction. Money and
support for the IRA went soft for a while. Laverty was a Catholic, devout, the second marriage wasn't because of divorce
– the first wife died of cancer. He had Boston connections.
Killing the wife and child made it that much worse.'

'This is all?' Meldrum held up the clipping: the headlined
account on the day it happened.

'I keep them hidden away. That one in particular. Look at
the date.'

'So?'

'It's the day before – the night I told you about.'

'The night Clay came storming in on you?'

'I told you he said he had something to celebrate.'

'Jesus Christ!' Meldrum said in disgust. 'I was told Clay
was a soldier. And not Irish. You're building all this out of
nothing.'

'Say what you like about me, I'm a bloody good journalist.
Don't tell me I can't stand a story up.'

'Fine, do it. I'm listening.'

But Worth, speaking so quietly Meldrum had to lean forward
to hear, said, 'I can arrange for you to meet somebody; until
then I've told you all I can,' and was not afterwards to be
persuaded.

CHAPTER THIRTY

When she saw Meldrum waiting, Harriet's first reaction was to go back inside. It was too late, though, she was through the doors and he had seen her. As she came down the steps, he said, 'I couldn't get through to you on the phone.'

'How long have you been here?' Her second reaction was to hope that no one had seen him. She restrained herself from looking up at the windows of the office. 'I go this way.' She began to walk so quickly it took him a pace or two to catch her up. 'I don't bother with the car. I like a walk at lunchtime.'

'I'd begun to wonder if you just had a sandwich at your desk.'

'Sometimes. Not today.' As they went by the railing of St Mary's Cathedral, the sun came out. A flickering among the grass became a butterfly and she followed its soaring until the turning angles danced against the sky and a brilliance of light struck her like a blow across the eyes. 'You should have phoned.'

'I haven't had much luck with phoning.'

She let it go. Last night she'd sat glass in hand watching the phone as it rang. It had rung twice earlier that evening and she had known it was him. If she could have been sure nothing more was wanted of her than sex, that would have been all right; she had found forgetfulness in that way, too. What made her afraid was the memory of holding him in her arms as he slept.

They walked to the French Institute. As they went down the stairs, he stopped in front of the window.

'I know,' she said. 'You wouldn't believe we were in the middle of a city.' The view was across a cleft gully clothed in trees. There wasn't a building in sight. She had seen it so often, most of the time, like a familiar painting, it no longer registered.

'Ten minutes' walk from Princes Street,' he said.

'You've never been here before?'

'I usually have a sandwich at my desk.'

She said that was bad for him and they found a table and read the board and collected what they wanted to eat. She drew the process out, and felt rather than thought that every minute used up left less time she would have to spend with him before she went back to work. As it turned out, the effort was wasted since she got up before the end of the meal and phoned the office to say she would be late.

'I just wanted to see you,' he said. 'I didn't mean to tell you all that.' He shook his head as if bewildered. 'I'm not someone who – I keep things to myself. I shouldn't have told you. It's not fair to you.'

But afterwards when they were outside again, walking aimlessly, he said, 'The thing is it felt natural.'

She had had her chance. All she'd had to do was go back to work. She could have left him. Left him, even him, after he'd confided in her; after he'd found it natural, Christ, natural, to confide in her. The natural thing to do should have been to go back to work, to run for it. Men made demands; with their eyes, their hands, their bodies. She accepted that. She didn't want to be asked to feel something for them as well; not love, or even affection; that was unfair.

They went along Princes Street. Busy pavements were no place for talking. They turned into the Gardens. The paths there were crowded too, but they made their way down until by the Norwegian stone they found an empty bench. People were picnicking on the slopes or spread face-up taking the sun. Under the nearest tree a man was lying half on top of a woman with his leg between her thighs. Music from the outdoor café kept a clattering time against the noise of distant traffic.

'Do you believe him?'

'He had the clippings.'

'You know that's not what I mean. I believe in the IRA. I know there's a place called Lebanon.'

'And the background on Laverty was real. I spent this morning in the library checking him for myself. Nobody spells it out, but there's one paper that talks about special responsibilities. I think he probably was Intelligence.'

'But if he was CIA—'

'One of the Intelligence agencies.'

'Whichever one – do they take their wives and daughters with them?'

'I don't know. Maybe he'd stopped. Maybe his wife wanted to see the old country. She was Irish-American too.'

'All right.' She tried not to think of the wife and child blown apart in a street. In a different city. A long time ago. It was Meldrum who had told her she only read of these things; as a lawyer, argued about them; she didn't see them. 'Suppose all of that's true. Why should the IRA kill Laverty? Even if they owed somebody like Gaddafi a favour. Even if they were being offered arms as payment. You say that it lost them support in the United States – that the contributions dried up for a while.'

'According to Worth it was some splinter group. Cowboys who were greedy and unsophisticated enough to take it on.'

'All the same . . . As a young lawyer, I was told if in doubt look for who benefits.' Told by John Brennan, of course. The thought confused her. 'Worth must have been terrified and ashamed that night. He's turned Clay into a kind of monster. All right, I believe a man like that might kill a lover. But as for what happened in Dublin—'

She realised Meldrum had twisted round and was looking up as if studying the Castle behind them as she spoke. He struck her incongruously as being like a child determined to avoid something he didn't want to hear. 'It's politics,' he said, spitting the word out. 'I don't want anything to do with it.'

'Let it go then,' she said. 'You can walk away.'

'They've transferred Hugh Keaney to Peterhead,' he said dully. 'I think he might be on hunger strike.'

* * *

'I'm sorry about this,' John Brennan said. He meant about having to talk to her in the back of the car. On his way home and with an appointment to keep that evening, there wasn't time to talk to her in his office. 'But whatever it is, you can tell me about it as we go. You're still in the same flat?' She nodded. 'Right, Ronnie, you know the way.'

Harriet caught the man's glance on her. She didn't know how long he'd been around, certainly since before her time. He acted as chauffeur, but didn't wear a uniform. Somebody had told her he was an ex-client whom John had got cleared on a murder charge. She'd heard him described as John's bodyguard; as a joke, of course, though he had the shoulders for it. For a period of just over six months, he had sat in the car outside her flat waiting while his boss was inside screwing her. He knew the way well enough. Watching her in the mirror, his face was without expression.

'Do you know Brian Worth?' she asked.

'The journalist?'

'Yes.'

'For twenty years. When he was useful to know. Not recently.'

'He claims to have information about a murder. There's this man Hugh Keaney—'

She paused and he said, 'I know who Keaney is.' His having defended Keaney was the reason she was here. Unless, of course, she was also trying to seduce him. The thought, which should have been simply ironic, made her wince. She had always been hard on herself.

'Worth thinks he can prove Keaney's innocent.'

He listened without interruption, something not many people could do. On the other hand, she told what she had to tell in order and clearly. After all she was a lawyer, a good one given the chance.

When she had finished, he said, 'I wouldn't like to go into an Appeal Court with no more than that to offer.'

'With no more than that,' she said, 'it wouldn't get to an appeal.'

'Your friend Meldrum should stop now. It's hard to see him getting anything but grief out of this.'

'He won't let Keaney down. I believe it just isn't in him to do that. But he's afraid. Not physically. He doesn't want to get involved with politics.'

'He could be right.' He ran a finger across his lips, a trick he had when thinking. 'Does he know you're talking to me?'

'No,' she said in alarm, 'I wouldn't want him to know.'

'He is out of his depth,' he said. 'If it comes to it, I'll get him to a sympathetic ear. Isn't that what you'd want? We'll keep in touch. Promise you'll keep me in touch with what's going on.'

CHAPTER THIRTY-ONE

The weekened began pleasantly enough for Farquhar Wood, however badly it ended.

He'd got to Gautmuir too late for dinner, but that had been a misunderstanding and he'd been provided with sandwiches, thick cuts of ham reared and cured on the home farm, eaten with pickles, as good a supper as he'd ever eaten. There had been no chance to talk about why he'd come. Feeling himself there on sufferance, he did not have it in him to be competition for Sir James's second guest. Bernard was as round-chopped and smooth as Sir James was wrinkled and skeletal, but the two men were exact contemporaries and friends from boyhood. In the end he'd given up, his departure for bed perfunctorily acknowledged as the two old men sipped whisky and recalled the terrors of yet another schoolmaster long dead.

Up early next morning he'd breakfasted alone; and afterwards, at a loss what else to do, set off to walk round the miniature lake that lay in front of the house. Birds on water he tended to think of as ducks if they weren't swans. Half-way round he stopped to watch them weaving patterns on the surface. The sun was warm on the back of his neck and he felt at ease for the first time since he'd arrived. When something clapped up out of the reeds at his feet, he jumped in fright. Looking around, he thanked God there had been no one to see him and strolled on, keeping away from the edge.

On the way back, he found a walled garden, espaliered pear and apple trees spreading across grey stones warmed by the sun. Beyond beds of vegetables and fruit bushes were lawns with trees set out like patterns in geometry. He was wandering at his ease up a long diagonal alley of flowers when Sir James and Bernard came towards him.

'I've been taking advantage of this beautiful morning,' he told them.

'You left the gate open,' Sir James said.

A cloud came over the sky.

'I'm sorry. Gate?'

'The one you came in through. We keep it shut for the rabbits. I told Bernard he'd to bring six to breakfast – and he did – shot them out of his bedroom window sitting up on the lawn. I've counted eighty of them out there before now.'

'As many as that?' It was the best he could manage.

'Great crested grebe,' Bernard offered and shook his plump jowels.

It was only when Sir James exchanged his petulance for the sake of joining in that he identified what was happening as laughter.

At his expense, as it turned out.

'I didn't realise I was being watched.'

'You have to know where to look.'

'How to look,' said Sir James.

'It came up out of the reeds so suddenly.' He spread his hands. 'About this size.'

'Balderdash.' Bernard measured air. 'More like this.'

Sir James seized his hands and adjusted their distance. 'More like that.'

The two friends studied the gap with a satisfied air.

'It seemed bigger,' he said.

'Big enough to put the shits up you,' Bernard said, and the old men laughed companionably.

Stung, he said, 'I'm surprised you can be so sure . . . I mean, at that distance, the distance you must have been.'

'Ah, but you don't have to be close. Every bird makes a different shape. A grebe, a chiffchaff, a buzzard.' Sir James angled his head, shrugged up his shoulders, trailed his arms and did just for the instant have something birdlike about him; some old bird of prey. 'A glimpse can be enough.'

A good lunch might have been a consolation; might have been, except that a conclusion was called to his visit before then.

Sir James's first response had been, 'Odd thing. I've met your police fellow. Goes to prove again, this is a small country. He was looking into the killing of a neighbour's widow. Made a hash of it – if that's any comfort to you.' But within moments, he was frowning and grumbling, 'Why do you feel you have to tell me any of this? I don't want to know such things. When I was Secretary of State for Scotland I made quite sure not to know them. It's the last Colonial Governor's job left now the Empire's gone. Do it properly and you get a better Cabinet berth. I got the Foreign Office. Reward of merit, you'll want to say, but I took care not to hear what I didn't want to. I'm not sure what kind of job you'll get next at this rate.'

'I'm thinking about the one I've got,' Farquhar Wood said. Brooding over his career, he had on occasion consoled himself with the reflection that Reith of the BBC and even John Buchan, later 1st Baron Tweedsmuir, had died disappointed in measuring themselves against what might have been. 'I mean, I'm concerned to do what's right.'

As he held the old man's stare, he felt that perhaps he'd earned some respect for taking a position. It lasted for a moment, then Sir James drew down his narrow chin, a strange movement like a turtle pulling its ancient head into its shell, and looked to where Bernard was coming down from the house with a shotgun broken across his arm.

'If you think by involving me you're protecting yourself in some way, forget it. I carry more weight than you do or ever will, and what I say I don't know I bloody well don't know. Understood?' Without looking round, still with his eyes on his friend's approach, he said more quietly, 'Try not to worry so much, my dear chap. Scandals don't last, they get muddled up somehow. Muddled, smothered, set aside, forgotten. They don't last – not for us. That's the beauty of the great British public, it can't keep anything straight in its head for five minutes.'

'The jizz,' Bernard called across the grass.

'Eh?'

'Size, wing angle, arc of the flight,' Bernard said joining them. 'Everything you put together to tell it's a grebe. Do it so fast you couldn't explain how. Soldier on patrol, same thing, come to think of it, enemy or one of ours? That's the jizz.'

'Christ!' Sir James said. 'Bloody yahoo kind of a word.'

CHAPTER THIRTY-TWO

'Money,' Brian Worth said. 'Isn't that all the motive most people need?' He was compulsively going over the story of the phone call he'd taken at the paper the night before Hugh Keaney went to trial. A man claiming to be a soldier in Ireland, wanting money for his story – a hell of a story, the voice said. About the killing of the American diplomat in Dublin, blown up in a car with his wife and young daughter. 'The way I felt then, it was just one more thing to be afraid of – I hung up on him. When he didn't try again, I told myself it was all right – he must be a fake. But I knew he wasn't. When I picked up the phone this morning, it was as if I'd been waiting all these years for him to call again.'

Meldrum didn't like any of it. He hadn't liked it when it was Worth claiming to have found the soldier; my contacts, Worth had said. He liked it less now it seemed the soldier was the one who had done the approaching.

The car bumped two wheels on to the pavement and stopped.

'We're too early,' Worth said. 'Sorry.' A slant of street light showed a muscle jumping on his cheek. Glancing away, Meldrum watched wind tease trash out of a tumbled bin and blow it over the waste ground. 'Out there on its own. That's it.'

Whatever had been above the ground floor had been sliced off, leaving the bar like a gun emplacement on a battlefield. It stood isolated in the middle of what had once been streets of tenements, a violent area in Glasgow of gangs and poverty, all pulled down now and left as a wasteland crossed only by roads in search of an escape. There would be a motorway not too far away; it was an easy city to get out of in a hurry.

'You go in at quarter past. At exactly quarter past, that's what he said. How long will it take you to walk across from here? Ten minutes? What do you think?'

'I think it would be easier to go over in the car.'

'I can only tell you what he said . . .'

Meldrum grunted. Walking him across open ground, that way a watcher could be sure he was alone. The idea didn't make him feel any better.

'I'd think ten minutes,' Worth said, 'to walk over.' He shot his cuff to look at his watch. 'I didn't mean to be early. From Edinburgh I thought it would take longer. I'm not a fast driver. Not usually. I'm sorry.' He checked the time again. 'I used to do things like this. Wait in cars. Wait for something to happen. Watching for somebody. Or like this waiting to meet somebody. I was younger then. I've been behind a desk too long. Bitch on the newsdesk told me that just before I got the bullet from the paper. She'd a picture of a family killed in a car. Wanted it on the front page. A family of tinkers on the front page, show some common sense, I told her.' Light gleamed off the face of his watch. 'Average age of that newsdesk was – what?—forty-two? Forty-three? Most experienced in Scotland. I'd built a good team. Remember a guy – did a bit for us – acted as a stringer for one of the dailies – never returned a tax form. Apparently, they don't hear from you, they charge you on an estimate. They were going to sell up his furniture. I sent him to see my accountant. He said, he's in a worse state than Lester Piggott. Look at the bloody rain . . . The Godforsaken middle of nowhere . . . What a place for a pub, eh? You ever see that film – the one about the gangs that attack an American police station?'

As he started to look at his watch again, Meldrum caught him by the wrist and pushed his arm down. 'I'm going.'

'But it's too soon.'

'I won't hurry.'

It was just on the hour when he got out of the car. He

forced himself to walk slowly. Half-way across, something
made him look back in time to see the car slide away in the
shadows between the lamps. How am I going to get home?
First thoughts were always stupid like that. Maybe Worth was
too nervous to sit waiting; maybe he would keep circling
and be there when needed. Maybe. Meantime there wasn't
anything better to do than keep going. Precinct Thirteen:
wonderful name for a Glasgow bar. It wouldn't have been
hard to imagine figures around him skulking across the broken
ground clutching Kalashnikovs.

Not yet ten past, but he shoved the door and went in.

It was like a blow in the face. He'd been braced to walk into
almost empty space, a few silent men, turning their heads to
watch him, as attentive as dogs in a pack. The noise came at
him in a wave. The place was crowded. As he eased through
to the bar, he drew some attention, but nothing that seemed
out of the way. To his left at the far end a fire roared in a wide
grate and against the wall a table covered with a white cloth
was laden with food.

'You've picked some night for a quiet drink,' a voice said,
the breath hot against his cheek, leaning close to be heard. A
big slack-faced bear of a man with long, dirty-looking yellow
hair. 'He's picked his night,' he announced, leaning across the
bar. 'Make it two wee goldies.'

While Meldrum was trying to catch a barman's eye on his
own account, one of the two whiskies that came was put in
front of him.

'To Tommy McGloag!' the bear man said. 'As decent a wee
fella as ever drew breath.'

He was wearing a black tie; so was the barman; other men
too. It looked as if Mr McGloag had gone into the oven that
afternoon. Meldrum wasn't usually so slow to notice, but then
he'd had other things on his mind. He nodded some kind of
agreement to the toast and drank.

The bear said something he didn't hear; nodding again,
deliberately vague, glancing round in search of the man he
was supposed to meet. There wasn't any way to identify his
contact. Worth said the man had claimed to be a soldier. Plenty
of men had been soldiers; and drink was more likely to leave a

mark on the face than being around a killer or even being one. He bought another whisky and laid it in front of the bear, who had turned away to talk to someone else. As he did so, a hand gripped him by the arm.

'Who are you? What are you doing here? You not know this is a sad occasion?' The questions rattled out from just above the level of his elbow. A little sliver of a man with a melancholy clown's face scowled up at him. There should have been something to say, something respectful to the particular departed or proverbial about the general condition of ending up dead, even a joke could work. Meldrum jerked his arm free, bar-room diplomacy not being one of his gifts.

And cursed himself as he did. Most of the people in the room were undersized; probably half of them were related on one side of the blanket or the other. Little men were touchy in their pride and this runt looked malevolent enough to try to muster the rest of the seven dwarves. Despite which, his mind stayed obstinately blank of words.

'That's not civil,' the little man said seriously.

'I'm saying every bullet has its billet,' said the bear, putting his face between them.

'Aye, but who the fuck are you?'

'Everybody's friend, friend. This is my friend Jim. I was a good friend of young Tommy's.'

'The boy that was killed?'

'The same one.'

'Old Tommy never got over that. He was never the same. I don't know what that boy joined the fucking army for.'

'It's a living.'

'Eh?'

But before the little man could work that one out, the bear was moving away. Meldrum followed him into a quieter space near where the women were gathered around the fire.

'Jim?'

'Jimmy, if you like,' the bear said, and his accent, which Meldrum had until that instant taken for granted as local, broadened as if in parody. At once, though, he grinned and went on, 'Isn't everyone in Glasgow called Jimmy?'

'You tell me.'

'Oh, it's well known.' He held out his hand. 'Name's Sharkey, nice to meet you.' And when Meldrum made no response, grinned and asked, 'Come with Brian?'

'What Brian would that be?'

'Is he sitting outside shitting himself?' And when Meldrum waited, 'Worth. Is Worth shitting himself?'

'What would you think?'

'We've spoken on the phone. I wanted him to meet me – but he wouldn't come. Like I say, a nervous man.'

'When would this be?'

'Did Worth not tell you *anything*?'

'He told me about a man who shoved a gun up his arse.'

'This arse bandit have a name?'

'The one I heard was Clay.'

The bear shifted; it didn't seem much of a movement, but his body blocked Meldrum off from the room. He had made a private space.

'That wouldn't be his real name,' he said. 'Stands to reason.'

'Maybe, maybe not. Pietro and him were lovers.'

At the word the bear made a face of disgust.

'You like to spell out what you're talking about?'

Meldrum thought for a moment, then decided. He said, 'I'm working on the theory Clay was careless, really careless. I think Pietro heard him shooting his mouth off so much that Clay had to kill him. And then he had to kill Arthur Hull to make sure.'

'You must think this guy Clay was a fucking idiot.'

'Maybe they did most of their talking in bed. I hear Pietro got people pretty excited. That can make a man careless.'

'What else did Worth tell you?'

'That he'd found somebody who'd talk about what Clay had done in Ireland.'

'Is that what he said?' He blew out his breath in a way that looked like contempt or surprise at how dishonest people could be. 'If I walk out of here this fucking minute, he wouldn't have a prayer of finding me. You neither.'

'But now after all these years you get in touch with him again. Why would you do that?'

'Because I was back in Ireland last month. First time since Laverty got killed. You know about Laverty?'

'The American who got blown up in Dublin. With his wife.'

'And his kid. Just a wee girl. That made it bad. We didn't like it.'

'We?'

'Keeping surveillance, that was our job. Part of our job. On Clay, on the locals he was involved with. Think we didn't know about the plan to take out the American? Shit, we were the best. Believe me, we knew.'

My contacts claim there was a top secret army unit in Ulster, Worth had said.

As a policeman, Meldrum didn't like the secret kind, in the army or anywhere else.

'So why didn't you stop Laverty getting killed?' he wondered.

'Because we weren't given a fucking chance. It was blue on blue.' He registered Meldrum's ignorance of the phrase with a sneer. 'Friendly fire. Our own side screwed us. And last month in Belfast I found out why.'

'Belfast?' Meldrum shook his head.

'I was setting up a drug deal. Met a guy who told me about Laverty. It was so long ago he thought it didn't matter.' He bent closer so that Meldrum caught the staleness of his breath. 'He was wrong. I'm talking about evidence – I mean stuff that would stand up in court. Worth tells me that's what you want.'

But before he could answer, the aggressive little man came at them, carrying drinks. 'No, no,' he insisted. 'I want you to have them. I'm a brother-in-law of the deceased. That's my sister, young Tommy's mother, nearest the fire there. I told her you knew young Tommy in the army. It was the first time her head's come up all day. I think it would really help her if you had a word.'

'In a minute, no problem,' the bear said. 'Be in touch about where and when, Jim.' He explained, 'Me and my friend here are treating ourselves to a wee fishing trip.'

'Lucky you can afford it – more than I could,' the little man complained.

'There's more important things in life than money. That's
how we feel.' The bear reached out and patted Meldrum on
the shoulder. 'Am I right?'

As he started over towards them, the women who had been
watching rearranged themselves to make a place for him beside
Mrs McGloag.

'See last Saturday,' the little man said, 'somebody stood a
cut out of Charlie Nicholas in the corner. Life-size. Monday
somebody asked Jimmy the barman, Right Charlie Nicholas
was in here at the weekend? Stiff as a board, Jimmy said.
Cardboard, get it? Are you listening? Listen. The *Daily Record*
rings him – Is it true Charlie Nicholas was out his skull in
your place Saturday night? Credit it? Somebody listening and
phoned the paper looking for a backhander. World's fulla
bastards.'

The bear had disappeared.

Meldrum's attention had lapsed only for a moment, but
looking round there was no doubt. As he headed for the door,
Mrs McGloag hurried after him to ask if he'd been in the army
too. That big pal o'yours is a gem, she said. He's promised he'll
keep in touch – see you do the same, son.

Outside there was no sign of life. A sheet of newspaper
drifted ahead of him across the waste ground, folding and
unfolding in the wind.

Solitary splashing drops of rain turned abruptly into a down-
pour.

It would be nice if the car appeared and Worth had come back
to give him a lift home, but he didn't expect it to happen.

BOOK FIVE

The Fields of Armagh

CHAPTER THIRTY-THREE

Queuing to get on to the plane, Meldrum listened to a conversation about how the flight didn't get into Belfast until mid-morning now. 'Before,' one of the men said, 'you could make a meeting for half-nine.' It was a small plane holding under forty passengers, and Meldrum took it for granted that they would be businessmen flying in for meetings at whatever hours of the morning would be left. He glanced through the headlines in the morning paper as they crossed Scotland, and when he looked down, he was in time to see cloud shadow slide across a field to where it ended in a drop to the sea.

'The Ayrshire coast,' the man beside him said, leaning forward to look. 'That's where most of the Scots came from to settle the Plantation in Uster. Ayrshire lairds taking their chance of some of the spoils after James Sixth got the English throne.' He was a thin man with a beard and nervous hands who seemed to require attention rather than response in a listener. He explained some other things; for example, 'The nationalist historians in the South blamed their past on the bloody English, now the revisionists decide everyone's a bastard and call that an improved view of human nature'; none of which Meldrum, who knew nothing about history, followed. Instead, he tried to place him: an unlikely businessman, an academic on his way to an interview? Would those opinions go down well in Belfast though? A journalist? Just possibly; a doctor, a vet or a— He'd got to that point in playing Sherlock Holmes when his nose began to gush blood. 'The cabin's not pressured, we're not supposed to fly above eight and half thousand feet,' the man said. 'Here, take these,' and he passed across a wad of paper handkerchiefs.

Meldrum was still clutching them when they came out of the concourse at the city airport.

'Sure you're all right?' the man asked. 'My sister would be glad to give you a lift.'

'No need,' Meldrum said. 'Thanks anyway. I'm being met too.'

'I try to get back two or three times a year. My parents are getting on. There she is. Annie!'

A plump, grey-haired woman came forward to his waving. She looked a generation older and held her face up while he dabbed at her cheek with his lips and explained about Meldrum. 'Are you sure your lift'll turn up?' she wondered. 'Everybody seems to be gone by now.'

'You'd be perfectly welcome,' the man insisted.

'No. I'll be fine.' Meldrum controlled his irritation. 'You'll be wanting to get home.'

'Home!' the man repeated and pulled a face that for a moment seemed comic before it went sour.

It was a relief when they went. Meldrum touched an unused corner of the handkerchiefs to his nostril. It stained red. His head ached ferociously and he asked himself why had he come. He watched the taxis come and go. He knew why he had come: what other chance did Keaney have? Feeling as bad as he did, he wondered if that was a good enough reason any more.

The bear came from the wrong direction, not from outside but from the concourse. He was shaved, the anorak expensive this time, his hair cut short; but it was the difference in the way he carried himself that delayed Meldrum's recognising him. As he came forward holding out his hand, he had the upright bearing of a soldier.

'Mr Meldrum. I have a car in the car-park.'

Meldrum fell into step beside him. 'I looked for you on the plane, Sharkey.'

'*Captain* Sharkey. I came yesterday. There were things to be arranged.'

The car was an old Astra with a dent on the door and rust showing along the sills.

'You hired this?'

'Borrowed.' The Captain smiled.

Getting in, Meldrum saw a teddy bear and a plastic truck on the back seat.

'Children?'

'Nothing to do with me.'

Sharkey put the key in the ignition but didn't turn it. Fat drops made rings in the dirt on the smeared window. They'd been lucky making it dry across the car-park. If Sharkey had something to say, it was up to him to speak first. Meldrum waited him out.

'That man, did you meet him on the plane?'

'What man would that be?'

'The one I saw you talking to – a woman met him.'

'He was on the plane.'

'I saw the two of you getting off.'

'Yes.'

'Who was he?'

Rain began to drum on the roof.

'Some kind of academic. He had the seat beside me and started talking.'

'What did you talk about?'

'The fact my nose was bleeding. Do you have handkerchiefs?'

'No.'

Meldrum pulled down the drawer under the ledge and found a couple of crumpled paper handkerchiefs. As he took them out and held them against his nostril, the Captain started the car.

'Captain?'

'What?'

'Are you really a Captain?'

'I told you I was in the army.'

'I suppose calling yourself Captain wouldn't have been clever, not in that pub in Glasgow.'

There he had sounded like a Glaswegian; here since the airport his voice had been more clipped, with a different tune to it that suggested an Englishman and one not from a town but born in the country, some southern shire perhaps. In any case, driving with a ferocity of concentration, whether as bear or Captain, Sharkey seemed disinclined to talk. Among all the other items of his ignorance, Meldrum hadn't been given a destination. At first they were driving north; he saw a sign for Larne. Later, at a junction, they turned back on themselves. 'Are we going into the Republic?' It was as if he hadn't spoken. They took a side turn and swung right and left among a net of empty narrow roads where signs offered a village or the name of a farm at crossing after crossing until it seemed the flat landscape spun around them. They came without a transition to a busy road and sat while lorries threw up dirty water across the windscreen.

Sharkey missed an opportunity to pull out. Meldrum saw him looking into the rear mirror and twisted round to check for himself; the narrow road behind them was empty.

'You think we might be followed?'

For answer Sharkey swung out into what was almost a gap, the car behind screeching its horn.

Meldrum asked, 'Who would follow us?'

It made him uneasy that nothing he asked seemed worth answering. As if in deciding to come he had made his last decision that would matter.

Lurgan, Portadown, then Armagh; the names went by and he thought, yes, we're going to cross the border. He caught a sign for somewhere called Keady as they came on to a secondary road. Quarter of an hour later, Sharkey pulled off on to a layby. At the far end a double-decker bus painted with bright rainbows was parked beside a farm gate. In a slanted script THE GOSPEL BUS was marked in red and yellow letters along its side. A poster filled the nearest window. On it he could make out only the largest word, which was JOY.

'Open the gate,' Sharkey said.

'We're going up there?'

Meldrum got out of the car. Beyond the gate there was a road of packed earth and stones which went up in a curve towards a range of hills. He rested his hands on the top bar of the gate. There were sheep on the stony field and a black horse cropping the grass. Mist hung in grey loops about the tops of the hills.

'The gate's padlocked.' The voice came from a man hovering on the step of the Gospel Bus, half out to be helpful, half wanting to be back inside out of the cold. 'Unless, of course, you have a key. Assuming, that is, I was assuming, that you want to go through.'

Meldrum walked back to the car.

'What?' Sharkey asked. He'd cracked the door open and was squinting up through the gap.

'The gate's locked.'

'Can't you break it?'

'The chain goes round twice, the padlock's new, a big one. You could break it with a bar – if you've got one – but I don't know what he'd make of it.'

'Is he alone?' Sharkey's eyes slid across to where the man still stood on the step watching.

'I heard somebody else.' Meldrum lied without thinking about it.

'We'll wait till they go.'

But the man was coming over.

'Would you like to see inside? We have a little library of pamphlets and an exhibition we're proud of.'

On some instinct, Meldrum had gone forward to keep him at a distance, a safe distance, though for whom he couldn't have said. 'We wouldn't want to put you to the trouble.'

'Trouble? It's what we're here for! How could there be any trouble in spreading the Good News? We come from Huddersfield and we go all over. This is the third year we've come to Ireland. Anyway, we'd be glad of the company.' He peered past Meldrum's shoulder. 'We're going to have lunch in a little while.' Meldrum heard the car door bang shut. 'Why not join us? You could join us . . . if you're not in a hurry, that is.' Looking round, he was in time to see Sharkey jumping over the gate.

'He *is* in a hurry,' the evangelist said.

It didn't seem like hurrying, though; Sharkey looked almost lazy in pace. Meldrum remembered his first impression from the pub in Glasgow had been of a slob, a man carrying fat.

'Please, in case you don't come back!' The evangelist's voice sounded ominously behind him.

'What?'

'In case we're gone, I mean.' He was holding out a booklet.
On a reflex Meldrum took it. 'You'll find it isn't a waste of time.
If you get a quiet ten minutes to read it for Jesus' sake.' But
Meldrum was already moving away. As he climbed the gate,
behind him the voice cried, 'To die is gain,' and a hand touched
him on the shoulder. 'Paul said, For me to live is Christ, and to
die is gain.'

The evangelist had two faces. When he spoke about Jesus, the
eyes shone and his flesh seemed to tighten. Now, left behind at
the gate, sallow-skinned, cheeks deeply gouged, he looked like
a man who'd smoked and drunk too much in his time, been too
poor, worked too hard.

Struggling to catch up, finding it hard to close the gap, breath
coming fast as the track got steeper, Meldrum wondered if what
Sharkey was carrying might not be fat but solid muscle. 'Hold
it!' When he came level and grabbed at a sleeve, the thought
had him braced for trouble. As Sharkey put up a hand as if to
push him away, he set his weight to resist. Next moment he was
staggering forward. Sharkey had pulled him, not pushed.

'You want to watch for that,' he said. 'Don't they teach you
anything in the police?'

'Where are we going?'

'Up there.'

In the grey light the track vanished ahead as if rubbed out
between soft risings of green turfed banks.

'Easy walking,' Sharkey said with a sneer. 'You'll manage.'

'I'm going back.' The dull bulk of the hill above him,
the track narrowing ahead, between one step and the next,
Meldrum had come to feel like an animal hurrying into a trap.

Sharkey put his hand into his pocket. He tossed keys in the
air and caught them, put them back. Meldrum recognised the
keys of the car. 'Walk back to Belfast then.'

A friend had done that to him once. Pulled the keys out of
the ignition and challenged him to fight for them. Meldrum's
car, too, and the friend given a lift home to his door. It was
childish. You think I don't know what they're all hinting at,
the friend had said, with all their talk about what a happy
couple Carole and you are?

'I'll get a lift on the bus.' At once, it was a plan: get a lift to the nearest town, hire a car.

'Sing hymns on the way? Why would you do that? You want to do that, do that.' He chopped at the air like a man losing patience. 'If you do that, why did you come?'

They walked for what might have been another twenty minutes before Meldrum saw it. He had been looking round constantly as the track led them upwards. Hills of poor grass and bracken and heather and nothing alive but the little sheep and the occasional bird he couldn't put a name to. It was bleak to his eye, a stranger's eye. He heard the sound of his own breath as the slope steepened. Sharkey never slowed or paused. It had begun to seem to him as if there wasn't any reason why they shouldn't go on like this endlessly, in this wilderness without a destination. Die: people threw that word about too easily. A wind began to search across the slopes. He felt it cold on his cheeks and looked down to keep the snap of it out of his eyes. The track was rutted, stones embedded shone as if they had been polished; it would be easy to stumble. They came to a place where water had run across from the hill. Meldrum picked his way through mud stamped with rounds of hoofs and the interlaced circles left by tyres, not farm carts, he decided, the wheels of a car. He lifted his head to see a low building edge into sight out of its sheltering screen of trees.

Sharkey turned abruptly and began to walk back the way they had come.

'What is it?' Taken by surprise, he took a dozen steps to catch up.

'This'll do,' Sharkey said. There was a gap in the dry-stone wall and, both of them being tall men, the fence behind was low enough for them to step over.

A sheep was lying on its back, feet in the air. His first thought was that it was dead, but as they came nearer it convulsed and then subsided, the white front legs folding down and looking too frail now to support its weight. Its head lay flat against the ground. Too exhausted to lift it, it let it roll to the side and watched them with a dark, alien gaze. The obtrusion of its sex looked pink and somehow unwholesome. He remembered reading that crows picked out eyes, thought of foxes, wondered how long it could have been lying there helpless. There was a pile of fresh dung at its tail. Its belly seemed to him to be swollen. Perhaps that was what was wrong, some poisonous herb. Even while he wondered, Sharkey knelt and took a grip of one of the dark stretching rear legs. With his other hand he gripped the wool and with a heave turned it over on its side. Next moment it was on its feet and trotting away. A lamb hurried to its side and they moved off together.

As they headed across the field, Meldrum realised they had come back far enough so that their approach couldn't be seen from the building. Either Sharkey didn't trust whoever he'd come to meet or he wanted to make sure the people inside were the ones he was expecting.

'You've been here before?' Sharkey stared ahead, blank-faced. 'You didn't say if you'd been here before.'

Over his shoulder, Sharkey said, 'It's been a safe house for a long time.'

They came out of the trees about a hundred yards from a building, a long wall of undressed stone. Sharkey went along it to the left, walking quickly like a man who knew where he was going. Along the short wall that made the end of the building he moved more cautiously. At the corner he stopped. Meldrum looked past him into a narrow farmyard with buildings on three sides. The middle one had windows, some of them curtained. Clumps of machinery and discarded tools lay around and a car set up on blocks was rusting beside the front door. For a big man, Sharkey stepped quietly. Meldrum followed his example in keeping close to the wall. They passed sagging barn doors. Splintered wood gave glimpses of a grey interior out of which came a stirring of living things and the heavy stink of penned animals. He picked his way over a runnel drain carrying a trickle of brown liquid, and as he did heard a distinct sound in the stillness. It was the lifting of a doorlatch.

A man with a shotgun was watching them from the doorstep of the house.

'O'Toomey.'

'You got here then so, Captain,' the man said in a broad accent.

'It's been a while,' Sharkey said.

'I could have waited another fourteen years,' O'Toomey said. He came off the step to let them pass into the house. 'That wouldn't have bothered me at all.'

Meldrum followed Sharkey along a corridor; they passed a couple of doors and came into a room the centre of which was filled by a great slab of a table. A fire glowed low in the grate. Through an arch Meldrum could see a stove with a sink beside it and a door that must lead out to the back.

O'Toomey came in past them and took an easy chair set at the side of the hearth. He stood the shotgun up against the wall. Sharkey took an upright seat at the table near the fire. Meldrum hesitated, then sat opposite him; he felt better for having the table between them.

He waited for O'Toomey to look up from staring into the fire. A face gaunt with work and weather; fifty anyway, probably older. A big man in dungarees, a plaid shirt, boots crusted with mud. The chair went down under his weight until his knees, hands like shovels clasping them, came up almost to the height of his shoulders; fingers like a bunch of bananas, a phrase from childhood. Thumbs that bent back on themselves; you could cock them like a pistol, Meldrum knew, because his father had had the very same kind. In his mind that went with some notion of being handy, competent, a good tradesman. As a child, he'd wished his thumbs were like that.

On the mantelpiece above O'Toomey's head was a photograph of a man staring unsmilingly into the camera, sepia tones, heavy gilt frame. At the other end stood a statue of the Virgin Mary carved in flutings of wood on a base inside a wooden shell. The colour of her cloak was summer sky-blue. The wood sat out like wings and you could see they were made to close around the image. Even from where he was sitting, Meldrum could see how beautifully it was made. It looked expensive and he wondered who had bought it and when.

There was a plate on the table with a fork laid across scraps of congealing meat.

'Do you live here on your own?'

'My son was killed. Nineteen eighty-three. May fifth. In the morning at eleven-fifteen. According to the Brit patrol that shot him.' He spoke without looking up from the fire. 'They might have been out a minute or so one way or the other.'

Sharkey began to drum his fingertips on the table, one after another, two beats or three. Even when Meldrum began to question O'Toomey, he paid no attention, watching his hand as if encoding a message to himself. He hadn't taken off his glove, and the muffled slithering taps struck unpleasantly on Meldrum's nerves.

'Were you told why I'm here?'

'No idea in the world who you are,' O'Toomey answered. 'I imagine you know yourself.'

'I came to ask about a killing.'

'There have been plenty of those.'

'Not like this one. A man, his wife, his child.'

'. . . that's happened. Most things have happened.'

'His name was John Fields Laverty.'

'The American.'

'You know about it.'

'It was in all the papers.'

'Years ago it was in the papers. How many people would recognise it now?'

'Maybe not many where you come from.'

'Maybe not many here. Unless they were mixed up in it.'

'In Christ's name, what shape of a thing is that to be saying?' The reluctant growling monotone rose in resentment.

Abruptly, sick of the steady tapping, Meldrum reached across the table and put his hand over Sharkey's. He felt the raised finger resist and then subside.

'It's why I'm here.' He answered O'Toomey, but said the words to Sharkey. He lifted his hand away, but could sense the other's bone and integument like a map burned with wire on to his skin.

O'Toomey stood and went out.

'You're letting him get away,' Sharkey said.

The corridor was empty. Meldrum opened the front door; a thin smirr of rain slanted across the yard. The passage of the corridor was narrow, what had once been white paint peeling to show scabs of grey stone. Though he hadn't seen any, he could smell dogs. Their stench filled the house.

Going back again past the front room, he glanced in and saw Sharkey still at the table looking back at him without expression.

On the other side of the passage, there was a room about half the size of the one he'd left. It was cold; furniture pushed together, boxes piled on the floor; it was like a storeroom. A pedal sewing-machine in a corner had its cover off but was covered in dust. The car up on blocks outside filled the window so that it took most of the light. As he went back out, he heard a toilet flush.

O'Toomey with his hand at his crotch pulling up his zip came out of a door at the end of the corridor. He watched Meldrum approach.

Softly, leaning close, he whispered, 'Are you army too?'

Meldrum shook his head.

'Are you on your business or his?'

Asked the question, Meldrum didn't find it an easy one to answer. 'I want to know about Laverty's death,' he said.

O'Toomey frowned. 'Are you police? . . .' He looked past Meldrum. The corridor, though, was just as before. 'If I talk about Laverty, what will the big fellow in there make of it?' He weighed the question as if it was part of an argument with himself. Before he started back, he said one last thing, so softly Meldrum read the words in the movement of his lips more than heard them. 'I warn you, he's a dangerous man.'

Sharkey looked up as they came in. 'Was he holding it for you?' he asked.

'I'm thinking that'd be more in your line. I can piss on my own.'

O'Toomey's hand trailing over the arm of the chair was out of sight, so that Meldrum wondered if he was drawing courage from touching the stock of the gun where it stood against the wall.

'The Irish!' Sharkey said with a thin smile. 'Even the stupid ones. A nation of funny men.'

'Oh, I've been stupid. Would you like me to tell him the stupidest thing I ever did?'

'The day you decided to play the patriot game.' So matter-of-fact, Sharkey made it sound more contemptuous.

'For that I had a reason,' O'Toomey said, looking over to Meldrum who had gone back to his previous seat.

He supposed O'Toomey meant his son being shot by British soldiers. You could see that might be a reason. Even if it was an accident.

'It was one of yours shot Eoin,' O'Toomey said.

Meldrum looked at him blankly, not understanding.

'A Scotch gobshite.'

One of mine; what did that mean? He'd read over the years, over the decades now, without particular interest, of soldiers involved in killings in Ulster. And of them being killed. Some of them had been Scots. A country that couldn't find jobs for its young men. Join the army and get off the dole. Once he'd taken part in a search in a desolate housing scheme on the outskirts of Glasgow for an army deserter. On the run, twenty years old, he'd killed a woman in a bungled raid on a post office. They'd pulled him out from under his mammy's bed and dragged him off, screaming for her as he went. One of mine? A farm labourer from Lothian; a miner's son from Ayrshire where the pits had closed. From the Borders. From the Islands.

Out of the window he could see the steady rain falling. Rheumatism country; rain and mist and sodden fields you could squeeze like a sponge. It was strange that men would fight for it or think it worth dying for.

'Don't pay too much attention to Mr O'Toomey,' Sharkey said. 'He's no hero.'

'I had my wife to think of. If she'd lost me as well as the boy, it would have killed her.'

'You made the right decision.' Sharkey winked at Meldrum. 'What good would you have been in prison for twenty years? To her or anybody else?'

He was laughing, making no attempt at concealment, as if to share something. If it was a joke, Meldrum didn't know what it was.

'By Christ, I was some good to you. Listen, mister, you want to know about Laverty? Who do you think got him killed? Oh, not me, you heard the man, I'm no hero. I did what I was told. I didn't have any choice. The Captain there said to me, you don't have any choice. We know about the bomb in Coleraine, he said, you don't have any choice. So I found them for him, those that would do the job. I didn't know they'd kill the man's wife and child as well.'

'Laverty?' Meldrum said. 'You're talking about Laverty?' It was as if he'd taken a blow in the head so that his brain stopped working. He stared stupidly at Sharkey.

'If I lie in the flames of hell for the woman and child, the Captain will too.'

'What about this shithole?' Sharkey asked. 'Don't you think it needs a woman's touch?'

'If I'd never met you, my wife would still be here,' O'Toomey cried.

He wants to get us killed: it was the only clear thought Meldrum had in the confusion. Is he trying to get us killed? Goaded too far, O'Toomey wouldn't even have to reach for the gun to fetch it up. His hand might be touching it. Does he want to get us killed?

And just then Meldrum saw the joke. Two fat cartridges, red plastic and brass, on either side of the Virgin Mary, tucked against her where she stood between unfolded wooden wings. Guardian angels. Sharkey must have unloaded the shotgun while they were out of the room.

'A couple of years ago in London I looked across a street and saw your wife.' Sharkey said. O'Toomey wanted to believe him, Meldrum saw; despite himself, wanted hope. 'Under a lamp near King's Cross. I was in a hurry but I went back to look. A little skirt up to the crack of her arse. Not expensive, short time up against a wall. That's the O'Toomey cunt, I thought. It was only when I got close I saw it was a different whore altogether.'

The gun looked oddly small in O'Toomey's hands. He'd gathered it up and got to his feet in one movement with no sign of effort in getting out of the low chair. He pointed it at Sharkey. After what seemed a long time, he lowered it. Sharkey unbuttoned his Berghaus, one button at a time, not hurrying. O'Toomey watched as if hypnotised. Sharkey brought out a gun from where it must have been holstered under his arm. 'It takes guts to kill somebody,' he said. The big man cried out, not words, a noise like a goaded animal, as he levelled the shotgun

again. He pulled the trigger twice. Metal on metal, a little
sound, once, then again. He stared at the shotgun, dazed, and
then shook it. The little jerk up and down looked to Meldrum
like the shake you would give a broken clock.

'Sit down, you fucking clown,' Sharkey said.

The big man fell back into the chair. He sat with the gun
held across his knees.

'*This* one's loaded. If I pull the trigger, it'll keep going until it
cuts you in half.' He grinned at Meldrum and shook his head.
'Don't try it. The patriot here isn't worth it. I'd take you out
before you got started.'

Meldrum looked at the table. It was so broad, if he stood
and stretched over he would hardly reach to the other side.
He sat back.

'Cowards,' O'Toomey said. His voice was steady but thin, as
if it came from just a spoonful of air at the top of his lungs.
'You shot my son in the back.'

'Who's shooting? Who's talking about shooting? Nobody's
shooting. Nobody's going to shoot anybody. We'll just sit here
and wait till they come.'

Nobody's going to shoot anybody: Meldrum didn't believe him.
Then he took in what else had been said. 'Who?' And when
Sharkey ignored him, he asked O'Toomey, 'Who's coming?' And
getting no answer, raised his voice. 'Who? What's he talking
about? Waiting for who?'

'You've done so well, Jim,' Sharkey said, 'and now you're
shouting. I remember one time in Hong Kong a policeman took
me out for a meal. There was a queue but we walked straight
in. A German couple started complaining – if you were British
in Hong Kong then you were top of the heap. My cop friend
said to me, they'll pay for that. And they did. The Chinese
made them wait for every course. They'd lost face, shouting
like that.'

'I don't know who's coming,' O'Toomey said. He said it
slowly so that it sounded like something he'd just discovered.
Discovered and didn't like and might be frightened by if he let
himself think about it.

'You could guess,' Sharkey mocked him.

'Let me try,' Meldrum said. This time he kept his voice low.

'Would whoever's coming have something to do with what happened to Laverty?'

'"Something to do". You should say what you mean. With killing him, you mean?'

'Is it the army that's coming?' O'Toomey asked.

'You'll have him thinking the army killed Laverty.'

O'Toomey shook his head, bewildered. He said to Meldrum, 'Unit Ten. This man was in Unit Ten. Secret operations. Worse than the bloody SAS. Is it them that's coming?'

'Suppose,' Sharkey said, 'for the sake of argument, the people who're coming are the ones who put the bomb under Laverty's car.' He was very relaxed, with the air of a man enjoying himself. He had put the gun down on the table in front of him. 'Three of them. Wouldn't three of them be right?'

'Do you think I'm a fool entirely?'

When Sharkey contented himself with a nod, Meldrum intervened. 'The men who planted the bomb that killed Laverty, is that what you're saying? They're coming here?'

Sharkey glanced at his watch. 'In one hour fifty minutes. Assuming they're punctual. That's when we were due as well.'

Meldrum tried to think. 'Why would they do that?' Confess? Why would they do that? But if they did and if they would name Clay as part of it – Christ – 'Is Clay one of them? Is he coming?'

'You're getting warm,' Sharkey said. 'You know that game the kids play? Getting warm.'

'You're raving,' O'Toomey burst out. 'You're a fucking lunatic. How could those two be coming here and them dead? You know they're dead. Jamesie and Peter O'Connell died in a ditch. Didn't your lot get rid of them after they planted the bomb? Did you think I didn't know it was you killed them?'

'I'll let you into a secret. The O'Connells were too stupid to trust near a bomb. But *somebody* planted one right enough. *Somebody*'s coming,' Sharkey said. 'You'd better believe it.'

'Their pictures was in the papers. Jamesie with his eyes shot out of his head.' When he sighed, Meldrum thought it was for the dead Jamesie, but O'Toomey was sighing for himself. 'I

always knew my turn would come. I've waited a long time
for this day. You're going to kill me, aren't you?'

'You know what I'm here for,' Sharkey reasoned as if with a
backward child. 'You were told. Nothing to do with killing.'

'No, Captain – I don't know. I don't know why you're here.
Not after so many years. And I don't know why your man's
here. Who the hell is he, what's he after? I don't know – Christ,
tell me what to say to him and I'll tell him, any damned thing
so be you go away and it's done with.'

For more than an hour after that, though, it was Sharkey who
did the talking. It was a strange monologue, wandering from
one thing to another so that it was only gradually Meldrum
saw there was a pattern and what it might be. Strange in
the first place talking at all after being so taciturn on the
journey. Strange talking at the two of them, not looking for a
response; like a night of pub talk, but with everybody edited
out except the one voice. Strangest in what Meldrum gradually
caught under the flat monotonous tone, something that might
be excitement, an edge certainly, anticipation perhaps.

Sharkey on a talking jag while he waited, for whatever he
was waiting for:

'Eddy, my contact, acted as a bodyguard for one of those Loyalist politicians who go on tv to condemn paramilitaries. But
do you think he didn't know Eddy was a brigade commander
in the Ulster Volunteer League? Brigade was a joke, of course,
there never being more than a dozen at any one time of the
fucking idiots. When Eddy was a boy in Lurgan, his family
voted Unionist, but they got nothing by way of thanks, that's
what they were there for, the Protestant working class; now the
town of Lurgan has a swimming-pool – why? Because of the
Troubles. Eddy told me that himself; not that it had stopped
him picking up the gun in the Protestant cause, as he put it.
He was a desperate character, Eddy. Too much even for the
established paramilitaries, him and his friends. Did I say there
were never more than ten or so of them? Brigade, for fuck's
sake! Told Eddy one time there was new evidence that King
Billy was a homo. Pissed him off – and yet the little bastard
took it up the arse himself. Nowt so queer as folk. Nowt so
queer as queer folk.'

'If he's going to kill us,' Meldrum interrupted, saying it to O'Toomey, but not taking his eyes off Sharkey, 'he'll do it now before anybody else comes.' Thinking: he wouldn't want a witness, and if he's going to kill whoever comes as well, all the more reason to get rid of us first. But Sharkey didn't answer, just grinned and looked at his watch. Plenty of time, Meldrum thought, he's telling us – plenty of time.

'Back then, you should appreciate this, most of the Loyalist explosives came out of Scottish pits; they solved that by closing them down. Lived in Scotland, did I tell you that, Jim? Stayed in Edinburgh for a time; used to get letters from America addressed "Edinburgh, England". Makes you laugh. Say one thing for the Irish, they may be thick but they have some pride. Did you know for a bit now respectable money's been coming to the Loyalist paramilitaries? Smart businessmen taking out insurance against at some point down the line there'll be an independent Ulster, the three-county heartland maybe. With RCs forced out or "nullified", nice word that. Reminds me of how Eddy used to talk of the way he'd handle it if the British pulled out: take the hills above Belfast and throw shells into the town, turn the Catholic housing schemes into killing grounds.'

When it happened it happened suddenly. Meldrum listening to Sharkey, hearing every word, while he weighed the chances of making a move, calculations going on as it were in a corner of his mind where he hoped Sharkey wouldn't notice them, not believing there was any real chance, yet knowing he would have to try sooner or later, and not doing any more maybe than waiting for the courage to come from somewhere that would let him go for it.

'Like Sarajevo: it could work: and then all the halfwitted cunts could sit around in the ruins starving to death and singing "The Sash".'

When it happened, it happened suddenly.

'In the town of Dungannon,' Sharkey sang. Meldrum registered he was tone-deaf; so there was something else he knew about the big man. The plotter in the corner of his mind couldn't see how that helped. 'There's many a ruction—'

They came in the door behind Meldrum so suddenly O'Toomey

was startled into jumping up, which from their point of view was a pity. They must have been clear that Sharkey was the danger man, but for a while he'd been sitting with the gun held out of sight under the table. What they saw was O'Toomey lumbering to his feet and the shotgun that he'd caught up off his lap as he rose. Both of them shot him; both maybe in the face, since it gouted blood as he was thrown backwards.

Under the table Meldrum scrambled on all-fours in the direction of the kitchen. O'Toomey's destroyed face went ahead of him. He fought his way past chairs that struck him on the shoulder, bruised against his forearms. Solid wood, like the table above, a board inches thick to give him shelter as he fled. As he flung himself out into the kitchen space, the noise of gunfire struck him like clapped hands across the ears. Crouched, he reached up and pulled at the handle of the door. It didn't move. For ever it didn't move and he understood it was locked. He was going to die. He wrenched at it and the door flew open. On hands and knees he sprawled out. To his left a voice called, 'Eddy?' A man was peering in at the window. He must just have arrived, their timing had gone wrong, hardly time to turn as Meldrum came out of the door beside him crashing it open – 'Eddy?'

The glass of the window shattered as someone fired from inside. Meldrum was on his feet and running. At the sound of screaming he didn't wait to see, but took off as if to a starting pistol. He had seen one man dead. The ground was broken and he mustn't fall. Running for his life, floating, moving so fast and sure-footed across the broken ground. He tried to jump the low stone wall, but it caught his trailing leg, twisted him round and hurled him down on his chest and shoulder. As he lay, he heard the thump of running feet. He didn't have enough time to run again before it would be too late.

He rolled towards the wall and pressed the length of his body against it.

'Meldrum?' Sharkey's voice sounded somewhere to his left. And then it sounded further off as if he had turned away at once. 'It's all right!' And he began to cough, a wet retching. 'Meldrum!' And then quietly and sounding just above him, 'Where are you? I have something here to stick up your arse.'

Meldrum heard his breath go out and realised he had been holding it. That took a time. He waited. As he did, the stones of the wall close against his face changed in colour. He edged his head round until he saw a column of light stretch down to the earth from a parting in the clouds. On his belly, using his elbows, he began to inch along keeping under cover of the wall. Where it stopped, he took a chance and crouched up. Small and discarded at that distance, the body of a man lay under the window. He could see places where it was possible Sharkey might be concealed waiting for him to break cover. When he stood, the calf of his right leg balled in an agony of cramp. Staggering like a drunk, he made it to the shelter of the gable end.

Legs trembling under him, he edged along the wall towards the yard. He had known for an hour or more Sharkey had brought him there to kill him. Him and O'Toomey and whoever came afterwards. That had been the plan. Spoiled because those who came had their own schedule and killing agenda. The noise Sharkey had made coughing, a wet noise like somebody who'd taken a hit in the chest. It was possible all of them, Sharkey, all of them, were dead. That would be good.

Hiding would make better sense than going to look.

He went all the way round until he came to the car up on blocks. A tyre lever had been left on the bonnet. Rust flaked off under his grip when he lifted it. Through the dirty window it was hard to be sure, but the sewing-machine still sat in its corner and nothing in the room looked different.

The door of the house was open. On the frame there was a smear of blood, almost up to his shoulder-height, about where a man as tall as Sharkey might have left it if he'd swayed or leaned for support.

A man's body sprawled out of the door of the front room into the lobby. Trying to run for it, he had been shot in the back.

In the front room the second man had slid down the wall still holding his pistol with both hands. A gunman's grip. Probably it was Sharkey's first shot that took him in the chest, the big target. In that case, the second wound had been inflicted later just to make sure. The day's growth of beard and what was left of his hair was grey. If his name was Eddy, which seemed likely, Meldrum knew some of the things which had gone on in his head before the back of it above his ear was blown off.

O'Toomey's fall had tipped the chair and he lay back watching the ceiling out of what was left of where his face had been. The shotgun lay by the opposite wall as if he had thrown it there. Meldrum stretched across him for the cartridges, one from either side of the Virgin. He searched the house, all the way along the corridor expecting death in ambush.

When he stepped out of the back door, he was at the end of his tether.

It was a small noise like the suck of an open wound. It was only providence that stopped him from pulling the trigger of the shotgun, but he looked in time and saw the third man still dying with his arm outstretched as he clutched and released and clenched on a handful of the wet soil of Armagh.

BOOK SIX

Man in the White Hat

CHAPTER THIRTY-FOUR

T he phone was ringing, but Harriet hadn't felt able to answer, not right then with John Brennan making noises familiarity told her meant he was coming to a climax. She couldn't believe how heavy he was. He didn't ease any of his weight. All of it pressed down on her. It must be she'd forgotten how their lovemaking had been. The other possibility was that then the selfish burden of him had been part of her excitement. Carry me, his body had said to her, carry me like the animal you are. Smothering, fighting for breath, being ripped apart. Fighting for her life, it had seemed. And losing and dying as her body spasmed into oblivion.

Now she smelled the staleness of his sweat and his weight was a discomfort to be negotiated. He rolled off her with a groan and lay on his back. After a moment, he put a forearm over his eyes. The bush of white hair that was normally swept back stood on end and she saw the pink of his scalp shining through.

'No rest for the wicked,' he said. 'I'll have to go.'

But his voice was a throaty murmur and she knew that next he would sleep, a deep sleep that would last for no more than quarter of an hour. Then he would go. Up and dressed and gone, with not a hair out of place.

She got out of bed and he didn't stir, already asleep. The phone by the bed had stopped after four rings; the answerphone in the front room must still be on from when she had left for work that morning.

'Harriet? You're not there? This is Jim . . . Jim Meldrum. I'm at the airport. I wanted to – I'll try again later. I wanted to tell you what happened. I wanted to talk to you . . .' There was a silence, as if he was thinking of what else he might say, or couldn't bring himself to put the phone down.

The message ended there. She stood for a time by the desk. A draught searching the corners of the long room chilled her bare feet. From the bedroom she could hear the drumming of the shower. She was cured of John Brennan, but she didn't feel exorcised.

She felt unclean.

When he had paused and then given his full name, Jim Meldrum, as if she might have forgotten him, her eyes had filled with tears. She knew the griefs of lust, and that it wasn't to be mistaken for love. If love laid you more open to hurt, as it must, she had resolved that she would be armoured to deny it.

It had never occurred to her to take thought against the everyday unexpectedness of affection.

Meldrum put the phone down. There was too much to tell. Coming down from O'Toomey's farm in a cold rain watching for Sharkey, who must need to add him to the toll of the dead. Going by every dyke and scraggy tree with the expectation of a bullet.

When he had got down to the layby, the car was gone. Half a dozen cars sped by ignoring him before he realised he was still clutching the shotgun. He hid it in a hedge and the next car stopped for him.

In the first town he had searched out the police station. What else could he have done? He was a policeman after all.

They had given him a lot of grief, three days of it. Things had got better when a grizzled fifty-year-old called Campbell arrived from Belfast to take charge. 'Your man Ord puts in a good word for you. But, Christ, we both agreed that knock on the head's addled you,' he told him at last. 'And don't think you're out of the woods, not by a long shot. There could be charges. You've put your whole career at risk. Pension and fucking all!'

Which was fair comment.

They'd put him on the plane, and he'd expected to be faced by a reception committee of his own colleagues at the other end. When there wasn't, he'd decided sourly that they'd taken it for granted he'd trot along and turn himself in.

Now, putting the phone down, through the glass he saw Ord and another two hurry past. Maybe they'd got the plane wrong. For some reason the Irish didn't share with him, they'd flown him out on a Macair flight from Derry. He pushed at the door to call after Ord, then let it swing shut.

It wasn't his fault they were late. With his back turned, he wouldn't have seen them. Wouldn't even have known they were there.

He walked to the big swing-doors at the main entrance. He didn't hurry and paused for a moment, looking at displays of books and tourist bait carried round behind the glass of the dividers with each swing of the doors. By doing that, he felt he had given Ord his chance. Outside, the sky had cleared and he stood feeling the warmth of the sun. He went over to the first taxi and gave Worth's address.

As on his previous visit to Brian Worth, rows of cars were lined up in the court at the front of the flats. Half past two in the afternoon; did no one go to work any more? This time the door at the entrance was locked. He rang Worth's entryphone, waited, rang again. Glass door, he could kick it in. There was no way he would, even the thought took him by surprise, but he wanted to, having had the idea he wanted to so badly he could feel the juddering smash of it done.

Leaning close, he watched a woman crossing the hall. She couldn't not have seen the dark shape of him against the light, but she came on without breaking stride and opened the door. A well-dressed woman in her fifties, maybe she was hurrying to visit her sick mother; maybe she was a serious shopper.

The hall still needed a coat of paint. He took the wide stairs up from it two steps at a time, but on the first landing none of the doors was the one he wanted. Memory played odd tricks. He took the next flight more slowly, and found Worth's flat opposite the lift on the second floor.

After the entryphone there wasn't any reason to expect Worth to be in, but he tried anyway. The question then was what to do. There were two locks, and the tricks he'd picked up over the years didn't run to opening ones that good, not without tools. And even if he was able to . . . That felt too much like being on the wrong side of the law. He sat on the top step and thought about the difficulties of being a policeman. Rain ran down the long narrow panes of the half-landing window.

He took the lift back down and when the doors parted to let him out, the first thing he was conscious of was a heavy sweetness, blown roses drooped in a vase; then of men crowding towards him.

Big men, the shoulders of their coats dull with rain, they filled the lift.

'At least you didn't try to break in. I wasn't even sure of that any more.' They were the first words Ord had said to him. He opened the door with a key and Meldrum responded to his nod by going into the flat. He heard the door close and looking round saw that the other two had been shut out.

The room struck him in the same way it had before, long and full of light. Ord, though, as he picked his way among Worth's piles of books, was shaking his head in distaste. Didn't even know he was doing it, Meldrum thought, things had to be tidy for him. Ord lifted away a soiled plate, holding it fastidiously by the edge, and lowered his bulk into the leather chair.

'Tell me about it,' he said.

'I told them across the water. If you've talked to Campbell, you know it all. I didn't keep anything back.'

'I wouldn't expect you to.'

They looked at one another in silence. Meldrum went over to the door in the corner and pushed it back to see inside. A room in line with the living room so that it had the same extraordinary brilliance of light from the run of huge windows on the facade. The single bed was made, a plain cover drawn tight with the precision of a hospital ward. The whole effect was spartan, not much furniture and nothing lying about. A wall of door-length mirrors, some slid back to show shirts or a single suit on a rail. At a guess all the wardrobes would be half empty; so much space, designed for a couple. Or for someone vainer than Worth.

He turned back to Ord.

'You had a key to get in here.'

'So I did.' He leaned back, and like that looked just as aggressive as he seemed sat forward, hands braced on knees.

'Sharkey didn't take me to Ireland to meet anybody. He took me there to kill me. Me, O'Toomey, Eddy Patterson. All together. Nice and tidy. Dispose of the bodies, too – I can't be certain of that, but I think so. If things had gone to plan, it would have made sense. Suppose O'Toomey had been killed with his own shotgun – a guy with a son dead, wife run off, it would be suicide, no problem. The rest of us, graves in the hills. They'd have buried the past with us.'

'They?'

Before he could say he didn't know, confirm his ignorance, there was a knocking at the door. Not too loud, not too long, and when Ord went to answer it the voice talking to him sounded deferential enough though he couldn't make out what was being said. He hadn't any difficulty, though, making out Ord's response, every word of it, 'fucks' and all.

'Cunts,' he said. He sat in the chair, easing himself back with a grimace. 'What they? You said Sharkey was on his own.'

But the interruption had given Meldrum time to think. He asked, 'What about Worth? Has something happened to him?'

There was something familiar about the way Ord studied him. Then Meldrum remembered – I ask the questions, you're here for the answers; in the interview room; to a suspect.

At last Ord said, 'Fuck knows. He wasn't here when we came looking for him after the Irish guy Campbell passed on your story. He hasn't been here since. We're keeping an eye on the place waiting for him to come back.'

'He won't.'

'That right?'

'Something went wrong at the farmhouse. Sharkey thought Eddy Patterson was going to turn up like a lamb to the slaughter. Walk in and get his head blown off. But it didn't happen that way. Maybe he'd been warned. Or maybe, this is what I think, he was the one who'd been given the real killing job. It was Sharkey who was supposed to die with O'Toomey and me. If Sharkey hasn't bled to death somewhere, he's going to be an angry man wanting some questions answered.'

'He's not the only one.'

'I think it goes back to Laverty.'

'The Yank who got himself blown up donkey's years ago—'

'And his wife. And his wee girl.'

'Sad. Campbell told me you went on about that. He doesn't reckon much to it. Didn't he tell you this fellow Eddy Patterson was a small-time crook? Not a terrorist. Nothing to do with bombs.'

'No. That's not exactly the way I heard it, Billy. Patterson and the two with him had been in prison. Not political, on their own account—'

'What I said.'

'But he was inside for drug deals and extortion. Getting me to talk, meant Campbell did some talking too – you know how it works. You couldn't do that stuff, not in the last twenty years, not without paramilitary connections.'

'He was a Protestant. The IRA killed Laverty.'

'. . . Patterson came in shooting.' Meldrum felt sick. The headache had settled at the back of his skull. 'It's just luck Sharkey isn't dead meat. He knows he was set up. I think Worth's hiding from him.'

'And I think maybe Worth's away visiting his granny,' Ord said. He got to his feet. 'Now we'll go in for the official chat. All I can tell you is, the less you say the better. Facts okay, take my advice, keep your theories to yourself. You're suspended anyway, you know that? Special Branch is going to take you apart. Go on about Captain this and Captain Sharkey that and they might decide you think the fucking navy's after you. You could finish up in a straitjacket bouncing off rubber walls.'

There was nobody on the landing. It had been Meldrum's impression that Ord's subordinates had been told to wait, but he must have been wrong about that for there was no one in the car. Ord nodded him into the front passenger seat.

The sky had cleared and as they came down through Canonmills he glimpsed the nudes outside the Standard Life building warming their bronze rears in a blink of sunshine. Ord turned the wheel, checking to his right and saying something Meldrum missed.

'What?'

'I said Malcolm's named the day.' Malcolm? 'This girl he
met in London. Nice girl. Her father was a judge, retired now.
Malcolm's done well. He's a hard worker, like his father.'
Meldrum had a sudden image of a boy, eight or so, square-
faced, solid, like his father. 'Only he's working with stocks
and shares and all that shit. More brains than I ever had.'

'Wedding in London?'

'No! Her family came up here when the father retired. He
was a judge.'

'Aye, so you said.' Meldrum hid his amusement at Ord letting
his guard down. A bit of vanity; why not? The boy had done
him proud.

Ord said, watching the road ahead, 'You know the only thing
that matters to me now? My sons thinking well of me.' Getting
out of the world undisgraced. 'You're invited, remember.'

'Is that a good idea? Don't get me wrong, I appreciate it. What
about the brass? You sure you want them to see me there?'

'Fuck them,' Ord said. 'I don't take back invitations.'

They sat each busy with his own thoughts until the car
pulled into the reserved parking behind police headquarters.

'From here it's out of my hands.'

'I know that.'

Now they were there, Meldrum just wanted to get on with
it, but Ord sat on, rubbing the wheel between his fingers.

'Tell you something I thought about all the time on the plane
coming home,' Meldrum said. 'What if Sharkey and Clay are
the same man?'

'Christ, you never give up! Why?'

'Because lying behind that wall waiting to die, I knew I was
hearing the same man who'd jammed his gun up Worth's arse.
I knew because I could taste the fear, Billy.'

Poof. Try that on a court.

As soon as he'd spoken, he could imagine the big man's
response.

But showing no reaction at all, neither disgust nor disbelief,
Ord got out and headed for the entrance without a backward
glance.

But then he didn't have to look back to know Meldrum
would be following.

CHAPTER THIRTY-FIVE

Three mornings running they sent a car for him, and then it was the weekend. Meldrum would have preferred to drive in himself, that way he would have had the car to get home when they were finished with him. Car in the morning, nothing at night. When they finished with him each day, he was on his own. Clearly, if anybody's time was going to be wasted it wouldn't be theirs. The questioning went on, even during coffee and the occasional sandwich, going over the same ground until on the afternoon of the third day he floated above it all, looked down on himself and his interrogators and heard his answers. They didn't make sense. And then at night, waiting for a bus, looking for a taxi. It would have made a difference if he'd been allowed to drive himself in; give him a time to come in for questioning, he'd have been there and punctually; no risk of him not turning up. He wasn't stupid enough, though, to suggest it and give them the chance to shake their heads at one another in disbelief. There was no love lost between his kind of policeman and Special Branch. Local or from London, made no difference. He'd even glimpsed them gathered to the corners of occasions televised from Moscow or Washington, men with the same hallmark look, nothing so individual as arrogance, just a hard blankness.

He wakened without opening his eyes, crouched in the bed's warmth, thoughts like those churning, hands pressed between his thighs. The clock in the living-room chimed, but he started counting too late to be certain whether it stopped at nine or ten. It could have been eleven. He rubbed his tongue along the dry staleness at the back of his teeth and thought about the word 'home'. Somewhere he'd read that French didn't have an equivalent, which had been taken as proof of how rotten Frenchmen were in contrast to the good-hearted Saxons. Self-congratulatory shite. German was probably stuffed full of synonyms for home, dozens of them. Glad to be home. Odd. What would it usually be, anyway? Glad to be back, was what he'd say to himself. Get in at night, shut the door on a bad day: I'm glad to be back. The thoughts that went through your head.

The door-bell rang, jerking him upright like a shot of electricity, straight up in bed with his eyes open.

He pulled on a pair of trousers and went to the door barefoot. It's Saturday, you bastards, he was ready to tell them, but squinting at the figure bulky against the light, complained instead, 'I don't need a lawyer.'

'That's not what I hear,' John Brennan said. 'Are you going to ask me in?'

'What for?' And for a daft moment, he actually wondered if Brennan could be in trouble and needing *his* help.

'So I can take the weight off my feet while you make yourself decent. That dark suit you come to court to give evidence in would do.' He checked his watch. 'We don't have for ever. Farquhar said he'd be out of the place by twelve.'

'Farquhar?'

'Farquhar Wood. He'll see you, but only if you're there by twelve. He can't wait. A busy man.'

'Wait? Wait where?'

'The Scottish Office. Farquhar Wood, Secretary of State,' Brennan said as he marched in on the expectation the other would step aside, matching Meldrum's impatience with a touch of his own at having to explain the obvious.

And for a while Meldrum didn't ask any more, wanting to think about it, going into the bedroom and getting dressed, putting on the dark suit, sitting on the edge of the bed to put on his shoes, and with one on and the other in his hand staring into the mirror in what his mother would have called a dwam, a waking dream that had no thought in it at all or none

to remember when you wakened out of it with a tremor as if
time had stopped and started again.

When he came into the living-room, Brennan said, 'Fine.
Let's get on our way.'

'No,' Meldrum said. 'Not till I know what this is about.'

'We'll talk in the car.' And when Meldrum shook his head,
'To hell, man. You've put the suit on. What makes you think
you don't intend to go?'

At six foot plus, Meldrum tried to avoid back seats; but then
he didn't often travel in a Mercedes. There was no lack of
leg-room.

John Brennan filled his side comfortably; a big car for a
big man. He said, 'Don't misunderstand. Whether you need
a lawyer or not, it's not going to be me. I'm not about to ask
you any questions. I'm not going into things with you. And I
certainly won't be there when you talk to Farquhar. It's between
you and him.'

Meldrum studied the back of the driver's neck, thick red
flesh with the shirt collar loose round it in the way of wrestlers
or weight-lifters. Muscle built in a prison gym and ears like
snails tucked on either side.

'Why should Farquhar Wood see me?'

'What?'

He said it again, a little louder.

'Call it the old pals' act.'

'Because you asked him to?'

'Because I asked him to.'

'Why would you do that?'

Brennan looked at him out of the corner of his eye. 'A friend
of yours thought it would be a good idea. And I went along
with that since she was a friend of mine.' He broke off as the
car jerked to a halt.

'Sorry,' the driver grunted.

'World's full of clowns,' Brennan said.

A couple had jaywalked in front of the car. Meldrum watched
them edge through the traffic and go down into the Gardens
under a banner snapping above the gate. The same wind would
be tugging flags straight out from poles the length of Princes
Street and, high above, pressing the Castle's flag against the

sky. A wind blown off the dark open waters of the Forth. On the congested pavement, shoppers leaned into it. He imagined how on the other side of the glass the salt cold of it would burn against his skin.

'Do you see that?'

'Sorry?'

'The Academy. That great stone monument of a place with its columns and halls of paintings. Do you know it floats on a raft of wood? They had to build it like that because of the soil. Can you imagine trying to tell the youngsters, Get your arse off the steps, there's too much weight on the raft? Or warning the buskers, Look out, the Academy's sinking?'

And by the time Brennan had finished with that and had his laugh over it, a high chuckling that came out oddly from the size of him, they'd left Princes Street behind. They passed the High School building promised to house a Scottish Parliament in 1979, and the vigil of protest kept outside since the promise had been broken. The Scottish Office stood almost opposite.

On a Saturday morning, its long corridors had an empty feeling. Their escort from the reception area knocked, and as they went in, the Secretary of State got up from behind his desk. He held out his hand to Brennan who clasped it in both of his own before introducing Meldrum and in the same breath declaring that he would take himself off. He shook his head when told there was no reason why he shouldn't stay. On a note of apology, the Secretary said that in any case he only had twenty minutes to give, since something had come up and he had another appointment at the half-hour. All the same, Brennan thought it would be better if they talked without him, and with a nod to Meldrum and after a familiar pressure on the arm from the Secretary, turned on his heel and was gone.

Farquhar Wood sat down again and gestured to the seat opposite. Some leather chairs round a low table by the window looked pleasantly informal, but maybe he felt better behind his desk. They looked at one another across it until Meldrum began to worry how many of the twenty minutes were left. Behind the desk, the Secretary looked taller; he must be one of those men whose shortness comes, from their legs. He was a hard-working team player, noted for his unswerving

loyalty to the Prime Minister. There had been criticism of
him a few years back. He'd sold a hospital or college or
some other chunk of the public good to private enterprise
at a bargain price. As an ex-journalist he was popular with
the media; he did a good sound bite. Anyway, it hadn't been
much of a scandal; accusations of incompetence or ideology,
not a murmur about bribery. Thick dark hair, fleshy beak of
nose, head slightly too large for his body: he might have been
designed for television.

'You must be wondering why I agreed to see you,' he said.

'I'm grateful you did.'

Reading upside-down, Meldrum saw the form laid at the
side of the desk was a 'SPEAKING NOTE FOR USE OF THE
MINISTER' at the launch of a road safety campaign. He'd
seen similar NOTES as part of the guidance from the Scottish
Office to make sure some good-cause photo-opportunity went
off smoothly. Non-secure: unclassified: so they came by telex.
'Mr Jackson, Councillors, Ladies and Gentlemen. I am most
grateful to Mr Jackson for his kind introduction; and to both
the Director of Planning and—' Every word of it spelled out
by some bright boy who must have been pleased when his First
got him into the Civil Service.

Maybe that's what Farquhar Wood was missing: his Speaking Note.

'John Brennan's been a good friend to the Party. He's a
constituent of mine, you know.' He fiddled with a pen from
a set that stood on the corner of the desk. 'It's a small world.
Anyway, a small country. Norman Buchan's argument against
Home Rule used to be that Scotland was so small he met
everybody who mattered on the Monday morning plane to
London. The Man on the Monday Morning Plane. That would
make a nice little folk song, I told him.' He put the pen back in
its holder, aligning it carefully before sliding it back into place.
'I doubt if I can do anything for you. I'm not sure it would even
be . . . appropriate for me to try. But I told John I was willing
to listen.'

The problem was what to tell him. There was a patch of blue
sky with a cloud edging across it. Sunshine, and ten minutes
later it could be raining. He tried to pull his thoughts together.

'I went to Ireland – looking for information . . . But things went wrong . . .'.

'I know what happened. Well, something of it, enough. Can we begin before that? Why go in the first place?'

'I was pursuing a line of enquiry.' That had a comfortingly familiar ring. By his sceptical look, it didn't impress Farquhar Wood. 'I was approached with information about a murder. It involved a man called Hugh Keaney, he was given a life sentence.' Did Farquhar Wood recognise the name? He'd been the latest in a line of Secretaries of State to turn Keaney down for parole. The rule was no parole without repentance; and how could you be repentant if you claimed to be innocent? A busy man, of course, lots of decisions to be made; he gave no sign. 'I believe it's just possible there's been a miscarriage of justice.'

'What business would that be of yours?' There wasn't any easy answer to that. Some notion of right and wrong? Something about living with yourself, something about being honest, the duty of an honest man? He couldn't hear himself saying any of that stuff out loud. 'I don't mean that we shouldn't be concerned about justice. Of course not. I can say frankly *I* care about justice.' Leave rhetoric to the politicians. 'What I'm asking is why should you more than anyone else be concerned about Keaney? Were you involved with the case?'

Sharp questions, not at all rhetorical, cutting to the point. It didn't do to underestimate anyone.

'I was, then I was pulled off it—'

'Why?'

'It happens. I was put on to something else.'

'Is that usual? Did you resent it?'

'I was put on to another murder case. No, I didn't resent that.'

Farquhar Wood let the answers hang in the air, so that they could both consider them. No, it wasn't usual. Yes, he'd resented it.

'And then after so many years . . .' Farquhar Wood allowed himself to be puzzled.

'Hugh Keaney didn't let anyone forget him.'

'Climbing out on to roofs in the winter, you mean?'

'He's always claimed to be innocent.'

'Aren't our prisons full of men doing that? It's just that every so often someone like Keaney comes along with a gift for catching the newspapers' attention.'

'He's on hunger strike now.'

'Exactly. I mean, are we at cross-purposes here? I thought you wanted to get back to normal. It was my understanding that you wanted to find a way of putting all this behind you.'

'I do.'

'That's not quite what I'm hearing.'

It seemed like a moment of choice, and what Meldrum felt was panic. The implicit reproof, the sense of being judged, of an authority with power over him, the father, the head teacher, the superior officer: he longed for the reassuring certainty of obedience; and in the very moment of wanting it felt something harden in him, unwilled, unwelcome, opposed.

He said, 'They wouldn't let me in to see Keaney at Peterhead. If I could talk to him, it would help. Could you arrange that?'

And perhaps what he had in mind was that if he could do that, take one more look at Keaney, he might find some way of persuading himself it would be best to leave the man to his fate. Perhaps he had that somewhere in mind. God knows, he wanted to get back to where he'd been before all this started. There might have been something Farquhar Wood could have found to say which would have made that possible.

Perhaps.

'No.' The Secretary stood up. 'In your present situation, even to suggest that— No, I couldn't.'

He walked Meldrum to the door.

'It wouldn't be right just to let it go,' Meldrum said.

'Glad we had a chance to talk. There aren't enough hours in the day, I'm afraid.' He smiled, unruffled, as if some automatic pilot had been reset to blandness.

'It goes back to an American diplomat who was killed in Dublin. There should be an enquiry—'

Farquhar Wood reached out, but not to shake hands. Instead, he grasped Meldrum by the upper forearm.

'I believe your daughter and her friend had difficulties with the police. That demonstration at the prize-giving. I took an interest – having been there. I don't know the rights and wrongs of it, but I can understand you might have been angry. Any father would be. That kind of thing can put you off the rails for a bit.'

The odd thing was that the grip on Meldrum's arm wasn't felt as threatening but friendly; it was the same gesture Wood had used to send off Brennan. It belonged to a man with the habit of wanting to be liked, so that apart from the words, lurking under them was an unforced impression of something human and even benign.

CHAPTER THIRTY-SIX

After his phone call from the airport Harriet expected to hear from Jim Meldrum again that day, but didn't. The following day was Wednesday and she hurried home and waited. She thought of calling him. Nothing easier. He had called her after all, so that she knew he wanted to talk to her. All she had to do was to pick up the phone. She sat beside it waiting. It would be better if it rang. The simple spontaneous gesture of getting in touch with him was beyond her. If he had been a friend in trouble, who had come back from a journey full of risk, she would have lifted the phone. What happened? Is something wrong? Are you all right? With friends, you knew about them, about parents, school, what made them lose their temper, you shared a history. She had been to bed with him, she thought about him all the time, but she didn't know him like that. By the Friday as the evening dragged on, she wanted to ask him, the first thing she wanted to ask him was, Why didn't you phone? . . . Why didn't you come? The more time passed, the harder even to imagine touching the phone. When it was impossible, she went to bed. It had got to be late and she spilled her last drink and lay down without undressing.

And after all that, when he did appear the next day it all went wrong.

Meldrum had gone straight from the Scottish Office to the rank in Waverley Station through the busy Saturday morning crowds and got a taxi to Harriet's flat.

And they had quarrelled and afterwards he walked the streets blinded by more misery than he had ever expected to feel again over a woman.

It had been late afternoon, then, before he opened his own door and found behind it the note from Carole with the ticket enclosed. It was totally unexpected. The note didn't explain anything: just asked him to phone her.

When he did, there was no answer.

His room seemed uninhabited or as if a stranger might live there. He heard the silence and watched dust settle through a shaft of sunlight; put the ticket in his pocket and went out again.

He put the car in the park beside the McEwan Hall and cut through to Nicolson Street. This would be his first visit to the Festival Theatre, but nearby was the Italian restaurant where he used to take Carole before a film at the Odeon. He chased spaghetti bolognese round a bowl and drank coffee till it was time.

The bar space to the right was crowded, but as soon as he came up the steps on to the first floor at the Festival Theatre he saw her. Sitting at a table by the glass wall, Carole had all the lit street behind her as a backdrop. As he watched, she turned her head as if someone had called her by name. Once, at the corner of a street, not long after they had met, before they were married, she had made just that gesture of turning to him. Flustered by being late, hurrying to join her, he broke step among the crowd for it was the moment when he fell in love. In the bar of the theatre, walking towards her, he could not have found a difference between that smile from the twenty-year-old girl and the one she gave him now.

'I'm so pleased you came,' she said.

'I only got your note a couple of hours ago. I've been out of the house all day.'

'I wondered. I kept phoning. You don't even have an answering-machine!'

What was so urgent? He found he was smiling at her; nothing more natural with someone known so long, they had made a child together, married, flesh of my flesh. There had been a time when there had been no shadow, nothing hidden

between them. There had been no reserve or calculation in
his talk with her, and one Sunday morning in bed with the
breakfast tray balanced between them, chatting out of a lazy
content, it had ended when she turned away from him and
said, You're waiting for the phone to ring about some bloody
case. An unfair thing to say, a stupid thing, though he didn't
get angry until she said, Don't worry, somebody'll get killed
somewhere. After that, the bad times had begun.

Sitting opposite her, he was disoriented. That turn of her
head had blurred past and present for him. That smile when
she saw him; her face had lit up. What was so urgent? He
didn't ask. Until he asked her, anything was possible.

'Sorry, would you like a drink? Can I get you something?'

'They're coming,' and this time, together with her stress on
the pronoun, the energy of her smile puzzled him. What's
so wonderful about these drinks? That foolishness popped
into his mind and then the obvious question, Who's bringing
them?

He saw his daughter, fists curled round glasses, making her
way to them. 'Betty's here?'

Disappointment took him by surprise, but Carole grinned
and cried, 'Of course, that's the *whole point*!'

'Dad,' Betty greeted him. 'Our treat, what would you like?'

And as she spoke she was setting not two but three glasses
on the table. As if she'd read his mind, which happened with
his daughter, she pushed the glass of beer past him to the empty
place. 'Lager – I know you wouldn't want that.'

He didn't recognise the gangling boy, self-conscious in a
white linen jacket and a tunic shirt without a tie until Betty
called his name.

'Sandy!'

It was the scarring he recognised; not so obvious as it had
been, but for the rest of his life cold weather would bring it
up as a brand seared around the curve of the nostril.

Sandy Torrance.

From what was being said, it seemed he'd arrived with them
but had to go to the loo; and Meldrum was feeling irritation
at the lack of courtesy that had left the two women to make
their own way – and Betty to buy the drinks – when he

took it in he was being told his daughter was engaged to be
married.

'This is a celebration,' Carole said. 'It would've been nice if
Sandy's parents could've been here. Thurso's a bit far away
for an overnight, but we're hoping to see them soon. I didn't
say in my note to you. I wanted it to be a surprise.'

'Are you glad for me?' Betty asked.

And the boy must have said something too, but afterwards,
going over it, for the life of him all Meldrum could recall was
his own moment of hesitation before he took the hand held out
to him and the dry papery feel of it in the clench of his fist.

There was an interval that passed in the business of getting
drinks and talking about the show. It was a variety programme,
singers, dancers, comedians, arranged in a format television
had killed off two generations earlier. Camped-up nostalgia
so long out of fashion it came over as a novelty. Towards the
end of the second half, the compere, an ebullient man with
a moustache, took the audience through 'Shout' on a giant
songsheet lowered from the flies; they sang it, did it again better
and all together, did it stalls against the cheap seats upstairs.
Distracted, he opened and closed his mouth on broken words.
To add to the fun, they sang while snapping fingers, while
clapping, while doing both alternately. All round him people
snapsnapsnapped clapclapclapped snapclapsnapped. Off the
beat, out of step, finally defeated he sat waving his hands in
tiny circles.

They walked back to the car-park together. Carole took Betty
and Sandy Torrance and he followed in his own car.

At the house the young couple went into the kitchen to make
supper. The boy seemed at home; that must have happened
very quickly, perhaps he had a gift for that kind of thing.
Meldrum, who had known this house for years, felt like a
stranger.

Carole and he were left looking at one another from either
side of the hearth; the proud parents. 'I don't understand,' he
said. 'I thought she'd fallen out with him because he dropped
the police assault charge.'

For answer, she fetched a Sunday newspaper from where it
had been tucked into the bookcase. The piece built a shaky

tower of allegations against half the Forces in the country on the narrow base of a judge's criticisms of the Glasgow police in a recent trial. It spread across two pages and among the photographs clustered round the fold was one of Sandy Torrance.

Bad enough, but then, bottom of one column top of another, Betty's name together with quotations which made him wince. Among the four names on the by-line he recognised that of Kaye Short, fifty-plus, an old pro, good enough to get him on occasion to say more than he'd intended. She must have had a hint from somewhere and chased it up to fatten out the piece.

Had she spoken to Harriet? If so, there was no mention of it: Harriet would have known how to handle her. Not so Betty and the boy; baits, hooks, a delicate touch on the line, she must have played them like fish.

'How could they have been such bloody fools!'

All smiles, they came out of the kitchen with trays just in time to catch that outburst. He never did get supper.

At one point in the altercation, it occurred to him that whatever else she might be, for Betty and Sandy Torrance, yes, and to Carole's delight, the hard-bitten Kaye Short had also and most importantly played the improbable role of Cupid.

At another point, the phone had rung. Carole went upstairs to take it: 'I'll only be a minute.' The silence as they waited sang like a stretched fiddle note. At last, breaking it, Betty said, 'That'll be Phil. Mum's friend. He's an advisor with the Education Department.'

Am I supposed to be impressed, Meldrum might have asked, but didn't.

They'd all said too much already.

'Why would John Brennan do that kind of favour for me?'

It was only when Meldrum asked the question that Harriet understood it had been waiting between them from the moment he arrived at the door of her flat. As soon as it came, though, she knew she had been expecting it. How could it not be there? Why shouldn't he suspect the worst of her? And now it had come she was on his side in despising her. Of course she was.

'I asked him to,' she said.

'And he went off to Farquhar Wood because you asked him?' She tried to find something to stop this before it would be too late. 'Was that before or after you climbed out of his bed?' Her business was advocacy, and she couldn't find the words. Goaded by her silence, he cried, 'Are you telling me you were drunk?'

'If you like.'

'For Christ's sake, don't try and tell me you did it for me.'

'I wouldn't.' She meant that she had too much pride to tell him that.

'Anyway, he must have had some other reason. It's not as if you were a novelty. It's not as if it was the great love affair.'

'I wish you'd get out of here,' she said. 'Now. Please.'

Did you ever think you might not have good taste in men? Somebody had asked her that, or she'd asked somebody, and not long ago. It was a question women put to one another.

He couldn't despise her more than she despised herself. She didn't want to think about it any more or go through such misery again.

After their quarrel, she wanted to be done with him.

CHAPTER THIRTY-SEVEN

It broke up and was gone before he could take hold of it. All he had left was that there had been a town, or a village, anyway streets and houses, and people in a meeting hall who were told, 'This isn't being done for you.' They would have the mess or danger; that was their role. 'This isn't being done for you.' Obey, keep your mouth shut, you don't matter. Nothing to ring the bells about there. But the bells were ringing; church bells – he saw the heavy swing of them to and fro in grey stone towers. A call to rebellion? In a swimming-pool a man was being led along the edge by men in black uniforms, hands drawn up behind his back. Boot-heels beat on tiles, drums echoing under the wavering sea-green roof. He opened his eyes and willed a defiance of church bells until the bells turned into the ringing of the phone by his bed. Hours still before light and the streets of the little town were as real to him for a time as anything else that might belong to the dark.

The voice whispered, 'Sorry.'

He thought it was Harriet and said 'Don't be. It's my fault.'

'You could have been killed. When I heard, I was sick. Physically sick.'

'Worth? Is that you?'

'They made me. I never even met the man.'

'What man?'

'Where I took you. When we went to Glasgow.'

'Sharkey – you mean Sharkey?'

'Was that his name? They didn't tell me.'

'The one he gave me. But I've wondered if he could have been the man you told me about, the one called Clay.'

He said Worth's name several times but the phone had been put down.

Who are *they*? he thought, that's what I should have asked.

He switched on the lamp and hit 1471 to get the number from which the call had been made. It was a service which let anyone play detective: except for the facility which existed to put in a code before calling to bar a 1471 enquiry. He doubted if Worth would have been thinking clearly enough to do that, and sure enough in a moment the voice of a robot woman gave him the number which had been stored. He scribbled it on the pad and looked at it as he dialled.

No answer: he let the ringing go on and on until an image came to him of Worth staring at a phone that had exploded into life. Sweat and the sour smell of fear. At that he gave up and switched off the lamp.

He opened his eyes. Full of unease, he looked at the grey light across the ceiling. Morning and people would be going to work. Perhaps that was why he felt bad. If you had no work, you lay in bed and let the day drift by. Work was who he was and they were keeping him from that. Something was wrong, he felt something had gone wrong, already he was too late.

A turn of his head let him see the bedside table.

The pad was by the phone, for messages, notes; a policeman, you were often called during the night.

After a time, he lifted it and angled it so he could see.

He rang the number before he got out of bed, and again after he had dressed, and once more when he was ready to leave. Then he made one more call and risked using his police identification to get the address for that phone number. He recognised the name of the village. Not far outside the city, a dozen houses one side of the road, hills on the other, blink and you'd miss it.

He passed the ski park at Fairmilehead, lines of matting marking the hill like dried wound scabs. At the junction he swung south; just before seven on a fine morning. The road rose steeply and below him the Lothians spread flat as a table top off to a blue haze of distant hills. He remembered on the Margaret Hannah murder the journey back to Edinburgh after being taken to see Sir James. Because he'd found the pawn ticket that proved whoever killed Mrs Hannah it couldn't have been William Hawthorne. The dry grip of the old aristocrat's hand, skull-head, bloodless gash of lips; the fury of Baird the local politician; and Ord later laughing at him, You've upset the country cousins. What made me think of that, he wondered, switching off the radio in mid-keening of a Country-and-Western song. Hard times and unlucky lovers; poor white trash blues. Would it have suited them all better if he'd let an innocent man be sent to prison? Perhaps innocence or guilt mattered less than having someone to punish, as if punishment was the point of it all, the thing in itself that would let them draw a double line, be done with it, make their peace with the worst that might happen.

Down into the dip by the Flotterstone Inn, then climbing again, one long haul after another until he began to look for Carnethy. The top of the highest hill in the range was clouded in mist. Often after two or three warm still days, the haar off the Forth estuary would shrug itself like a blanket over the shoulder of the Pentlands. As he watched, it rolled down and covered the road ahead. It came without any warning change of weather, so that he ran out of the sun to be sealed in whiteness.

He put on the screen-washer. The blades wiped back and forward. He almost missed the village's name set on a narrow sign. Next moment he glimpsed a fence and sensed rather than saw the bulk of a house at the end of a garden. There was a strip of pavement and he bumped two wheels up on to it and stopped.

The air touched cold, all the warmth wrung out of it by the haar. His lips imagined the taste of salt. He leaned on the fence. There didn't seem to be any lights showing at the front of the house. What his memory retained of driving through the village was a line of grey wall, the houses set somewhere behind it. In fact, as he made his way slowly forward his knuckles brushed the little windows of cottages built to the pavement's edge. A car roaring blindly towards town set the mist tumbling. Stupid bastard! He felt his heart pounding. No light in any of the windows: it would make sense if people lived their lives at the back away from the traffic. When he came to the corner, though, and round the gable wall to a lane along the backs of the houses, he found what seemed to be an endless tangle of unbroken hedging.

When he came to a gate and found it pushed open, he didn't hesitate about going in.

Once, on holiday, in a wood by the river under the shadow of Durham Cathedral, Carole had left the path to pick a bunch of white flowers. He stepped cautiously, the path underfoot uneven crazy paving. Wild garlic, the stalks broken in her hand traced a sudden pungent oil on the air and he heard young voices murmur together as student boats drifted by under the branches. A triangle of concrete slab rocked under his weight and he stumbled through an arch of hedge into a sweet heaviness of roses that seemed to come from the mist itself like a blanket releasing scent from its folds.

There was a glow of light ahead. He thought of what excuse he might make, but was determined to ask where he'd find Worth. He went carefully forward, and realised he was mistaken in assuming the light came from a window. It spilled from an open door, and he saw the corridor beyond and a man hurrying away along it.

'Excuse me!'

The man spun round. Light shone on his face.

Meldrum stared in astonishment.

'Bell?'

The Special Branch man put out an arm bent as if to fend off an unexpected blow.

'It's Jim Meldrum. Is Worth here? Are your lot looking after him?'

'Fuck's sake fuck's sake,' Bell said. His breath panted like a man in a race.

'What? Christ's sake, man, what is it?'

'Nothing.' Bell spread his lips in what might have passed for a smile. Meldrum's flurry of alarm seemed to have calmed him. In a voice that was almost normal, he said, 'You'd better come inside.'

Meldrum took a step forward, then stopped. Bell's forehead shone with sweat.

'Is Worth here?'

'Come in,' Bell said again.

And Meldrum almost did. What stopped him was how Bell's face had looked as he turned into the light. Not just surprised, or even alarmed; no wonder if he had been both at a voice behind him, totally unexpected, from the deserted garden. Instead, rage and fear, for an instant he had looked like nothing so much as a trapped animal.

'Worth phoned me. During the night.' He thought about it. 'Did you have a tap on my phone? Is that why you're here?'

A man stepped out of a room at the far end of the corridor. He wasn't anybody Meldrum knew, average height, heavy-shouldered, a face you wouldn't notice passing in the street. From somewhere behind in the garden a bird began calling, a double note, rising, repeated. The man made an odd wrenching motion with his jaw, like the stifling of a yawn. Nerves maybe, or he might have been tired. It was possible his night's sleep had been broken.

'Come on,' Bell said, with a kind of coaxing impatience. 'We can talk inside.'

The second man made Meldrum even less inclined to do that. Common sense told him it was reasonable to go in. Instinct gave him a strong impulse to turn and run for it. Tugged between them, he froze. The next move was Bell's, but before he could make it sirens clamoured on the front road. All of them listened, waiting for them to pass. One cut off, then another. They had stopped; it sounded like just outside.

The other man squeezed by Bell and, as Meldrum braced himself, simply walked past down the path. Bell followed without a word or a glance. Meldrum watched them fade into the mist.

In the rooms inside everything was tidy, even the bedroom, but that wasn't different from the way it had been in Worth's own flat. It was more surprising to see books not open or scattered around but in neat piles on one table or another. It occurred to him that it was only amateur searchers who tore a place apart.

He found Worth sitting on the floor, swung round so that his arms were under the water in the bath. It looked an uncomfortable position, but it had let all the life bleed out from his wrists so it had worked in that way.

As he crouched beside the body, the banging at the front went on until it was joined by voices calling in the back garden. After that they were loud in the corridor and then softly gathered in the doorway behind him.

CHAPTER THIRTY-EIGHT

'He could be an awkward shit. Not to speak ill of the dead, but he could be. I'd this idea, I was getting married, why not on a cruise, in fact, why not on the *Queen Lizzie*? And get the captain to marry us. Be worth a few column inches. Done right, I mean, and who could do it righter than I could? Shit wouldn't pay for it.'

The organ was playing, too softly for Meldrum's taste. For this woman's voice, even on half-throttle, it was no contest. Sitting beside her had been an accident. He'd wanted to sit at the back of the church and had slipped into the first empty space he'd seen. Now it felt as if half the congregation was eavesdropping on what Kaye Short felt about the late Brian Worth. What he needed was a Sousa march. Played by a brass band.

'He told me captains don't marry people at sea any more. But what he said to Norrie Turner – bloody fool not realising Norrie and I were mates – was that I was getting past the orange-blossom bit. Little poof!' And grinned as Meldrum swung to look at her. The word took him by surprise, remembering what efforts Brian Worth had made to keep his secret. 'A woman can always tell. Not that it would have taken a rocket scientist to guess. I thought everybody knew. Anyway, I suppose he did me a favour. No wedding bells, I mean, Mr Right as it turned out being an awful utter self-centred complete bastard. Like most men. Not to speak ill of the dead.'

On cue, the organ paused then soared into the Wedding

March, while in front of the altar Billy Ord's son Malcolm cast one backward glance at the girl pacing the aisle to him on her father's arm.

When it was over, Meldrum sat in the car swithering about whether he should go to the reception. Lines of cars were pulling away. The church had been full. Afterwards, in the crowd milling around outside he'd recognised lawyers, John Brennan among them with a little dowdy woman who must be his wife, businessmen, journalists, at least one MP, councillors. It amazed him how many people Billy Ord knew, all sorts of people. A full turn-out from the Lodge, he thought sourly. And policemen, of course, no lack of them or of hard looks coming his way. He'd paid his respects, seen the boy married. Obviously, it would be a mistake to go to the reception.

On the other hand, if he didn't he must go back to an empty house and brood about Worth's death, which he'd gone over a hundred times in the last two days. He swung the car out and joined the procession making its way down the hill.

In the Roxburghe Hotel, he sipped a glass of what he assumed was champagne, plenty of bubbles anyway, and watched them cut the cake. Both left-handers, her hand on his holding the knife. Pretty girl. The groom had rugby player's shoulders, soccer wouldn't be played at that expensive school his father had sent him to, good-looking boy, apart from inheriting Billy's thick brooding mouth, hint there he might be a bit of a bastard, inherited that too.

For the meal, he was put at a table with strangers. That was all right, mixing people round so they got to know one another. He remembered Rab Finlay (one night years ago, the two of them in a car keeping watch outside somewhere or other, had spent half his life doing that) talking about a wedding in Inverness; 'It was about fifty-fifty, the bride's side and ours, and my cousin Donny was looking round and looking round and he turned to me and said, No point in waiting, let's just get stuck into the buggers now. And we hadn't finished our soup.'

He must have smiled to himself for the woman next to him responded and looked as if she might start a conversation till someone on her other side said something and she turned away. He cut himself a mouthful of steak and built greens on top. It would be nice if they let you take a bag of it away to enjoy by yourself. After a time he noticed that very same Finlay at a table by the wall and then that everybody at that table was police. Looked like they were having a good time. So much for mixing.

Like the food, the speeches were all right. At least the woman beside him laughed a lot. The bride's father, thin gold watch, expensive haircut, knew how to tell a joke, a man who'd made a few after-dinner speeches in his time. Billy's son had married well.

While they were getting ready for the band, he went to get a drink at the bar. Kaye Short glanced his way, and he wondered why she hadn't asked him about Worth's death. Would she do anything about it if he tipped her off to check back on the murders of Francis Pietro and Arthur Hull? Or if he told her about his visits to Hugh Keaney in prison? With her sources, she must know he'd been suspended from duty. Or was he exaggerating his importance? If he told her about Ireland, would she ask, This Clay, you get a picture of him? Though Doubting Thomas had wanted to touch a wound, maybe she'd be satisfied with a photograph of O'Toomey's blood on the wall.

He saw her eyes on him over the man's shoulder. He went over.

'Tell me—' he began.

'You've got it the wrong way round.' She grinned at her companion. 'I ask the questions.'

'Were you ashamed, what you did to my daughter?'

'Eh?' She glanced at the man again, but if she was looking for support he didn't want to know.

'Just because the boy Sandy Torrance was stupid enough to talk to you. All that crap you don't believe yourself, dragging that crap out does nobody any good.'

'You've got a headstart,' she said, waggling her glass in front of her mouth in the drinking gesture.

It seemed to him everyone was carefully avoiding his eye.

But he hadn't been drinking, certainly wasn't drunk. He broke out in a sweat at his own folly. What had made him so angry?

If the bloody woman hadn't stirred it up, if it hadn't gone into the papers, Betty might not have got together again with Sandy Torrance.

Christ! he thought. Is that it? Send for Mr Freud. And then that all he'd ever wanted was for Betty to marry someone who would love her – and be able to look after her. A penniless boy with a scarred face didn't fit the job description. The world was a tough place. He worried about her.

And what was wrong with that?

Without thinking about it, he had begun to gravitate towards the group of his colleagues. Finlay was there, Barry Cox, people he felt comfortable with. Then he saw the one with his back to him was Dyall, and changed his mind.

It was time to leave. Instead, he started to drink. He'd sat in crowded bars on his own. That wasn't so bad. He liked noise and the stirring about. From both parents he had inherited generations of the genes of Lowland Scots, which might have been why strangers would nod at him in the street as if in recognition. He'd lived his entire life in this country; and always felt an outsider. There were worse things than being left in peace in the middle of a crowd to drink on your own. He watched John Brennan dancing for a while. Never with his wife. Twice he thought Harriet Cook was there. Once it was the sound of a laugh, the way it began and broke off; the second time a glimpse of a seated woman, slumped a little to the side. He got up and carried his drink round until he could see her face.

It was on the way back Billy Ord caught him by the arm. He already had hold of Dyall, gripping him above the elbow.

'. . . so the guy gets married again. The priest can't believe it. Once is bad enough, but twice! But same thing again, couple of months and she's turned. A good Catholic, can't keep her away from Mass, four kids. All set for more, but she dies as well. So another year passes. And the guy goes on holiday to London again. Back to Kerry with wife number three. Same thing!' He swung his face from one to the other, breath smelling as if he needed to brush his teeth. 'Same bloody rigmarole. But the priest's just going through the motions this time, he's not really bothered. Only thing is four months pass, then five, six. And no sign of her turning. So he gets a hold of him – Michael, he says, what's going on? Those two Protestants you brought back from London turned good Catholic wives. But this one! It's a year since you brought her home. And she's never set foot over the door of the chapel. For God's sake, Michael, what's wrong? Ah, Father, he says, to tell you the truth the ould converter's not what it used to be.' Dyall smiled but, although they were face to face, managed to look past Meldrum, somehow not to see him. Even retired, he was a man with influence where it mattered. Ord coughed and laughed; 'The ould converter's not what it used to be! John Brennan told me that one. Hell of a bloody man.' He shook them each by the arm. 'Come back to the house afterwards. Both of you. Just the family and some friends.'

Dyall delicately disengaged himself. 'I'd like to—' But he couldn't.

And Meldrum knew he shouldn't, but at some point afterwards found himself in the back of a car with Ord's oldest son Donald and his wife in front. The grandson, little Billy, exhausted by all the excitement, slept strapped into his Britax seat beside him.

In all the years he'd known Billy Ord he'd never been in his house. It was semi-detached, but solid, built of grey stone and, following Donald up the path, he guessed at five bedrooms upstairs. It was full of people, full of noise, waves of laughter. Despite all the food that had been consumed earlier, piled plates were being ferried from a buffet table set up in the conservatory. He stepped out into the garden and came on Ord's wife, Jean. She was by herself, a shape under a tree, and perhaps he recognised her because he had gone through the house expecting to come across her. Her head was turned as if she was staring down the garden, though in the dark there couldn't have been anything to see. Drink made him benign, and he went over wanting to say something nice about the wedding ceremony, the reception, being asked to her home. When he was close, he saw she was in tears. They looked at one another and he couldn't find anything to say until she shook her head and went past him back to the house. Mothers must often cry over weddings. Tears of nostalgia, tears of joy. It could only be a deception that hers had looked like unhappiness. With tears, there wasn't any way of telling what kind they were.

What he remembered next morning was a room with a music centre and records, shelf upon shelf of them, records not compact discs, and being surprised that so much of it was classical music. He wondered if the wife was musical, maybe that was it. With his instinct for getting away, he had found the door at the end of a corridor and wandered in. It didn't fit, not the man he knew. He wondered if Billy Ord called it his study, and for some reason found that funny and was laughing when Ord came in.

'God's sake, man, sit down before you fall down,' Ord said.

He picked up Meldrum's glass from where he'd put it when he crouched down to check the records, and fastidiously wiped at the ring it had left on the surface of the desk.

'This not your seat?' Meldrum asked, taking the glass. He had subsided into a black leather chair by the desk. He stared at the glass Ord had handed him. It was full of whisky, pale as straw. He sipped.

'I think my phone was tapped, Billy,' he said. 'They were there when I got there. Bell and the other fellow.'

Ord shut the door. There was a little table with a bottle and glasses by a leather easy chair. He poured himself a drink.

'Nobody believes me, but I saw them . . . Or maybe they do believe me. But nobody'll admit it. Special Branch. Shutters down. Never mind the poor bloody infantry – Sorry.' Ord was picking up records from the floor. Meldrum realised he must have pulled them out to look at and left them lying. 'Sorry, Billy.'

Ord said, 'I don't know why you started this. A quiet man like you. Didn't you know the score?' His voice was muffled as he bent over, sliding the records back into place. 'As a detective, for me you were always the pick of the bunch.'

'I was lucky.'

Ord sat by the little table and picked up the glass he'd filled.

'What I always said, you were a good copper. No luck about it.'

But that wasn't what Meldrum had meant. He tried to get his thoughts clear. 'If that old woman— There was some old woman in that row of cottages. She couldn't sleep. Burglars on the brain. She didn't even know Worth was hiding out there. Thing is, if the police hadn't come . . .'

'What?' A hard, challenging noise.

'I might have been dead too.'

'Shite!'

'I'll tell you what shite is. Them saying Worth committed suicide. That's shite.'

In the way of old boxers, Ord squared his shoulders, ready for a challenge, not even knowing he was doing it. Next moment, though, he had picked out a record, slipping it out of the sleeve and settling it on the turntable. He must have had a lot to drink, but his movements were quick and neat. Violins. Slow. Other instruments joining in as the tempo quickened. Drunk, Meldrum could imagine he understood about music.

Ord said, 'I heard the other day Willy Cormack was dead.' Meldrum tried to place the name. It wasn't any policeman he knew. 'We were at school together. One time, this would be our first year, we climbed up and got out on to the roof. You know what we did? We ran from the ridge of it down to the gutter. Just stopping every time at the last minute. It was three storeys up. Right to the edge we went and you'd see the playground way down below. We were mad.' The whole orchestra was busy now, blowing and sawing away. You had to concentrate to hear what was being said. 'One time the two of us broke into church. The Henry Arthur Memorial Free Church. It was made out of wood, and everything inside very plain, but it didn't mean God wasn't there. You know what I did? I pissed in the font. I was defying God. Same way as when I ran to the edge of the school roof. I was defying Him to punish me.'

Meldrum yawned. His jaw cracked with the stretch of it. He said, 'If that old woman hadn't phoned the police—'

But Ord swept his hand out. It was the shape of a back-handed blow, but at the end of it he snatched the needle up off the record.

In the silence, he said, 'Leave it! You know what day this is?

It's the day my son got married. I want to leave a clean name, so they'll think well of me when I'm gone.'

He could have phoned for a taxi, but only thought of that after he'd set out. He walked along looking for one that would take him back to the hotel where he'd left his car. The night air gave him an impulse to sing and he tried that for a while.

The district was unfamiliar to him and soon the streets got meaner and darker. He felt no anxiety though, and went on firm in the persuasion that God looked after the drunk no less than the mad.

CHAPTER THIRTY-NINE

After over three hours' unbroken work in the University Library, Betty was dazzled by the Meadows' open space. She wandered from the straight path and lingered along the edge of an impromptu football game, jackets for goalposts piled on the grass. Pages turned still behind her eyes: chunks of fact, gobbets of background on the period and, the last thing she'd read, a short shrift of critics chewing jargon like gristle; a stew bubbling away until, to the muted sound of cricketers by the pavilion, 'Sitting on a bank, Weeping again the King my father's wreck,' came to her mind; 'This music crept by me upon the waters,' fragmentary music, words and ideas, which after all was what all that reading was supposed to be about.

Ahead, joggers wove a hemstitch between the trees.

She crossed Melville Drive and walked up Marchmont Road in the direction of the Grange. As a schoolgirl she had accepted a friend's invitation to her home in that district. She knew the girl's parents were much better off than her own, and on the way she had anticipated the size and grandness of their house. She was invited for a meal, and imagined a conversation which would range across books and the theatre and ideas; not music, she hoped; what if they talked about opera? She prepared an answer against being asked what she was reading at the moment; not a textbook or anything on the recommended reading list for the Highers, of course not. Something to show what she was made of. And not fiction, changing her mind at the last moment as her friend led her in through the gate. It wasn't long since she'd come across Vera Brittain's *Testament of Youth* in the school library; that would do. Her friend's father was there. He was an engineer who talked of how hard it was to train women – When I wash dishes, I rack them, go away and have a pipe, come back and they're almost dry. Who cares, she'd thought; and what do you do about pots and pans? My wife cut the hedge once, he'd said. I went out and took a ruler to it. It was two inches higher at one end than the other and up and down like waves in between. Oh, I just can't manage, the wife said quietly.

At the lights, turning left would have taken her along to the Grange. She went the other way.

She realised how fast she was walking. Sweat trickled down her spine. Four days of continuous sunshine and cloudless skies; not something that happened often in this country. She eased the T-shirt free of her skirt and let the air run cool on her back.

On the other side of the road, a high stone wall left the pavement in shadow. She had gone over to get out of the sun before she saw the men. They were in a straggled group along the pavement. They seemed to be together and yet apart, all of them silent. One was leaning on a rail set at the pavement's edge. Two or three stood and another two sat with their backs against the wall. One man lay flat out with an arm across his eyes. Apart from them there was no one in sight. The sun beat down on the empty street. Not a leaf stirred on the hedges opposite. The long wall pinned its length of black shadow. She had a strong desire to cross back over the road, but was too stubborn to give in to the impulse.

Nothing happened. Unshaven, disconsolate faces remained indifferent. The man lying on the pavement took his arm away as she picked her way over him, and followed her with his eyes. Face your fears, she thought, and smiled at herself.

In the Crescent, she looked for number nine. She had the address and the time on a piece of paper ripped from the phone pad. Her mother had taken the call last night. From one of your friends, she'd said, but she hadn't caught the name. 'Must be someone close, though. He knows you and Sandy are looking for somewhere. It sounds like a bargain.'

She started with the ground-floor flat and went up the stairs looking at the name on each door. On the top landing she glanced from one door to the other in disbelief. She checked the name and address on her piece of paper, then rang the nearest doorbell to seek help. As she waited, footsteps sounded coming up from landing to landing unhurriedly.

She had given up and was on her way down when the door opened. A woman came out, flustered by a baby and a pram and a toddler clutching her skirt. Betty offered to help with the pram. On the way down, the woman shaking her head at the name on Betty's paper, Betty struggling to manoeuvre the pram, they passed two men who made way for them on the landing below.

At the corner, Betty parted from the woman who was going to the park. She didn't know whether to be furious with the unknown caller, or her mother for getting the address wrong. Either way she had wasted the best part of an hour.

The dishevelled men hadn't moved; the one with elbows on the rail perhaps drooped even lower, a wax figure melting in the heat. Their stillness struck her more unpleasantly than before. Why were they there? What could they be waiting for? Unthinkingly she had come back on the same pavement, and would have to make her way between them for the second time.

She glanced back and saw two men strolling along behind her. In that glimpse they were young, clean, well set up. Reassured, she quickened her pace.

The group ahead stirred. The figure unbent from the rail. The man lying on the pavement got to his feet. There was the scrape of a door being set back. A nun appeared. Coming level with the convent gate, Betty saw a notice with a list of days. 'Alms will be served at—' Not sinister any more, the derelicts trailed in the nun's wake through the arch for their handout.

Then she had walked on. It was difficult to sort out later. She had been thinking how strange. In the middle of Edinburgh. Medieval charity. The poor, always with us. Redundant. Different word for it. Surplus to requirement. What you added in case the message got muddled—

Thinking something like that, when a hand took her by the

shoulder and turned her, and as she turned a second hand took her so that she was pinned against the wall. They had put on white cotton hats, the floppy kind gardeners wore, and outsize sunglasses with bright yellow rims – and should have looked funny, but didn't. They were the men who had been walking behind her; and afterwards, belatedly, she would realise they were the two men who had been waiting on the landing at the flats for her to come down.

The taller one said something like: 'Your boyfriend was warned,' so that at once she understood this was about the demonstration at which Sandy had been hurt. A car went past and stopped further up the street, but they paid no attention. We must look like friends, she thought, standing talking. The taller one talked, what about she couldn't remember afterwards. Threats. She'd kept thinking, they must be policemen.

'Look at this,' the shorter one said.

He held up his right hand. One of the knuckles was thickened and distorted. A medical student had shown her the same thing. The fifth metacarpal. You saw it a lot on the hands of young men in poor districts. They called it the boxer's break.

But he hit her with his other hand folded into a fist and she was falling and there was shouting and running feet and the two men were being smashed up against the wall with their arms twisted behind them.

She was helped to her feet, and a stout, sweating man was apologising and saying over and over, That wasn't meant to happen. He meant her being punched in the face. That wasn't meant to happen. Her mouth was full of blood. It wasn't meant to happen. She swallowed blood and felt sick. So many men.

She thought, They must be policemen too.

Up the street all the doors of the car lay wide open.

CHAPTER FORTY

Meldrum was at breakfast the next morning when Carole rang. She said his name and, though he'd been thinking about Harriet, there wasn't any doubt in his recognition. The one word was enough; their marriage had taken a lot of years before it was over.

He wasn't to be alarmed, she began. Betty had been attacked, but she was all right. Calm at first, she became upset as she talked. He couldn't get it into his head that it had happened the previous day. He wanted to go to the house at once to see Betty, but Carole said she was sleeping, leave it till after lunch. You're talking about *my* daughter, he wanted to tell her. Instead, he found himself making comforting noises.

He didn't even think to ask if there had been a motive. The wrong place, the wrong time: in cities now, being unlucky was reason enough. When she told him who the attackers had been, his first reaction was disbelief. Anger came later.

It was the anger, though, which grew as he made the familiar journey to Lennart Square. The sergeant on the desk opened his mouth as if to say something, then thought better of it. As an officer on suspension Meldrum had no more right of access to the areas of Headquarters where people worked and files were held than any other member of the public. As he went through and took the stairs, he noted it by habit as a breach of security, and one the sergeant shouldn't have allowed.

It was obviously the first thing Ord thought; looking up from his desk to ask, 'Where the hell did you spring from?'

'I just heard about Betty.'

'Ah.' He pushed the file aside. 'We got the fuckers.'

'You didn't tell me.'

'Don't be stupid.'

'She's my daughter.'

'A confidential operation. We're talking about officers under suspicion – men working out of this building. This one had to be under wraps.'

'You put her in danger.'

Ord shook his head. 'You try my bloody patience, man. I'm sorry she got hit. That wasn't supposed to happen. But I'll tell you this – it's that punch settled their hash.'

A thought occurred to Meldrum. 'Did Betty know about it?'

'What?'

'About the operation. She's such a fool, if you told her it was the right thing—'

'Sit down!'

It was an order. He kept a baleful silence, until Meldrum obeyed. From where the drink was kept at the back of a middle drawer in the nearest filing cabinet, he fished out the bottle and the two glasses.

'Pretend you've just come in the door,' he said, and poured. 'You want to thank me. You know how dangerous guys like that can be. They get sent to sort out some demonstrators, a nice bit of overtime – so they tear some cunt's nose half off, that any reason to lose the job and the pension? They think they've got it quietly sorted out, and then suddenly there it is in the papers again. It's not fair. They're pissed off. You can see that. But your daughter and the boyfriend don't know, couldn't tell shit from custard, haven't a notion the trouble they're in. But Uncle Billy sorts it out. Because the cowboys – as cowboys do – shot their mouths off. In the canteen, would you believe? I get the word. And I move on it. All of which takes time. But I *took* the time. Right?'

It was a long speech, designed to be long enough to let a man cool down and think. In the middle of it, the phone had rung and he'd kept on until it stopped.

Meldrum sighed. He picked up his glass and drank.

'Thanks.'

'You see,' Ord said, 'that wasn't so hard to say.'

When the big man leaned back, it gave Meldrum a view of the window. He wondered again why with his rank Ord should have chosen an office that faced a brick wall.

'Do I know them?' he wondered.

'The cowboys? A couple of nobodies. You might recognise their faces.'

'You'll charge them?'

'Don't worry. We'll put them the whole road.' Ord sank his drink in one and grimaced. 'Talking of pensions,' he said, 'you heard anything?'

'I imagine you'd know before I would.'

'Special Branch.' And Ord shrugged as if that said it all. 'They haven't talked to you again?'

'Since?' But Ord just stared, and Meldrum, knowing how useless it would be to try to outwait him, went on, 'They wrung me dry when I came back from Ireland.'

'What about since Worth?'

'No, they haven't spoken to me since I found Worth.'

'You don't think that's funny?'

'Special Branch,' Meldrum said, and carefully matched Ord's shrug.

'Not even when you claim they were at Worth's cottage, Bell and whoever? Your phone being tapped. All that shite.'

'I said that to you, Billy.'

'Not just to me.' Ord made a chopping gesture of dismissal. 'Don't fuck me about. There were other people there. I'll show you the tapes if you've forgotten.'

From the interview room one floor below.

'One thing you won't see on them,' Meldrum said. 'That I think Worth was killed. I'm not that stupid. I only said that to you, Billy.'

'You think you're not stupid,' Ord said and shook his head. 'Are you waiting for a fucking good conduct medal? You know better than that. How it works.' Behind him Meldrum heard a door open, and close again as Ord shook his head. 'It's grinding away and when they're ready they'll put out their hand for you.'

'When they do,' Meldrum said, 'I'll want to talk about Hugh Keaney.'

Saying that, he had felt defiant; he had felt like a gambler laying down an unexpected card.

'I thought you might,' Ord said, quietly matter of fact, eyes still and watchful.

'He's on hunger strike.'

'So what's new? He's tried that before.'

'They won't let me in to see him. I can't find out how he is.'

It seemed to Meldrum that he had to trust somebody. Finally he wanted it all out in the open. He didn't want to be on his own. He was a policeman, not an outsider, not an agitator, not some kind of politician. In his heart of hearts he believed in the system, and that where it had been at fault there wasn't anything else you could use to correct it but itself.

He wanted his life back the way it had been before. He wanted Hugh Keaney to be proved innocent. He wanted an enquiry, and for that sooner or later he had to trust somebody.

He had told Ord part of it before, and now he gave him everything, gave what Brian Worth had told him, not holding anything back so that he described again how Clay had caught Worth with his lover Francis Pietro. He told how the night before that a car bomb in Dublin had killed the American John Fields Laverty and his family. Again he went over what had happened at O'Toomey's farmhouse, and gave an accurate professional description of Captain Sharkey, whose real name might have been Clay.

He ordered the list of the dead like beads on a string: the spy Laverty and his wife and eight-year-old daughter, the homosexual Pietro, the blind man Hull, O'Toomey and then the man who had killed him together with his companions, and Worth slumped over with his life draining from cut wrists.

Giving it all, he described his visit to Arthur Hull's neighbour Mulholland, how he'd had to have the minister help because of the old man's stroke, and how the Reverend Tommy Wright too had brought up the name Clay. Laying out everything he had, he offered the girl Tracey Connolly who claimed Keaney had been sleeping rough with her when Arthur Hull was killed; and that the landlord's thug Andrew Fisk had perjured himself in court when he said Keaney had boasted of the murder.

And through it all as he listened, Ord rubbed at a mole on the base of his middle finger, rubbed and rubbed, back and forward as if at last by trying he might wipe the brown stain of it from the back of his hand.

It felt like making an appointment. Not before lunch. Betty will sleep until lunch, Carole had said. He stopped the car and walked round the park, looking at his watch until it seemed to be time.

Betty herself opened the door. Carole, of course, must be at work.

'Mum said she'd try to get back before five.' As a head teacher, it was after six o'clock or later before she came home; and sometimes only to rush out again to a meeting of parents or the School Board. And yet he was the one blamed, because work took up too much of his life, for breaking up their marriage. Against a possible criticism of her mother, for any hint of which she had thought-police antennae, Betty put in a pre-emptive strike. 'There wasn't any need for her to stay. I'm all right.'

He was shocked by how she looked. Whoever had punched her had worn a ring, splitting the lip and leaving scabbed wounds above and below the mouth. Either that blow or one in falling had swollen her face and left a bag of bruised blood under one eye.

'It was worth it,' she said.

They spent the rest of the afternoon circling around that notion. He knew her better than to imagine she was thinking about revenge. Neither had she properly realised the kind of risks she and Sandy might have been running: Ord was right about that. As far as he could make out, she had in mind some kind of abstraction like justice.

'I won't ever be on the side of authority. Not like you.' She frowned and said, 'Sorry. That came out wrong.'

It didn't matter. He was content to be with her. For years, telling her stories, explaining things to her, later arguing ideas with her, had been among his greatest pleasures. He couldn't put his finger on exactly when or how that had been lost.

He didn't need her to tell him not everything was right with the police. 'It's a job with temptations. There was this young guy—' He took the goodness of his memory for granted. Forgetting a name felt like having his pocket picked. 'Time. Brain cells are going . . . Gemmell! Brian Gemmell – started same time as I did. Four o'clock in the morning, this wee shop had been robbed. Him and a sergeant and another fellow were first there. Sergeant gets them organised to load the boot of the car with cigarette cartons. Done all the time, he tells them, the insurance'll cover it. This is a sergeant, remember. Take a lot of guts to say, no. Anyway, who'd see you at that time of the morning? Somebody who couldn't sleep, that's who. End of wee Brian.'

He broke off to make them a coffee, but the kitchen had been changed round and he had to come back and ask her where the jar was kept now.

When he brought the cups through, she said, 'There but for the grace of God, eh?'

He'd have felt it ridiculous to say the idea offended him.

At something in his look, though, she said, 'Just kidding. I know you never would,' and he had to frown to conceal the pleasure she gave him.

At one point he told her, 'I thanked Billy Ord. You know, I didn't want them to get away with it.'

'You were busy with other things.'

It was then he started talking about Hugh Keaney. Having in mind, perhaps, that Keaney was innocent and starving himself for help and to the danger of his life. Sufficient defence surely, even if implicitly, against any idea that he had been too busy with just the routine of his job to care. It turned out, though, she didn't know anything about Keaney. The name meant nothing to her. It had never occurred to him Carole wouldn't have told Betty about something that gave him so much concern.

That she hadn't mentioned it upset him, and he was still coming to terms with the idea when first Carole came home and then within five minutes of that, while she was still taking her coat off, the doorbell rang.

It was Sandy Torrance, who took one look at Betty's face and nearly in tears said, 'Oh, the bastards!'

Carole could be heard speaking with someone in the hall.

Meldrum looked at the two youngsters side by side on the couch. The boy had his arm round the girl's shoulder. With his free hand he touched her on the cheek and then with an unconscious gesture stroked the line of the scar on his nose. She took that hand in both of her own and laid her head against him. A couple, two made into one, with not a gap between to admit another.

He was taken completely by surprise to see Harriet Cook come in behind Carole. For her part, she froze at sight of him, but recovered at once. He wasn't sure if Carole realised what was happening; Betty being the focus of attention helped. Sandy, it seemed, had gone to Harriet to see if she knew any more than the police were telling about the trapping of the two assailants. She had come back with him to visit and see how Betty was.

Meldrum misunderstood. He said to Sandy, 'I thought you'd have come here first to see Betty when you heard.'

The boy looked puzzled, then explained, 'I was here last night.'

Carole said, 'When he heard what had happened, I couldn't keep him away.'

He stayed for the best part of another hour. They talked about what might happen to the two policemen, and then by some transition he missed they were talking about plutonium in the River Dee. Scotland, it seemed, rich in coal and oil and hydro-electricity, was the last country in the world that should have needed to burden its children with the risks of nuclear power. Pressed for an opinion, he shrugged it off with the word, Politics; and Betty cried, 'Everything is! You want crime in a neat box. Preferably committed by the poor.' And after a moment, said, 'Sorry.' He wanted to talk to her about that, think about it, try to make sense of what he felt. She sat entwined with Sandy except when they went into the kitchen to make coffee. In his years in the police, had things got better? You didn't float somewhere in the air above a job seeing the whole thing, you did it up close day after day, and what you remembered were disputes about pay, things like that, and people, respected or disliked, people you worked with. And if he had to think about it, over a drink with someone he trusted he might have said, There were the ones who came into the job for the wrong reasons: you knew all about them, who didn't? Maybe it was just a coincidence that the guys he'd had most time for had come into the police by accident and before that been tradesmen, a plumber maybe, like Peter Wilkie, something like that. Sandy came out of the kitchen carrying a tray and he took one of the cups and sipped at it and listened.

Then he went home.

The last thing in the world he expected later that evening was to open his door and find Harriet there.

By way of explanation, but not at once, 'I've never seen anyone look so alone,' she said.

In the night he wakened with her arm round him, and gently so as not to disturb her, eased up the sheet to keep her warm.

A couple, two made into one, for the moment with no gap between them.

CHAPTER FORTY-ONE

It would have been good to spend the next morning together, but Harriet had an advocate briefed for the defence, Number Three Court, ten o'clock, assuming her client turned up and the victim turned up and a sufficiency of witnesses turned up. The jury almost always put in an appearance.

When he woke, he found her note on the bedside table. She'd got up early and breakfasted and gone home to change into her court outfit. A woman with a sense of duty. Her note ended, 'I'll be back about five, if nothing turns up. Harriet.' And then she'd drawn a line from 'nothing' to the bottom of the page and written, 'will stop me – I'll be back' and underlined the last two words. She had signed just with her name, not 'Love – Harriet'. Yet women in particular signed 'Love—' all the time now without thinking twice about it.

He rolled up and sat on the edge of the bed. The clock showed nine-fifteen. He yawned and wondered at himself for falling asleep again after having wakened. When you didn't have a job to go to it was as if some spring inside slackened. The thought depressed him.

He was shaving when they came for him.

In the car he sat beside the driver, whose name according to his identification was Brown. The other one sat in the back.

The signs told him they were travelling south but not why.

As they went through Jedburgh, the one behind said, 'Let him hear the tape.'

'You just like to listen to it,' Brown said, but he put it on all the same, sliding it in one-handed as he drove. There was a hissing that grew louder as he turned up the volume. 'It's a copy of a copy,' he explained. 'Man's voice we're interested in.'

It started abruptly. Perhaps the first part hadn't recorded or for some reason had been edited out.

A woman spoke and then the man.

'. . . married twice and divorced. I'm a blonde and at the moment I have a live-in lover. I'm thirty-eight. You don't mind that?'

'No. I'm waiting for my wife to come home.'

'Oh, she's late.'

'She won't be coming back. She's spending the night with her boss.'

'With who?'

'With her boss.'

'Does she do that often?'

'He comes here for the weekend sometimes. I look after them. Make the meals. Tidy up. Make the beds.'

'You have a very modern marriage.'

'Eh?'

'Young, is he?'

'He likes to use me as a punchbag before he makes love to her.'

'What age is your wife?'

Silence.

'My wife is in her early thirties. I'm . . . about fifty.'

'I see.'

And her voice trailed off, as if tired even of pretending to care.

Silence.

'He punches me.'

There was a pause and then in the same abrupt fashion the voice of another woman, picking up it seemed in the middle of a conversation.

'If you got me earlier, it must have been phone three. I'm on phone one now. Phone one's the popular one. It rings all the time.'

'My wife's left me kneeling in the bedroom.'

'Why is that?'

'To punish me.'

'I see.' Unsurprised. 'How long have you to stay like that?'

'Until she comes back.'

'When will that be?'

'Three o'clock. About three o'clock. Usually she tells me not to speak. But this morning she just said kneel and don't move, so it's all right to phone.'

'What did she punish you for?'

'She sent me to clean her sister's flat. And her sister said I was cheeky to her.'

'And does your wife get you to keep other people's places nice, too?'

'She gets me to do her best friend's flat as well.'

'Does she ask you for sex?'

Silence. When his voice came again, it sounded flat.

'No. She punishes me.'

'Do you have your clothes off when you do the cleaning?'

'. . . yes.'

'Does she whip you?'

'. . . Punches me.'

'Does that turn you on?'

'. . . yes.'

'She'll be able to see you're excited. Does she touch it?'

'She lets me touch it.'

'While she watches . . . While she watches, eh? . . . You can tell me. I mean, there's not much sense in phoning and not talking. Tell me right now!'

'I could crush her head between my hands.'

'Sorry?'

'I could smash her voicebox with the side of my hand. I could put out her eye with my finger. I could squeeze it out so it hung on her cheek. I could kill her a dozen ways. I know how. I've killed people.'

There was no answer, only a faint sigh that might have been the woman taking a breath.

Brown reached across and hit the off button.

'That shut her up,' he said. 'Recognise his voice?'

No; and yet there was something.

The one in the back asked, 'Sound to you like a military man?'

'Sharkey? You mean Sharkey?'

'Captain Sharkey. He kills people. According to you.'

He thought about it. 'The accent . . .' But then he'd heard Sharkey use different accents, in Glasgow, in Ireland.

'Newcastle,' the one in the back said. 'Like mine.'

'A Geordie,' Brown said. 'You know, Scots with the brains knocked out.'

The Newcastle guy said, 'Funny. I heard it the other way round.'

With the backchat, it didn't seem they were much bothered whether he recognised the voice or not.

After a pause, Brown glanced across and prodded; 'Anyway.'

'It could be. But I wouldn't have thought of Sharkey. I don't think I would have.'

'No lawyer'll get funny about it,' the voice twanged from behind him. 'Don't you worry.'

'There was a resemblance,' Meldrum said. 'But the voice on the tape sounded older.'

'Give the man a coconut.'

'You've a good ear,' Brown said.

What that was about, he'd no idea, and didn't ask – any more than he'd pressed them after their first noncommittal response to find out where he was being taken. Partly that was superstition: don't ask in case you won't like the answer; partly that he would find out soon enough. Anyway, when Special Branch asked, not going wasn't an option. Better to save his energy.

They left the A68 south of Consett and headed west.

'Not long now,' Brown said, and Meldrum caught his sly sidelong glance.

The man was bored with driving and wanted to play games.

He stared ahead impassively. He tightened his left hand, down at his side where the driver couldn't see it, into a fist and then let it uncurl slowly. It was an old trick for easing tension out of his body.

'I said not long now.'

'Hmm.' Meldrum grunted just the barest acknowledgement.

'You haven't asked where we're going.'

Forcing that out of him counted for Meldrum as a small victory. He picked his reply carefully.

'Seems it won't be long till I find out.'

The man in the back seat snickered as if he recognised what was going on.

'Can't argue with that,' he said.

'Are you watching the map?' Brown asked abruptly.

'What?'

'For the fucking turn-off.'

'Now! It's now!'

Meldrum was thrown forward as the car braked sharply and swung right. As he settled back he saw Brown was grinning.

Another stupid game.

As they came off a hill and over a bridge, he saw flags and a large building set low by the river. They took the third exit off a small roundabout, turned right across the traffic and into the car-park behind the hotel.

It was a long narrow area with parking on both sides. Brown reversed into the first empty space and got out. He stood at the front of the car, looking around. A man got out of a car parked further up on the other side. Brown walked across. They spoke, the man held out his hand, Brown shook it.

'Dr Livingstone, I presume,' the voice behind him twanged ironically.

Brown turned and gestured. The man in the back seat reached over and switched off the engine.

'Let's join the party,' he said.

More handshaking. It turned out back seat's name was Warner. The man out of the other car was Detective Inspector Knight of the Northumbrian Police.

'We've been waiting for you,' Knight said. 'Surveillance's been watching out for a car, but target just walked up the hill and turned in the gate. Out of nowhere, they said. Almost didn't eyeball him.'

He glanced from Brown to Meldrum.

'This is another colleague,' Brown said. 'He's here to make an identification.'

'Shit-hot on voices,' Warner said seriously.

The four of them got into Knight's car. As it turned right out of the car-park, going uphill from the roundabout, Meldrum experienced a familiar tingle of excitement. From about then, and it didn't matter whether it made sense or not, he felt like part of the team. He leaned forward to catch voices from the radio – Yellow One in position/in position/he's still in there/in position.

When he sat back, he saw that Warner beside him in the back seat had taken out his gun and laid it on his lap.

Brown in front must have done the same, for Knight said suddenly, 'No need for that.' And then, 'There's no record of him being armed.'

'Fuck's sake,' Brown said in disgust.

Looking past Warner, he saw trees and then a field with goal posts and overgrown grass. On his own side, a narrow pavement, a length of chainlink fence, beyond it a concrete yard and the end of a low one-storey building; a factory, deserted, with a For Sale board at the gate.

When the houses started on the right, they looked like respectable council rentals, semi-detacheds or four in a block with well-kept front gardens. On the left, a school, old village-style, and then another building and a notice-board on the grass at its entrance that went by too quickly for him to read.

'Off! Off! Off!' Knight was shouting. Brown was scrambling out, the car still moving. Christ, what was happening?' 'All units, off, off, off!'

They were almost at the top of the hill. Two men in overalls who'd been trimming a hedge had dropped their tools and were sprinting across the road. Meldrum had a glimpse of men jumping fences as they came from the street that lay behind the houses. Then he was part of the hunt, running with clenched fists.

The door lay burst open before he got to it. He was surprised to see the hall empty. The hedge-trimmers came from a room on the left. He saw a wardrobe, doors lying open, a bed tipped over on its side. They ran down the passage towards the sound of breaking glass. He went to go through the opposite door, but Knight coming out pushed him aside and ran for the stairs. As

early as that, some instinct told him they'd made a cock-up of it.
He went into the living-room, a little crowded space of sideboard,
yellow sofa and stuffed chairs. An old man holding a cup and
saucer stood beside a table placed under a window with a view
of the back garden. There were two plates on the table, ham and
eggs half eaten, a wedge of mop-up bread abandoned in a smear
of yolk and grease.

Overhead the banging and shouting stopped. The cup could
be heard rattling in the saucer. Using both hands, the old man
put it down. He bent and tipped a chair up on to its legs from
where it had been knocked back from the table. There was the
tramp of feet coming down the stairs.

The old man said, 'Catch our John?' and blew out his cheeks
in contempt.

Brown leaning through the dining-hatch from the kitchen
struck him on the shoulder with his gun. 'Where the fuck is
he?'

A question echoed by Knight as he and the others crowded
in from the hall.

CHAPTER FORTY-TWO

It occurred to Meldrum he hadn't eaten. After the fiasco of the raid, Knight had brought all of them back to police HQ in Newcastle. Since then, like a parcel to be called for, he'd been abandoned in a corner of the squad room.

Searching the house, Brown had found a photograph of the son, John Clay, beside the old man's bed. What about it? he'd asked: Is this him? The thing was, the only answer was maybe, it could have been. He'd seen the man who called himself Sharkey once in a pub in Glasgow, and then when he'd been in fear of his life from him in Ireland: two occasions, and from one to the other Sharkey had altered the impression of how he looked. He had that trick, same as with the accents. In any case, it would have been hard to compare a man to the pictured image of a boy with wide eyes and an uncertain grin, a boy of maybe twelve.

It had been the only photograph in the old man's house of his son.

The red-headed detective constable at the next desk, who'd been hammering away at a typewriter, stretched and rubbed at the base of his neck.

'Still waiting, then?'

The way it happened across the twenty-four hours in every squad room in the country, the room which had been busy had gone quiet.

'Getting hungry,' Meldrum said.

'Could get a roll. Not anything hot. Not at this time.'

'I don't suppose they'll be long.'

'Tell me about it. Nothing but waiting – and writing up. Never mind catching villains, get the paperwork right.' He rolled in another sheet and stared at it balefully. 'Paper's killing bloody job.'

Meldrum grunted. He'd heard it all, innumerable times, the job was full of dyslexic one-fingered typists.

The detective hunching forward tapped in some kind of a heading and slumped back.

'That was a good bloody laugh,' he said. 'Outside, like. With your mate.'

It had happened as they'd got out of the car in the private park at the back of Headquarters. All the way, the old man had talked about his son. 'You were lucky our John didn't wait around. Us Clays are hard. None of you lot have been in Killing Room at Hereford. Don't bloody tell me. If he'd wanted to, he could've fought his way out. Bodies all over place.' And over and over again even after being told to shut his mouth, 'I'm hard, our John's hard, and me, I'm just the same.' Getting to their destination had been a relief. Scrambling from the car, the old man yelled at Knight, 'And you didn't have a shooter!' Brown, following, agreed, 'That he didn't.' Taking this as insult added to injury, the old man had gone for Brown as he was half in, half out, and in best unarmed combat style tried to bite off his nose.

'Out of sight, man,' the red-headed detective said. 'Old Eddie Clay! My brother won't believe it.'

'You know him?'

'I wouldn't say know. I come from there. My parents still live about four doors away. I've heard my dad talking about old Clay off and on for years. Always shooting his mouth off about his son did this, his son did that. Nobody paid any mind to him and his army patter. Truth is, old cunt was in the Catering Corps during the war. Saw fuck-all action, my dad said.'

'What about the son? You must have known the son.'

'John Clay?' The detective shook his head. 'He was older than me. Five years or more. And he got out of it sharpish. Glad to get away from that old bastard Eddie.'

'You know where he went?'

'He finished up in the army, didn't he?' He grinned. 'Fighting the IRA on his own, if you believe his old man. But that must have been later. He was only about fifteen when he took off. He'd got tired of having the shit beaten out of him . . . Pity he couldn't have taken his mother with him.'

'She got the same?'

'Nights I've stood at our back door and heard her screaming. People our way mind their own business. But he did do time for her, little bits of time now and again when he'd gone over the score. She didn't last long after the boy left.' He made a sour face. 'After that, according to my father, he was just plain disgusting. Crying, nose dripping into his pint, telling anybody that'd listen how much he missed her. And some believed him. Always somebody sending a drink over for poor Eddie. Till even the mugs got sick of him.'

There had been one photograph of the wife, a smiling girl on her wedding day. One photograph of the son as a boy of twelve.

When Warner appeared at last and took him out to the car, Meldrum was chewing over how odd that was.

'Did you know Clay was always boasting about his son? All the time to the neighbours. Till they were sick of it.'

Warner eased the car to a stop at the lights. 'Mouthy old cunt. Wouldn't like his phone bill. You should hear some of the shit—' He broke off and grinned. 'You did.'

'So why only the one photo? I'd have expected him to have photographs all over the place of his son in uniform.'

'Maybe the son got rid of them when he came home,' Warner suggested.

It was possible. A man with secrets, not wanting to leave—

'But if he was as careful as that, he wouldn't tell his father anything that mattered.' There wouldn't be anything to be got from the old man's boasting. It made depressing sense.

Warner glanced across. 'It's a daughter you have?'

'Yes.'

'Fathers and sons,' Warner said, and grinned at his own thoughts.

At the station, he waited while Meldrum bought a single ticket for Edinburgh and then walked him to the platform.

'I doubt John Clay was even in the bloody house,' he said. 'We only had the word of those fucking clowns.' By which Meldrum took it he meant Knight and his men. 'A total fuck-up. Down to them.'

'Why did they want him?'

'Some pisspot assault and robbery. Only an accident, we even heard.'

'What'll happen to the old man?'

'Let him go in the morning, I suppose.' He smiled. 'Meantime the Boss is making him pay through the nose. He's letting the old cunt hear how he sounds talking to those women on the phone. Playing him some bits over and over again. Time I left, the hard man was crying.'

Paying through the nose.

He sat in the carriage watching Warner walk away. He could still hear the crack as the old man's rotten teeth snapped under the pressure of trying to bite off the tip of Brown's nose. The Special Branch man had been lucky, though he might need a rabies shot.

When he thought he'd given it enough time, he got out of the carriage and walked back down the platform. No one paid him any attention as he went through the station and out again to the street.

CHAPTER FORTY-THREE

The bar of metal glowed yellow. He lay trying to work out what it might be, but undecided drifted back to sleep. When he opened his eyes, time passed and he understood it was light coming in under a door. Lifting his head, he made out a mirror glimmering beyond the foot of the bed and beside it the shape of a television set. It was dark. The middle of the night. Was the radiator on? Had he forgotten to open a window? He sighed and turned in a dry, oppressive heat.

A hotel room. He got out of bed and twitched back one of the curtains. A wall of windows and patio doors, the dining-room probably; a small garden under a couple of lamps; murmur of unhurrying summer water; a bridge arched against the sky.

The hotel with the flags; by the stone bridge; low-set by the river.

And in the morning he was going to talk to Eddie Clay about his son.

The hair rose on the back of his neck. Behind him someone was trying to get into the room. He could hear the metallic tick of lock against retainer and a soft bumping, wood on wood, as the door was shaken.

But when he snatched it open, the corridor both ways was empty and night-still.

He went along to the swing-doors that led outside. Here at the side of the hotel a second glassed-in corridor led to the leisure complex. Concrete slabs struck cold on his bare feet. Looking across, he could see all the lights were on, white chairs set by a pool, and the water strange as if waiting for a swimmer to break the surface.

In the morning, scrambled eggs, sausage, bacon, tomato, toast, three cups of coffee; he never ate like that except in hotels. He took the last coffee out of the deserted dining-room into the lounge. In there, too, he had his pick of the seats and took one by the window. He looked at the garden and the traffic going by on the bridge. There wasn't any hurry. After the police let him go Eddie Clay would still have to travel from Newcastle to get home.

Just after half-eleven, he went back up to his room and got his coat. No luggage to pack. He paid his bill and went out by the side entrance to the car-park where they'd rendezvoused with Knight for the raid on Eddie Clay's. Yesterday seemed a long time ago.

The air was heavy, inland air overheated and still, air to push against. As soon as he started to walk uphill from the roundabout, he began to sweat. The small factory that had flicked by from a car took longer to pass on foot. He had time to see boards over windows, a lidless drum for paint or oil tipped over and rusting. When he came to the village hall, he stopped and read the board by the gate: gifted by a local magnate in memory of a son dead 'for his country'. First World War. A long time ago; the grieving father dead by now, too. A date for the son's death; for a place nothing more particular than France, so a skirmish or a sniper's shot or a battle not big enough to have a name. Hugh Keaney didn't have a rich father or a building named after him or much luck; but at least he was alive. In prison; on hunger strike; not perfectly sane any more; but alive. When last heard of.

He should be thinking of questions for Eddie Clay. He should be working out a strategy of questioning. It was difficult to think in the dazing heat. He didn't stop again, but went on slowly.

From across the street, the house looked much like the rest in the neat, well-kept row, up and downstairs, roughcast, with a little concrete lid jutting out above the front door to keep a visitor dry till the bell was answered. Only thing to pick it out by was the front garden. The grass was knee-high.

To give himself time to think, he went on to the junction, crossed and walked down the street behind the houses. Clay's looked worse from the back, but there was still no way of telling if he was inside.

When he was tired of looking, he walked slowly back. At the junction a two-bungalow-sized health centre was set on the slope. He stopped and read the notice outside, and then read it again. The notice said: Please take off muddy boots before entering waiting-room.

Either Eddie Clay was in or he wasn't. It was that simple.

It was twenty to one. He looked at his watch as he got to the gate. In the next garden a man in shorts and a baseball cap marched behind a mower scowling, perhaps on general principle or as a sign of disapproval of the grass jungle on either side of the path Meldrum was walking up. It would be understandable if Eddie had that effect on his neighbours.

He pressed the bell, but couldn't hear it ringing though the sound of the mower from next door had stopped. The man stood watching, then wiped his forehead and went into the house leaving the mower in the middle of the lawn. It was possible he'd gone in for a drink of water. On the other hand, after all the activity yesterday he just might have gone in to make a 999 call.

At the second try, still no sound from the bell.

Hand raised to knock, on impulse he tried the handle. The door was unlocked. That was all right; people did that in the country; over his shoulder he could see fields.

He stepped inside and closed the door.

'Eddie? Mister Clay?'

He glanced into the bedroom on the right. It was dimly lit with the curtains drawn across. He went into the living-room.

A man was at the table by the window. He wasn't doing anything, just sitting looking out at the back garden.

'I thought that might be you,' he said.

He had the burr of the local accent, but he was Captain Sharkey, which made him also John Clay, the missing son.

If it had been less unexpected, Meldrum, given the terror of his life at their last meeting, would have turned and run for it. Instead, surprise held him just long enough so that he took in through some battery of animal indications, none of which he could have identified, that the man did not threaten him. It might have been no more than that Clay had greeted him so casually, seemingly hardly able to rouse himself from the torpor of whatever was occupying his thoughts.

It might be the impression was mistaken or the condition temporary; for the moment, Meldrum was convinced.

'Have you been here all the time?' he blurted.

'Just got here.'

'Yesterday – how the hell did you get away?'

'Spotted them watching the house. Took off.'

'But there were police all over the place, back and front.'

'Not when I left.' He turned his gaze from the garden. 'Did my Da tell you something different? Like as if I was Houdini? He always liked to build me up.'

Not always, Meldrum thought, remembering what he'd been told. The boy who'd run off at fifteen to get away from the beatings. As a child, in one of the gardens a door or two down, the Newcastle squad room detective had heard the mother's screams.

The memory games people played.

My Da.

Happy families.

He hadn't expected to despise Clay.

'Apparently your father likes to talk,' he said. 'Special Branch had some tapes to play him.'

'What did they do to him?'

'I wasn't there. But he'll be talking to them now.'

'No,' Clay said. 'No, he won't.'

'Why not? Oh, because he's a hard man. I'd forgotten.'

'He's not hard,' Clay said. 'When I was fifteen, I saw him getting into an argument about the war. But he'd picked the wrong man. This soldier, just a little guy, beat the shit out of him. That's when I decided, Fuck this, and got out. I felt he'd let himself down.'

He yawned, mouth stretching as he took in air and let it out in a long, gasping exhalation.

'I saw him break my mother's fingers,' he said. 'No reason.

You just had to be around when the beatings were being handed out . . . Wouldn't think to look at him now . . .'

'What?'

'In there.'

He nodded at the door to the hall, and when he didn't get a response turned away as if losing interest.

To Meldrum it seemed like a trick: if he went to look, Clay would disappear. As before, though, he was persuaded by the other man's seeming indifference, his lethargy, by something he couldn't place but recognised.

Grief.

It was easy to see why he'd missed the old man the first time he went into the bedroom. Even knowing there was something to look for, he had to come all the way round the bed before he found the body. Eddie had taken off his clothes. The trousers he'd worn yesterday, the shirt, vest, underpants, socks tucked and folded, all laid on the bed, the shoes side by side on the floor. It was neat, though he hadn't seemed like a man who would be tidy.

There was blood and not much space. To get a look he went in across the bed. The knife that had been used to stab the groin and upper thighs was still clutched in the corpse's left hand. Blood under pressure had hosed the side of the bed. There was something strange about the eyes. As he reached down to touch, he knocked the phone off its stand.

'Christ!' he heard himself saying.

From the doorway, Clay asked, 'What did they do to him? All I want's a name.'

The dialling tone buzzed like insects and the smell of blood choked him as he realised the old man had closed his eyes and sealed them shut with superglue. – *Please replace the handset and try again.*

The voice said the same thing over and over.

A woman's voice, reasonable, but firm.

CHAPTER FORTY-FOUR

As for any duty to report the old man's death, one day or the next made no difference to a suicide, and there wasn't any doubt that's what it had been. Brown if anyone was responsible; but humiliating a man wasn't a crime, and a tape of phone calls wouldn't qualify in any court as a blunt weapon.

Revenge and Clay would operate by different rules; he couldn't risk telling him what the Special Branch man had done.

No mention either, then, of old Eddie's attempt to bite off Brown's nose. That seemed a pity, Clay giving the impression he was short of positive memories of his father.

Meldrum was in shock. There was a difference between examining a body at a crime scene, other people there, colleagues, the flash of cameras, jargon, shop talk, and what he had stumbled upon in that bedroom. How could he have gone in the first time and not smelled the blood?

Maybe after Ireland he had lost his nerve.

Maybe there was a total of the number of bodies you should look at in one lifetime, and he had reached his.

Whatever, he had left the house and walked with Clay, and when they came to an old Suzuki four by four parked opposite the disused factory and Clay took out keys for it, he'd got in on the passenger side without a word spoken. It had been like that all the way walking down the hill, the sky high, blue and cloudless, coming out of the house the air even hotter than when he went in, and children playing in gardens as they went by, side by side, not talking or hurrying because of the heat.

The sun beat in on the driver's side. Clay was in a sleeveless T-shirt, a weightlifter's arms and shoulders, sweat pouring down his cheeks. Behind the wheel, intent on the road and his own thoughts, he didn't look like a man in mourning, but Meldrum had learnt faces hid as much as they revealed.

No more than earlier did he feel afraid. They came to a sign for Sedgefield and shortly after that turned into a drive with a board at the side marked Hardwick Hall. There was a road winding up between trees and signs off at intervals on the right to car-parks. When Clay turned off at the third or fourth sign they parked at the end of a line of cars. On the grass people were eating at picnic benches. They cut down to a path and there was a long narrow lake and couples walking and children paddling their hands in the water. Some kind of country park. How could you feel threatened in a place like that?

Fenland Trail, the arrow said. Clay followed it on to a narrow boardwalk fenced on either side. It ran out and bent across swampy ground. Every hundred yards or so the path widened at one side to make a small observation platform. At one of these Clay stopped, leaned on the rail and seemed to read the information board. It had illustrations and explained things in simple language. Meldrum could imagine children crowded here with a teacher who would question them about it later. He leaned on the rail beside Clay. The board explained about fens and marshes and places with 'sedge' in their names or 'carr', which meant wet ground with trees round, and how there might be alders first and then birches overshading them as peat rose and the marsh sank.

'What do you want?' Clay asked.

'What I've wanted since I got into this. To prove Hugh Keaney's innocent.'

It was odd how you could walk five minutes from a place busy with people and be lost to view. Bushes crowded close at their back. In front, the space of open wetland ended in a line of trees to shut them in. No one, it seemed, wanted to look at the fen, which anyway was drying up. Under their

feet at the walk's edge a stagnant shallow fold of black water
shone between rotting trunks.

'And I'm guilty? You think I'd help you to do that? . . . I
might do that,' Clay said. 'You'd have to come with me to see
somebody.'

'Go with you?' He straightened in disgust. Clay moved too,
the couple of steps to the end of the platform. He held the
rail on either side of the walkway, blocking the way, wads
of muscle shifting on his forearms with the fierceness of his
grip. Meldrum thought, he's like a bomb, primed, wanting
to explode into violence. 'You think I'm stupid enough to
go anywhere with you?'

'You came here.'

He heard insects hum like a summer meadow about the fen.
From somewhere on the other side of the trees children were
calling.

'It would mean going abroad,' Clay said.

'Back to Ireland?' He shook his head in disbelief. 'With you.'

'I was the one nearly killed in Ireland,' Clay said, and
touched his chest under the shoulder.

'No way.'

'Not Ireland. Europe.'

'Not anywhere.' But that was automatic. Part of him couldn't
help catching up the scrap of information and probing. 'Europe's
a big place.'

'I can take you to the man who paid to have the American
killed in Dublin,' Clay said.

'It was the Palestinians wanted Laverty killed.' He saw
clippings scattered across Worth's carpet. 'It was all in the
papers at the time.'

'Not all. I can take you to him. The Palestinian who set it
up.'

'I'm going to get an Enquiry.' Hadn't he seen Farquhar Wood,
the Secretary of State? What he had done once, he could do
again. 'I found witnesses – I can show Keaney had an alibi.
I don't need you or anything from you.' One Arab country
or another; one terrorist faction or another. 'What difference
does it make who the people were that ordered Laverty was
to be killed?'

'It would make a difference,' Clay said, and his lips pulled back in a spasm that resembled a smile.

Meldrum heard a noise behind him. A woman came into sight trundling a go chair that filled the width of the boardwalk, followed by a white-haired man and woman.

Clay moved fast. Meldrum didn't catch up with him until the car-park.

'Tell me one thing.' As he spoke he saw there was a couple, little chairs and a folding table, looking round from their picnic at the open boot of the car beside the Suzuki. He lowered his voice and asked, 'Did you kill Worth?'

'I don't know why you care what happens to Keaney. What's one less person on the face of the earth? If it was me I'd walk away.'

Clay unlocked the driver's door and got in. Meldrum went round to the passenger side, but it had been locked and the Suzuki was already reversing out.

CHAPTER FORTY-FIVE

T he week he came back was a strange one. It began with the picnickers in the car-park at Hardwick Hall who, full of wary guesses as to what had been going on between Clay and himself, showed their broad-mindedness by giving him a lift to Durham. After a wearisome journey home, he lost the first day. It was late in the afternoon before he came awake and even then he let go of sleep reluctantly. He tried repeatedly to get Harriet on the phone. Finally he went and waited outside her flat and was there when she got back, after eleven and not entirely sober. By that time, unreasonably, he had a grievance that almost matched hers, and they fought loud-voiced and strident, and at some point he got through to her why he had disappeared so suddenly, and they lay in bed holding one another while he told her all that had happened and afterwards they made love and next day she didn't go to work. They stayed in the flat and talked all the time in bed and out of it. When it got to be evening, they ventured out for a walk. The air was mild, the pavements crowded, and it made them smile to see how many couples went hand in hand as if the neighbourhood was a conspiracy of lovers.

That day or the following he saw a news item about the old man's body being found. It didn't say who by or, for what that was worth, anything about neighbours seeing Clay or him there.

On the fourth morning, Harriet had a court appearance. He knew it was stupid but it felt like a castle wall being breached. He hated that she had to go and he had to take up his life again.

It was like a sign of that when she suggested they eat out and named a restaurant and a time to meet for dinner.

They had talked, however, about what he should do next, and decided the best way to prepare for an Enquiry would be to get signed statements from the Hull murder witnesses.

That was when everything fell apart.

TOMMY THE GRASS

The painted words stood out even more white and clear from the fire-blackened gable end than the last time. Maybe the dry summer had helped. The other possibility was that the letters had been retouched.

Nobody round here liked a police informer.

He needed a signed statement from Tracey Connolly that she had spent the two vital days around Hull's murder with Hugh Keaney. It wouldn't guarantee a result – she would make a lousy witness: a fifteen-year-old runaway who'd grown up to be a streetwalker. Living in a flat with Keaney and the others who paid over their social security giros to Andy Fisk, the bully boy who took her own rent in kind: lawyers would love all that. Any half-competent one would take her apart.

Still, she was the best bet he had. If nothing else, her evidence cast doubt on Fisk's story of Keaney confessing the murder to him. He had to start somewhere. For the moment, never mind that being beaten, getting pregnant, the loss of the baby, all of that mess could be presented as motive for her lying now, looking for revenge on Fisk.

As he went up the path, it was difficult to believe anyone could live behind those dirty, uncurtained windows. Round the boarded-up ones of the flat above, the fire had blackened the roughcast in stripes like dragged make-up.

It was the mother who answered his knocking.

'Tracey? You want to see her? Listen, I'd like to fucking see her.'

She turned back inside, but didn't close the door on him.

He made a deliberate effort not to examine too closely the kind of detritus he was picking his way through on the floor. Inadvertently, he caught a glimpse of what looked like cat shit under the table. A mewing sound drew his attention to where the four-year-old was lying on her side on the couch. The woman caught her grand-daughter by the arm and jerked her upright.

'Have a seat.'

He shook his head in refusal.

'You want a cup of tea?'

Christ, no!

'Where is Tracey?'

'God should have struck her dead. She walked out the door with a wad of money that thick. I saw it! She tried to hide it, she turned her back so I wouldn't see when she was taking off some to give me. Sleekit wee cow, twenty quid, she'd hundreds there, I tried to hold on to her. She shoved me out the way, there was a car waiting for her. I thought, she's away to London. I've always wanted to go to London. So I think she's in London, how would I know, not even a postcard. She could be dead.' And she screwed her face into a grimace experience had taught him might be intended to signal maternal concern.

She didn't connect any of that with Andy Fisk, whom her daughter hadn't seen for years and she'd never set eyes on at all. Anyway, neither Fisk nor anyone else had come to the house. Whatever had happened had happened elsewhere. Tracey had got in tow with somebody when she was at the shops or out for a drink or doing a bit of business. 'A wad of money that thick.' Where it had come from, why it had been given, she had no idea. When he asked if there had been any hint it might have been to persuade her to disappear, the mother stared at him blankly. 'Who'd stay in this hole if they'd money?'

As he left, the four-year-old slipped over without a sound and lay again on her side. He was outside before he remembered the baby held on Tracey's hip and wondered where it might be.

When he got back to his house, it was some time before he opened the anonymous letter.

There had been a scatter of mail behind the door which he gathered up and carried with him into the kitchen. He put on the radio, heated a can of tomato soup and ate a heel of bread, dipping into the soup to soften it. The lunchtime news was half through by the time he got to the letter. To the left of his plate he'd laid the junk offerings, magazine subscriptions, football coupons, to put in the bin, on the right a gas bill. He began to read the letter, then turned the page to look where the signature should have been. After going back to the beginning, he reached across and turned the radio off.

Dear Mr Meldrum,

There was something odd about the handwriting. Perhaps an attempt had been made to disguise it. Told to find who had written it, though, as a professional using the internal evidence he wouldn't have had much difficulty. Somebody with daily access to Hugh Keaney in the prison infirmary. A man with some medical knowledge: *fat and muscles are wasted away in keeping up the work of his heart . . . his body is poisoning itself and more quickly every day . . .* Not a doctor – and that for more than one reason, knowing prison doctors. From someone working as an orderly perhaps. Another prisoner. One of the Born Again brigade. *He is a true Christian. Isaiah, Nineteen, verse twenty, he said. That is the message he wanted sending to you.* 'Wanted sending' instead of 'wanted to send': so an Englishman. A long-term prisoner, in for murder perhaps or armed robbery, a convert to Jesus, a man with a compassionate heart. He wouldn't be hard to find – not that there would be any point.

I don't know why he is still here, it's wrong, he should be in a proper hospital. They'll take him when it's too late, you'll see, did all we could they'll say.

The date stamp on the envelope was three days earlier; but the address was written in a different hand from the letter. There was no telling when it had been smuggled out.

Since Carole left, there hadn't been a bible in the house, but he wandered around looking for one just in case. Like so much else he'd done, it was a waste of time. Time that was running out for Keaney.

On his way to the street where Arthur Hull had lived and died, he got it into his head he was being followed. He drove in circles, speeded and slowed, made an abrupt right turn across the traffic, stopped the car and waited. Starting again, he decided nothing was wrong except his own guilt about the days he'd lost. Ten minutes later he found a parking slot, bought a ticket and walked back.

The last time he had been here, communicating with the stroke-afflicted Mulholland without the minister Tommy Wright to act as interpreter had been hard. He had blamed himself for distressing the man. This time he didn't hesitate. Mulholland was the one who had spoken to Francis Pietro; he was the one who had been told of Clay. His evidence was important.

It was a young woman who opened the door.

'I'm sorry,' she said. She rubbed her finger on the name-plate: tarnished brass, MULHOLLAND, the incised letters worn down, faded almost away. 'So much to do, we haven't got round to replacing it yet. I believe he'd been ill a long time. We've just moved in.'

Slowly he mounted the next flight.

Morton, the upstairs neighbour, opened the door so quickly he might have been standing behind it waiting for someone to ring.

'Oh . . . It's you,' he said, taking Meldrum by surprise, who introduced himself anyway and asked if he could go over the events of the murder day again.

'You asked about my wife, when you were here before.' He made no move to step aside.

'I told you I was sorry she's dead.'

'That's it, she isn't. I was ashamed to tell the truth. She's left me.'

The wife – very round and soft – with something about her that turned the mind to bedrooms in the afternoon. And Morton, the insurance man, who had taken note of Hugh Keaney's National Insurance number 'just to be on the safe side' – a precaution which had led Keaney by one step and another to his confinement for murder.

'I'm sorry to hear that.'

'It's been on my mind that I lied about it. I don't know why I did. I have nothing to be ashamed of.'

He looked worse than he had the last time. Unshaven, but he'd been unshaven then; not a matter of grooming, something about the eyes. He had the eyes of a man who was ashamed.

'Could we go inside?'

'No.'

'I think we should. I wouldn't take up much—'

'I don't have to talk to you. You're suspended from duty. You don't have any right to ask me questions.'

Meldrum was too astonished to do anything but put out an arm with an idea of stopping him from closing the door. As he did he caught a whiff of his own staleness; he had been wearing the same shirt for days. And in the same way of everything slipped unexpectedly out of kilter, Morton's nose wrinkled; it seemed of its own prissy volition out of a memory of fastidiousness.

He said, 'If you come here again, I'll send for the police. The real ones, I mean. You shouldn't tell lies.'

The sergeant on the desk, a different one this time, stopped him.

'Sorry,' he said. 'You know how it is. I can't let you just walk in. Are you here to see somebody?'

'Ord. He's expecting me.'

'. . . is he? Give me a minute to check that.' There was something in that paused, quizzical enquiry which made Meldrum uneasy. He was a man who abhorred lies, and hearing his claim to be expected he had taken himself by surprise. He leaned on the desk, then thrust his hands out of sight into his pockets. It was important to hide his anger while he waited. The tight pressure of fists clenched against his thighs. Tracey Connolly had been paid to go away. Someone had told Morton about his suspension from duty. He'd given it all, every witness he'd talked to, every link of evidence, to one man, only one. Billy Ord. He was blocked. Any chance of an Enquiry was blocked.

Why did you do it, Billy?

He waited for more than half an hour. The sergeant came back and made himself very busy. People went by, not seeing him or pretending not to see him. It was a busy place; everybody was busy. A white-haired man came to the desk with a letter. He was told to wait, but tried to explain himself. 'I didn't see him. I look out for people on bikes. I wouldn't drive off if I'd hit someone. I just wouldn't. This is the first I knew about it.' Perhaps he was rehearsing. After a time he was taken off to find out how it would play.

When an inspector appeared, it wasn't Finlay or even somebody like Turner, but a new promotion, a face he hardly knew. Maybe that's what had taken so long, them arguing over who would go down.

'I think there must have been a mistake.'

'Take Ord a message, tell him it's me. He'll see me.'

'I can't do that.'

It was the tone that did it, quiet but firm, and the round, bland face.

'Don't tell me what you can't fucking do!'

Nothing of anger in response showed in the face or manner of the new promotion. Still quiet and polite; allowing for the fact there was no way of knowing how a suspension might resolve itself in the end. A careful boy who should go far.

'You obviously haven't heard, sir. He collapsed in his office a week ago. You'll have to go to the Southern General. Since he's in intensive care, though, they might not let you see him. Detective Chief Superintendent Ord has cancer.'

CHAPTER FORTY-SIX

A nd it shall be for a sign and for a witness unto the LORD of hosts in the land of Egypt: for they shall cry unto the LORD because of the oppressors, and he shall send them a saviour, and a great one, and he shall deliver them.

In James Thin's bookshop, he had glanced at the verse but then bought the bible on the theory he needed time to look at the whole chapter. It didn't help. He could have saved his money. Isaiah, chapter 19, verse 20, if it had meant something to Keaney defeated him as a message, a code that wouldn't break for him. He was no saviour, God knows not one of the great, and as for deliverance all he could do was try. It seemed to him that was all there was to find in it, not being a religious man. He was so little anxious to be mistaken for one that it would have embarrassed him to read a bible in the open at a restaurant table while waiting for Harriet to arrive. Instead, he'd slipped it into his pocket and gone to the lavatory, where he sat on the toilet seat and read the chapter for a second time with the same result.

Help me!

Hadn't he known that was all Keaney had to say?

He left the bible on a ledge behind the toilet, between a soap dish and a framed cartoon of a sports car. Maybe someone else would pick it up and it would alter his life. That wasn't impossible. It was also possible to imagine that he'd bought that particular book, a bible, out of despair because now there didn't seem any way there would be an Enquiry to help Hugh Keaney.

Why did you do it, Billy?

And then, too, there was the possibility that he had bought a bible on impulse because he'd been told Billy Ord had cancer. Maybe it was a way of praying for the dying. Belief gone, you were left with superstition.

He came out of the lavatory checking the time on his wristwatch, and looking for Harriet saw a man sitting at his table. There were only seven tables in the place, four of them unoccupied. The man was at the table by the flight of steps that came down from street level. He had his back to the room, and Meldrum was beside him before he realised it was Clay.

It was the first time Meldrum had seen him in a suit, and despite the warm weather a shirt and a tie. The shirt white, the tie sober stripes: he could have walked down from one of the offices off Hanover Street.

'It's as cheap sitting as standing,' he said.

The young waiter lugged over a blackboard on which the evening's menu was chalked.

'I'll wait until my friend arrives,' Meldrum said. He saw the waiter glance at Clay. 'The lady who made the reservation. She shouldn't be long.' Harriet was late.

'Would you like something to drink while you're waiting?'

'The same as I'm having,' Clay said. 'Bring him what I'm having.'

'Another bottle?'

There was a bottle of red wine already on the table. Clay laid a finger on top of it. 'If that's what this is, that must be what I want,' and he smiled, broadening it until the waiter smiled back uncertainly.

From the corner of his eye, Meldrum had an impression of a woman. The window by this table looked into the basement area and through the railings above he could see passers by on the pavement. The woman was gone but he thought it might have been Harriet and turned to the door half-expecting to see her come down the steps.

'Where did you get to the last two days?'

'What?'

'Suppose I should ask where you were these last two nights.' Clay emptied his glass and poured again. 'It was unreal standing in that street again after all this time.'

'Outside my house?'

'No!' he said scornfully. 'Just luck I came back to your place in time to see you coming out of it, I'd nearly given up.'

'You followed me.'

'Anybody else, driving like that, you'd have got rid of them. I was impressed. Where the hell's he going that's so important, I asked myself.'

He fell silent as the waiter came, not just with the second bottle of wine but with a plate of fanned slices of duck breast and side dishes of new potatoes, vegetables, a tossed salad. Meldrum watched as he started shovelling it in. Clay wasn't a pretty eater.

'I didn't recognise the street at first,' he said through a mouthful of food. 'I was walking behind you, not far back, I was waiting for you to look round. Then I realised where we were. It stopped me in my tracks – it was like a time trip. I expected you to go into the old man's – I can't remember his name.'

'Hull. His name was Arthur Hull.'

'I only saw him one time.' He stopped. Meldrum tried to keep his face expressionless, struggling to hide the excitement suddenly going through him, cop thrill, the moment of capture. Clay grinned. 'You've got it,' he said. 'I'm confessing to murder.'

Meldrum looked round. The couple laughing together in the opposite corner were too far off, but the elderly couple only a table away might have heard. If they had, they gave no sign, heads down, grazing with gloomy earnestness.

'Pietro too?'

'First one, then the other. I should have told the old man, same knife as I used on Francis – he'd have liked that. Same knife on you both. That would've got his rocks off.'

'Somebody else as well – Worth was killed with a knife.'

'Not that one.' But whatever the value of that as a denial, he chose to qualify at once. 'I lost that knife. A couple of years ago. You know how it is, losing things. Sooner or later.'

The first bottle was well down. Meldrum poured a glass for himself. He lifted it to his lips and sipped from it.

Clay said, 'To success, eh?'

'You want to tell me about it?'

'If only it was that easy. I know – I talk, you write it down, I sign it.'

'I haven't had much luck with that today.'

Clay folded a slice of the duck on to his fork, built vegetables on top and pushed the lot into his mouth. As he chewed he began to nod, as if he had something important to communicate. When his mouth was empty enough, he said, 'You should order. You never know when you're going to get food as good as this again. When you get the chance, you enjoy it. That's what life is about. I told Jamal, life brings you a bonus, you take it. It doesn't interfere with the operation. When we got into bed, there was a misunderstanding. I said to him, no, you've the wrong idea – you're the horse. We got on like a house on fire after that.'

'Jamal?' With the word, Meldrum concentrated. His mind cleared to listen and assess, thoughts moving fast, weighing possibilities. In an interrogation, he always arrived at a moment like this. 'A Palestinian?' Clay nodded, an almost grin turning up one corner of his mouth, chewing and watching. 'Was he the one wanted the American killed? Was that the operation – killing the American?'

'John Fields Laverty. A name I do remember, but then I worked on the thing for months. Let's be clear on this, Jamal came to me. He'd been turned down even by INLA. None of them wanted to touch it. But while he was sniffing around, our people got wind of him, and he was led to me – led by the nose. I did a fucking Rolls-Royce of an Irish accent then. As far as Jamal was concerned I was a terrorist – he didn't care what label hung on me. I put a group together through O'Toomey and took Laverty out. Make it look like those Irish nationalist bastards killed the nice American. I laid the evidence out so neatly in plain sight even the Gardai couldn't miss it. Really harmed the fuckers in the States. Not for long maybe, but every little helps. Coming back to see Francis I was walking a foot above the ground, I had such a buzz going. And he's

in bed with Worth. Real little slut Francis was.' He paused.
'No questions? Listen and let me talk? You're good. From one
who knows, eh? Anyway, it was that night did the damage.
Woke up next morning, Francis has his head round on the
pillow watching me. I thought, something's wrong. Tried to
remember. Bit of fun with Worth, Francis and me drinking,
we made love, drank some more. Fuck it, it was a celebration!
Although I knew I'd said something I shouldn't, shot my mouth
off, I lied to myself. Couldn't get enough of him, understand?
All the same, I kept laying traps trying to make sure, every time
I saw him. And he'd just close his eyes and say, Sssh, he'd say,
listen to the music. Then one morning the phone rings – the old
guy what's his name?—Hull, yeh – and I just listened same as
the music. Seems Francis wasn't to be trusted.'

He talked through mouthfuls of food so that Meldrum lost
words here and there.

'You killed both of them. Then what? Back to Ireland? And
nobody knew.'

Clay was offended. 'I reported to my superiors. That's what
a soldier does. I'm not saying they were happy. It was a breach
of security. A fuck-up. But they took care of it.'

Meldrum didn't like anything about it. 'Your superiors—'

Clay shook his head. 'Don't even try. By then it was alphabet
soup time. RUC Special Branch, MI5, MI6, 22 SAS had been
in Ireland since '75, NITAT had been going for years. 14th
INT – army blokes, they were trained near Hereford, very
hush hush.'

'Was that your lot?'

'To us they were amateurs. Like I say, don't even try. I'm not
giving you any of that stuff.'

'What are you giving me?'

'Jamal.'

As Meldrum stared at him in astonishment, Clay, satisfied
with his effect, swung round for the waiter, gesturing him
towards the blackboard that stood in the corner. When it was
lifted over, he checked on which was the largest and sweetest
pudding on offer. 'One of them, then. Oh, and here,' as the
waiter turned away, 'more wine as well.'

Two bottles had been emptied.

'I'll bring the wine list.'

'Bring that, bring that!' rapping the bottle in front of him.

'I thought you might want white with the pudding.'

'You what?' Clay reached up and took a pinch of the young man's shirt. He held it about where the nipple would be, not having hold of any flesh, but rolling the cloth between his fingers. The waiter was held bent slightly forward until just enough time had passed to make it clear that he lacked the courage or resolution to break free. Only then did Clay let go, turned away as if the space by his side had emptied, said indifferently, 'Just bring the red.'

It had the bully's trademark.

'You're giving me Jamal?'

'Where he is. What he's calling himself now. And a letter to him, explaining why he should talk to you.' He took an envelope out of his inside pocket and laid it on the table. 'We could be there tomorrow.'

As he glanced down at the letter Clay had written to Jamal, Meldrum said, 'Are you seriously asking me to go to Ireland again with *you*?'

'No, I fucking told you. Jamal hasn't been back to Ireland in ten years. Those boys get around. I met a lot of Palestinians when I was in Denmark. And, no, he isn't in Denmark either.'

'How would you know where he is after all this time?'

'Because he feels about me the way I felt about Francis. Put it this way,' his left hand squeezed along the length of his right thumb, 'we kept in touch. If I tell him to spill his guts to you, that's what he'll do.'

'He hasn't anything I want to hear.'

'Yes, he has. About me telling him I'd had to kill Francis and the old man. And why. Statement from him, your friend Keaney might walk.'

'You must think I'm stupid,' Meldrum said bitterly.

'Why would I drop myself in it? I know exactly what's going through your mind. I'm not saying, move over, Mr Keaney, you've kept this cell nice and warm, now it's my turn. Statements is what you get, you don't get us. Jamal's people are retiring him home to live like a prince. I've seen pictures of the house. No more grey skies. We'll have servants. It's going to be a nice life.'

'What are you after?' Then for a moment Meldrum thought he had it. 'You want to go public on Laverty. That your mob killed him, not the IRA.'

'Why would I do that?'

'Revenge for your father's death.'

'You sure you met my father?' Clay asked incredulously.

'That wasn't the way you were talking the last time we met.'

'Leave it,' Clay said.

Watching him spoon up the last of the pudding, a thick sludge the colour of excrement, Meldrum retched and had to swallow.

Clay smacked his lips in satisfaction. 'You've got it arse to front. What I'm offering you is a bargain. You get Keaney out of jail. And in return accept Jamal's story that I was an Irish terrorist. That's what he believes to this day. You bring that story back, and I can go off, they'll leave me alone. They'll say, fine, old Clay isn't going to be trouble. Forget him.'

'They?'

'I've been in hiding since what happened at O'Toomey's farm. Here – I've this for you as well.'

'What is it?'

'Tickets.'

Meldrum tore open the second envelope. Inside were two sets of flight tickets: Edinburgh to Paris; and two sets of rail tickets departing south from Paris.

'Plane leaves tomorrow morning. He'll meet us at the station in Issoudun.'

Meldrum dropped the envelope on top of the first, the one with the address and letter to Jamal.

'I wouldn't walk across the street with you at my back.'

Clay picked up both envelopes and stood up as if to leave. Instead he crossed the room and went into the lavatory. At once, Meldrum found the old lady at the next table was watching him. She stared without any attempt at concealment, eyes fixed on him. Perhaps she was one of those old ladies who could sit with her husband and catch scraps of talk for miles around; or maybe the waiter reminded her of a son and she disliked Clay's bullying. As far as he'd noticed till that moment she hadn't looked up from her plate.

A thin man and a tall thin boy, father and son, came down the steps from the street. As they got themselves settled at a table, Clay came back carrying the bible that had been left in the lavatory.

'That's bad luck,' he said, handing it over as he sat down again, 'leaving that behind. And new, I saw you buy it.'

The two envelopes were tucked into the middle of it.

'Suppose you didn't have to?' Clay asked.

'What?'

'Worry about having me at your back. Would you keep the bargain? I think you would.' He called, 'Here!' The waiter standing by the newcomers' table with his blackboard glanced over uneasily. 'When you've a minute!' Again his voice was a near shout. There was a silence, then a commentary of lowered voices in response. 'Suppose I got myself into jail, you could go then. Catch the plane in the morning.'

As he spoke, he swung round in his seat. The waiter, who had taken the newcomers' order and was heading for the kitchen, lost his nerve and made the detour to him.

Clay took out a money clip with notes folded in it. 'No credit cards. No wallet. No driving licence. No nothing. Look,' he held out his wrist, 'not even a watch. But there's eighty, a hundred quid there. Here, take it! Keep the extra. It'll help pay for the damage.'

The waiter opened his mouth to speak. His eyes screwed up into a frown. He knows, Meldrum thought, somewhere in his head he knows, it's just that he won't believe it. The young waiter was like the straight man in an old slapstick movie. He bit his lip. He frowned. There was no way he wasn't going to end up by asking. Inevitable. Like keeping on falling once you're over the edge.

'What damage?' the waiter asked.

With a sweep of his arm, Clay cleared the table. It was the glasses smashing into the wall under the window that made the noise. In the same movement, he was on his feet and hitting the waiter. The blows were very fast and all to the head. It was over before Meldrum could move. The man lying in a huddle on the floor. The bottle knocked over, rocking to and fro on the table, red wine spilling and dripping from the edge to the floor.

A woman appeared in the kitchen door and vanished.

'Off you go,' Clay said. He hadn't stopped smiling since the waiter spoke. 'Nobody else hurt, promise. I'm just going to wreck the place a little.'

Meldrum was in the street walking away before he came to himself. He stepped off the pavement at the corner to cross – and stopped. What about everyone else? What about the old lady at the next table who had watched him so intently, before the violence began? He had an image of her crouched against the wall, afraid.

On his way back, the police car passed him. When he got there, he saw through the basement window the two policemen hitting Clay. It was hard to be sure, but he seemed to be smiling and not defending himself.

As Meldrum watched, he went down finally.

CHAPTER FORTY-SEVEN

H arriet didn't know how long she had been sitting motionless. There had been a knocking at the door, but she
couldn't have said whether that was five minutes or an hour
before. The whisky bottle was full, but the top was off. It had
been off for a long time. The liquid inside was the wrong colour,
too dark, caramel-coloured, not the pale straw of the expensive
stuff. It would be sweet, too, cheap blended whisky. Since her
diet had taken her off sugar, she tasted it added to everything,
even tins of beans. The sweet liquor smell made her feel sick.
She had been sitting for a long time feeling sick.

'Failed in her duties as an officer of the Court.' Of all the
things that had been said to her that day, this was the one she
hadn't been able to keep out of mind.

A glass sat beside the bottle. It wasn't one of the crystal
glasses from the sideboard, just a cheap tumbler fished from the
back of a shelf in the kitchen. Cheap and nasty and untempting.
Side by side, the empty glass, the bottle full.

She attended them, in waiting.

She had arrived at court. No, before that: she'd kissed Jim
and said she would see him at the restaurant. He was to go and
talk to whoever he could find among the Keaney witnesses;
that was what she had advised him to do. She was a lawyer,
she gave advice. To do that took a certain kind of person. She
had never thought of any other profession.

The first time, a student, she had gone into a court to observe,
it had felt right; she had been at home. This morning home had

turned strange, gingerbread castle, side glances, stepfathers, a pot of water boiling on the hearth for the orphan child. Come and be cooked.

Every lawyer was an officer of the court, with a duty to justice as well as client. When she was in love with John Brennan, she had gone back and read in one of her law books: 'The code which requires a barrister to do all this is not a code of law. It is a code of honour.' That was how she saw Brennan then, a man big enough to be a hero.

At some time after the room darkened, she had crouched under the noise of knocking at the door, knowing it must be Jim Meldrum. How could she describe to him the stillness after they had accused her of perverting the course of justice? Or how police had broken into her office? Or that the search had been undertaken on information laid by John Brennan, Counsel for the Defence? How could she explain what was impossible to understand?

Yet she had wept when the knocking stopped. An accessory, art and part of the crime itself, if she was that, she would be jailed. She had wanted to be comforted by him for she was afraid.

She reached for the bottle but stopped herself, less by will than allowing the impulse to lapse. Her hand lay open beside the glass. The pad of the thumb belonged to Venus; cross-hatched lines of life, heart, fate. Chirognomy, chiromancy: character is destiny. Loving was a mistake. Father, mother, lovers, it didn't matter; a husband . . . children. Anyone you might love gave the world another hostage to hold against you. And if you resiled from all of that: a gaunt woman of sixty alone naked before a mirror searching her breasts for cancer.

It was the ringing of the phone that wakened her, jerking up her head from where it lay on her chest. Light spilled from the three high windows at the end of the long room. It was morning and she had slept in the chair all night. As she stretched her aching neck and pulled herself up in the chair, the phone stopped. Nothing had changed.

But the bottle on the table was still full.

That much she had won.

CHAPTER FORTY-EIGHT

As the path came over the crest of the hill, instead of coming into view of Gautmuir House as he had expected, Farquhar Wood found himself on the edge of a steep drop. It fell a hundred feet into a bowl cut out of the hillside.

By his side, Sir James had mounted the slope with a light step, so that it had been a repeated strangeness turning to confront the taut parchment of skull and yellow teeth pressing forward as if out of a dead man's mouth. Relaxed and affable, he talked of lines of alliance within the inner workings of the Party and of past friendships and rivalries: 'I was there, dinner after some function or other, when this university type asked Jephson, what achievement would you say you were proudest of? I don't think in those terms, he told him. With a scrap of manners, fellow would have left it at that. Didn't, of course. He rephrased it, isn't that what they say? *Rephrased* it more than once. Been in three of the great offices of state, he persisted, long life in politics, blah blah what were you proudest of blah. Finally, Jephson, who'd been giving it some thought, said, I'll tell you what gave me most *satisfaction*. We got a contract for twenty million to build a hospital in Africa. And ten years later we got another contract which paid as much again for tearing it down. University fellow's mouth opened, then shut, he didn't know what the answer to that should be. Jephson. Jew, of course.' The old man made him uneasy standing so close to the edge. 'Quarry for aggregate, for roads and suchlike. Worked out thirty years ago but worth a bit to the estate in its time.' He saw now there was a stock fence strung along the edge; out of repair, though, with sections missing and posts and wire fallen over. 'That business,' Sir James went on with no alteration of tone, 'is on its way to being more or less settled, I understand.'

'Business?' Then he realised he was being obtuse. 'Ah, you mean Keaney and—'

Sir James accompanied his nod with an impatient gesture of the hand as if to sweep names aside. 'Stuff you were worrying your head about last time you were here.'

'Things seem to be happening. I don't know about settled. I have no details.'

'Nor should you have. Details aren't our concern. Best that way. Settled is what matters.'

Coming upon the fall into the quarry like that, so unexpectedly, had been a shock. As his breath slowed, he became aware of the noise. It was soft, like the rubbing of fingers close to his ear. A stream of little stones was running down the slope. Puzzled, he leaned forward and had a glimpse of rabbits before they flicked away out of sight. Just under the edge of the overhanging drop he saw the open mouths of burrows. Tunnels must honeycomb the ground under them. Under the old man's sardonic gaze, he took himself carefully back from the edge.

For his grandfather, a foreman moulder in an ironworks and a Kirk elder, the deceptiveness of seemingly solid ground under your feet would have been the stuff of a sermon. He shook his head, as if to shake out of it this remnant of ancestral moralising.

His was a different world.

Bathed and changed, that evening he turned to the girl sitting beside him. His luck was running in this as everything for the moment. She was the one who had caught his attention when they all burst in, young, noisy, on their way south again after attending a wedding. Sir James had accepted their arrival with a good grace.

For his part, he was content to be in this room, about which with the possible exception of Sir James he would

bet he knew more than anyone else sitting round this table
– carved, incidentally, from a single piece of walnut. He could
name the provenance of the Belgian tapestry on the wall which
depicted the encounter of Jesus with the brother fishermen by
the Sea of Galilee. He knew the value and rarity of the bronze
patera on the side table, could have told how the Hogarth and
Allan Ramsay paintings had come into the family and that the
carved embellishments of the wall panels were after the style
of Grinling Gibbons. Under the elaborate plaster ornaments of
the ceiling – mid-seventeenth-century, birds, beasts, flowers –
he sat at meat: had he been a cat he would have purred.

In the Party, he was thought of as one of the new breed,
self-made men, rising schemers, pliant yet hard. That inside
dwelt this romantic was his secret. It was true that Britain was
not the power in the world which once it had been. For himself
he would have been happiest as the servant of a great empire.
In the imperial ideal, it could even be said, there was the germ
of the new idealism of today which sought to transcend the
nation state. Taking a different turn, he thought, Who in any
case could read the future? It was possible that Britain might
find a fresh destiny and be in some way great once more. As
a public man he was circumspect, the mouthpiece of smaller
times; privately, he dreamed of greatness of which he might
be a part. He had made himself the man he was, and in the
making left behind friends and even family. He had sacrificed
what it had been necessary to sacrifice. He needed no one to
tell him he had lost as well as gained over the years of rising
in the world. The girl confirmed him in the rightness of his
choice. She took away his doubts, for there were times when
he doubted.

She was the embodiment in flesh of that which he struggled
towards.

It must have been some of this going round in his head
which led him to remark to her what a fine thing it was
to be dining in a room where so many remarkable men had
eaten 'and among them the Duke of Cumberland on his way
to Culloden'.

She looked at him thoughtfully. It occurred to him he had
neglected to add 'and women' after 'remarkable men'.

She said, 'My brother Simon finds all that kind of thing fascinating.'

A moment later she was discussing with her neighbour on the other side how the investment house of which yesterday's groom was a director had been approached to put money into a film, 'And Prue was doing their Public Relations. And it went on from there. If I'd been told those two would ever marry, I'd have said, sorry, just not on. Not Prue, not when Dickie hated him so much at school.'

And listening to her chatter, he was pleased by her. He'd been a fool to talk history to her. To her history wasn't something to be learned out of books. It was the element she moved in; and so she talked not of kings or battles but of weddings and children born and, yes, even, as now, of a loved nanny dead. History was what her connections had been making for generations and made still. Bending forward to speak, she laughed at something which had been said and he was conscious of how under the pressure of her leaning the flesh of her forearm spread a little, slender, white, dusted with fine hairs. He wondered how it would feel to brush its length gently with his fingertips. He had a vision of himself naked on hands and knees, being ridden by her, his sides gripped between the lean muscled tautness of her thighs. And then he was on top, driving down on her, crushing her with his weight, splitting her apart. The images blended and confused together so that he could not tell which of the two he desired.

If he had hoped again to have Sir James to himself, he would have been disappointed. In the library he found whisky set out on a tray, but after a while it became obvious he was to be on his own. He poured himself a glass and then another. Getting up, he found the switches and tried them until only one lamp, by the corner seat of a black leather couch, was left on. Then he went back and sat with the decanter by his elbow looking out from an island of light to where the farther ends of the long room were mysterious in shadow, imagining himself to be at home.

Getting ready to leave next day, he took a turn into the wrong corridor. Doors lay open giving glimpses of rooms, being vacated he supposed like his own after the weekend.

These would be the rooms occupied by some of last night's party of young people. Perhaps one of them by the girl who had sat next to him at dinner. He stole glances inside as he went along until a maid coming out backed into him, spilling the armful of bed linen she had been clutching.

'Sorry!'

A courteous man, and the girl was pretty, without a thought he bent to help her gather them up. And as he did, stirred the sheets so that an acrid tang rose to offend his nostrils.

'They all do it,' the girl said, and grinned. 'Pee the beds. Like kids. They drink too much. But that's not the only reason, of course.'

It was disconcerting that she should feel free to speak to him like that. She hadn't the accent of a country girl. Perhaps she was doing this as a vacation job. A student, yes, if she was a student that would account for it. It came to him with a shock of recognition that the maid's accent belonged not just to anywhere in Glasgow but exactly to some bleak housing scheme on the outskirts, perhaps even the one in which his parents had been allocated a house after the war. He had hated growing up there. Hated the featureless streets, mile after mile of identical housing, steel-framed, rough-cast walls, hated the mean little shops, hated the blank slope of straggling grass where a cinema might have been if television hadn't come along, hated as he got older the long journeys into the city on Saturday nights, smoke-filled buses, drunks coming back. And found his escape, to university, into journalism, at last, like a fish into water, to politics.

He had spent his life getting to where the valuable people were. He needed no one to tell him what the rest were like. He'd been there.

For her, escape might not be so easy. A student in these days. Debt. Jobs hard to come by. Young, reckless, didn't she understand?

At the door of the breakfast room, he paused. The faint smell of something bothered him. A scent on the air resembling nothing so much as the lingering smell of urine. He sniffed at his fingers.

It was hard to be sure, but his hands seemed to be clean.

BOOK SEVEN

Blue on Blue

CHAPTER FORTY-NINE

Meldrum was pleased to see the water tower as he drove into town. He used it as a marker, turning right and running along until he came to the bakery where he bought baguettes and *pain raisin*. He had the French to ask for them memorised, though he forgot to add *s'il vous plaît*. He took them back for breakfast and by then he was hungry, but he liked that too, driving back through fields where sunflowers were in harvest, the clusters that were left nodding and darkening on the long stalks.

He liked the smell of fresh bread coming from where it lay on the back seat, and taking the side road smoothly as old habit though this was only the third morning.

He was holding on to the shreds of the spell. The one that should have been over or never started. The one that had begun on the station platform.

He had expected to be met by some swarthy thug, not this elegant slim smiling man, ring-laden hand extended in greeting.

'Mr Meldrum? You have presence – your photograph does you no justice. I'm so glad you could come.' Jamal's voice was light and soft, and hearing that accent in Britain it would have been recognised as the one that told about school not birthplace, a matter of class rather than geography. At a guess Meldrum put him in his late forties.

That was in the middle of the afternoon, and next morning was a different kind of wakening. For weeks, he had jerked out of sleep like a canoeist paddling to stay upright, thoughts already in spate. Unhurriedly then as sun rising on a bedroom wall he had retraced that first day. From the station, being driven round the edge of the town and into the countryside. Long perspectives to the horizon, open sky, a sign set up in a field – BLOCUS DE PARIS. A side road narrow enough to make him think of passing places. Sunflower fields on either side, the road bending through them like a drawn bow. A stretch of densely packed trees and bushes and a glimpse of a path running steeply down. It was a landscape that tucked such hidden pleasures into its folds. One house set back in a wide garden, then another, a corner, turning in at the open gate of a third. 'Coffee first. Make yourself comfortable.' And that was part of the laying of the spell, that ritual of coffee in little cups and chatting of planes, train connections, journeys and weather. There had been a meal and a bottle of wine. 'Time enough to talk in the morning.' But he had talked, all through the meal Jamal had talked.

'I rent this house from a man in Chateauroux. It was his family home. Where I put the car in? That was the forge. For shoeing horses and so on, they were blacksmiths. If you walk back the way we came there's a path down to the river. I'm told it has good fishing. The village is quiet even in the summer, most of the houses are only used by families at the weekend. I don't think I've ever been in a more peaceful place. In winter, out of the world. I've liked it very much.' And at some other point: 'A little argument with Paris about agricultural subsidies. A certain dislike of Algerians on welfare. My neighbours, apart from such preoccupations, aren't political people. They enjoy life.'

That first morning when he'd finally got up, it was still only seven o'clock. There was no sound in the house, so he'd dressed and taken the path down to the river. It was sluggish and not very wide and there was a little jetty with broken planks and a boat pulled up among reeds with the bottom rotted out of it. He had come to it along an avenue of young pines, and crouching to feel the water cool between his fingers he looked over his shoulder and saw the trees throw elegant shadows and the sun make haloes among the leaves. Going back, he peeped over a hedge at a place with the look of a farmhouse. An old woman huddled in long skirt and jersey was wheeling a barrow through high uncut grass towards the back door. She stared at the sight of him. From the house a second woman hurried to her support. Nothing to be done but grimace and flee, grateful to get off without barking dogs. His fault for startling them like a fool. Malicious and afraid, outside that shabby secretive house, the women might have been bonneted peasants caught in a time warp. Yet near Jamal's front gate, he met a villager who responded to his 'Good morning' in English, nodded at the house, 'Ah, yes, the Greek gentleman,' and went off smiling, sleek length of dog at heel, as if strolling a Parisian boulevard.

'One of the weekenders,' Jamal said.

'Who thought you were Greek.'

'Which I'm not.' He touched his breasts with fingertips, then stretched out open hands spreading the fingers. 'A father who was Palestinian. An English mother. See what confidence I have in you. Come on, I want to show you something.'

He led the way from the kitchen through the garage to the outside. On the same wall there were two sets of double doors. To open, the nearest had to be lifted and dragged sagging on its hinges. In the dim light of the interior Meldrum made out stalls, cribs for fodder, a couple of old bicycles hung one under the other. 'Watch your step. There's all kinds of rubbish lying about.' At the back a flight of steps ran down into the dark. As Meldrum hesitated, a light went on below. 'Come and see!' He went cautiously down into a cellar with an arched roof of roughly cut stone. 'This is where they baked bread.' And there was an oven with a rusted round iron door. 'Wonderful, eh? Progress means I fetch my loaves from town. I'm going in now, would you like to come with me? And if you're an early riser, you might like to fetch it by yourself tomorrow.'

It wasn't a difficult run to memorise. To the water tower and turn right. Along to the traffic lights. Round the corner; park; cross the road to the baker's. 'Remember to look left.' The bread was warm to the touch. On the return journey the smell from the back seat was wonderful.

That day, they lunched in the open. Afterwards he found

the garden continued into a quarter-acre of rough grass lined by trees. He walked around the edge of it until he paused and looking up recognised he was standing under a walnut tree, apples scattered on the grass nearby, a harvester rattling somewhere beyond in an adjacent field. He was out of sight of the house. Open paddock, windfall apples, walnuts. He felt free, irresponsible, escaped; whether or not it made sense, that was how he felt, even if it was only a measure of the fear and tension he'd brought with him. Escaped, for the moment. He picked up one of the apples and took a bite. It tasted pulpy and dull, which was often the way with windfalls.

For dinner, Jamal had taken him to the next village. They ate at the restaurant run by the commune. There was no choice, everyone got the same dishes – a soup, little fish with the heads on, steak, sweet fruit tart – good food, wonderfully cooked, and bottles of wine between them as they ate. 'We arrived in London in nineteen fifty-one,' Jamal said. 'My mother, my father, myself and my little brother, who was waiting to be born. Within days my mother was dead giving birth to him. You know how some women show a lot of gum when they smile? Sometimes, when I see that, I think, yes, perhaps. But really I don't know. I was too young when she died, and there were no photographs. After my uncles were killed, our family joined the hundreds of thousands who fled from this new place called Israel. Father took us to Egypt, where he had a sister and cousins. Then to France. As a young man he'd been a student at the Sorbonne. We stayed with a friend he'd made at that time. Between Jaffa and Cairo or Paris or London, somewhere on those journeys like so much else photographs were lost.'

It was late when they got back. As they went into the house, Meldrum asked again about the assassination of Laverty. Jamal pleaded tiredness, and it was agreed they would talk in the morning.

It had been in the street market at Issoudun that afternoon that he had raised the question of Laverty. 'Later, at home in comfort, I promise.' They were wandering to and fro between stalls weighted with cheeses and bearded scallops and oysters in baskets. Meat, fish, honey.

If he was impressed, it wasn't by any cliché about abundance

in comparison to his own northern home. Meldrum tramping
in the Pentland Hills had passed hives tucked in by dry-stone
dykes: heather honey sweet as any. He had walked East Lothian
lanes with not a summer breath stirring and fields on either
side heavy with wheat. The bother was that in the back of his
mind he knew an unneeded nuclear plant squatted where
those fields met the sea; knew entire hills on the opposite
western coast were hollowed out and stuffed with warheads;
knew, as even unpolitical men knew, that the radioactive spew
of Cumbria was carried by drifting tides always north.

Far from home, on the other hand, he saw only how good
the living was: fish, meat and honey. In the Issoudun market,
ignorant of language and history, he heard words he didn't
understand, and it seemed to him a place where it should be
easy for men to be happy.

Returning from town at the end of the afternoon, Meldrum
had begun to work out the questions he would ask about the
Laverty affair. Jamal, however, instead of taking the side road
to his house, had kept on towards the next village. 'We will
dine out this evening.'

Meldrum, then, got up on the morning of the third day
determined to have his questions answered. The house wasn't
large. He came out of his bedroom into the living area with its
table by the window, open fire and easy chairs. The door to
the other bedroom was in the opposite corner; still closed,
Jamal not being an early riser. Apart from that, there was a
corridor which beyond the entry to the tiny kitchen led to a
bathroom.

In the kitchen he found the car keys on the hook where Jamal
had shown him they'd be left. He was half-way to town before
it occurred to him that he had no insurance to drive. A fine
dry morning; empty roads; a two-door Renault with plenty on
the clock. Safe enough; and if illegality ran against his grain,
still some latitude should be allowed a man far from home.

There was still no sign of Jamal when he got back. He sat for
a while at the table then went outside, coffee in one hand and
a twist torn from a baguette lined with butter and cheese in
the other. He wandered round the grassy area at the side of the
house. A playhouse big enough to sit inside stood near a hedge,

a leftover from the owner's family time. Chewing on a giant mouthful, he stood for a while contemplating dust tumbling through slants of sunshine from the patched roof of a lean-to set up to cover gathered branches and wood cut for the fire.

It was only when he went back in that the time registered and he became suspicious. He knocked on the bedroom door, and getting no answer checked the bathroom and kitchen. He went back and knocked again more loudly, then opened the door.

The bed was unmade, tumbled about as if by a restless sleeper. White curtains drifted back from the open window.

He went looking in every room. He went into the side garden where he had already been. He walked the circumference of the open paddock under the trees. He went out on to the road and walked first in one direction then the other. He even looked into the garage to see if the car was where he had left it, though it couldn't have been moved without him hearing.

There wasn't a phone in the house. He went all through it to make sure. And if he had found one, who would there have been to call?

The book lying open beside Jamal's bed was in French, a language he couldn't read. He had carried it with him into the living-room before he admitted the futility of turning its pages and threw it down.

In the bedroom, he began again with a policeman's thoroughness and at the end of an hour had nothing. No address book. No letters. A suitcase in a cupboard with marks where luggage labels had been scraped off. A bit of paper in a compartment of a scuffed briefcase that turned out to be a restaurant bill; in Greek, so that all he could make out was 8% and 18% – for tax? – and the total 2100–drachmas presumably.

No photographs, either, though the lack of them might have been a habit Jamal had kept from his childhood.

It struck him since the car was still there that either someone had come for Jamal or he was somewhere nearby. With that in mind, he walked the half-circle of the side road both ways until in each direction it joined the road to Issoudun. Few houses, some with the windows shuttered. At one point a car passed, and later a tradesman's van. Near one end of the road a farmhouse had been deserted to collapse into itself.

He found tomatoes in a basket in the kitchen, cheese and cold meat in the refrigerator, and carried them out with a bottle of beer from the garage shelf to the table in the garden. As he ate, he went over everything he could remember of what Jamal had said. Certainly, he had given no hint he was about to disappear.

Walking down from the market, they had been caught by a flurry of heavy rain outside a museum. Whitewashed walls, a chapel with a screen from behind which tight-packed bedfuls of the sick had watched Mass, a pharmacy with mortars and stills, a book of drug recipes: *take*, the caption in English quoted, *scorpions, honey, oil from a small dog.* 'I love this town.' 'So why leave it?' 'Is that what I'm going to do?' 'According to Clay, leaving it with him.' 'And did he say where?' But that question, the soft fluting of it, the raised eyebrow, made Meldrum feel as if he was being laughed at. He lost his temper, the strength of his reaction taking him by surprise. 'How the hell would I know? I'm not an expert on terrorism. Libya?'

And what had Jamal said then? Looking at him, shaking his head. 'No, not an expert. Iran, Iraq, Syria. The list goes on. Many regimes have made use of the Palestinians.' And then said? With the edge of his hand Meldrum brushed together crumbs scattered on the table. 'Believe me, I won't be setting foot in any of them.' Crickets chirped in the grass. 'I wouldn't be so rash.' And then? He raised his head and felt warmth on his cheek. When they came out of the museum, the rain had stopped and the sun was shining.

'I'm pensioned off,' Jamal had said, smiling down at him from the steps. 'I think you and I are more like one another than either of us resemble Mr Clay.'

Sitting at the table going over it, he knew he was missing something important. He tried to think about it, just as it had happened, then he let himself be distracted by the formality of calling a lover Mister Clay.

The rest of the day he waited. Twice he thought he heard a car and went out to the front. He searched the house again, and when he found a torch looked through the old stables. He went down into the cellar, and even tried to open the round door of the bread oven, but it was rusted tight. He walked the road again, both ways, with no more success than the first time, and it was getting dark when he got back.

He dreamed he was walking in Issoudun. On a wall there was a plaque, a memorial to the dead, tortured by the Gestapo, hostages punished for the courage of others, the men of the Resistance. It was in French but he read it and understood every word. Boulevard Roosevelt. Boulevard Stalingrad. In his dream he thought of Edinburgh: Princes Street, George Street, Charlotte Square: dead Royals.

And wakened to see a torch waving its light over the window as someone approached along the path. It was Jamal come back in the middle of the night. 'I have all you need now,' he'd said. 'Tomorrow.'

In the morning, he checked that Jamal was there, that he hadn't dreamt his return during the night, edging the door open until he could see him curled on his side in bed asleep. He stood looking at him for a long time. Tomorrow, he had said. He had no fear of him disappearing again.

Coming back with the bread, he saw BLOCUS DE PARIS – and on a hillock a sign Jamal had translated for him: PAS DE PAYSAN, PAS DE PAYS. No country folk, no country.

He sat at the table by the window and spread honey and peach jam and washed it down with cup after cup of coffee. 'You didn't use the car. Someone came for you – and brought you back.'

Jamal was in the chair beside the fire. The hearth was grey with wood ash. He turned a page and looked up. 'Hard to believe this was written two and a half thousand years ago. He divides spies into the living who come back with their reports; and the expendable used to spread false reports among an enemy. They are a ruler's treasure, he says. High praise for the profession. Pity you can't read it.' It was the book Meldrum had taken out of the bedroom.

'Today,' Meldrum said. 'I want this finished today.'

'It will be.' Jamal closed the book. 'You'll be told who was behind the death of the American Laverty, and you'll get information which will finish the Keaney matter once and for all. I'm sorry you've been kept waiting, but a meeting had to be arranged. We're going to meet someone today.'

'Was that what you were doing yesterday?'

'In part.'

'Was he there – this person we're going to meet?'

Jamal put up his hands, smiling. 'No, no. He has some way still to travel.'

'Was he directly involved in killing Laverty?'

'Oh, yes.' He stood up. 'And now you have to trust me. Believe me, Meldrum, I am well disposed to you. Put up with me for a few more hours – take a little tour, there's no question of meeting here – and then it is finished.'

As the day went on, Meldrum decided that Jamal was being sent from one place to another, and in each place being told where to go next and given a number to phone once he was there for fresh instructions. Maybe that wasn't what was happening, but it was how he worked it out. For whoever they were going to meet it would make sense to be careful or frightened.

He didn't trust Jamal. Why should anyone else?

At first it seemed straightforward. They went south to Chateauroux and as he was led this way and that through its crowded streets Meldrum was on the alert for a contact, expecting it to be made at any moment. They went in and out of shops, sat in a church, stood in front of busts of Napoleon in a museum. When they were eating lunch Jamal excused himself and left the table. As he waited for him to come back – began to wonder if he was coming back – two elderly couples came in. They stood behind their chairs watching one another across the table. It looked like an uneasy moment until younger ones arrived, plus a carry-cot with blue flounces and white frills. There was what must have been the parents and another couple who might have been a sister and her husband or a brother and his wife. Two young men last in to complete the family party smiled and nodded at Meldrum sitting on his own and one offered, 'Bon appétit!' As the mother laid the baby out to be changed on the table, Jamal reappeared. 'We're going to Bourges,' he said, which was when Meldrum worked out his idea about the phone calls.

They left town on the ring road, going north past lines of barracks with broken windows and a gate guarded by soldiers in uniforms that fitted as badly as if they had been asked to make them themselves.

BOURGES 65km, the sign read.

Bourges didn't just have churches, it had a cathedral. Tipping back his head to look at the figures writhing above the portal, Jamal said, 'I went to a dance once in Camberwell that looked like that. I was nineteen years old and the Israelis had just been defeated at the battle of Karameh.'

What was going on around them on the steps, the circling up and down for a camera viewpoint of a tourist busload, seemed to Meldrum more like a dance than anything in the carved stone. Beside him, an earnest American lectured to his wife, checking occasionally with the book he carried. It was the portal of the Last Judgment and that figure holding the scales was Christ. To His right the saved looking smug, and at the end under a canopy a figure like an older god holding a blanket in his lap from which tiny heads peeped out – of babies? notions of the need for baptism stirred vaguely, were they the unbaptised who could not be saved? And to the left where the scales fell heavy, a grinning devil and his attendants pushing the damned along and stuffing them into a pot, the mouth of hell, and at its base a little devil pumping away with a hand-bellows that might have been exactly the one he'd used the night before to get the logs going in the open hearth. And Christ in Majesty was there too, up at the very top flanked by angels, arms spread above a writhing of naked supplicants looking up more in dread it seemed than hope.

'Sorry. You were saying about a dance?'

'No, please. I understand. Take your time.'

But Meldrum was already turning away. The unexpected effect for him had been how childish it seemed, a bogey tale for all the craft and the years of toil.

What he thought of these things was none of Jamal's business.

'Karameh?'

Jamal didn't supply an answer until they were comfortably seated with coffee and pastries ordered.

'After the' Sixty-seven War, the Palestinians were in a bad way. Arafat had no more than four hundred fighters under his command gathered in the town of Karameh. With the connivance of King Hussein, the Israelis invaded Jordan to wipe them out. Infantry, tanks, artillery, planes. Against men and boys with grenades and sticks of dynamite. But Fatah stood its ground and fought them for six hours – until the Jordanian army joined in out of shame. The Israelis ran for home, and within a year twenty thousand volunteers had joined Fatah to carry on the struggle. A small battle over a little town, but to survive every cause needs its heroic moment.' He told the story unemphatically, an incident from history, then added, 'Think of the Just Men, the Jewish notion of the few who make a whole people worth saving. Wasn't it Graham Greene who wrote somewhere that you could tell a Jew by the shape of his paunch?'

'And you were in London when you heard about this?'

'Where else? My father had become a British citizen. He'd qualified as an optician, and had a shop where he sold spectacles. Nothing heroic about my father, which was why I was surprised to be told he was working behind the scenes to raise money for Fatah. I was dancing with this girl, more than one dance, we'd taken a fancy to one another. Her boyfriend asked my name, asked me to give him my full name, and then he drew me aside. Where I'd been to school, our last holiday to visit my aunt in Egypt, my father's activities – which, as I say, came as a surprise to me. My father and I didn't get on very well. It was astonishing how much that young man knew about us.'

'Special Branch file clerk,' Meldrum guessed. 'Drunk or stupid. How did you feel about that?'

'I was impressed,' Jamal said. 'I was impressed by a sense of power. Would you excuse me for a moment?'

'You have a phone call to make?'

He smiled and didn't answer, but within half an hour they were back in the car and leaving town.

Picking up on familiar features of the road, Meldrum asked, 'Are we going back to Chateauroux?'

'A little further south. Have you heard of George Sand?'

'Should I have?'

'A writer. She was Chopin's mistress. The composer?'

'The composer,' Meldrum repeated, 'and when I go to Nottingham Robin Hood is an outlaw.'

Jamal turned his head and studied him interestedly. 'What?'

'I'm not a tourist. That's not what I'm here for.'

'We have a destination,' Jamal said, 'and till then let us pass the time pleasantly.'

'How much time?'

'Before dark.'

In the next town there was an Avenue George Sand and a museum George Sand, which for some reason was full of stuffed birds, though Meldrum's French didn't run to knowing whether or not it had been the lady writer who stuffed them. Of all the voices round him, Jamal's was the one he understood, talking more than ever and of everything, it seemed, except George Sand. Disoriented, there wasn't any choice but to listen. The truth was that, tiring as the afternoon went by, he had a sense imposed upon him of the Palestinian as rational, cultured, and drawing for his view of politics and the future upon a wider experience than his – and an experience reflected upon as his had not been.

'It's not a common thing to risk private comfort, Meldrum, for some public good. To risk safety even. We hear so much about the passivity of modern man, his feeling of helplessness. But when did the ordinary man ever influence events? During the Thirty Years War? Riding behind Genghis Khan into Baghdad? He didn't expect to, the idea wouldn't have entered his head. Perhaps it's a democratic illusion, and one held for only a brief time in a few countries. And even then, what influence did the ordinary man have? In 1914 men volunteered for the armies of Germany, France, Britain. They were the first generation of mass schooling, the best-educated foot soldiers since warfare began. It didn't take them long to work out what was going on, but they couldn't stop. They ran into the grinder, like mice on a butcher's counter. Man needs to give himself, to the Mongol Horde, Islam, the Workers' State. Let men be all together to shape a piece of history and they'll swing away with a will, until they hear bones breaking and swing harder, their own bones breaking, for they are the anvil as well as the hammer. A man like you is rare. The one who says, this is wrong, even if he has to stand alone. When I heard what you were doing, I wanted to meet you.'

But Meldrum felt he was being treated as a fool and scowled.

'At my public school, we were reared on the ideal of service. Some of us took it so seriously we did voluntary work in Africa. Boiled goat and banana for eight weeks. No imagination. Even the Mexican, hardly the peak of evolution, thought of tacos. It was a relief when term started and we got back to Kipling. But don't think we were disillusioned. No, we were well pleased with ourselves. Service, you see. This was before AIDS, of course, so the worst we brought back was the odd case of clap and no harm done. That the Empire had folded in on itself was a secret our schoolmasters kept from us.'

When they left La Chatre, it was to head north again. This time Meldrum couldn't see where there had been an opportunity for Jamal to make a phone call, and that worried him. They didn't go far before the car pulled in to a village square. The sky was overcast and the square deserted. Looking around, Meldrum realised that for the first time that day he wasn't surrounded by crowds of people.

Off the square there was a church, a tiny place like a child's toy after the pomp of cathedrals. He had followed inside tentatively, suddenly convinced that this was where they would be met. By a table at the door Jamal pointed to a notice in different languages; this toy of a building had survived from the twelfth century. Laid out on the table were paper rolls held by elastic bands; copies of murals, according to the notice, and beside them a saucer for coins left in payment. On either side of the aisle were wooden benches, their puppet congregation folded away. From the nave to the altar led through an arched wall, but each space was no larger than a room in a house. The murals, found and uncovered, seemed already to be fading, on the edge of being lost for a second time. Dusty, silent, the trustful saucer by the door for coins, with its air of being abandoned it seemed more like the house of a god than anything he had seen in Bourges.

Even in the glimmering light there was no place where anyone could be hidden.

As they left, Jamal picked up one of the rolls from the table. Meldrum, seeing that he had no intention of paying, took a handful of coins from his pocket and laid them in the saucer.

In the car, Jamal unwound the roll. It was a detail in dark earth colours. A man reaching up to kiss another on the cheek. Enormous almond-shaped eyes. Painted on the wall of the church 800 years ago. In the corner the legend: *Le Baiser de Judas*. 'It's for you,' he said, 'a gift.'

It was getting dark now. Heavy clouds covered the sky. They had crossed into a countryside of forests. Trees hemmed in the road on either side. And Jamal was talking again. 'In nineteen seventy-four Yasser Arafat offered to settle for Gaza and the West Bank, a little homeland in exchange for peace. But the Baathists in Iraq didn't want a democratic Arab state, however small. All those Arab kings and dictators think democracy's a contagious disease. The Baathists initiated terrorist attacks in France and elsewhere by Palestinian groups they controlled. End of peace initiative. I knew what was going on from my father, who was in despair. I was twenty-five then and drew a different lesson. It seemed to me my father's was a lost cause.'

What did this matter to him? Meldrum felt he was being taunted by some elaborate mockery he didn't understand. All he had to take comfort from was the coins he had laid in the saucer in the church. That had been the day's first assertion by him of his own will.

He was thinking about this assertion when the car came to a stop.

'Here at last,' Jamal said.

They got out. The road on one side was open fields, on the other woods. The car had stopped by a path that led into the trees. Jamal indicated it and smiled. With a grunt of rage, Meldrum spun him round and slammed him against the car. The bones of the shoulders felt delicate as if they might break between his hands. 'Hold still.' He rubbed him down, chest, hips, legs.

'I don't carry guns.' Jamal shivered delicately like a cat offended in its dignity. 'Tomfoolery over, can we get on?'

'In there?' It was dark under the trees. 'Who was behind the killing of Laverty?'

'I arranged it, you know that. The question is, who was I working for? You're supposed to be a detective. I've been telling you since we set out this morning. All you had to do was listen. Come or not, as you wish.'

There was a path, broad at first. They seemed to be skirting the edge of a lake, for there were glimpses of a great spread of dark water and rushes flattening under a rising wind. Hurrying, Jamal had drawn in upon himself, neatly shod feet splashing through the wet grass. 'I thought so well of you, Meldrum. I didn't expect you to behave badly like that. During the war, my aunt in Cairo had British officers to stay. They taught her to say, What a fucking beautiful morning, and thought it was very funny. My father would tell that story and get furious. I said to him, you can't expect every officer to be a gentleman, not in wartime.'

Meldrum had never been in woods like these. Everywhere under the trees there were blackened trunks melting back into the earth. The air was dank with the stench of rotting wood. Hardwick Hall in England was a domesticated miniature, fen, marsh, carr, sedge, birch, alder, of this appalling reality. They waded the surface of an ancient swamp.

'I'm tired of this now,' Jamal said. 'Go home. But you have to be reasonable. Put Laverty and everything connected with him out of your head, and your job will be waiting for you. Everything as it was before.'

'How can you tell me my job will be waiting?'

'You know why. You've been listening, you're not stupid. Unlike poor Clay, who never understood he and I had the same employers – ultimately the same. If you don't go home quietly, your friend Miss Cook goes to prison.'

'What?'

'She concealed incriminating evidence given to her by a client. A man, of course, who was bedding her for her trouble – at least that's the way it will seem. No violence, please! Take your hands from me.' Meldrum released his grip. 'I can't tell you how much I dislike you doing that.'

He stalked off stiff-legged as a spitting cat. Shaken grass sprayed water. Meldrum hurried after him.

'She's been set up. Why? For God's sake, why?'

'As an indication of how uncertain life is. But it can be repaired. You can be reasonable and go home to her. And be like two birds in a nest. And a word of advice, sometimes it's best to keep things to oneself even in a happy marriage. Explain to her all that's happened with anything but the truth, and if sometimes she drinks a little too much it will not matter since she will have nothing to say – that will be your gift to her.'

'I haven't told her anything.'

But Jamal only shook his head at that and increased his pace so that Meldrum had to catch up with him again.

'If they would let Keaney out—'

'He shouldn't have kept climbing on to roofs. He draws too much attention to himself.'

The path was overgrown or they had wandered from it, but then Meldrum saw red slashed on to the side of trunks and realised they were following some kind of trail. It had been raining here. As they stepped into an open space by the edge of a pool, drops showered down on them from branches stirred by the wind.

'You want justice,' Jamal said. 'There it is.'

Clay had been hung by the wrists between two trees, but one was rotted and had given under his weight so that he was held up by one arm with his head dropped to the side and his cheek resting as if in thought against the palm of the other hand.

Meldrum went to him. As he circled the edge, his foot slipped into the green slime that coated the surface of the water. The wet hair of the corpse shone in the light of the open space. He had recognised who it was, who it must be, but as he got closer Clay had the look of an older man.

For the first time, he saw the father in the son's face.

The voice came to him quietly from across the pool.

'He killed Pietro and the old man. He's paid the price. It's over.'

'For Christ's sake, he was your lover.'

'I've had better,' Jamal said.

Behind him shadows approached through the trees.

Meldrum turned and ran. Low bushes clung around his thighs. A voice shouted. A tree branch struck him on the shoulder. Everything added to his panic. He ran until his legs gave way under him.

In the forest there was no certain path. He found trunks slashed with yellow and followed that trail until he scrambled across a gully and lost it between one side and the other. He ran down a wide avenue until it divided at a fork, chose left and that way came to nothing. Twice he came out on the side of the lake. Pines on an island in the middle were bending to the wind. The surface chopped into broken waves. The second time a flight of birds heading to the opposite shore lost themselves against the clouded sky. The light was going. He wanted to keep by the edge of the water, but was driven from it by tangled bushes and inlets of mud treacherous underfoot. He went forward with his hands held out. Every tree was wet sick and rotted. He choked on the smell of decay. His hands closed on soft bulging growths. Putting his face close to a trunk, he saw it was marked in red and he went round it and stood by a pool. It wasn't the first he'd come upon, pools were everywhere, but he thought it might be the one. There were two trees, one with a broken branch. It was too dark to see if the scum of the surface had been disturbed. All it would have taken was to cut the cords and let Clay slip under the water.

Shortly afterwards the trees thinned and he crossed a field and climbed over a low gate. He had walked along the road for a mile or less, when the headlights of a car came towards him. It had been driving back and forth searching for him. Jamal was alone and the easiest thing was to get in.

'You think I wish you harm? A man who said, this is wrong, even if he had to stand alone? My schoolmasters taught us to admire such men. Others might want you dead, but I've argued your case. I want you to go back and live your life. We all have to compromise. Why should you be different from the rest of us?'

'I'm not different.'

'Let me tempt you to take your chance then,' Jamal said. 'The evidence against Miss Cook has been set up in two ways. With the second, her client the criminal only will be found responsible. He will get an addition to his sentence. That is a miscarriage of justice. But one, I think, you should leave alone.

Yours would not be the only happiness based on such a thing. Go home, your life waits for you.'

And every part of his heart and mind needed to say, yes. He wanted to be with Harriet for the rest of his life, eat with her and lie beside her at night. His job was the largest part of who he was; there was nothing else he wanted to do. Sweat broke out on him. He groaned in anguish.

'I can't do that to Keaney.'

'You owe him nothing. Explain to me why you can't. It would be so easy. Who is to say it wouldn't be the right thing to do? There is as much right on one side as the other. Why won't you do the sensible thing?'

'I can't.'

Couldn't abandon him. Had no words to explain why.

Jamal sighed.

'Keaney's dead. He died two nights ago. Forced feeding, glucose, Complan and water, milk. He lasted a long time. But his heart gave out.'

It was years since Meldrum had wept.

'I let him down.'

All of it had been for nothing.

Light from below shone on Jamal's face. Ahead of them the forest streamed back on either side into the dark.

'No,' Jamal said. 'I don't think you did.'

BOOK EIGHT

In the Belly of the Whore

CHAPTER FIFTY

By the graveside, they were all there to pay their last respects to Billy Ord. Dyall was there, and Finlay who was probably thinking he should go for the pension before it was too late, and Barry Cox, yon brute Gowdie, a couple of Lodge Grand Masters.

A working policeman again with a file of cases to deal with when the funeral was over, he was among his own.

In the kirk, he'd sat at the back and listened to the minister read. *Wherefore, if thy hand or thy foot offend thee, cut them off, and cast them from thee; it is better for thee to enter into life halt or maimed, rather than, having two hands or two feet, to be cast into everlasting fire.* Why pick that? Was it supposed to be a policeman's text? A touch of the Old Testament? Except that it wasn't, those words were spoken by Jesus. And while he was thinking about that, the minister was arriving by some route or other at a familiar destination, *William Ord lived for his family.*

And that was when he'd remembered Billy's story of pissing in the font as a wild kid.

Great timing.

There was no way of controlling your thoughts.

Only the very lucky, or the ordinary lonely unlucky, could get to Meldrum's age without a funeral being a palimpsest of all the ones gone before, whether by burial or burning. The cleric there by the grave had other men at his elbow, a sleek minister plump as a partridge, a fierce old one like a shabby eagle, preachers of the Word, bibles fallen open in their hands, wind ruffling pages, sunshine into an open grave, a smirr of rain, snow in a cemetery beside a Borders kirk. And the dead too were shadowed by the dead, killed in the line of duty, killed in a crash, died of heart disease, of mountain falls, of old age. Suicide, some of that too.

When cops killed themselves in America, they talked of eating the gun. One time in the canteen wee Finlay had told them that and then wondered, What would a Scottish cop do? Eat the battery oot o his torch, had been one suggestion. Stick his baton up his erse! Tam Gowdie had offered.

Die of cancer. That was another way.

Offering his condolences as they came out of the church, he'd been taken aback when the widow clasped him to her as an old friend. 'You know what Billy was like,' she wept. 'By the time he admitted something was wrong, it was too late. It was all through him.'

The minister was finished and the gravediggers were moving discreetly forward. The older son Donald was shaking hands and thanking people for coming.

'I know how much Dad thought of you.'

'He was a fine policeman,' Meldrum said. 'You should be proud of him.'

From this high on the cemetery slope, he could see over Rutherglen and all the way across Glasgow. He had never given it a thought one way or the other about Billy being originally from the west, though he'd heard him talk of starting out on the beat in Moirhill. It turned out this was where his mother and father were buried and he'd chosen to be near them. A long way for his widow to visit from Edinburgh, but Billy had always thought of himself first.

He started to follow the crowd winding between the graves making their way down to the Mill Hotel. In the hotel, he would find a phone and her secretary would say she was putting him through and he would wait and at last he would hear Harriet's voice. Then he'd tell her how the day had gone. He would ask her when she would be home, and tell when he would be home to her. He would say how much he loved her.

The afternoon had turned cold with raw gusts clapping as if to fill sails. The air's taste though far from the sea released memories of going up by heather slopes to hill crests in the Pentlands above Edinburgh. Clouds unravelling across an open sky and church spires and terraces and a castle laid out below him as if to be a model on a table of an ancient city. On winter days there the gale could be fierce as justice in which he believed, salt as forgiveness after which he hungered – though knowing it as hard to hold as the wind itself.

In the group ahead, someone turned and was calling him. He began to hurry.

Down below, there would be a meal and stories about Billy, and some joking too, before they set out on their various journeys.